RAVE REVIEWS FOR

OUT ON THE RIM

"*Out On the Rim* is really good. I mean it's *really* good. Ross Thomas takes us *Out On the Rim* with a stunning array of characters working on a plot that twists and slithers, never stops."

—**Elmore Leonard**

■

"Fuse the dark humor of Evelyn Waugh with the knack for chicanery and suspense of a Graham Greene entertainment and you'll get a pretty good idea of what Thomas is up to . . . quite irresistible."

—*Newsweek*

■

MORE . . .

"Thomas has great moves, and the reader who supposes that he or she has outguessed the author and seen ahead to any single position in—much less the end of—this game had better think again."

—*Washington Post Book World*

■

"Ross Thomas was terrific when he started, and he just gets better with every book. *Out On the Rim* goes straight to the bull's eye."

—**Donald E. Westlake**

■

"Mr. Thomas' new, high-polish excitement could hardly be more topical . . . Mr. Thomas has never been more devious and duplicitous."

—*The New Yorker*

■

"Thomas' intricate, rapid-fire story may be the best piece of suspense fiction this year . . . Once again, Thomas deserves his title of master of mystery."

—*Philadelphia Inquirer*

■

"A black comedy of greed . . . a first-rate thriller."

—*New York Times*

■

"Everybody else watch out! Ross Thomas writes with a switchblade knife. *Out On the Rim* dazzles!"

—**Ed McBain**

■

"*Out On the Rim* is vintage material . . . The writing is crisp, clear, and very contemporary, though the greatest attraction of Thomas' style is that he never forgets he is out to tell a story."

—*Boston Globe*

■

"With a motley crew of characters that might make lesser authors quake, Thomas keeps the reader guessing right until the end. What else would you expect from this two-time Edgar Allan Poe Award winner?"

—*Indianapolis News*

■

"It has all the Ross Thomas trademarks: a fast-paced plot heavy on corruption and treachery, a couple of juicy murders, and the snappiest dialogue in the business . . . *Out On the Rim* might be the best of Thomas' books. Higher praise than that you won't find anywhere."

—*Cleveland Plain Dealer*

■

MORE . . .

Also by Ross Thomas

Cast a Yellow Shadow
The Singapore Wink
The Fools In Town Are On Our Side
Chinaman's Chance
The Eighth Dwarf

Published by
THE MYSTERIOUS PRESS

OUT ON THE RIM

ROSS THOMAS

THE MYSTERIOUS PRESS

New York • London • Tokyo

MYSTERIOUS PRESS EDITION

Copyright © 1987 by Ross E. Thomas, Inc.
All rights reserved.

Cover illustration by Pamela Noftsinger

Mysterious Press books are published in association with
Warner Books, Inc.
666 Fifth Avenue
New York, N.Y. 10103

W A Warner Communications Company

Printed in the United States of America

Originally published in hardcover by The Mysterious Press.
First Mysterious Press Paperback Printing: November, 1988

10 9 8 7 6 5 4 3 2 1

The three who survived the ambush on the black-sand beach were the 19-year-old second lieutenant of infantry; the five-foot-four guerrilla; and the huge, somewhat crazed medical corpsman who had sweated, starved and raved away 16 pounds in the week that followed.

Yet it was Hovey Profette, the Arkansas medic, who first noticed the two Imperial Marines in the valley below, some 40 or 50 yards away, as they slowly emerged from a grove of neglected coconut palms. "Shoot the little fuckers," the medic urged in a hoarse whisper.

Booth Stallings, the second lieutenant of infantry and putative leader of the ambushed intelligence and reconnaissance patrol, flattened himself between the pair of sun-baked black rocks. After brushing away what seemed to be four dozen flies he squinted down through the afternoon haze at the two figures in their mustard uniforms. Both Imperial Marines had stopped and were glancing around with the apprehensive air of point men who suspect someone is about to shoot at them.

"I'd say that second little fucker's at least six-two, maybe even six-three," Stallings said.

"Imperial Marines, " the guerrilla murmured. "There is a minimum height requirement."

For the fourth time that day the medic's terrible rage exploded without warning. It surged up his 18-inch neck in a bright wave, turning his curiously small ears a lipstick red and twisting his face into a fat pink angry knot that Booth Stallings thought might never be untied.

"You ain't even gonna try and shoot 'em, are you, Lieutenant Pissant?" the medic said, enough menace in his soft question to make it a death threat.

Booth Stallings shook his head no as he continued to gaze down at the two Imperial Marines who were now moving slowly across the clearing that once had been planted to maize. "They're scouts, Hovey," Stallings said, forcing a measure of reasonableness into his answer. "They've got a squad behind them at least. Maybe a platoon. Maybe even a company."

"Probably a company," the guerrilla said in the flat, almost toneless Kansas accent he had acquired at the hands of a Thomasite maiden lady who had landed on his shores in 1901 and spent the next 40 years teaching little brown boys to speak and write American English the way it was spoken and written back in Emporia.

Hovey Profette, still crimson-faced and seething, ignored the guerrilla and stuck out his right hand for Stallings' rifle, the sole community firearm. "Gimme the piece," he demanded. "I'll shoot the fuckers."

Stallings again shook his head no, trying to insert a trace of unfelt regret into the gesture.

"There's no rear sight, Hovey," said Stallings. "That dead guerrilla I took it from must've pried the sight off and thrown it away. Guerrillas think rear sights just fuck things up—right, Al?"

Alejandro Espiritu, the five-foot-four guerrilla, smiled—

politely. "An old and much observed military tradition in my country."

"You know what you are, Lieutenant Stallings, sir?" the medic said, his voice almost too loud, his color far too high. "You're just a . . . a great big pile of yellow shit, that's what."

Hovey Profette lunged for the Garand, tore it easily from Booth Stallings' grasp, jammed its butt into his own right shoulder and was sighting down the sightless barrel when the blade of the guerrilla's bolo sliced almost halfway through the 18-inch neck.

The medic made a sound that was part sigh, part wheeze and collapsed atop the unfired rifle. A gurgling noise followed that Booth Stallings thought went on forever but lasted only seconds. When it was over, Hovey Profette, infantry medic and failed conscientious objector, lay dead on the tropical volcanic ridge that afforded Imperial Marines on one side and a fine view of the Camotes Sea on the other.

Stallings jerked the sightless Garand from beneath the dead man. Not bothering to wipe away the blood, he flicked the safety to off and aimed the rifle at the squatting guerrilla who ignored it and went on wiping Profette's blood from the bolo with a handful of wild monkey grass.

"Why the hell didn't you just nick him a little?" Stallings demanded.

Espiritu the guerrilla carefully examined the two-foot bolo before shoving it back down into its homemade wooden scabbard. "He might've screamed," he said finally and pointed with his chin down into the valley where a long line of Imperial Marines was now moving quickly across the clearing. "A company at least," he said. "Just as you and I thought."

Booth Stallings shifted his gaze to the hurrying Japanese Imperial Marines, then to the dead American medic, and back to the Filipino guerrilla. It occurred to him that this was the second Filipino he had come to know well, the first having been Edmundo something or other from San Diego who, like a robin, had appeared each spring near Stallings' grade and junior high schools, dispatched by the Duncan Yo-Yo people to demonstrate their product. Edmundo could make a Yo-Yo do anything, and for three childhood springs Booth Stallings had taken a limited number of private lessons at an exorbitant 50 cents an hour until, turning thirteen, he had discovered masturbation, Lucky Strikes and girls in approximately that order.

"So what the fuck do we tell the Major?" Stallings asked.

The 22-year-old guerrilla seemed to ponder the question with care. "We—you and I—will tell Major Crouch that our fallen comrade died bravely defending the rear." He paused to gaze thoughtfully at the dead Profette. "The wild pigs'll eat him by morning."

For a dozen seconds Booth Stallings stared at the still squatting guerrilla with a frozen expression that agreed to nothing. For during those twelve seconds Stallings had stumbled across what to him was a new and comforting credo, an epiphany of sorts, that neatly excised the moral imperative and left him not only comforted, but also wiser and older. Much older. At least 26.

Still wearing the frozen expression and oblivious to the sweat that ran down over it, Stallings spoke in his new cold grown-up voice.

"You've got a whole lot of elastic up in that head of yours, don't you, Al? I mean, you can make it stretch and wrap around just about anything you want it to."

"I think," Alejandro Espiritu said, almost smiled, thought better of it and started over. "I think we should recommend poor Profette here for a posthumous medal—a Bronze or Silver Star perhaps?"

Booth Stallings gazed down at the dead medic and lapsed Quaker. "What the fuck," he said. "Let's go for the DSC."

CHAPTER ONE

A t three in the afternoon they summoned Booth Stallings, the terrorism expert, to the library in the foundation's seven-story building just east of Dupont Circle on Massachusetts Avenue and fired him over a glass of fairly good Spanish sherry. It was the Ides of March, which fell on a Saturday in 1986, and exactly two months after Booth Stallings' sixtieth birthday.

The firing was done without any qualms that Stallings could detect by Douglas House, the foundation's 35-year-old executive director. House did it politely, of course, with no trace of acrimony, and with about the same amount of regret he might use if calling the *Washington Post* circulation department to put a vacation stop on his home delivery.

It was the foundation's 51-year-old chairman, Frank Tomguy, who administered the pro forma ego massage while wearing an apologetic, even deferential air and one of his $1,100 three-piece suits. Tomguy went on and on about severe budgetary restrictions and then turned to the quality of Booth Stallings' work, which he swore had been brilliant. No question. Absolutely, totally brilliant.

Tomguy's massage completed, Douglas House spoke of money. There would be three months' severance pay in lieu of notice and the foundation would keep Stallings' health insurance in force for six months. There was no talk of pension because the terrorism expert had been with the foundation only 18 months, although that was three months longer than he had ever stuck with any other job.

As the dry talk continued, Stallings lost interest and let his eyes wander around the black walnut paneled library, presumably for the last time. He eventually noticed the lengthening silence. Now that they've canned you so nicely and apologized so handsomely, you're expected to say something appropriate. So he said the only thing that came to mind. "I used to live here, you know."

It wasn't what Douglas House had expected and he shifted uneasily in his leather wingback chair, as if apprehensive that Stallings had launched into some kind of sentimental, even mawkish goodbye. But Tomguy, the chairman, seemed to know better. He smiled and asked the obvious question. "Where's here, Booth?"

"Right here," Stallings said with a small encompassing gesture. "Before the foundation built this place in—what? seventy-two?—there used to be a big old four-story red sandstone mansion that got cut up into apartments during the war." He glanced at Douglas House. "World War II." House nodded.

"I rented the third floor one in February of sixty-one," Stallings went on. "Partly because I could walk to work and partly because of the address—1776 Massachusetts Avenue." His lips stretched into what may or may not have been a small smile. "A patriot's address."

Tomguy cleared his throat. "That walk was to the White House then, wasn't it, Booth? And you were back from Africa or some such."

"I was just back from Stanleyville and the walk was to the old Executive Office Building, which wasn't the White House then and still isn't."

"Heady times, those," Douglas House said, apparently just to be saying something.

Stallings examined House briefly, not blaming the executive director for having been ten years old in 1961. "Ancient history," he said and turned back to Tomguy. "What happens to my Angola survey?"

Tomguy had a square and too honest pink face and not very much gray-blond hair whose sparseness he wisely made no attempt to conceal. From behind rimless bifocals, a pair of wet brown eyes, slightly popped, stared out at the world's perfidy, as if in chronic amazement. Still, it was a face to inspire confidence, what with its stairstep chin, purselike mouth and an aggressive Roman nose that was altogether reassuring. A perfect banker's face, Stallings thought, if only it could dissemble successfully, which it seemed incapable of doing.

The question about the Angola survey made Tomguy turn to the executive director for guidance. With a slight smile that could have meant anything, Douglas House gazed steadily at Stallings who prepared himself for the inevitable evasions.

"We ran it by some people downtown," House said, the smile still in place, the gray eyes indifferent.

Stallings returned the smile. "Did you now? What people? The Georgetown boys? The folks in the Building? Maybe some of the Langley laddies? Did everybody love it?"

"They all thought it could use a bit of restructuring."

"That means they don't mind my calling Savimbi brilliant, but they'd just as soon I didn't call him a brilliant back-slid Maoist crook, which they damn well know he is."

Tomguy, the prudent conciliator, offered soothing noises. "It's still scheduled for summer publication, Booth. Our lead item."

"Restructured though."

"Edited," House said.

Stallings shrugged and rose. "Then take my name off it." He gave the handsome library another last glance. "Thanks for the drink."

Tomguy rose quickly, right hand outstretched. Stallings shook it without hesitation. "Sorry it had to wind up like this, Booth."

"Are you?" Stallings said. "I'm not."

He nodded at the still seated Douglas House, turned and headed for the door, a tall lanky man who used a kind of gliding lope for a walk. He wore a thatch of short ragged gray hair that hugged his head like an old cap. Under it the world was presented with a face so seamed and weathered that many looked twice, not sure whether it was ugly or handsome and, finding it neither, settled on different.

After Booth Stallings had gone, Tomguy watched silently as House rose, went to the telephone and punched a local number from memory. It rang only once before being answered. "It's done," House said into the phone. "He just left." House listened to either a question or a comment, replied, "Right," hung up and turned to Tomguy.

"They're all extremely grateful," House said. "I'm quoting."

Tomguy nodded, his expression sour. "They fucking well better be."

•   •   •

Booth Stallings sat on his favorite bench at the north end of Dupont Circle, sipping from a half-pint of Smirnoff 80 proof that came disguised in the de rigueur brown paper sack. One bench over, a pretty young mother took yet another apprehensive look at him and quickly stuck her twin 18-month-old sons back down into their elaborate top-of-the-line stroller where they would ride home facing each other.

Stallings tried a reassuring smile that was obviously a failure because the mother shot him another black look, gave the stroller a shove and hurried away. The forward-facing twin started to bawl. The backward-facing one burbled merrily and waved at Stallings who toasted him with the half-pint of vodka. He had another sip and tucked the bottle down into a pocket of the eight-year-old suede jacket he had bought cheaply in Istanbul.

It was then that Stallings noticed the weather and the time. It had grown chilly and was almost dusk, which presented the problem of what he should do with the Saturday night that stretched out before him like a slice of infinity.

Stallings' choices were limited. He could spend the evening alone with a book or a bottle in his sublet apartment on Connecticut Avenue across from the zoo, or he could drop in uninvited, unexpected and possibly unwelcome on either his Georgetown daughter or the one who lived in Cleveland Park.

In Georgetown the food promised to be fancier but the dinner guests (six at least on Saturday night) would spend the evening handicapping the 1988 presidential race, divining signs and portents from the same printed entrails that each had studied during the past week in the *Post* and the *Times* and whatever else they had happened to read.

Booth Stallings, child of the Depression, had never really much cared who was President after Roosevelt died. He had voted only once, and that was back in 1948 when, at 22, he lightheartedly had marked his ballot for Henry Agard Wallace. Whenever he thought of it now, which was seldom, he congratulated himself on the youthful folly.

Stallings had a final sip from the vodka bottle, rose from the bench and went in search of a pay phone, having decided to call his Cleveland Park daughter. He found a bank of pay phones near the Peoples Drugstore on the southwest arc of Dupont Circle. Using the only one that hadn't been ravaged, he called the 33-year-old Lydia who had married Howard Mott shortly before he left the Justice Department in 1980 to specialize in the defense of wealthy white-collar criminals. Mott liked to describe his practice as a growth industry. After two slow years, Mott was growing wealthy himself.

When Stallings' Cleveland Park daughter answered the phone, he said, "What's for dinner?"

Lydia Mott gasped. "Oh my God, it's all over town!"

"What?"

"You got fired. You drunk yet?"

"Not yet, and all over town means Joanna, right?" Joanna was Stallings' 35-year-old Georgetown daughter. She had married a car wax heir whose wealth and political leanings had won him an appointment to the upper reaches of the State Department. Stallings sometimes thought of his son-in-law as Neal the Know-nothing.

"She's called three times," Lydia Mott said.

"What for?"

"Because she made this tentative dinner date for you. It's about a job and he wants you to have dinner with him around seven-thirty at the Montpelier Room in the Madison and, Jesus, that'll set him back a few bucks, won't it?"

"Lydia," a patient Stallings said. "Who's he?"

"Right. That is kind of pertinent. Well, it's one Harry Crites."

"The poet."

"Poet?"

"He gets published."

"Yeah, but what does he *do*?"

Stallings hesitated. "I'm not quite sure. Anymore."

"I see. One of those. Well, you want me to call Joanna and have her say when he calls back that you'll meet him there at seven-thirty?"

Stallings again hesitated, debating the rewards of a Saturday night in the company of Harry Crites. The internal debate went on until his daughter grew impatient and said, "Well?"

"Sorry," Stallings said. "I was just trying to parse that last sentence of yours. But okay. Call Joanna and tell her yes."

There was a brief silence until his daughter said, "Look, Pappy. If you don't want to eat with the poet, why don't you come out and have lamb stew with us and listen to some of Howie's real-life dirty stories?"

"What a solace and comfort you are in these pre-Alzheimer years."

"No thanks, huh? Okay. How come they fired you?"

Stallings started to shrug, but stopped when he realized she couldn't see it. "Budgetary restrictions, they said."

"*Budgetary?* With all those millions?"

"I'll call you," Stallings said.

"Tomorrow."

"Okay. Tomorrow."

Booth Stallings hung up the pay phone, crossed to one of the drugstore's lighted windows, and used its reflection to examine what he was wearing: the old suede Istanbul jacket; the too wide black and brown tie he remembered buying in Bologna; a tan shirt from Marks and Spencer in London that he thought of as his thousand-miler, having once heard an old-time traveling salesman describe a similar shirt as such; and the gray flannel pants he couldn't remember buying at all, but whose deep pleats suggested they hadn't been bought in the States. As for shoes, Stallings knew without looking that he was wearing what he always wore: cheap brown loafers that he bought by the half-dozen, discarding each pair as it wore out.

Still, it was an outfit that would get him into the Madison. And it was certainly adequate for dining with Harry Crites who had worn an aging blue suit with shiny elbows and a glistening seat when Stallings had first met him 25 years ago. Thirty minutes after they met, Crites had borrowed $35 to make an HFC payment that was a month overdue.

As he turned in search of a cruising taxi, Stallings tried to remember if Harry Crites had ever repaid the $35, and finally decided that he hadn't.

CHAPTER
<u>TWO</u>

ooth Stallings sat in the lobby of the Madison Hotel near a couple of bored-looking Saudis and waited for Harry Crites who was already 19 minutes late. But Crites had always been late, even back in the early sixties when he would burst into a meeting a quarter hour after it had started, wearing a big merry smile, an inevitable King Edward cigar, and clutching a file of hopelessly jumbled documents. He would then disarm everyone, even the punctuality sticklers, with a wry, self-deprecating crack that had them all chuckling.

After Kennedy's death in 1963, Harry Crites had resigned from what he later always referred to not quite accurately as "my White House stint" and moved over to Defense, where he wasn't at all happy, and from there to State where he landed a slot in the suspect Public Safety Program of the Agency for International Development. AID dispatched Crites to seven or eight lesser developed countries from which came mutterings about some of the deals he had cut with their premiers, presidents-for-life and prime ministers. But Stallings had never paid much attention.

Besides, it was around in there—1965—that Stallings, his wife and two young daughters, cushioned by a $20,000 foundation grant, had left Washington for Rome where he would continue his research on terrorism.

In the seven or eight years that followed, Booth Stallings only returned to Washington and sometimes New York when forced to wheedle additional funds out of mostly unsympathet-

ic foundations. And occasionally he would bump into Harry
Crites at some unavoidable cocktail party or embassy reception.

By then Harry Crites' shiny blue suit and King Edward cigar
and the old Ford Fairlane with its rusted-out rocker panels were
long gone. Instead, the suits were from J. Press and the cigars
smelled of Havana and the car was a beige Mercedes sedan,
not the most expensive model, but not the diesel either.

At these infrequent encounters Harry Crites and Booth
Stallings never said much more than hello and how've you
been, although Crites almost never gave an answer, or waited
for one, because there were always others he wanted to talk to
far more than he did to Stallings, and usually he was already
waving and smiling at them.

But once there had been nobody—nobody worthwhile
anyway—and Harry Crites said he had left government and
was now doing liaison work, which meant he was peddling
what back then was still called influence but in later years was
softened to access. Stallings had sometimes speculated about
who might be retaining Crites and his conclusions had left him
as depressed as he ever got.

       •   •   •

Harry Crites was 22 minutes late when the muscle walked
into the Madison and read the lobby with the standard quick
not quite bored glance that flitted over Booth Stallings,
lingered for a moment on the two Saudis, counted the help and
marked the spare exits. After that the muscle gave her left
earlobe a slight tug, as if checking the small gold earring.

Booth Stallings immediately nominated her for one of the
three most striking women he had ever seen. Her immense
poise made him peg her age at 32 or 33. But he knew he could
be five years off either way because of the way she moved,
which was like a young athlete with eight prime years still
ahead of her.

She was at least five-ten and not really as slender as her

height made her out to be. She carried no purse and wore cream gabardine slacks with a black jacket of some nubby material that was short enough to make her seem even taller, but loose enough to hide the pistol Stallings somehow knew she was wearing.

Her hair was a thick reddish brown with the red providing the highlights. Worn carelessly short, it looked perfect. It also looked as if all she had to do to make it look like that was run her fingers through it. Stallings suspected that nothing perfect was that easy. The red-brown hair framed a more or less oval face whose features seemed to have been placed precisely where they should be—except her forehead, which was a little high. Her eyes were green, although Stallings couldn't decide whether they were sea green or emerald green. But since she looked expensive, he finally settled on dollar green.

A few seconds after she tugged at her left earlobe, Harry Crites made his entrance, wearing a nine-dollar cigar and a thousand-dollar camel's hair topcoat. The coat was worn like a cape, much as a rich poet might have worn it, if there were such a thing, which Stallings doubted.

The woman nodded at Crites. It was a noncommittal nod that could have meant either have fun or all clear. Crites paused. The woman removed the coat from his shoulders with no trace of subservience. Stallings wondered how much her services cost and what they included. With the camel's hair coat over her left arm, the woman turned and left the hotel through the 15th Street entrance.

When Harry Crites caught sight of his dinner guest he narrowed his blue eyes and twinkled them behind what Stallings suspected were contact lenses. The wide joke-prone mouth, a shade or two paler than a red rubber band, stretched itself into a delighted smile, revealing some remarkably white teeth that Stallings knew were capped. After remembering that Crites had been 27 when he had borrowed that still unpaid $35 back in 1961, Stallings put his present age at 52.

Rising slowly, Booth Stallings extended his right hand

Crites grabbed it with both of his and pumped it up and down as he spoke from around and behind the immense cigar. "Goddamnit, Booth, too many goddamned years."

"Fourteen," said Stallings who had that kind of memory. "June seventeenth, 1972."

Crites removed his cigar, flipped back through his own mental almanac and made his eyes dart from side to side in mock panic. "The Watergate break-in. Christ, I didn't see you here."

Stallings couldn't hold back his grin. "My daughter Joanna's twenty-first birthday. She's the one you talked to today—the one married to Secretary Know-nothing of the State Department."

"Neal Hineline," Crites said and nodded gravely. "A great fourteenth-century mind. Sound." He frowned then. "But I don't remember Joanna's birthday."

"That's because you weren't there. You were going into that fancy place that closed down and almost got turned into a McDonald's. The—uh—"

"Sans Souci."

"Right. And I was heading for a birthday lunch with Joanna at the Mayflower and you looked right through me."

Crites touched his finger to his right eye. "That was before I found the miracle cure for vanity. Contacts. Now if you're through fucking me over, let's eat."

"Your friend going to join us?"

Crites glanced over his shoulder in the direction the tall woman had gone and then looked at Stallings with a faint smile. "She's not exactly a friend."

"Then let's eat," Booth Stallings said.

They gave Harry Crites the choice northeast corner banquette in the almost empty Montpelier Room. He and Stallings had a drink first, Perrier and bitters for Crites, vodka on ice for Stallings. They both ordered a salad and the veal and a double portion of the first-of-the-season green beans, which the waiter swore had been picked only that morning in Loudoun County,

Virginia, although Stallings suspected it was the day before near Oxnard, California. After that, Harry Crites ordered the wine, which required a grave five-minute conference with the sommelier.

Once the wine was ordered, Harry Crites leaned back, sipped his drink, and examined Stallings as if he were still something that would be a wonderful buy despite a doubtful provenance.

Stallings returned the stare, mildly disappointed to find Crites had aged so well. There was just a bit of fat around the middle, although the well-tailored vest helped conceal it nicely. The round face had yet to grow another chin. The color was also good, the broken veins few, and the controlled expression still ranged from glad to gladdest.

There were a few new lines, of course, but apparently none from worry. The hair had stayed light brown, a shade or two off true blond, and what was left was just enough. Only youth was missing. It had fled—along with its twin pals, spontaneity and carelessness. What remained was a careful, if not quite cautious middle-aged man, obviously prosperous, who still planned on getting rich.

"So they bounced you," Harry Crites said, not making it a question.

"Did they?"

Crites shrugged. "This is Washington, Booth. Where do you think you'll light?"

"No idea."

"Interested in a one-shot?"

"Why me?"

"You're sole source."

"That means I can charge a lot."

"A hell of a lot."

"All right," Stallings said. "First I eat; then I listen."

Following the veal, which turned out to be particularly good, Stallings and Crites ordered a large pot of coffee, passed up dessert, and vetoed a cognac recommended by the waiter

After two sips of coffee, Booth Stallings put his cup down and smiled at Crites. "Isn't it curious though?"

"What?"

"That I got fired at three and by eight-fifteen I'm sitting in the Madison, eating twenty-six-dollar veal and listening to you offer me a sole-source one-shot. Who put the fix in, Harry? At the foundation?"

Crites went on lighting his after-dinner cigar, taking his time, obviously enjoying the ritual. After several puffs he contemplated the cigar fondly. When he spoke, it was more to the cigar than to Stallings. "If I said me, you'd think I was bragging. If I said not me, you'd think I was lying. So I'm going to let you think whatever you like."

"Let's have it then," Stallings said. "The proposition."

"The Philippines."

"Well now."

"You've been there."

"Not recently."

"A long time ago," Crites said. "During the war."

"Right. A long time ago."

"We—and we means some people I'm associated with—" Stallings interrupted. "What people?"

"Just let me tell it, Booth, will you? When I'm selling I like to maintain the flow."

Stallings shrugged.

"Well, these people would like you to go back."

"And do what?"

"See the man."

"Who?"

"A guy who read that book of yours—the one that got all the raves."

"I only wrote the one book, Harry."

"Yeah. *Anatomy of Terror*. I read it. Some of it anyhow. But our guy read it all and is very, very impressed. You could say he's a fan."

"So what would I do, if I saw him?"

"Convince him to come down from the hills."

"How?"

"We'll go as high as five million U.S. deposited in Hong Kong."

"What's his name, Aguinaldo?"

"Who's Aguinaldo?"

"A guy who came down from the hills for a lot of money a long time ago and went to Hong Kong."

"Never heard of him," Harry Crites said. "What happened?"

"He was double-crossed."

"Then what?"

"He went back to the Philippines and turned himself into either a terrorist fool or a revolutionary hero, depending on what source you consult."

"When was all this?"

Stallings looked away and frowned, as if trying to remember exactly. "About ninety years ago. Around in there."

"Don't go looking for historical parallels," Crites said.

"Why not? They're useful."

"Not this time. Our guy's ready to deal, but we need a closer; an authenticator. You."

"Me."

"He knows you."

"From my book, you mean?" Stallings said, trying not to anticipate Crites' reply.

"Not just through the book. Personally."

"Has he got a name?"

"Alejandro Espiritu. You do know him, don't you?"

"We've met," Booth Stallings said.

CHAPTER
THREE

During the next half hour Stallings and Crites drank three cups of coffee and discussed the recent not quite bloodless February revolution in the Philippines. They touched on Ferdinand Marcos' exile to Hawaii; Imelda's shoes; the shambles the Filipino economy was in; the disastrous world price of sugar; Mrs. Aquino's prospects as President (dicey, both agreed); and whether it was four or eight billion dollars that Marcos had managed to squirrel away. After discovering that neither apparently knew much more than what he had read, or seen on television, they returned to Alejandro Espiritu.

"How well did you know him?" Crites asked.

"Fairly well."

"What was he like then?"

"Short. About five-four."

"Come on, Booth."

"Okay. He was smart. Maybe even brilliant. About twenty-two or twenty-three then and tough. He was also kind of flexible—for a guerrilla."

"He was one of those commie guerrillas, wasn't he —what they called Huks?"

"The Huks were mostly up north—in Luzon. We were down south. Negros and Cebu. Most of the time Cebu."

"What'd Huk stand for anyway? I forget."

"For *Hukbong Bayan Laban sa Hapon*," Stallings said, pleased he could still remember the Tagalog. "That translates into something like, 'People's Army to Fight the Japanese.' It was shortened to Hukbalahapa, which finally got cut down to Huks so it'd fit in a headline. Then Lansdale came along in the fifties and helped Magsaysay put the boot to them. You remember General Lansdale, don't you, scourge of the Orient?"

Crites ignored the question and said, "They're calling themselves the NPA now—the New People's Army."

"Not the same bunch. Most of what was left of the Huks turned into mercenaries and strikebreakers."

"You sure?"

"Christ, Harry, if they were still the same guys, you'd have some pretty superannuated guerrillas puffing up and down those mountains."

"But the NPA's also red as a rose."

Stallings shrugged. "So?"

"You ever talk politics with Espiritu?"

"I was nineteen. My job was to kill people, not discuss dialectics."

"Let me tell you what Espiritu is to the NPA," Crites said and drew on his cigar. He inhaled a tiny portion of the smoke and then blew it all out—and away from Stallings. "He's their secular archbishop. Their grand panjandrum. Their oracle. Their high lama. Their keeper of the sacred and everlasting flame. Some claim he's even been to Moscow."

"Moscow," Stallings said. "Think of that."

"Listen, Booth. If Espiritu comes down from the hills and exiles himself to Hong Kong, my people figure it's eight to five that Madame Aquino can cut a deal with the NPA and keep on being President."

Stallings studied Harry Crites' expression, looking for guile and deception, but finding only a crack salesman's normal greed and unassailable confidence. "With the token communist or two in her cabinet, right?"

"Why the hell not?"

"Because then it would be all over for the NPA, Harry.

Capitulation. Surrender. Defeat. And for what? So they can come down and starve in the barrios? They can do that up in the hills. Look. If the NPA makes a deal with Aquino, they won't've won anything and they'll've lost what power they had. It doesn't work like that. Not in the Philippines. Not in Afghanistan. Not in El Salvador or Lebanon. Not in Peru. Not in the Basque country or Northern Ireland. Not anywhere."

Crites put his cigar out in the ashtray, taking his time, tamping it carefully, making sure no spark was left. When he looked up, it was with an expression from which all friendliness had vanished. The blue eyes had come down with a chill and the wide joke-prone mouth had slipped from glad into grim. A faintly surprised Stallings realized that the son of a bitch didn't like me—surprised not so much by the realization as by the surprise itself.

"They say you're the expert," Crites said, not bothering to keep the disbelief out of his tone. "That's what they say. Everybody. But my people're willing to bet five million bucks you're wrong."

"Five million could buy the NPA an awful lot of M-16s and AK-47s and Uzis—maybe enough to bring back martial law."

"My people figure five million's not enough to buy anything but one guy."

"And just who the fuck are your people, Harry?"

"Money people, who else?"

"I think they're the duck people."

The frost suddenly melted from Crites' eyes and the wiseacre smile returned. "The Langley ducks, you mean."

Stallings nodded. "You sure quack like one."

"No ducks," Crites said.

"Who then?"

"Suppose there was a bunch of people," Crites said slowly and carefully, "a consortium, let's call it, that has a billion or so already invested in the Philippines. And this consortium is still hoping to make a return on its investment, or break even, or maybe just cut its losses a little. But its only hope in hell of doing any of that is with a stable government."

Crites paused, as if waiting for encouragement. Stallings gave him an impatient go-on nod.

"Okay. So if this consortium spends another five million—which is maybe one-half of one percent of what it's already sunk out there—well, it just might bring it off. And that's it, Booth. The whole plate of fudge. Tranquillity instead of trouble. A few years of peace and quiet. And my people're willing to spend a few bucks to get it."

"And buy off the chief troublemaker."

"Pension him off."

"You're going to bribe him, Harry, and you want me for your bagman."

"Not me. Him. Espiritu. Like nine-tenths of the world, he doesn't much trust or like Americans—God knows why, wonderful as we are. But he will deal with his old asshole buddy from World War II. So that means you'll be our authenticator, our bona fides, and convince him the deal's really kosher. Then he can retire to Hong Kong, spend his money and watch the Chicoms take over."

"He's already nibbled then, hasn't he?" Stallings said. "If he hadn't, you and I wouldn't be talking."

"He's nibbled."

There was a long silence as Stallings drew careful cross-hatch patterns on the tablecloth with the tines of his unused dessert fork. The patterns turned into a Filipino nipa hut. A smile of anticipated victory spread slowly across Crites' face. "Well?" he said and then went on without waiting for an answer. "You want in, don't you, Booth?"

Booth Stallings looked up slowly from his tablecloth sketch. "I want ten percent."

Crites' victory smile vanished and his mouth formed a small shocked O. The eyes widened with what Stallings judged could only be horror. Nor was there any mistaking the fury in the whisper. "You want half a million dollars?"

Stallings smiled. "I'm sole source, Harry, and I get to charge a lot."

They used the silence that followed to stare at each other: Stallings with amusement; Crites with something that resembled rage. Then the rage, if that's what it was, suddenly went away, replaced by what Stallings interpreted to be an utter and alarming confidence. Crites reached for the dinner check. He studied it and when he spoke his tone was neutral and businesslike. "You'll pay your own expenses, right?"

"Sure," Stallings said.

"Then let's start right now," Crites said and dropped the check on top of the nipa hut sketch.

•   •   •

After they left the Montpelier Room, Booth Stallings $126 poorer, they headed across the lobby to the 15th Street exit where the tall woman was waiting, camel's hair topcoat over her left arm, quite ready, in Stallings' opinion, to spring and kill. He indicated her with a nod. "Why the nanny?"

They were still a dozen feet away when Stallings asked his murmured question and Crites didn't answer immediately. First, he had to turn so the woman could drape the topcoat over his shoulders like a cape. After that he had to cock his head to one side and give Stallings a careful head-to-toe inspection. Only then did Harry Crites smile and answer.

"Enemies," he said. "What else?"

Without waiting for a reply or even a farewell, Crites turned and sailed through the open 15th Street door, his camel's hair topcoat billowing out behind. The tall woman with the dollar-green eyes looked at Stallings, nodded to herself as if reconfirming some previous assessment, smiled pleasantly, said, "Goodnight," and followed Harry Crites out the door.

CHAPTER
FOUR

At 11:08 that night Booth Stallings waited under an old elm across the street from the three-story vanilla house with the black shutters on the south side of P Street in Georgetown. He waited until the last two guests came down the five wrought-iron steps and headed west toward their car.

When the guests were 30 yards away, Stallings crossed the street, mounted the steps and rang the bell, which was actually a loud buzzer. He heard footsteps on the parquet floor of the entrance hall behind the door. The sound of the footsteps stopped, but the door didn't open. Stallings hadn't expected it to. Instead, from behind the door a man's deep baritone said, "Yes," managing to make it neither a question nor an answer.

"It's your father-in-law, Mr. Secretary," Stallings said to the man behind the door who was either deputy assistant secretary of state or assistant deputy secretary of state, a pair of rankings whose fine distinctions Stallings had never bothered to fathom.

"Jesus, Booth, it's past eleven," Neal Hineline said from behind the still closed door. "You sober?"

"Close enough."

The door opened and Stallings entered into a reception hall whose parquet floor creaked nicely with age. A remarkable stairway curved up to the second floor. His son-in-law stood— or posed—beside the delicately carved newel post, a man so handsome it was difficult for Stallings to believe that he was as dim as he seemed. Difficult, but not impossible.

Stallings sometimes hoped it was all an act, and that beneath the wavy blond hair and behind the puzzled puppy eyes was a magnificent brain, busily thinking up all sorts of elegant international schemes. This was, Stallings sometimes thought, one of his last remaining fantasies.

"Joanna's right through there," Hineline said, indicating the living room's 150-year-old double sliding doors that had been carved by the same craftsman who had created the newel post.

"It's you I need to talk to, Neal."

"Me?"

"You."

"Oh. Yes. Of course." Hineline's right hand strayed automatically toward the inside breast pocket of his gray tweed jacket. "Sorry about the foundation, Booth. How much—"

"Not money," Stallings said, stifling a sigh. "Advice."

Hineline's hand stopped its slow journey toward the inside pocket where the checkbook presumably lay. "Advice," he said.

Stallings nodded.

"Did you see your Mr. Crites? The one who called Joanna?"

"I saw him."

"Well, then, why not just pop in and say hello to Joanna and then come on back to my study where we can talk."

•   •   •

Joanna Hineline was prettier than her dead mother and, at five-nine, two inches taller. But there was still the uncanny resemblance that always disturbed Stallings until his daughter opened her mouth. After that there was no resemblance at all.

She turned now, smiling—although not very much—as Stallings entered the living room that was long and narrow and contained many of the French antiques she had begun to collect after she married Neal Hineline and could afford them.

Her slight smile was not one of welcome, but of amusement—as if something unexpectedly quaint had just strayed in. Stallings thought it may well have. As always, the uncanny resemblance to his dead wife vanished when his daughter opened her mouth and said, "You're looking chipper for an unemployment statistic—or do we call it jobless now?"

"I'm neither."

"You've already found something else?" Joanna Hineline said, signaling disbelief by cocking her left eyebrow to an almost amazing height, just as Stallings' dead wife had when she'd wanted others to know they'd said something ridiculous, fatuous or dumb.

After Stallings replied with a shrug and a maybe, Joanna Hineline said, "Then that dinner with your friend paid off."

"He's not exactly a friend."

She nodded, as if expecting the comment. "You could say that about almost everyone, couldn't you? 'He's not exactly a friend.'"

"Almost," Stallings said.

"So tell me about the new job. Does it pay a lot?"

"Ask Neal. If State wants it spread all over town, he'll tell you. But he'll probably say it's none of your business."

"In that unlikely event, I'll simply have to pry it out of him later. In bed."

"He'll like that," Stallings said, turned and headed for the small downstairs back room that Neal Hineline liked to call his study.

•   •   •

The room faced south. It had French doors overlooking a tiny garden that night had made invisible. But Stallings knew that with the early spring a fine stand of azaleas might be in bloom. The study also boasted a wall of photographs and a wall of books—mostly history, biography and polemics. There was an old desk fashioned out of beautiful black cherry. The desk sat in front of the French doors. Neal Hineline sat behind the desk, looking important, handsome and complacent.

Stallings, now seated in a leather club chair, crossed his legs and asked, "How much do you really want to know?"

Hineline frowned, aiming for thoughtful but hitting puzzled. "What d'you think, Booth? The bare essentials, I suppose. Just do me a fat paragraph and if you start to say something naughty, I may cut you off."

It took Stallings less than a minute to outline Harry Crites' proposition. Hineline listened carefully without interrupting. He then pursed his lips, managing to look judicious. "Yes, well, I don't see us having any trouble with that. Some private citizens of this country want to make a gift to a private citizen of another country, providing he accepts the gift in yet another country—although I suppose Hong Kong's still a crown colony and not really a country, is it?"

Stallings sighed. "It's a bribe, Neal, and I'm the bagman."

Hineline denied the charge with a small smile. "Gift-giver, actually." He turned then to examine his wall of books. He asked his next question with eyes averted and tone elaborately casual. "How much are you getting, Booth—or should I even ask?"

"Five hundred thousand and I don't know if you should ask or not."

Shock dropped Hineline's mouth open a half-inch. "Good Lord! That much?"

Stallings smiled. "I'm sole source."

"But you will report it—to the IRS people, I mean?"

"Every dime."

"I see no problem then. Nothing insurmountable, at any rate."

"What about Harry Crites? Is he a problem?"

"Har . . . ry Crites," Hineline said slowly, stretching the first name out with almost devoted care. "Your Mr. Crites looks out primarily for Harry Crites. But then don't we all? You know him well?"

"Well enough."

"I know him by reputation only and he is, I'm afraid, always something of a problem."

"Who's he working for, Neal?"

A long pause was followed by a careful answer. "It could be—I repeat, could be—just as he says: a consortium. Nuclear power people. Electronics guys. Some sugar and pineapple people. Mining interests. And possibly several others who have capital tied up in the Philippines."

"Is he fronting for Langley?"

The pause was longer this time and the answer even more careful. "I wouldn't quite rule that out—not altogether, if I were you."

"What the hell's that supposed to mean?"

"Exactly what I said."

Stallings rose from the club chair. "Thanks, Neal. You've been a great help." He turned to go, but turned back. "By the way, Joanna's awfully curious and thinks she's going to fuck it all out of you in bed tonight."

Hineline smiled and rose. "She's more than welcome to try, of course."

Stallings nodded, turned again and headed for the study door.

"Mind how you go, Booth," his son-in-law said.

"You bet," Booth Stallings said.

•   •   •

After his younger daughter, Lydia Mott, greeted Stallings with a neck-wrenching hug and a smacking midnight kiss in the foyer of the old Cleveland Park house on 35th Street Northwest, he was led by the hand back to the kitchen, seated at the big round scarred table, and forced to eat a slice of lemon meringue pie. Since there was no coffee ready and she didn't want to make any, Lydia Mott mixed her father a bloody mary, assuring him that it went amazingly well with lemon pie. To his surprise, it did.

Stallings was halfway through the pie when Howard Mott, the criminal lawyer, entered the kitchen, wearing an old plaid bathrobe. He winked at Stallings, served himself some pie along with a bloody mary, nodded encouragingly, and sat down at the table to eat, drink and listen.

"All ears?" Stallings said, looking first at Mott, who nodded again, and then at Lydia Mott, noticing not for the first time that she wasn't nearly as pretty as her older sister. For one thing her face was so mobile and her emotions so transparent that friends and utter strangers liked to tell her their most godawful secrets just to watch the light show her face put on as sympathy, consternation, amazement, concern, grief and joy blazed across it. Stallings often thought his younger daughter's pathologically forgiving nature made her the perfect mate for a criminal lawyer.

When he was finished with his tale—a slightly longer version than he had spun Neal Hineline—the awed Lydia Mott whispered, "Oh, my God, Pappy!" She then turned to her husband and said, "What d'you think, sugar?"

Sugar was short and chunky and 36 years old with a curiously unfinished look. Just a few more blows from the DNA chisel and Howard Mott might have looked distinguished, if not exactly handsome. Instead he looked as if he had been put together by someone who hadn't bothered to read the directions.

His intimidating half-finished look was complemented by a magnificent mind, not much hair and countersunk black eyes that some thought could peep into souls. He used a silken bass voice to thunder, cajole and produce a rumbling confidential whisper that an often mesmerized jury could easily hear from 30 feet away. He won most of his cases.

"What do I think?" Mott said. "I think the shit's deep and rising."

"That's understood," Stallings said.

"It's also illegal, despite what my brother-in-law, the beloved simpleton, says. I can think of a dozen laws you'd break. But what's most important is this: nobody ever pays a bagman half a million to deliver five million unless the deal's dirty."

"Another given," Stallings said.

"But you're still going ahead and doing it, aren't you?" Lydia Mott said.

Stallings nodded and then said, "But I'm also going to need some help."

"Handholders," Mott said.

"You know any?"

Mott put the final bite of pie into his mouth, chewed thoughtfully, put down his fork and rose. "Come on upstairs."

Stallings followed his son-in-law up the stairs and into a room that held a very old rolltop desk, a couch for Saturday afternoon naps, and an elaborate stereo system to play the operas that were Mott's passion. He waved Stallings to a chair, sat down at the desk, and began rummaging through its drawers and pigeonholes until he found the business card he wanted.

Mott read the card, tapped it against a thumbnail, read it again, looked at Stallings for a long moment, turned to the desk, picked up a ballpoint pen and wrote two names on the back of the card.

"These two guys are probably about what you need," Mott said as he wrote. "I hear from the usual unimpeachable sources that they're very good, fairly honest and awfully expensive. You willing to pay?"

"I expect to," Stallings said.

Mott again turned to his father-in-law. "The last I heard they were out on the Rim someplace. Hong Kong. Singapore. Bangkok. Malacca. They move around. But this is their stateside contact. Sort of their agent." He handed the card to Stallings who noticed it was engraved and that it read:

Maurice Overby
House-sitter to the Stars

The only thing on the card was a phone number with a 213 area code that Stallings knew meant Los Angeles. He looked up at Mott. "How's he pronounce it? Maurice or Morris?"

"Close friends and slight acquaintances usually call him Otherguy. Now why would they call him that?"

Stallings smiled. "Because some other guy always did it, didn't he? Whatever it was."

"Exactly," Howard Mott said.

CHAPTER FIVE

A shirtless Otherguy Overby, wearing only baggy chino walking shorts and a pair of laceless New Balance jogging shoes, stood in front of the open four-door garage, waiting for water and trying to decide what to drive to the Los Angeles International Airport. He could choose from a Mercedes 560 SEC sedan; a Porsche 911 cabriolet; a seven-passenger Oldsmobile station wagon; or a high-sprung, four-wheel-drive Ford pickup.

He had almost decided on the Mercedes when he heard the truck grinding up the long gravel drive. He turned to watch as the Peterbilt tractor-cab nosed around the corner of the enormous house and shuddered to a stop, air brakes hissing. Coupled to the Peterbilt was a tanker containing ten thousand gallons of fairly pure water that wholesaled at two cents a gallon.

Luis Garfias, the young Mexican driver, lit a cigarette and stared down at Overby for several seconds, as if trying to place him. He finally nodded in the self-satisfied way some do when they've managed to match a face to a name. "Your water, Señor Otherguy."

"You're late, Luis."

Luis Garfias smiled and blew out some smoke. "Your mother," he said, put the Peterbilt in gear, and started creeping toward the ten-thousand-gallon water tank that rested on a man-made earth mound just to the right of the drive. The mound was high enough to raise the bottom of the tank level with the roofline of the two-story house, thus permitting gravity to do its work and send water flowing to the nine bathrooms, two kitchens, three wet bars, two Jacuzzis and one laundry room, not to mention the octagonal swimming pool that twice a year required twenty thousand gallons all for itself.

*   *   *

Now wearing a paisley tie, starched white broadcloth shirt, well-tended black oxfords and what he thought of as his gloom-blue suit, which seemed a size or so too large, Overby opened one of the two large refrigerators, removed two bottles of San Miguel beer, snapped off their caps and served one of them to Luis Garfias who sat slumped in a chair at the round kitchen table whose top had been fashioned out of two pieces of invisibly bonded rare old maple and would easily seat eight.

Garfias looked at the beer's label. "Who likes this Flip beer—you or Billy?"

"Me," Overby said, pouring his own beer into a tall glass. "Billy doesn't drink."

"Anymore."

"Anymore."

Garfias drank two swallows of beer from the bottle. "Mex beer is better." He had another swallow. "But this ain't bad. So when's Billy getting out?"

"Friday," Overby said, sitting down on one of the custom cane-bottomed chairs that surrounded the table.

"She coming back?"

"No."

Garfias glanced around the huge kitchen, obviously pricing an O'Keefe & Merritt restaurant-size gas range, two micro-wave ovens, a commercial freezer, the twin refrigerators, a double rack of copper pots and pans, and an assortment of other appliances that may or may not have been used in the past year or two. "Christ," Garfias said, "he built this fucking place for her."

"He's going to sell it," Overby said.

"How much it cost him—to build and everything?"

"About two point seven."

"What's he asking?"

"One point nine, I think."

Garfias shook his head regretfully, as if he had just decided not to make a counteroffer after all. "Never get it. Not without water. Tell me this. How come somebody smart as Billy, when he's not on the shit anyway, how come he builds a place without no water?"

"There was water when he built it. Four wells."

"How long'd it take 'em to go bad—one month? Two? Three maybe?"

"A year."

"They lasted about as long as she did."

She was Cynthia Blondin, the estranged 23-year-old companion of Billy Diron who was a founding member of Galahad's Balloon, a rock group that had made him a multimillionaire by the time he was 28. Now 39, Billy Diron had nearly completed the prescribed four weeks at the Betty Ford Center in Palm Springs for his addiction to alcohol, cocaine and the occasional toot of heroin.

"So what're you gonna do when Billy gets out—stay on?"

"I'm a house-sitter," Overby said. "Not a nursemaid."

"Whatcha got lined up—anything?"

Overby glanced at his Cartier tank watch. "I'll know this afternoon."

"But you're still paying the house bills—the gas, phone, electric and all?"

"Yeah."

"Then you mizewell pay mine."

Garfias reached into a pocket of his faded blue Levi's jacket and brought out a pink statement. He passed it to Overby who saw that the bill was $100 more than the $200 it should have been. He rose, walked over to the kitchen counter drawer, took out a three-tier checkbook and brought it back to the table. Then he filled out a check—already signed by the incarcerated Billy Diron—for the exact amount of Garfias' pink statement.

When finished, Overby put down the pen, neatly tore the check out and extended both hands, his right offering the check, his left prepared to accept the $50 dollar bill Garfias had almost finished folding lengthwise into fourths. The check and the $50 dollar bill were exchanged simultaneously.

•   •   •

When Booth Stallings walked off the United flight at 3:46 P.M. and into the arrival-departure lounge of Los Angeles International Airport, the first thing he noticed was the sign that had been neatly lettered on the coated side of a shirtboard by a sure hand with a felt pen. The sign read: Mr. Stallings.

The man who displayed the sign without any visible self-consciousness was somewhere in his early forties and had one of those too still and too careful faces that are frequently worn by men who have something to do with the law—either its enforcement or its avoidance.

Stallings also noticed that the man's expensive dark blue suit seemed to be a size or so too large, as if he had lost ten or even 15 pounds and, by grim resolve, had made sure the weight stayed lost. Stallings automatically classified the suit as a patently false testimony to steadfast character.

Carrying his only luggage—a scuffed buffalo hide Gladstone he had bought in Florence years ago—Stallings walked toward the man with the sign. When they were seven or eight feet apart they made eye contact, an act of mild bravery that Stallings had noticed fewer and fewer Americans were willing to perform.

The man's cool blue-green eyes seemed to slide over

Stallings, dismissing him. Stallings walked 15 feet past the man, stopped and turned.

The man with the "Mr. Stallings" sign stood patiently, examining each of the 200 or so male economy passengers who were still filing off the Boeing 747. The man stood with his feet a little less than 18 inches apart, his back straight, his pelvis tipped slightly forward. It was the posture of someone who knows all there is to know about waiting.

Stallings retraced his steps until he stood just behind the man with the sign. "Otherguy Overby, I'll be bound," he said.

If he hadn't been watching for it, Stallings might not have caught Overby's slight start that was really no more than a twitch. But Overby didn't turn around. Instead, still watching the arriving passengers, he said, "I figured it was you from what that son-in-law of yours told me over the phone. An old crock, he said, who'll be wearing funny cheap clothes, a barber college haircut and walks with kind of a waltz. Hard to miss, he said." Overby turned, with no discernible hurry, and examined Stallings with the same time-wasting care. "He was right."

"Where do we talk?" Stallings said. "Here, there or in the bar?"

"Unless you're all done with the ha-ha stuff, we don't. If you are, I've got somewhere in mind."

"Let's go."

"You check any luggage?"

With the look of one who has just been asked a particularly stupid question, Stallings turned and headed for the escalator where a four-color photo of the mayor who would be governor beamed down on arriving passengers.

•   •   •

When they reached the Mercedes on the second level of the parking garage across the street from the United terminal, Stallings gave the car a dour glance and then turned to Overby. "Yours?"

"No."

"Good."

"You still got something against the Krauts?" Overby said, unlocking the car's doors and slipping behind the wheel.

Stallings opened his own now unlocked door, tossed the buffalo bag onto the rear seat and climbed in. "I just don't much like dealing with anyone who needs to wear fifty-five thousand dollars worth of car."

Overby started the engine, shifted into reverse, changed his mind, shifted back into park and stared at Booth Stallings. "What are you, Jack—some kind of act?"

Stallings smiled his smallest smile. "Didn't that son-in-law of mine mention it? I do the old coot."

Overby put the car into reverse again. "It kind of gets on the nerves."

"It's supposed to," Stallings said.

Neither spoke again until they were on the San Diego freeway and heading north. It was then that Stallings finally asked, "Where're we going?"

"Malibu."

"Jesus," Stallings said.

When they neared the off ramp to the Santa Monica freeway, Stallings spoke again. "Which way's Pelican Bay from here?"

Overby flicked a glance at Stallings and then looked back at the road. "South."

"Tell me about it—you and Pelican Bay."

"You already know or you wouldn't be asking."

"What I know," Stallings said, "I got out of the California newspapers in the Library of Congress. It lacked a certain savor."

Overby didn't reply until he reached the Santa Monica freeway and had the Mercedes over in the far left fast lane, heading for the Pacific Coast Highway at a steady 60 miles per hour.

"I'll tell it just once," Overby said, "and if you want more, then you'd better try the library again."

"Fine."

"Okay. The chief of police of Pelican Bay and I made a little money on a certain deal that there's no need to go into. His name was Ploughman. Chief Oscar Ploughman. So we decided to invest in a political campaign and run him for mayor. Of Pelican Bay. I'd be campaign manager and later share in the satisfaction that always comes from good honest government."

"The graft," Stallings said.

"You want to tell it?"

"No."

"Then just listen. The chief wants to build himself a real old-timey political machine. And since I'm bankrolling about half the campaign nut, he's even started calling it the Ploughman-Overby machine, at least to me and him, if not to anybody else—except he always calls it the *powerful* Ploughman-Overby machine. The chief was a case."

"Apparently," Stallings said.

"Well, we put on one hell of a campaign and then he goes and dies on me Election Day afternoon."

"Of a heart attack," Stallings said. "Or so I read."

"Yeah," Overby said. "Of a heart attack. But the old bastard still won, lying in the morgue there with a tag on his toe, and if you think they really don't tie the toe tags on, then you haven't been to the Pelican Bay morgue where I went to make sure the asshole was really dead." Overby gave the steering wheel a hard thump with the heel of his right palm. "But we by God won it going away—fifty-three point seven to forty-six point three—and him dead as Sprat's cat."

"He did have a bad heart then."

"What he had," Overby said, "was a yen for cupcakes—fifteen-, sixteen-year-old cupcakes. Election afternoon, right up there in the victory suite I'd already rented for him, two of 'em gave him what must've been one hell of a ride—his last one anyhow—because he died in the saddle, probably smiling that big yellow smile of his, and that was it for the powerful Ploughman-Overby machine."

"And you became house-sitter to the stars."

Overby glanced at Stallings. "I like to live well even when I can't afford it."

"Who got you started—in the house-sitting trade?"

"A guy I once did a favor for."

"A guy with a name, I bet."

"A guy named Piers who's married to the Lace in Ivory, Lace and Silk. Remember them? The Armitage Sisters?"

"I seem to recall they sang awfully loud."

"Yeah, I always thought they were pretty good, too."

Stallings nodded thoughtfully and then spoke more to himself than to Overby. "Piers and Ploughman. Piers, Ploughman."

"No connection," Overby said.

"There was in a poem a long time ago."

"When?"

Stallings tried to remember. "About six hundred years back."

"You jacking me around again?"

"No."

They drove on in silence until they neared the Third and Fourth Streets off ramp that led to downtown Santa Monica. It was then that Overby asked, "You really a Ph.D. like that son-in-law of yours claims?"

"I really am."

Overby nodded comfortably, as if the last few pieces had clicked into place. "After I talked to him, what's his name, Mott, I went down to the Malibu Library and checked out that book of yours, *Anatomy of Terrorism*."

"*Anatomy of Terror*," Stallings said, unable to resist the correction.

"Yeah. Right. Well, I read it. Most of it, in fact, but then I quit about three-quarters through. Want to know why?"

"Not really."

"Because I couldn't figure out whose side you were on."

"Good," Booth Stallings said.

CHAPTER
<u>SIX</u>

S tallings disliked Billy Diron's house the moment he saw
it. He was offended by its Disney-like mock-Tudor
design and its tinted mullioned windows. He thought its
weird eight-sided blue swimming pool was awful. But what
bothered and dismayed him most of all was its total lack of
trees and greenery.

Yet Stallings couldn't fault the view. The house was built on
a high sloping bluff. A thousand feet away and a hundred feet
down were miles and miles of Pacific Ocean. The view was
from Trancas on the right to Santa Monica on the left and then
out to Palos Verdes, Catalina and beyond. Stallings knew it
was a view most could only dream of and of which few would
ever tire—unless they developed an aversion to 97 shades of
blue.

Standing beside the Mercedes in what he took to be the
courtyard, Stallings looked from ocean to house, back to ocean
and then at Otherguy Overby. "He hasn't got any view from
the house," Stallings said. "He's only got those tiny little
windows the English thought up to let in some light and still
keep out the cold but never do either."

Overby nodded in agreement as he too glanced from the
ocean to the house and back to the ocean. "Billy didn't want a
whole lot of view. He figured it'd be a distraction."

"From what?"

"His music."

"He's a musician?"

Overby cocked his head to the left, the better to study Stallings. "You never heard of Billy Diron?"

"No."

"What about Galahad's Balloon?"

"I'd guess it's a rock group. But that's a guess from someone who no longer sings his country's songs."

"That's like guessing the Rams play—" Overby broke off when he heard the unmistakable whine of a Volkswagen engine. He turned toward the noise, clamping his lips into a stern line and folding his arms across his chest. A certain amount of forbidding crept into his eyes.

Both men watched the open white VW cabriolet speed around the corner of the house too fast, skid on the used brick paving, and buck and shudder to a stop when the woman driver applied the brakes but forgot to throw out the clutch. Stallings saw that she was young, quite young, no more than 22 or 23, and rather pretty once he got past the spiky silver hair and manic eyes.

The man who sat next to her in the passenger seat was older, at least 30 or even 32. He had a journeyman surfer's tan, more ripe-wheat hair than he really needed, and jittery blue eyes so pale they seemed almost bleached. The man's gaze flitted about, darting straight ahead to Overby, right to Stallings, left to the house and then back to Overby where it hovered with a hummingbird's bold resolve.

The woman opened the car door and got out. She was barefoot and wore half a blue T-shirt that just covered her breasts and ended eight inches above her navel. She also wore skimpy white shorts that hadn't been washed in a while. The wind had made a mess of her spiky silver hair. But even with the bird's-nest hair and the forest creature eyes, Stallings thought she could pass for a standard Hollywood beauty if only something would iron the sullen rage out of her expression. He thought he knew what that something might be.

As though feeling Stallings' gaze, she looked at him but

directed her question to Overby. "Who the fuck's he, Other-guy?"

"Nobody."

"He's somebody. Everyone's somebody."

"He isn't."

She moved several steps closer to Overby who still stood guard, arms folded, eyes implacable, his mouth all set to say no.

"I wanta go in and get my shit," she said.

"I work for Billy, Cynthia, and Billy says you don't go in."

Cynthia Blondin's wide unpainted mouth twisted itself into what began as an ingratiating smile but ended as a snarl. "I gotta have it, Otherguy."

"It's gone," Overby said. "I flushed it down the john. Just like Billy said to."

"You fuck."

Overby nodded his indifferent agreement.

"The lady thinks you're lying, Ace," said the man in the car as he opened the door and stepped out, his lower body concealed by the car door.

Overby glanced at the man without curiosity. "Who cares what she thinks?"

"I do," the man said as he stepped around the car door and aimed a short-barreled five-shot revolver at Overby. "She goes inside."

Overby first studied the pistol, and then the man's face. After that Overby turned and walked slowly to the rear of the Mercedes sedan, produced a key and opened the trunk lid. He reached into the trunk and brought out a tire iron. Stallings wondered if the tire iron came as standard equipment with a Mercedes and decided it didn't.

Holding the tire iron down at his side in his left hand, Overby walked over to the man with the pistol. "You better take Cynthia and get in the car and leave," Overby said. "I think maybe you better drive."

"You've just about cost yourself a knee, fuckhead," the man said and pointed the pistol at Overby's left knee.

Overby brought the tire iron up fast and smashed it into the underside of the man's right wrist. The man yelped as the pistol flew up and out of his grasp and landed at Stallings' feet. Stallings bent down, picked it up, examined it briefly, and then aimed it at the man who now stood, slightly bent over, left hand clutching his right wrist.

"Go get her what she wants, Otherguy," Stallings said.

A surprised Overby stared at Stallings. "Why?"

"Because if you don't, she'll be back, and I don't want her here."

Overby thought it over, acquiesced with a nod to superior logic, turned and entered the house. Cynthia Blondin took two happy dance steps toward Booth Stallings. "Who're you, Pops?" she said.

"I'm Daddy Goodtimes," Stallings said, looking not at her but at the man with the injured wrist who had now straightened up and was gently massaging the hurt wrist with his left hand.

Cynthia Blondin giggled happily. The man with the hurt wrist glowered at her. She giggled again. The man turned his uncertain gaze on Stallings. "I want my piece back."

Stallings replied with a head shake and a slight smile.

"Bet I can take it away from you." This time there was no smile when Stallings again shook his head no.

The man took a slow hesitant step toward Stallings who cocked the revolver, pleased with the ominous sound it made.

"Old fart's gonna shoot you, Joey," Cynthia Blondin said and again giggled. "You'll shoot him dead, won't you, Pops?"

"You bet," Stallings said.

The man with the hurt wrist started to say something else but stopped when Overby came out of the house, still carrying the tire iron in his left hand and, in his right, a small brown paper bag that was folded over into a packet and wrapped with two rubber bands. Overby stopped in front of Cynthia Blondin who bit her lower lip, staring greedily at the packet.

"I want you to listen to what I'm gonna say, Cynthia. You listening?"

She nodded, not taking her eyes from the packet.

"Billy doesn't want you back. He doesn't want to see you. He doesn't want to talk to you. If you've got something to say to Billy, call Ritto and Ogilvie and talk to Joe Ritto. Am I getting through?"

"Gimme my shit, Otherguy."

Overby sighed and offered her the packet. She took it with both hands, gently, carefully, as if taking a baby bird from its nest. She turned then, humming something, and hurried toward the driver's side of the Volkswagen.

The man with the hurt wrist started toward the passenger side, changed his mind, and turned back to Stallings. "You really ain't gonna gimme my piece back?"

"No," Stallings said.

The man nodded sadly, turned again, and climbed into the car. Cynthia Blondin, now holding the packet in one hand as if it might shatter, opened the driver's door. Before sliding behind the wheel, she looked at Overby who stood, tapping the tire iron against the palm of his right hand.

"Tell Billy," she said. "Tell him I'll always love him and I'll always care for him and that I wish him all the success in the world."

"Okay," Overby said.

Cynthia Blondin slipped behind the wheel, gently placing the packet in her lap. After starting the engine she leaned her head out and called to Overby, "You won't forget?"

"I'll tell him," Overby said. "Billy likes stuff like that."

Cynthia Blondin nodded, backed the car around until it faced the drive, ground the gears twice and drove off. Just as the car reached the corner of the house, the man with the hurt wrist twisted around and used his unhurt hand to give Stallings and Overby the inevitable finger. Overby waved goodbye with the tire iron, turned to Stallings, indicated the revolver and said, "You want to keep it?"

"What for?" Stallings said, handing it over.

A relieved Overby said, "Now what?"

"Now? Well, now we'll go inside and talk about Wu and Durant."

CHAPTER SEVEN

B ooth Stallings sat at the large round table in Billy Diron's elaborate kitchen and watched Overby make two canned corned beef sandwiches. He made them with the quick economical moves usually learned in either a delicatessen or an institutional kitchen. Since he suspected Overby would starve before working in a delicatessen, Stallings decided not to ask for the name of the institution in which he had trained.

Overby served the sandwiches on two plates, each containing exactly seven potato chips and three slices of dill pickle. Stallings had watched him count out both the potato chips and the pickles. To drink were two more bottles of San Miguel beer.

After Overby sat down, Stallings took a bite of the sandwich. Between the slices of dark rye he found not only corned beef, but also several leaves of Boston lettuce, a thick slab of Bermuda onion, and a dressing of mayonnaise and two kinds of mustard that Overby had carefully measured out and blended together.

After Stallings swallowed his first bite of sandwich, he said, "Tell me."

"What?" Overby said.

"How old are they?"

Overby tried to recall. "Well, Artie must be—"

"That's Wu, right?"

Overby nodded. "Arthur Case Wu. He must be around forty-four now, but it's kind of hard to tell about Durant on account of there was never any birth certificate. But Durant thinks he's about the same as Artie. Forty-four. Around in there."

"What else?"

"Well, they were both raised in this San Francisco Methodist orphanage, ran away when they were fourteen, wound up at Princeton for a while, and they've been partners ever since."

"They went to Princeton—to college?"

"I never got that quite straight. Artie went on a scholarship and Quincy sort of went as Artie's bodyguard."

"Dear God," Stallings said. "Their specialty is what exactly?"

"This and that. But most of the time they probably do pretty close to what you'd want 'em to do."

"I haven't said."

"Maybe you should."

"I'll get to it," Stallings said and ate some more of his sandwich, washing it down with the Filipino beer. "They married?" he asked.

Overby produced one of his sly grins that displayed no teeth. "To each other, you mean?"

"To anybody."

"Durant's not married and fools around. But Wu's married to this lady from Scotland, and by lady I mean she's got some sort of thoroughbred bloodlines—eighteenth cousin to the Queen twice removed or something—which suits Artie just fine on account of he's still pretender to the Emperor's throne."

"Emperor?" Stallings said. "What emperor?"

"The Emperor of China, who else?"

"Sweet Jesus."

"He's even got genealogical charts and everything. He also

figures if there were about two revolutions, three wars and maybe ten thousand deaths of just the right people, his oldest twin boy could be both King of Scotland and Emperor of China."

"He has twin sons?"

"Twin sons *and* twin daughters. Cute kids—or were the last time I saw 'em. The girls are younger than the boys."

Stallings slowly poured more beer into his glass and tasted it. "He's not . . . obsessed with this emperor thing, is he?"

Again, Overby smiled slyly. "Artie figures he's the last of the Manchus."

"How about a straight answer?"

Overby's frown managed to make him look both grave and highly proper. Stallings thought it must be one of his most useful expressions. "Artie knows exactly who he is," Overby said. "More'n anybody I ever met."

"And Durant?"

"He doesn't much give a shit who he is."

"When'd you meet them?"

"The fourth of July in sixty-eight, Bangkok. At the Embassy reception." He paused. "The Ambassador'd invited everybody who even looked American. Even us."

"What were you doing in Bangkok?"

"Looking around. I'd bumped into Wu and Durant and they needed a crimp for a little something they'd decided to play off against the chief of station."

"The *CIA* chief of station?"

"Who else."

"So what happened?"

Overby looked puzzled. "What d'you mean what happened? We ran it and walked away with about sixty-three thousand. That was major money back then, in sixty-eight."

"And what did he do about it?"

"The chief of station? He ate it. What else could he do? He sure didn't go around bragging about the bad case of greed he'd come down with."

"Were either Wu or Durant ever hooked up to Langley?"

Overby's answering shrug was a bit too elaborate to satisfy Stallings. "Is that a maybe yes or a maybe no?"

"Artie says that a couple of times they were maybe unwitting assets. But Durant always says they were half-witted assets and no maybe about it. They moved around a lot and sometimes they just took whatever turned up."

"When's the last time you worked with them?"

"Seven or eight years ago. We went in on a deal together and we all got well."

"Where?"

"Here. In California."

"What kind of deal?"

"That's none of your fucking business, is it?"

They stared at each other for long moments, each searching for the other's weakness, only to find there was none. Stallings finally replied to Overby's question. "No," he said, "I don't guess it is. Any of my fucking business."

Overby drank some of his beer and said, "Tell me about your deal."

"All right." Stallings was silent for perhaps ten seconds as he edited what he planned to say. "Somebody," he said, "and I don't know exactly who, wants to pay me half a million dollars to bribe a Filipino freedom fighter and/or terrorist to come down from the hills and light out for Hong Kong where five million dollars U.S. will be waiting for him. Or so they say."

Although Overby's face and eyes remained calm and even impassive, his nose betrayed him with a long, long sniff as if he suddenly smelled sweet profit. After the sniff came the white, wide and utterly ruthless grin, which Stallings found curiously merry.

"You need help," Overby said.

"I know."

"You need Wu and Durant."

"So it would seem."

"You also need me."

Stallings raised his eyebrows to register surprise. "I hadn't thought of that."

Overby's ruthless, merry grin returned. "Like hell."

"It's an interesting notion."

"Where's this freedom fighter and/or terrorist of yours holed up—central Luzon?"

Stallings shook his head. "Cebu. Know it?"

Overby's grin grew even wider. "Lapu-Lapu land. Yeah, I know Cebu. Like my name. Not to get too commercial and all, but what kind of split are we talking about?"

"You're negotiating for Wu and Durant now, right?"

Overby nodded. "For both them and me."

"I was thinking in the neighborhood of fifty-fifty."

Overby's feigned disappointment took the form of a sorrowful frown. "I think we'd need just a little more taste than that."

"It's take it or leave it, Otherguy."

The frown went away and the grin came back. "Well, hell, half of five hundred thousand split three ways, less expenses, is about eighty thousand each, which isn't bad. Not good, you understand, but not bad."

"I guess I didn't make myself clear," Stallings said. "I intend to split the entire five million—not just the five hundred thousand."

Overby didn't try to disguise anything. The big white smile was back, never more ruthless, never more merry. "You're talking interesting fucking money now."

Stallings didn't return the smile. Instead his eyes took on the look of someone who has dipped into the future and is dismayed by what he's seen.

"It's poisoned money," Stallings said.

"Money's money."

"Not this time."

Guided only by his almost infallible con man's instinct, Otherguy Overby came up with exactly the right measure of reassurance.

"In that case, friend," he said, "you sure as hell got off on the right floor."

CHAPTER EIGHT

The pretender to the Emperor's throne stood in the innermost sanctum of the deposed ruler's palace and listened, beaming with pride, as the younger of his ten-year-old twin daughters finished reading the framed poem aloud. The poem had been left behind on the wall when the deposed ruler fled into the night.

"'Yours is the earth and everything that's in it,'" she read, "'And—which is more—you'll be a man, my son.'"

The ten-year-old girl had read Kipling's "If" with what at one time was called expression. The Filipinos in the line behind her applauded enthusiastically. She turned, curtsied prettily—despite the jeans she wore—then looked up at the big Chinaman (as she and her sister always thought of him) who was not only her father, but also pretender to the throne of the Emperor of China.

"Very, very nice," said Artie Wu who stood six foot two and three-quarters inches and weighed 249 pounds, only six percent of it pure blubber.

His younger daughter made a face at the poem on the wall. "God, that's dumb."

"Mr. Kipling had an unhappy childhood," Agnes Wu explained. "To make up for it he sometimes became a trifle optimistic and overly sentimental."

Her daughter nodded wisely. "Mush, huh?"

"Mush," agreed Agnes Wu whose Rs were tinged with a slight Scot's burr. Everything else she said sounded like the

English spoken by those who have gone to proper schools that place a high premium on received pronunciation. But none of the schools were able to do anything about the burr of Agnes Wu who had been born Agnes Goriach.

The older of the twin daughters (older by 21 minutes) turned on her sister. "It wasn't half as dumb as 'Invictus' that you got out of and Mrs. Crane made me memorize last year. You want mush? 'Out-of-the-night-that-covers-me-black-as-the-pit-from-pole-to-pole-I-thank-whatever-gods-may-be-for-my-un-conquerable-soul.' *That's* mush."

"You're holding up the line, ladies," said Artie Wu as sternly as he ever said anything to his daughters. Totally incapable of assuming the heavy father role, Wu continued to be surprised at his daughters' reluctance to take advantage of his faltering will. His twin 13-year-old sons were something else. His sons would flimflam a saint.

The Wu family moved out of Ferdinand Marcos' small private study whose shelves still contained scores of pop histories, biographies and steaming political exposés, writ-ten—for the most part—by American authors. The study was a windowless room tucked away in the Malacañang Palace on the banks of the Pasig River in Manila. The Wus had already toured the discothèque, the throne room, and were heading for Imelda Marcos' bedroom when Agnes Wu turned back to the trailing Peninsula Hotel limousine driver who was also visiting the palace for the first time.

"How much time do we have, Roddy?" she asked.

Rodolfo Caday glanced at his watch. "Plenty, ma'am. The flight's not till four and I fix it with A and A to meet us here outside."

A and A were the twin 13-year-old Wu sons, Arthur and Angus, who already had toured the palace twice on their own. "Then we don't have to go back to the hotel for them?" Agnes Wu said.

"No, ma'am."

With a small gesture that took in the palace, Agnes Wu said, "Well?"

Rodolfo Caday frowned, then shrugged. "Much foolishness."

•   •   •

In the bedroom of Imelda Marcos one of the volunteer Filipina docents was commenting in a not quite bored voice on several of the room's more interesting items, particularly the huge red satin bed. Some ten thousand Filipinos were trooping through the palace each day and the handful now in the bedroom made no effort to disguise their voyeurism. Some of the men nudged each other. Some of the women giggled. Others kept handkerchiefs over their noses and mouths as if to strain out any of the remaining bad-luck germs that had infected Imelda Marcos.

Artie Wu's younger daughter looked up at him. "How come they bought so much—well, muchness?"

"It may have been a way to keep score."

"You mean the lady with the most shoes wins?"

"Maybe."

"But she didn't."

"Maybe that's the point," Artie Wu said.

•   •   •

Standing in the center of the bedlam that was the Manila International Airport, Wu peeled off 50-peso notes and handed them to sons and daughters, porters and self-proclaimed expediters, and to the driver, Rodolfo Caday, dispatching them all on real and imagined errands that would give Wu a few minutes alone with his wife.

Almost everyone liked to stare at Mr. and Mrs. Arthur Case Wu. They especially liked to gape at the tall woman with the pale yellow hair, the big smart gray eyes, and the not quite perfect features that seemed almost regal until she grinned. When she grinned she looked just a bit wacky.

The gapers also liked to dart quick and, they hoped, undetected glances at the big Chinese in his white silk suit and Panama hat who carried an ebony cane—a walking stick, really—that they all knew concealed a sword, although it didn't. Agnes Wu always referred to the white silk suit as the "get out of here and get me some money suit" because Wu almost never put it on unless they were broke or nearly so.

Agnes Wu ran a hand down the suit's immaculate lapel, smoothing out an imaginary wrinkle. "So riddle me this," she said. "When you get up to Baguio, what if you and Durant still can't find the Cousin?"

"We'll find him," Artie Wu said.

"You're going to have to face it sooner or later, Artie. The Cousin took you and Durant."

Wu nodded. "That's why we have to find him. After all, Quincy and I have our reputations to think of." Then he smiled—the great white Wu smile behind which laughter bubbled, threatening to erupt. The smile told Agnes Wu she could disregard everything her husband had just said.

She grinned back at him, again making herself look just a few charming bubbles off level. "So when you don't find the Cousin and your reputations are in shreds, then what?"

"Then we come back down here and take the next plane to London and the fast train up to Edinburgh. Durant likes trains."

"Bring money, Artie."

"Don't I always?"

"Bring bagsful this time."

"Bagsful," he promised.

"Take care of yourself."

He nodded.

"And look after Durant."

"Or vice versa," Artie Wu said.

•   •   •

The Peninsula Hotel in the Makati section of Manila was owned and operated by the same organization that operated the Hong Kong Peninsula. About the only difference Artie Wu could detect was that the Hong Kong Peninsula sent a Rolls-Royce to pick you up at the airport whereas the Manila Peninsula made do with a Mercedes.

As Wu entered the many-sided lobby he saw that most of its tables were filled as usual by well-dressed Manileños who had gathered to gossip and drink coffee or maybe something with ice in it. And, as usual, many of them stared at him when, swinging his cane, he strode across the lobby toward the concierge. Wu looked left once and right once, checking to see if there were any faces out of his past.

The only familiar one belonged to the Graf von Lahusen whose ancestral estates lay unfortunately on the wrong side of the Elbe. The 37-year-old count had dropped out of the Sorbonne at 19 to take the hippie trail to Southeast Asia where he soon discovered that his title, looks and four languages could earn him a decent if questionable living.

Wu was remembering the time the count and Otherguy Overby had run the ancient Omaha Banker wheeze, Overby playing the role of the remorse-stricken banker to perfection, when the Graf von Lahusen looked up, saw Wu, rose and bowed gravely. Artie Wu stopped and bowed gravely back. The count's mark, a middle-aged Japanese, twisted around in his chair to see who was doing all the bowing and scraping. He seemed visibly impressed by the Chinese gentleman in the splendid white silk suit and Panama hat who carried what obviously was a sword cane.

Wu continued to the concierge's desk, pleased to see that Mr. Welcome-Welcome was on duty. The assistant concierge's name was really Bernard Naldo but Wu always thought of him as Mr. Welcome-Welcome because that's what he always said to Wu, even when they had seen each other only minutes before.

"Welcome, welcome, Mr. Wu," the assistant concierge said

as Wu reached the counter and leaned on it, noting that Naldo still looked like a genial brown frog, all dressed up in a black coat, white shirt and striped pants, who would turn back into a prince once he had answered the millionth tourist's millionth dumb question.

"Got my bill ready, Bernie?" Wu said.

Naldo reached beneath the counter and came up with a thick sheaf of computer-printed billings. "As requested," he said. "The total is, let's see, sixty thousand two hundred and nineteen pesos."

"Settle for three thousand U.S., cash money?"

"Of course."

Wu took out a fat roll of $100 bills and started counting them onto the counter.

"Wife and kiddies get off safely?" Naldo asked.

Wu nodded and kept on counting.

"You had a visitor."

Wu stopped counting and glanced up. "Who?"

Naldo sniffed his disapproval. "Boy Howdy. He was looking for either you or Durant."

"What'd you tell him?"

"That you were out sight-seeing and that Durant was touring somewhere down south. Mindanao, I told him, around Zamboanga."

"He believe you?"

"No."

"When he comes back tell him I checked out and Durant's down on Negros, dickering for a sugar plantation."

"He won't believe that either."

"I don't want him to believe it; I just want him to feel unwanted."

Naldo sniffed again. "Terrible man. But I suppose he really can't help it, being Australian."

"Three thousand," said Wu, sliding the money toward Naldo who picked it up and counted it with amazing speed. "Three thousand two hundred," he said.

"I know."

"Oh," Naldo said, pocketing two of the $100 bills. "How can I be of service?"

"I need one of the hotel Mercedes for a few days."

"Of course. Would you like Roddy to drive again?"

"No driver."

Naldo was instantly dismayed. "You want to drive yourself? The hotel can't be responsible."

"It's my kind of traffic, Bernie. I'm like a fish back in water."

"No, I'm sorry, but we can't permit it."

"Bernie, let me ask you something. How much money have Durant and I spent with you guys the last three or four months?"

"You're both highly valued guests, but—"

"I want the car outside at seven tomorrow morning, all gassed up and ready to go."

Naldo sighed. "Do you mind if it's our oldest Mercedes?"

"As long as it has wheels."

"And your suite?"

"Run a tab on it."

"When can we expect you and Mr. Durant back—should you both survive?"

"A few days."

"You wouldn't reconsider and—"

"No," Artie Wu said. "I wouldn't."

CHAPTER
NINE

Wearing a yellow People Power T-shirt, seersucker pants and a pair of sandals, Artie Wu ate a large buffet breakfast in the Peninsula Hotel's La Bodega—where they always lost money on him—and by 7:05 A.M. was slipping the hotel's black Mercedes sedan through Manila's demented traffic. As always, the Filipino drivers relied exclusively on their horns to signal their uncertain intentions. Artie Wu matched them toot for toot.

At a long red light two professional beggar children approached him. The older child was a girl of no more than ten who carried her emaciated four-year-old brother in her arms. Their eyes were enormous; their expressions pitiable; their minds possibly retarded by malnutrition. Although suspecting that all beggar children stood for hours in front of mirrors to get their woebegone looks down pat, Wu nevertheless rolled down his window and put a 20-peso note into the four-year-old's palm.

He knew the children would be lucky to get a dime out of the dollar he had just handed them. The rest would go to the cops and the syndicate they worked for. Wu also knew if they managed to live another year or two, the syndicate might fatten them up and turn them into child prostitutes.

After leaving Manila, Wu didn't stop until he reached Angeles and was past both the sprawling Clark Air Base and the long line of open-air shops that offered black market PX goods. He stopped at a McDonald's for coffee and watched the

18- and 19-year-old U.S. airmen and their 15- and 16-year-old whores put away the Big Macs and the Cokes and the french fries at ten in the morning.

Later, not far from Tarlac, which was Corazon Aquino's hometown, Wu again stopped, locked the car, and walked up a short hill to inspect the memorial built on what was said to be the exact spot where the Bataan Death March had ended in 1942. Wu had passed the memorial several times, but had never stopped and was curious about what its plaque said. But there was no plaque. None that Artie Wu could find.

The only other visitor was a lanky red-faced man with thinning gray hair and a limp who wandered around taking pictures with his Instamatic.

"Where's the plaque?" Wu asked him.

"Guess somebody stole it," the man said in an accent that Wu thought could be from either of the Dakotas or possibly Minnesota.

"Hell of a thing," Wu said.

"Hell of a walk."

"You weren't old enough."

"My daddy," the man said. "That's how I still think of him. Daddy. He shipped out to the P.I.'s in thirty-nine. I was two then. Don't even know if he made it up this far. Never did find out what happened exactly—to him, I mean. But I thought I'd stop by and, you know, kind of pay my respects."

Wu nodded. The man glanced around, not much liking what he saw. "Looks like they could spruce it up a little."

"People like to forget lost wars," Wu said.

The man nodded. "I guess." He squinted at Wu through the 90-degree glare. "You're not Japanese, are you?"

"No," Wu said.

"For a second there I thought you coulda been one of the Japs that might've known my daddy and—aw hell, you know what I thought."

"Sure."

The man turned as if to give the Death March memorial one

last look. "Well, what the fuck, I don't even remember him anyhow."

* * *

Wu stopped for a late lunch at a resort called Agoo Playa that offered a fine black-sand beach facing the South China Sea and enough luxury rooms to sleep 140 guests. The town of Agoo in La Union province was near the foot of the Cordillera Mountains in northern Luzon and almost as far north as Baguio itself.

Wu assumed the hotel-resort had been built by the Marcos government, or by some of the ex-President's closer cronies. He sat, the lone guest in a dining room that would seat 80, and ordered a beer and the seafood salad from one of the five young waiters who hovered close by. When the beer came, Wu asked, "How many guests do you have?"

"In the rooms?" the young waiter said.

Wu nodded.

"Four."

"Think business will pick up?"

The waiter shrugged. "When it gets hot."

"It's hot now."

"Hotter," the waiter said.

* * *

Wu's last stop before Baguio was the Marcos Park clubhouse that served an 18-hole golf course. He had a cup of coffee and admired the empty golf links and the nearly empty clubhouse. He was high in the mountains now and the temperature had dropped from 90 degrees to the mid-70s. The course below looked green, tough and inviting, and Wu thought it a shame nobody was playing.

When he finished his coffee Wu went out on the stone verandah and gazed up at the great stone head of Ferdinand Marcos who glowered down at him. He had seen pictures of the head before, perched up on its own mountain, but had never been able to get a fix on its true size. He now guessed it was either five or six stories tall.

Next to Wu was the only other tourist—a fiftyish man who was using a pair of binoculars to inspect the Marcos head. Still gazing through the binoculars, the man said, "Look at that, will you?"

"What?"

"The nose," the man said in his New Zealand accent.

Wu looked at the Marcos nose with its flared nostrils. He could just make out two small figures, suspended by ropes as they swung from the left stone eyebrow toward the nose. One of the figures was carrying something white.

"What're they doing?" Wu said.

"Here. Take a look." The man handed him the binoculars. As Wu put them up to his eyes and adjusted the focus, the man said, "Unless I miss my guess, those kids're shoving a booger right up the old boy's nose."

The binoculars came into focus. "Maybe it's dynamite," Wu said.

"Mmm," said the man from New Zealand. "Didn't think of that, did I?"

• • •

Artie Wu sometimes estimated that 50 percent of the Filipinos he met had been to San Francisco. And of those who had, 100 percent always insisted the California city reminded them of Baguio.

He didn't buy the similarity. Both cities had hills and cool, even chilly, weather, but Baguio always reminded Artie Wu of some southern U.S. piney woods town during a spring cold snap. Asheville, maybe.

Still, Baguio deserved its Summer Capital title because all Manila had once migrated there when the hot season began in March. All Manila meant the President, the Cabinet, select members of the National Assembly, the generals, the press, the new and old rich—and the swarm of civil servants and hangers-on who followed in their wake. Durant had once called Baguio the place where "the elite meet to eat and fuck up the country."

But that year the President was spending a hot March in Manila, trying to nail her country back together. As Wu drove past the presidential summer residence (where some kind of topiary spelled out "Mansion House" in ten-foot letters), he became stuck in a traffic jam and noticed the soldiers who guarded the mansion entrance were selling film to tourists. Wu took it as a sign of the new entrepreneurial spirit abroad in the land.

Because he would rather drive 100 miles the wrong way than ask directions, Wu took a wrong turn and wound up going downhill on Sessions Road, which was Baguio's steep main commercial street. This led him down into the gridlocked market area that he had to honk and swear his way out of. Finally, by luck and guesswork, he wandered onto South Drive and found the Hyatt Terraces where Mr. Welcome-Welcome had reserved him a room.

Once up in the room, Wu took a bottle of beer from the mini-refrigerator, drank half, picked up the phone and called the woman he always thought of as the Rich Widow. A servant answered on the second ring. Then Emily Cariaga came on with a warm and low-pitched, "Artie! How nice."

"How've you been, Emily?"

"Let's talk about that later. Here's Quincy."

The first thing Quincy Durant said was, "Where are you—the Pines?"

"Quincy," Wu said. "The Pines burned down two years ago."

There was a brief silence until Durant said, "I blocked it, I guess. So. If you're not at the Pines, you're at the Hyatt."

"Right."

"I'll pick you up downstairs in ten minutes and we'll go see him."

"See who?"

"The Cousin," Durant said. "Who else?"

.   .   .

Camp John Hay served primarily as a country club for the U.S. airmen and officers stationed at Clark Air Base. In addition to its kilometer-and-a-half altitude, it offered golf, tennis, swimming, bowling, American films, a wealth of PX goods and an ocean of beer. But mostly it offered an invigorating change of climate. Well-behaved Filipinos could also use certain sections of the carefully tended grounds as a public park.

It was almost dark when Quincy Durant stopped the Honda Prelude he had borrowed from Emily Cariaga at the camp gates and asked the MP on duty how to get to the post hospital. The MP handed Durant a map marked with a red X. As they drove on, Artie Wu asked, "Who're we?"

"Business associates," Durant said.

At the post hospital an enlisted orderly steered Wu and Durant into a small office where a young uniformed Army doctor, wearing a captain's bars, sat with his feet on a desk, reading *Time*. He looked up at Durant, then at Wu and back at Durant.

"You the Durant who called?"

Durant nodded. "I'm Durant; he's Wu."

The Captain put his *Time* on the desk, his feet on the floor and rose. "I'm Doctor Robbie. Let's go."

Wu and Durant followed the Captain down a hall, a flight of metal stairs, and along a short basement corridor. The Captain used a key on a lock and tugged open a thick door. Wu and Durant felt a rush of cold air.

Captain Robbie reached around the door and switched on a light. Wu and Durant followed him into the room, Wu closing the door behind them. It was cold inside and the only furniture in the 9 × 12–foot refrigerated room were two gurneys. On one of them was a man, naked except for a bath towel with

Camp John Hay stitched across it in red letters. The towel covered the man's crotch. He had light brown skin, a handsome playboy face, and appeared to be about 30. His throat had been cut. Captain Robbie lifted the towel to give Wu and Durant a glimpse of the man's crotch. "They got his balls too," Captain Robbie said as he let the towel drop and turned to Durant. "Well?"

"What was he wearing?" Durant said.

"Why?"

"When they cut off his balls did they take his pants down, off or what?"

Captain Robbie gave his head a small shake, as if he didn't understand Durant's questions. "They found him just like that, naked as a jaybird, at oh-three-hundred this morning down by a post beer joint that's called the Nineteenth Tee. His throat was cut and his balls were gone. No socks, no shoes, nothing. Just him. Buck naked and stone dead. You guys know him or not?"

Durant looked at Wu. "I'd say that was Ernie, wouldn't you?"

Wu nodded. "Poor old Ernie."

Captain Robbie took a ballpoint pen and a small spiral notebook from a shirt pocket and clicked the pen into write. He opened the notebook and looked at Durant. "Ernie what?"

"Ernesto Pineda," Durant said and spelled the surname slowly.

"He was what to you?"

"We did some business with him once," Wu said. "We thought we were going to do a little more, but I guess we aren't."

"I guess not," Captain Robbie said. "Who's his next of kin?"

"The only kinfolk I ever heard him mention was a third cousin," Durant said.

"Nobody closer?" Captain Robbie asked. "Wife, parents, brother, sister—even a niece or nephew?"

Durant shook his head regretfully. "That third cousin was the only one Ernie ever mentioned."

The Captain shook his head and asked, "What's the cousin's name?"

"Ferdinand Marcos," Durant said.

Captain Robbie's smooth young face wrinkled itself into lines of worry and disbelief. "Tell me you're kidding."

Wu solemnly shook his great head from side to side.

Captain Robbie winced and turned to stare down at the exiled President's dead third cousin. "Goddamnit, Ernie, what a pain in the butt you've turned out to be."

CHAPTER
TEN

Quincy Durant sat propped up in the Hyatt hotel bed, smoking a rare cigarette and drinking Scotch and water, when Artie Wu came out of the bathroom, shrimp pink from his shower and wearing only a pair of voluminous white boxer shorts. Wu started putting on the pants to the white silk money suit. He spoke only after he had the pants on and was buttoning a tent-size blue chambray shirt. "How much?"

"About a thousand," Durant said. "I spread it around town with the word that I was trying to locate Ernie. I got a call at six this morning from a taxi dispatcher. One of his drivers took an Air Force CID major to that post beer joint, the Nineteenth Tee, where they'd found Ernie. The Major's car wouldn't start, which is why he called a taxi. The driver recognized Ernie."

"But didn't say anything."

"Not to anybody but the dispatcher."

Wu, looking into the mirror, carefully continued to knot his paisley tie. "What d'you think?"

"What or who?"

"Who."

"A cuckolded husband. A disappointed bankrupt maybe."

"Christ, that second one's us."

"The list goes on," Durant said and took another swallow of his drink. "A spurned lover, male or female. Some guy who didn't get the job in the ministry of works, or whatever, that he'd paid Ernie to get him. An NPA sparrow team."

"Sparrow team. That's nice."

"You prefer hit squad?"

Wu shrugged. "Not really, but you may be right at that. Let's say Ernie's out cruising. He meets this young sparrow, male or female, in a bar and they agree to a quickie in the front seat of Ernie's BMW. The second sparrow's already down behind the back seat. He cuts Ernie's throat, they drive out to the camp, strip him, cut him some more and leave him in the neo-colonialists' playground as a warning to whoever they're mad at this week. If you needed a symbol of corruption, you couldn't do much better than Ernie."

"I always kind of liked him," Durant said.

"So'd I, until he stiffed us." Wu crossed to the mini-refrigerator and took out a bottle of beer. He twisted off the cap, had a swallow and looked at Durant. "It's a write-off, isn't it?"

"The three hundred thousand? Total."

"How much've you got?" Wu asked.

Durant finished his drink, put the glass down, ground his cigarette out, locked his hands behind his head, leaned back against the bed's headboard and stared at the ceiling. "Three thousand two hundred and twenty-three dollars and a Gold American Express card that'll lie still for a couple of months if we don't beat it too hard. You?"

"About the same," Wu said. "Maybe two or three hundred more. I'm afraid to count it."

"If we needed to front something, I could probably borrow ten thousand from Emily."

"Front what, for Christ sake?" Artie Wu said as he put his beer down, picked up the white money suit's jacket, flicked something from its left sleeve and slipped it on.

"No idea."

Wu turned to examine himself in the mirror that hung over the bureau. "Boy Howdy's looking for us."

Durant's long face went still. Nothing moved. Not the green-gray eyes or the wide mouth that always stayed turned up at its ends. Artie Wu watched him in the mirror, trying to detect some reaction. It was no use looking for a flush because Durant wore one of those hot country tans that takes years to acquire and never seems to fade, not even in cold climates.

Durant at last unlocked his hands from behind his head and rose slowly. He stood an inch taller than Artie Wu but weighed at least 60 pounds less. At first glance most found him skinny until they realized their mistake and tried slim. When that didn't quite work either they resorted to lean and left it at that because they couldn't think of anything else.

In addition to his permanent tan Durant wore a pair of chino pants and a V-neck navy blue cotton sweater but no shirt. On his feet were a pair of expensive but sockless tasseled loafers that hadn't been shined in a while—if ever. He walked over to the mirror and stared at Artie Wu's reflection. "I don't work with that Aussie git," Durant said, using an offhand tone that Wu long ago had learned to interpret as adamant.

"Okay," Wu said. "Forget it."

There was a brief silence while they stared at each other in the mirror. Finally, Durant asked, "What's Boy got?"

"I don't know. He might be just the post office."

"With a hell of a lot of postage due—as always."

"So?"

"So we don't have much choice, do we?"

"None at all," said Artie Wu.

. . .

Emily Cariaga, reared by a great-grandmother in Manila who had insisted on speaking only Spanish to her great-granddaughter until the child was six, studied the ridged network of 36 pale scars that crisscrossed Durant's back. He sat naked on the edge of the bed, smoking a breakfast cigarette. She reached over and ran a gentle forefinger along the longest scar. Durant shivered.

"What time is it?" she asked.

Durant looked at his stainless-steel watch on the bedside table and then slipped it onto his wrist. "Five past five."

"At dinner last night Artie seemed so—well, I would say pensive, except I'm talking about Artie."

"Artie's broke," Durant said. "When he's broke, he thinks a lot."

"You should've asked me about Ernie."

"Probably."

"I've known him all my life."

Durant put his cigarette out in the ashtray. "And?"

"And Ernesto Arguello Bello Pineda was always a perfectly charming bastard. Utterly untrustworthy."

Durant turned around to look at her as she lay on the bed, staring up at the ceiling, her small breasts bare, the rest of her covered by the sheet. "He checked out okay," Durant said.

"With whom?" she said. "You and Artie talked to the wrong set. You talked to those who hoped to get a few crumbs from Ernie's table. You should've talked to the ones who own the table."

Durant smiled. "Your set."

"My set."

He shrugged. "It's finished."

"Whatever did you pay him all that money for?"

"To grease the skids; cross a few palms. The deal was a casualty reinsurance pool."

"To insure insurers, right?"

"Right. Poor old Ernie claimed he knew people who'd cut us in for a twenty percent share of the pool. For their kindness, they'd be rewarded with two hundred thousand U.S., all cash. Ernie'd get one hundred thousand for all his hard work. Once we had it signed and sealed, Artie and I knew some money guys in London we could've laid our twenty percent off on. We were figuring on doubling our money or better."

Emily Cariaga smiled. "Little lambs." She ran a forefinger down the inside of Durant's forearm. Again he shivered. "Didn't anyone ever warn you against well-spoken strangers?"

"That's what was really bothering Artie last night," he said. "You see, until we bumped into Ernesto Pineda, Artie and I were always the well-spoken strangers."

"Poor you."

Durant nodded his agreement. "Poor is right."

"You need money?"

He smiled, leaned over and kissed her. "That's sweet of you. But no. Not yet anyway."

"Let me know."

Durant nodded and rose. "I'd better get dressed."

She propped herself up on one elbow and stared at him. Spanish blood had bequeathed her a nicely boned chin and a straight thin nose that was large by Filipino standards. Above the well-shaped chin was a wide and perhaps overly generous mouth that grinned more often than it smiled. Best of all, Durant thought, were her eyes—enormous black ones that looked solemn until the grin came and they narrowed themselves into mischievous, faintly mocking arcs. With skin almost as dark as Durant's dark tan, she stood five-three, except her posture was so perfect it seemed to add a couple of inches. With heels, she could pass for five-seven, even five-eight.

"Do you really want to find out what happened to Ernie and your money?" Emily Cariaga asked.

Durant didn't reply for several seconds. "I really don't give much of a damn about Ernie, but I was rather fond of the money."

"Then I'll ride down to Manila with you and Artie. Talk to a few people. It shouldn't take me long to learn something."

Durant nodded. "Okay. Fine."

"When's Artie coming by?"

"Six."

"And it's what now?"

Durant looked at his watch. "Five-fifteen."

She patted the bed. "Then we just have time, don't we?"

"Yes, I think we do," Durant said as he slipped back into bed.

•   •   •

Durant said he'd already seen the great stone head of Ferdinand Marcos more times than he really needed to, so Artie Wu took the traditional Kennon Road back down through the mountains to the highway that ran south to Manila. The narrow two-lane Kennon Road twisted, curved and turned back upon itself. Traffic was light that early in the morning and Wu drove expertly, if too fast, making prodigal use of his horn on the curves.

Because riding in the back seat made her carsick, Emily Cariaga sat in front with Wu. Durant sat braced in the back. Whenever a curve came up he closed his eyes. Artie Wu's driving was one of the few things that absolutely terrified Durant.

The old Jeepney formed the roadblock. Positioned across the narrow road, the Jeepney's red and yellow paint was faded and peeling, but it still boasted two small chromed rearing horses on its hood. The hood and its radiator were all that still resembled the surplus Army jeeps after which it had been named.

They had parked it exactly right. When Wu came speeding around the curve he had just time enough to slam on the brakes. The Mercedes skidded to a stop a foot away from the Jeepney. In the rear seat Durant said, "Shit."

They came out from behind the Jeepney then. There were five of them—four men and a woman, all in their twenties. Durant thought most of them were under 25—at most, a year or two older. The woman seemed to be in charge.

The five wore what Durant had come to think of as standard international guerrilla gear: jeans, the inevitable jogging shoes, some kind of fatigue jacket with camouflage markings or, lacking the jacket, a dark T-shirt. Two of the men also wore Timex gimme caps.

The two with the caps and the M-16s took the right side of the Mercedes. The other two men, armed with sawed-off repeating shotguns, took the left side. The woman wore dark aviator glasses and carried a .38 semiautomatic down at her side. She walked slowly up to the driver's door and stared through the dark glasses at Artie Wu who, after a moment's hesitation, rolled down the window.

"Hi, there," Artie Wu said with his friendliest smile.

"American?" she said.

"American."

"Her?" the woman said, indicating Emily Cariaga.

"Filipina," Wu said.

"And him?" she said, giving Durant a nod.

"American," Wu said.

"Passports and ID, please."

"Right," Wu said and reached slowly into his inside breast pocket for his passport. The woman brought up her pistol and aimed it at him. Wu noticed it was of Colt manufacture; that it looked too large for her hand, and that the one safety he could see had been switched to off. He handed her his passport, collected Durant's, an ID card from Emily Cariaga and passed them over. The woman backed up two steps. One of the men with a sawed-off shotgun took her place.

The woman stuck the semiautomatic pistol down in the leather belt that ran through the loops of her jeans. She was not very tall, no more than five-two or three. Her straight black hair had been cut off into a kind of Dutch boy bob. Wu couldn't see her eyes behind the dark glasses, but he thought what he could see of her face was attractive, even pretty.

The woman studied the ID card and the two passports carefully. She then took out a small notebook and used a ballpoint pen to copy down some particulars. After she put the notebook and pen away, she looked at her watch, nodded in a satisfied way, took the pistol from her belt and walked slowly back to Wu's window.

"What is your occupation, your work?" she said. "You and the one in the rear. American passports don't reveal it."

"Businessmen."

One of the men with the shotguns said something to her in Tagalog. "He wants to know how much your company would pay for you," she said.

"We don't have a company," Wu said. "We're private investors."

"If you have money to invest, you must be rich. You wear a fine white suit and drive an expensive car."

"Alas," said Artie Wu. "The suit is old, the car is rented, and our last investment turned out badly."

The woman smiled. She had extraordinarily white teeth. "Did you really let Ernie Pineda take you for three hundred thousand U.S.?"

Artie Wu didn't try to hide his astonishment. He swallowed as much of it as he could and said, "I don't know what—"

Durant leaned forward, interrupting. "It was around in there. Three hundred thousand."

The woman nodded and tapped the two passports and the ID card on the car windowsill. "What happened to Ernie could happen to you. You understand what I'm saying?"

"Not exactly," Durant said, still leaning forward.

"This is a corrupt country with a new government that

promises to end corruption. Although we don't believe those promises, we do believe the new government needs to be reminded of what can happen unless those promises are kept. Poor talkative Ernie was such a reminder. I'm still trying to decide if three additional reminders would be useful or counterproductive."

The woman again tapped the passports and the ID on the windowsill several times and suddenly thrust them at Artie Wu who accepted them with a grateful nod.

She backed away as one of the men with an M-16 climbed into the old Jeepney and began grinding its starter. The battery was low and the grinding grew weaker and weaker. Just when it seemed that the battery was doomed, the engine caught and spat out a black cloud of diesel smoke from its exhaust. The man with the M-16 raced the engine several times and then backed and filled until there was enough room for the Mercedes to get by.

Wu put the Mercedes into drive and crept slowly forward. Durant stared out through the rear side window at the woman with the semiautomatic pistol. She reached up with her left hand and removed her dark aviator glasses. She had shining brown eyes that stared at Durant. After a moment, she nodded at him. He thought the nod could have meant goodbye, or we'll meet again, or remember what I said, or even nothing at all. He nodded an equally equivocal reply. Wu fed the engine more gasoline and the Mercedes shot past the Jeepney.

When they were safely around the next curve, Wu broke the silence with, "What the hell was all that about?"

"It was about just what she said it was about," Emily Cariaga said.

Wu wrinkled his forehead into an unbeliever's frown. "Maybe," he said.

"Tell me something, Artie," Durant said. "Did you really say 'alas' back there?"

Wu sighed. "Alas. I really did."

•   •   •

At seven that evening Wu and Durant were up in Wu's suite in the Manila Peninsula, debating whether to go to dinner at a new German restaurant that had been touted to them by the Graf von Lahusen, or wait for Boy Howdy to return their call. Waiting for the call meant dining on room service fare, which appealed to neither of them. They had almost agreed to give the German restaurant a try when the phone rang. Durant answered it.

Boy Howdy's harsh Australian accent crackled over the line. "That you, Artie—or that fucking Durant?"

"That fucking Durant."

"Listen, Durant, I've really got a ripe one for you lads this time."

"Tell it to Artie," Durant said. Wu rose from the couch and took the phone.

"How are you, Boy?" Wu said and began to listen. He listened for nearly two minutes without making a sound except for two noncommittal grunts. When he finally spoke, his tone was cool and indifferent.

"Tell him we're interested, that's all," Wu said, listened some more and then said in a new hard tone, "No, you sure as hell do *not* tell him it's on, Boy. You tell him exactly what I told you: that we're interested."

Wu went back to listening and when he spoke again there was nothing but deal-breaking finality to his tone. "Absolutely not," he said. "Your cut comes out of his end, not ours." There was some more listening until Wu broke in with an indifferent, "Okay, Boy. As you say, the fuck's off."

Wu hung up the phone, smiled pleasantly at Durant, and waited. Twenty seconds later the phone rang. Wu picked it up, said hello and again listened. Finally, he nodded, as if with satisfaction, and said, "Right. I think we finally understand each other now, Boy."

After he hung up this time, Wu turned to Durant, smiled

again, took a cigar from a shirt pocket, eased himself down into a club chair and squirmed around in it until he was comfortable. He lit the cigar and carefully blew three perfect smoke rings up into the air. Durant watched it all with an amused smile.

"Tell me," Artie Wu said. "Do you still believe in the good fairy?"

"Has the good fairy got a name?"

Wu blew another perfect smoke ring. "Otherguy Overby," he said.

Durant's smile widened and he began to clap slowly and softly. "I believe," he said and, still smiling and clapping, said it once again.

CHAPTER ELEVEN

Otherguy Overby explained that the very early breakfast meeting in the Beverly Hills Hotel's Polo Lounge was simply a matter of edge.

"This guy Harry Crites—the poet I've been reading up on— well, he flies in from Washington late last night and he's still on East Coast time, right? So this morning we're getting him up at say, six, six-thirty, and this'll throw his biorhythms all out of whack and that gives us the edge. Not much, but some."

"His biorhythms," Booth Stallings said.

"Yeah."

Stallings glanced at Overby who was behind the wheel of the yellow Porsche 911 cabriolet they had borrowed from the stable of the still incarcerated Billy Diron. They were rolling down the Pacific Coast Highway in Malibu, approaching the Getty Museum. It was 7:04 A.M., a Saturday, and the third day of spring in the year 1986.

"So you think his out-of-whack biorhythms are somehow going to help us pilfer the five million?"

"Pilfer? You don't *pilfer* five million bucks. You . . . liberate it."

Stallings chuckled. "Maybe I should recite the names of two or three dozen countries that've been sacked and plundered under liberation's bright banner."

Overby gave him a quick frowning glance. "Look," he said. "Let me ask you something you don't have to answer. But have you got funny politics? Not that I give a shit, but I'd kind of like to know."

"Funny?"

"Red. Rouge. Pink." He paused. "Moscow, Peking, maybe Havana?"

"No," Stallings said with a smile. "In that sense I have no politics at all." He chuckled again. "What're yours—if I may be so bold?"

Overby seemed to give the question serious thought. "Well, you'd have to say I'm kind of a Republican, except I don't bother to vote much anymore."

"Don't—or can't because of a past felony rap or two?"

Overby sealed himself away in that remote and frozen place where Stallings had seen him go before. It's his fuck-off retreat, he thought.

"I don't see how that's any of your goddamn business," Overby said with his always surprising dignity.

"You're right," Stallings said. "It's not."

* * *

The parking attendant gave the yellow Porsche a look of recognition when Overby brought it to a stop in the Beverly Hills Hotel drive. The attendant opened Overby's door and said, "When's Billy getting sprung, Otherguy?"

"Tomorrow or maybe the next day and watch the fucking paint," Overby said, getting out of the car.

As they went up the hotel steps, Overby turned to give Stallings a quick up-and-down inspection. "Let's stop in the john," he said.

"I'll wait for you."

Overby let a little exasperation flicker across his face. "Look. When I say something like that, it's not just because I need company."

The corners of Stallings' mouth went down in a facial shrug. He gestured for Overby to lead on and followed him down the corridor and into the men's room.

•   •   •

On that third day of spring, Stallings was wearing a new tan poplin suit and a blue tab-collar shirt with a gold bar pin and the striped brown and gold tie of some disbanded regiment. The suit, shirt, tie, pin and a pair of lace-up cordovans were part of a wardrobe Otherguy Overby had picked out for Stallings two days before at Lew Ritter's haberdashery on Wilshire Boulevard, paying a premium for next-day alterations and delivery.

Overby had then driven Stallings to a hairstylist on Melrose and contracted for $85 worth of haircut, facial and manicure. On their way to the barber, an amused Stallings had listened as Overby revealed his tactics.

"I don't know how long it's been since you were out on the Rim," Overby had said with a wave that included the world west of Catalina and east of China. "But when you're working it like we'll be working it, you've gotta look like you can buy the mark and have change left over. Out there, marks don't fork over to shabby because shabby doesn't inspire confidence and that's all we've got to sell. What does inspire confidence is front—not flash, but front. You know the difference?"

Stallings had smiled and nodded that he did.

"Well, begging your pardon all to hell, but you look like some freshwater college prof who didn't make the tenure cut. I mean, like some guy whose wife barbers him every seventh Friday while they're watching *Washington Week in Review* and pissing and moaning about the fascist in the White House."

Stallings had nodded again, still amused. "My daughter cuts it," he had said. "My Cleveland Park daughter. She'd also support any calumny you might aim at the occupant of the White House who, incidentally, is not a fascist but an actor."

"Well, that's almost as bad."

"My daughter wouldn't think so were he Gregory Peck."

Overby had nodded agreeably. "Yeah, Peck does look more like a President at that."

●   ●   ●

After checking the men's room stalls to make sure they were vacant, Overby gave Stallings a final up-and-down inspection, sighed and said, "Let's begin with basics. Zip up your fly."

"Christ," said Stallings and did as instructed.

"And fix your fucking tie."

"Never cared much for ties."

"It's your uptight badge. So make it look like you're used to it."

Stallings slipped the knot up until it was snug and refastened the gold bar pin he thought silly. Overby grunted his approval and said, "Now you look like the man who says no."

Stallings smiled. "To Harry Crites?"

"Why not? Like most guys from back east, he'll probably walk in wearing his version of L.A. casual, which is what he wears back home when he's barbecuing the weenies. He'll see us all dressed up and there he is, all dressed down. So what does that give us? The edge, that's what."

Overby turned to inspect himself and his gloom-blue suit in the men's room mirror, looking pleased with what he saw, even after Booth Stallings said, "You don't know Harry Crites."

* * *

They sat over coffee at a table with a clear view of the Polo Lounge's entrance. Overby kept watch on the doorway as Stallings examined the other early morning breakfasters, trying without much luck to distinguish the talent from those who peddled it.

As he glanced around, Stallings saw Overby's expression change. Until then Overby had been wearing what Stallings had come to think of as his baited trap look—one that spoke of quiet confidence, keen awareness and infinite patience. It was the same look Overby had worn while waiting at the airport.

Stallings grew curious when the look vanished and was replaced, if only for an instant, by a flicker of something closer to apprehension than fear. But then the baited trap look returned, even more pronounced than before, and Stallings turned to look at what Overby saw.

The tall woman with the short reddish-brown hair stood in the entrance, quartering the room. When her dollar-green eyes reached Stallings she almost smiled and almost nodded. When her gaze reached Overby it stopped. Nothing changed in her face. But the mutual stare went on long enough, Stallings decided, for her and Overby to catch up on the last few years. The woman then turned abruptly and left the Polo Lounge.

"Know her?" Stallings said.

"Who?"

"Come on, Otherguy."

"You know her?"

"She's with Harry Crites."

Overby relaxed as a calculating smile wiped away the last vestige of apprehension. "Well," he said, "what d'you know." Since it wasn't a question, Stallings made no reply.

* * *

Five minutes later Harry Crites came striding into the Polo Lounge followed by the tall woman who now carried a thin

black leather attaché case. Harry Crites was wearing a polo
shirt, riding breeches and polished boots that nearly reached
his knees.

"A polo outfit in the Polo Lounge," Stallings murmured.
"We just lost the edge, Otherguy."

Overby's confident expression hadn't changed at the sight of
Harry Crites, and all he said was, "He forgot his horse."

With the tall woman watching his back, Crites reached the
table and nodded at Stallings but didn't offer to shake hands.
"Hello, Booth."

"Harry."

Crites turned to Overby. "I hear they call you Otherguy
Overby."

Overby smiled. "I've read some of your poetry, Mr. Crites,
and—" He broke off and stopped smiling, as if he'd thought
better of what he had been about to say. "Well, never mind."

Before Harry Crites could do anything but glower slightly,
Stallings said, "Sit down, Harry, and introduce us to your
friend. Or did you tell me she's not exactly a friend?"

Crites indicated Stallings with a small gesture. "Miss Blue,
Mr. Stallings." She and Stallings nodded at each other. Harry
Crites then gave Overby a quick look of disapproval. "You
already know him."

She nodded at the still seated Overby. "Hello, Otherguy."

An unsmiling Overby said, "Georgia."

A waiter pulled out a chair and Georgia Blue sat down next
to Stallings and across from Overby. Harry Crites took the
remaining chair. The waiter passed out menus. Crites automatically handed his to Georgia Blue without a glance and said,
"Order for me." She began reading the menu.

"Didn't know you played polo, Harry," said Booth
Stallings.

"Why should you?"

"Been playing long?"

"Ten years. I picked it up down in B.A."

Stallings leaned toward Overby. "B.A. is Buenos Aires, Mr.

Overby. Mr. Crites was down there a few years back, briefing the generals on internal security techniques."

Overby looked at Crites with interest. "Must've been like teaching old ducks to swim."

Crites aimed a forefinger at Overby but glared at Stallings. "What the fuck's he?"

"My guide to the world's wicked ways."

Crites grunted. "From what I hear, he drew the map."

The waiter returned to take the orders. Georgia Blue ordered only melon and black coffee for Harry Crites but something more substantial for herself, as did Stallings and Overby. After handing the waiter the menus, she said, "Would you bring the melon right away, please?"

When the waiter had gone, Overby smiled another too pleasant smile at Crites and said, "Georgia must be quite a Handy Annie to have around."

Harry Crites leaned forward, his voice a rasp. "I want you to butt out, Jack. I made a deal with Stallings here. If he wants you along, fine. But I don't want to hear any more of your crap."

Overby added a pleasant nod to his pleasant smile. "Mr. Stallings has retained my services, such as they are, to give him my best counsel. If I decide your project will, one, put him in grave jeopardy, or two, fuck him over, I'll tell him to walk."

They stared at each other for seconds until Crites turned to Stallings and said, "Okay, Booth. Let's talk money. You got fifty thousand in Washington. There's another two hundred thousand in that attaché case Georgia's got—half of it in unendorsed Amex traveler's checks. That's so you can spread 'em around any way you want. But if, for some weird and wonderful reason, you decide to do a flit, I can trace you through them—eventually. Okay?"

"Where's the other half?"

"In Hong Kong. When you deliver the package, Georgia will hand over the other two-fifty. That means you might as well get used to her because she's along for the whole cruise. If nothing else, she can keep an eye on him." Crites jerked a thumb at Overby without looking at him.

"You didn't mention Miss Blue in Washington, Harry."

"Yeah, well, that must be why I'm doing it now."

Stallings smiled at Georgia Blue. "Mind if I call you Georgia?"

"Not at all."

"Tell me something about yourself."

"I was with the federal government for seven years."

"Agriculture, perhaps?" Stallings said. "Commerce? Housing and Urban Development."

"Treasury," Georgia Blue said.

Stallings shot his eyebrows up. "Not the dread Secret Service?"

Georgia Blue's mouth formed a slight amused smile as she nodded.

"And now you're with Harry here?"

"No, Mr. Stallings. I'm with you."

The waiter arrived with Harry Crites' honeydew melon. The others watched silently as he ate it in two minutes, patted his lips with a napkin, had a final sip of coffee, patted his lips again and turned to Stallings.

"Okay. That's it. I've told you what you need to know and if there's anything I forgot, Georgia can handle it. When're you leaving?"

Stallings looked at Overby who said, "Tonight. The ten-thirty flight. Philippine Airlines." He looked at Georgia Blue with what seemed to be concern. "I'm not sure we can get you a seat."

"I already have a reservation, Otherguy," she said.

Overby smiled. "Together again."

Harry Crites looked at his watch and rose. "I've got a match in forty-five minutes, Booth, so I suppose I'll see you when you get back." His eyes went to Overby. "You, too, maybe."

Georgia Blue also rose. "I'll go with you to the car."

Harry Crites turned away from the table, then turned back. "By the way, Booth. I really like that new suit."

When they were gone Stallings asked Overby, "Where'd you know her, Otherguy?"

"Around."

"Around where?"

"I'll let her tell it."

Georgia Blue was back in five minutes. She had taken the thin attaché case with her and Stallings now noticed she had brought it back. She sat down, poured herself fresh coffee, took a sip and leaned back in her chair, looking first at Overby and then at Stallings.

"I think we may as well get down to it, don't you, Mr. Stallings?"

"Why not?"

"Good." She leaned forward, rested her elbows on the table and smiled at Overby. "How many ways are you planning to cut up the five million, Otherguy?"

Nearly a minute went by as they again stared at each other, silently exchanging what Stallings felt were new confidences, ancient secrets and bad memories.

Overby finally looked away, not at Stallings, but at something miles off. "Four," he said. "Four ways."

Georgia Blue turned to Stallings with a cool stare that he thought he could feel poking around in the secret recesses of his mind. "And now it'll be five ways, right, Mr. Stallings? A million each."

"I guess I'm supposed to ask why it should be split five ways," Stallings said, "and you'll come back with some compelling reason that'll make me agree."

"The reason's simple," she said. "It'll be far easier for you to pull it off with me than without me. In fact, without me it'll be damned near impossible."

"Not much on preliminary bullshit, are you?" Stallings said with a twitch of a smile.

"It's a waste of time," she said, continuing to study him. "Well?"

"Okay," Stallings said with a shrug. "Five ways—a million each."

Otherguy Overby let out the breath he had been holding and nodded comfortably. "Makes more sense all the way around," he said.

CHAPTER TWELVE

For the second time in his life Booth Stallings flew first-class. The first time had been nearly five years before when a Swedish small-arms manufacturer had flown him to a sales conference in London to deliver an ill-received paper Stallings perversely had entitled: "Terrorism: the Exciting Hot New Industry."

Otherguy Overby had insisted on first-class to Manila as a matter of front and, by chance, Stallings had two seats to himself. Across the aisle were Overby and Georgia Blue who scarcely spoke to each other. After the 747 was 30 minutes out of Los Angeles, and after an overly solicitous flight attendant had pressed a second martini on him, Stallings rose, tapped Overby on the shoulder and said, "My turn."

Georgia Blue watched as Stallings slipped into the vacated seat with his drink and said, "Tell me about the money."

"The five million," she said.

Stallings nodded.

"It's real," she said.

"Where is it?"

"It'll be in the Hong Kong and Shanghai Bank—their new headquarters on Des Voeux Road."

"That's where it'll be. Not where it is."

"Right now it's where it can be wire-transferred without bothering Washington."

"Not in the States then, right?"

She smiled.

"When'll Harry wire it?"

"When I tell him to."

"By code?"

Again, she smiled.

"Like to share the code—since we're partners and all?"

"Not just yet."

"Whose money is it?"

"Who cares? Which means I don't know."

"Harry gave me some crap about it coming from a business consortium."

"Crap's a fairly apt description."

"Think it's Langley money?"

She shook her head.

"Why not?"

"They wouldn't go through Harry. They've got their own proprietary false fronts."

"Like to hear what I think?" Stallings said after ten seconds of silence.

"Of course."

"I think the money's coming from someone who won't send after it when it disappears."

"Harry'll send after it," she said. "And if we work it just right, he'll send me."

Stallings grinned. "Now there's a pretty notion."

"Yes, isn't it though," she said.

Stallings leaned back in his seat, closed his eyes and said, "Now tell me about you and Otherguy."

Georgia Blue thought before replying, "He was a bad accident that happened in Guadalajara when I was twenty and he was thirty-one, or so he claimed, except you never can tell about Otherguy because he lies so much."

"But he's good at what he does," Stallings said, opening his eyes.

She shrugged. "He's in the top forty anyhow."

Despite Stallings' encouraging nod, Georgia Blue volunteered nothing else. After 15 seconds went by, he said, "So what did Treasury have you doing?"

"I guarded the bodies of the wives and mistresses of visiting prime ministers, premiers, presidents, potentates and what have you. Actually, I was the maid who carried the gun. So when a certain stark-naked madame told me to give her a massage, I told her to fuck off and got fired and Harry Crites hired me three weeks later."

"To watch his back?"

She nodded.

"Just curious, but what does Harry really suffer from— enemies or paranoia?"

"They sometimes bunk in together, you know."

"So I've heard," Stallings said as he rose and returned to his seat across the aisle.

•　　•　　•

Booth Stallings had managed to sleep only three of the 15 hours it took to fly from Los Angeles to Manila. Overby somehow greased their way through customs and immigration and Stallings sleepwalked across the international airport terminal and out into the heat. The heat woke him up. That and the horde of Manila taxi drivers who were all yelling that they drove the coolest cabs and offered the lowest fares. Overby himself contributed to the clamor. He stood, coat off and tie loosened, bellowing, "Manila Hotel! Manila Hotel!"

The taxi drivers cheerfully took up the cry. Seconds later, an unusually small Filipino, wearing a white shirt, black tie, dark pants and a chauffeur's cap, rushed up to Overby and began alternating apologies for his tardiness with assertions that he, in truth, was Romeo, the driver of the Manila Hotel limousine. The taxi drivers vouched for him with shouts of, "True! True!"

•   •   •

Stallings hadn't been to Manila in more than 40 years. He had arrived then to find it virtually destroyed by some of the fiercest and most senseless house-to-house fighting of the war. Seated now in the front seat of the black Mercedes on his way to the Manila Hotel, he saw they had rebuilt almost everything; that everything looked pretty godawful, and that he recognized almost nothing except the slums. The slums were just as he remembered them.

•   •   •

In late August of 1945, Booth Stallings and Alejandro Espiritu had been flown in an Army C-47 from Cebu to Manila where it was rumored that MacArthur himself would present the medals during what a PRO handout predicted would be "a brief but stirring ceremony."

The chief purpose of the ceremony was to give the dead T/5 Hovey Profette of Mena, Arkansas, a posthumous Distin-, guished Service Cross for his exceptional gallantry in action. Bronze Stars were to be pinned on Espiritu and Stallings for their lesser valor. The trip to Manila was the first time either had flown in an airplane.

MacArthur didn't show, of course, and the task of handing out the medals to a dead medic, a live second john and a raggedy-ass guerrilla with suspect politics fell to MacArthur's amanuensis, Major General Charles A. Willoughby, who later in life would become a close and valued associate of yet another singular American, H. L. Hunt.

Espiritu was given his medal last. As the General pinned it on, he murmured congratulations in English. Espiritu smiled and murmured back in Tagalog or Cebuano—nobody was quite sure which. Years later Willoughby was to claim that Espiritu had said: The real struggle is yet to come, General.

The brief and not very stirring ceremony had been held in one of the few untouched rooms in the nearly bombed-out Manila Hotel, the same hotel Booth Stallings would return to more than 40 years later. When the lowliest public relations officer had gone and none was left save the second lieutenant of infantry and the guerrilla, Booth Stallings looked down at the medal on his chest, took it off and stuck it down in his hip pocket. Espiritu did the same with his and asked Stallings, "Where do you go now?"

"Looks like Japan," Stallings said. "The occupation."

"I mean this afternoon."

"I'd kind of planned on getting kind of drunk."

"May I accompany you?"

"You don't drink, Al."

"I can find you cheap gin, bargain with the whores, keep the binny boys away and otherwise entertain myself."

"Okay," Stallings said. "Let's go."

The drunk lasted two days and three nights. When they finally said goodbye on August 28, 1945, Stallings was sure he would never see Alejandro Espiritu again.

•   •   •

They knew Otherguy Overby at the Manila Hotel and his welcome was warm and effusive. As he crossed the huge rare wood and fine marble lobby, Overby handed out crisp new five-dollar bills to bellhops and porters and door-openers, greeting some of them by name. Stallings estimated Overby had parted with close to sixty dollars by the time he reached the assistant manager and another elaborate welcome.

But when Overby turned to run a practiced eye over the lobby, the well-dressed assistant manager's expression changed from one of welcome to the fatalistic look of someone who knows he's about to be sandbagged.

Overby turned from his inspection with a sympathetic smile. "What's the occupancy rate running, Ramon?" he asked.

"About forty, forty-five percent now all the excitement's over?"

The assistant manager shook his head. "It's better than that, Otherguy. Much better."

"I sure hope so." Overby turned, gave the lobby another skeptical look and turned back. "Tell you what we need. We need a suite for Doctor Stallings and two big rooms for Miss Blue and me. We want 'em all on the same smoking floor because even though Doctor Stallings doesn't smoke, he'll have guests who do."

The assistant manager nodded. "We'll be happy to do that."

"The only other thing we need is a twenty-five percent discount for a week's guarantee in advance, all cash, all U.S. dollars. But if you can't handle that, Ramon, just say so and we'll take a cab over to Makati and try the Inter-Continental or the Peninsula."

The assistant manager shook his head regretfully. "I can't give you twenty-five off, Otherguy. This is still a government hotel."

Overby shrugged and turned to Stallings and Georgia Blue. "Let's go."

"But I can give you twenty off," the assistant manager said. "Providing it's in dollars."

Overby reached into a pocket and came up with a roll of $100 bills. As he started counting them onto the mahogany counter, the impressed assistant manager picked up a pen and offered it to Georgia Blue along with a registration card. "Welcome to the Manila, Miss Blue."

*   *   *

They met three hours later in the sitting room of Booth Stallings' fifth-floor suite. Stallings, wearing a pair of chinos and a dark blue short-sleeve shirt from Lew Ritter's, still felt groggy from the flight. But Overby seemed rested and wide awake in his well-worn jeans, gaudy Hawaiian shirt and scuffed running shoes that he wore without socks. Stallings wondered why Overby wanted to look like a budget-bound tourist but decided not to ask.

Georgia Blue also appeared rested and alert in her white skirt, tan cotton blouse and brown and white spectator pumps, which Stallings assumed were back in style—or would be shortly. He and Overby drank San Miguel beer out of cans. Georgia Blue sipped a vodka and tonic. The drinks had come from the room's mini-refrigerator. On the low coffee table was a huge untouched basket of tropical fruit with a "Compliments of the Management" card.

Stallings glanced around the big sitting room whose windows offered a view of Manila Bay and asked, "How much?"

"Regular price is two-eighty a day, U.S.," Overby said. "But you're just paying two thirty-four and you can charge it off to front."

"Only two thirty-four," Stallings said. "Imagine."

"Since we're on money we might as well stick to it for a minute," Overby said. "Okay?"

"Fine," Stallings said.

"Georgia and I have to go see a guy who'll try and hold me up for ten thousand, but who I'm going to beat back down to five. I need the five."

"This your contact?"

Overby nodded.

"What's his name?" Georgia Blue asked.

"Boy Howdy."

"Sounds American."

"Australian," Overby said. "Except he may be Filipino now. He married one about ten or twelve years ago."

"What is he?" she asked.

"A first-class asshole who owns a snakepit over in Ermita. Runs whores, beggar kids, a protection racket, does a little strikebreaking, stuff like that. He also takes messages and that's what I use him for. Messages."

"Five thousand," she said. "Must be some message."

"I believe it concerns the whereabouts of our other two partners," Stallings said.

She looked first at Stallings, then at Overby, her disbelief apparent. "You guys don't even know where they are?"

Overby shrugged. "They move around."

Something happened to Georgia Blue's face then. It lost all animation and expression. Stallings decided it was her Secret Service look. When she spoke her lips scarcely moved.

"Have they got names?" she said.

Overby's eyes wandered the room for a moment or two until they landed on Georgia Blue. "Wu and Durant," he said.

Stallings watched as the surprise that was almost shock struck Georgia Blue. Her eyes widened and her face paled. Her mouth opened to suck in a lungful of air. For a moment, Stallings thought she might hyperventilate. But then an angry crimson erased her sudden paleness and she used her breath to swear at Overby.

"Goddamn you, Otherguy!"

"What's up?" Stallings asked.

Overby turned an unpleasant smile on Stallings. "All four of us worked a few deals together in Mexico a long time ago. Her, me, Durant and Wu. When Georgia and I sort of broke up, Durant caught her on the bounce for a while and I guess she's not over him yet. Right, Georgia?"

"You shit."

"You can't work with them?" Stallings said.

"For a million I can work with anybody," she said. "Even Overby."

"And Durant?"

"Him too."

"A rather nice coincidence, isn't it?" Stallings asked. "Your knowing Otherguy and also Wu and Durant."

Georgia Blue stared at Overby but spoke to Stallings. "Who sold you the package, Booth?"

"A man named Howard Mott in Washington. Know him?"

She ran the name through her memory. "Lawyer?"

Stallings nodded.

"I've heard of him but I don't know him. Should I?"

"He's my son-in-law."

The look Georgia Blue gave Stallings was one of pure malice. "Yes, well, I can see you must be relieved that I don't know him. Your son-in-law."

"Very relieved," Stallings said. "Extremely so."

CHAPTER THIRTEEN

O verby worked it so that he would carry the $5,000 and Georgia Blue the small flat Walther semiautomatic. She wore it stuck down behind her jeans, concealed by the tails of the Hawaiian shirt Overby had found for her in one of the Manila Hotel specialty shops. The Walther was her own.

It was nearly 10 P.M. when they rode the elevator down to the hotel lobby. "We're Mr. and Mrs. Average B. Tourist," he said. "The B is for bored and we're out for a halfway dirty night on the town."

"Gosh, it's like a disguise, isn't it?"

Overby sighed. "If I have to carry a chunk of money around Ermita, I want to do it so nobody notices me. And when I try and beat Boy Howdy down five thousand, I want to look as hard-up as possible." He inspected her critically. "Trouble with you is, you can't even *look* hard-up."

"My God," she said as the elevator door opened. "I think you just paid me a compliment."

"Think again," said Overby as he walked out of the elevator ahead of her.

Outside the hotel the doorman tried to sell Overby on the safety and security of a hotel limousine. When Overby refused, the doorman shrugged, whistled up a taxi, wrote something down on a small pad, tore it off and gave it to Overby who passed it to Georgia Blue without a glance.

The slip had the name of the hotel printed at the top. Below was the cautionary statement: "Dear Guest: For your Safety and Convenience the vehicle you are now taking bears the following information." After that the doorman had written the taxi's name and plate number.

"In case we get banged on the head and dumped in the bay, right?" Georgia Blue said.

Overby nodded as the five-year-old Toyota taxi pulled up to a stop and they climbed into its rear. When Overby said he wanted to go to Boy Howdy's in Ermita, the driver offered to take them to a much nicer place, his cousin's, where they wouldn't be cheated nearly as much. Overby had to decline the offer twice before the driver put the taxi into gear and crept down the hotel drive to Roxas Boulevard.

The trip was short in distance but long in time because of heavy traffic and the sin and sex customers who jammed the short narrow one-way street in Ermita. At the street's far end was a big flashing pink neon sign that spelled out Boy Howdy's name. At least a dozen clubs lined the block and outside each of them was a barker, hawking the delights that lay within. About half of the barkers were Australians in their forties and fifties with mean mouths and disappointed eyes.

Prospective customers included Japanese businessmen, wearing stylish sports clothes and foolish grins; American servicemen, all of them young and many of them drunk, and a scattering of European males who seemed torn between apprehension and desire. The rest of the crowd was made up of adult and child prostitutes of both sexes plus a variety of pimps, beggar kids, transvestites, pickpockets, all-purpose grifters and a sprinkling of middle-aged American tourists who looked as if they had bought the wrong guidebook.

When the taxi was fifty yards from Boy Howdy's, it became

stuck in a traffic jam. Overby paid off the driver. Once his passengers were out of the taxi, the driver switched off his engine, rolled up the windows, locked the doors and resigned himself to a steam bath of indefinite duration.

Overby led the way with Georgia Blue slightly behind him and to his left at curbside where the trouble, if any, would come from. Overby ambled along, sticking to his tourist role, his eyes wide and a know-it-all grin plastered across his face.

The trouble came from a big drunken American sailor who wore a T-shirt that read, "All-American Fuckup." He grabbed Georgia Blue by her right wrist, proclaiming: "Just can't help it—I'm in love!"

Overby turned to watch impassively as Georgia Blue allowed herself to be spun around. She almost laughed when the sailor told her that tall women turned him on. But then her left hand darted to the big right hand that still clutched her wrist. Her fingers sought and found the nerve that lay just below the pad of his thumb. She clamped down on it. The sailor yelled. He kept on yelling as she forced him to his knees, released him and walked away. A small crowd quickly gathered to discuss whether the kneeling man was damaged enough to roll.

"Durant taught you that, didn't he?" Overby said as Georgia Blue rejoined him.

"Did he?"

"I saw him do it in Bangkok once to some big special forces ape."

"I'm just fine, Otherguy, but it was sweet of you to ask."

Overby gave her a quick puzzled glance. "I wasn't worried, if that's what you mean. It's what you fucking well do."

She nodded slightly, looking away, and said, "You're right. It's what I fucking well do."

•   •   •

The barker outside Boy Howdy's was a jockey-size Australian with too few teeth and a loud-hailer voice. He had one good eye and one milky one. He turned the good eye on Overby.

"Been a while, mate," the barker said.

"Tell him I'm here."

"Tell him yourself."

It wasn't quite tar black inside Boy Howdy's because of the pink light that came from a small stage where three nude women—two Filipinas and one Chinese—were engaged in a listless, vaguely aerobic orgy. Below the stage a three-piece band, consisting of piano, drums and saxophone, played "Moon River."

There were two walls of booths, a long packed bar and two dozen very small tables where restless bar girls prowled in search of prey. The place was a little more than half full and most of the customers were Japanese men who watched the show and giggled into their Coca-Colas and Scotch.

A Filipino with an acromegalic chin and thick black hair down to his shoulders stepped up to Overby and nodded. He was a smallish giant of six-seven or eight and wore the confident air of a veteran bouncer who still delights in his trade. Three jagged scars ran down his right cheek like badges of office.

"Who's she?" the bouncer said, using his brickbat chin to indicate Georgia Blue.

"Wanda Mae," Overby said.

The bouncer frowned. "Boy didn't say nothing about no Wanda Mae."

"She's all night and all paid for and I don't want her to skip," Overby explained.

That was something the bouncer could understand. He jerked his head toward the rear. "Come on."

Overby and Georgia Blue followed him down a short hall that had two doors leading to toilets. At the end of the hall was a third door made of metal. The bouncer turned to Overby. "Raise your arms."

Overby raised them. The bouncer started at Overby's

armpits and patted his way down. When he reached the knees, Overby said, "That's far enough."

The bouncer looked up, shook his big head, and would have kept on going if Georgia Blue hadn't stuck the Walther into his left ear. "He said that's far enough," she told him as he slowly rose, the muzzle still partly buried in his ear.

Overby examined the bouncer. "If we go in with that thing growing out of your ear, you'll look pretty silly. So why don't you just open the door and we'll go in and you can stay out here and keep an eye on things. Okay?"

Because of the gun in his ear, the bouncer could only nod a fraction of an inch.

"What do I do," Overby asked, "ring the bell?"

"One long; two short," the bouncer said.

Overby pressed a black button as instructed. A moment later the unlocking buzzer sounded. Overby opened the door a crack and waited until he felt Georgia Blue's back against his. "Okay?" he said.

"Okay," she replied, using the Walther to wave the bouncer back down the short hall.

Overby opened the metal door wide and stood there, momentarily shielding Georgia Blue. She turned quickly, facing Overby now, and stuck the Walther back beneath her Hawaiian shirt.

The room they entered was no larger than a large rug, about ten by fifteen feet. All of its furniture seemed to be made from plastic, chrome and leather. There were no windows. One wall was painted a flat black and boasted a large acrylic-on-velvet painting of an idealized tropical beach with lots of coconut palms and a fat tiger stalking an even fatter carabao.

Boy Howdy stood in front of a chrome and plastic desk, wearing a long-sleeved *barong tagalog* that revealed an old-fashioned net undervest. Red chest hair going gray poked and curled its way through the vest.

At least six-one or two, Howdy had a street brawler's thick sloping shoulders and loose-hanging arms. His face seemed to be made out of pink knobs. One ear, his right, had had its lobe bitten off. Small blue eyes, a bit faded, burrowed back into his head beneath thick red bushy eyebrows that were also going gray. The hair on top of his head was short and wiry and seemed to have been crimped into place. It was much redder than his eyebrows and Overby guessed he was dyeing it.

"Who's she?" Boy Howdy said by way of greeting in a voice that always sounded to Overby like a wood file's first bite.

"Georgia Blue."

Howdy grinned, revealing two gold teeth. "That anything like Sweet Georgia Brown?"

"You know, that's never come up before," she said.

"I bet," Howdy said and made an awkward gesture. "Well, sit down—anywhere."

Georgia Blue chose a chrome and leather chair. Overby took a straight-backed one—the only one in the room. He sat with his feet planted firmly on the floor, his arms folded across his chest. He looked around and nodded at the acrylic painting. "That's new," he said.

"Sort of says it all, don't it?" Boy Howdy said.

"Sums it up."

"Well, what'll it be, Otherguy? A drink and some business, or some business and then a drink?"

"Business."

Boy Howdy nodded and leaned his rear against the desk. "I don't mind telling you I went to a terrible lot of trouble and expense to locate your two mates. Terrible trouble and beaucoup expense."

"I'd guess two phone calls and maybe fifty pesos to a bellhop."

Howdy turned a coconspirator's smile on Georgia Blue. "Ever notice what a fast lip old Otherguy has?"

"Frequently."

"But I did it, Otherguy. It cost me time and it cost me money but I ran 'em to earth and talked to 'em both."

"What'd Durant say? Hello and goodbye?"

"Just because Durant and I rub each other wrong don't mean we can't do a bit of business."

"Boy," Overby said. "Listen. Durant won't talk to you. I know it and you know it. So what did Artie say?"

Howdy forced a measure of warmth into his reply. "Old Artie. Offer me the choice of who to do business with and I say give me a Chinaman every time. They tell you something, you can stick it in the bank. So when I tell Artie about all the time and expense it cost me to find him, he says he appreciates my efforts and would fair take care of me himself personally, except he ain't got any deal with you yet, Otherguy, and he figures my share'll have to come out of your share."

"Sounds like Artie."

"So I says, 'Artie, what d'you think I should ask old Otherguy for? Name me a fair price,' says I, 'one that'll send him away humming to himself.' And Artie says he thinks a fair, rock-bottom price'd be ten thousand U.S."

"Artie's full of shit then," Overby said.

A melancholy look spread slowly across Howdy's knobby face. "I know you, Otherguy. Known you for years. And I know Artie and that fucking Durant. And I know they don't come cheap and neither do you—and never have done. So what you lads've got cooking is something rich and tasty and I think I oughta get my spoonful."

Overby sighed, stared at the floor for long moments, and then looked up, his eyes brimming with honesty and pure intent.

"Boy, let's get one thing straight. I'm here to pay you some money. I called you from L.A. and asked you to find Artie and Durant. You did that and I appreciate it. But what I've got going is all on spec—except for bare expenses. And that's all I can offer Wu and Durant: bare expenses plus a slice of some sweet by-and-by. So how many phone calls did you make? Two? Three? Okay. Let's say three. I'll pay you one thousand

U.S. per call. Three thousand dollars. Now if that's not more than fair, by God, I don't know what is."

Howdy's face took on a look of utter dejection and wounded pride. "Otherguy, you're not paying me to pick up the blower and dial some numbers. You're paying me because I know what numbers to dial and because I run the best fucking message drop between Honolulu and Sydney. So you owe me for unique services, professionally rendered. And if that ain't worth eight thousand hard cash, I'll eat my butt."

"For professional services, I'll tack on a thousand."

"Four thousand? That's a . . . a professional insult. But because you're an old customer I'll drop her to six."

Again, Overby sighed and again studied the floor. When he at last looked up he said, "By digging into my own pocket, I can go five." His tone turned cold. "But that's tapping my own case money."

"Five, you say?"

"Five."

"Five it is, then."

"Okay," Overby said. "Where're Artie and Durant?"

"Could I see a bit of the money first, Otherguy?"

Overby bent over and started pulling up the right leg of his jeans. Georgia Blue leaned forward in the chair and reached behind her back, as if to scratch. Boy Howdy walked behind his chrome and plastic desk and opened a drawer.

Taped to Overby's bare right leg with a strip of Velcro was a fat number ten envelope. He ripped away the Velcro and tossed the envelope onto Howdy's desk. Howdy grinned, picked up the envelope and looked inside.

"I've got their address and phone number right here," he said, reaching toward the open desk drawer with his right hand.

"Don't!" Georgia Blue said, snapping the word out.

Boy Howdy looked at her with surprise that could have been either real or pretended. "Don't what, Miss Sweet Georgia Blue?"

Georgia Blue's right hand came out from behind her back. In it was the Walther. Boy Howdy's surprise turned genuine.

"Don't reach into the drawer," she said. "Just tell Otherguy what he wants to know and count your money. He'll phone to confirm Wu and Durant. If you're not lying, we'll leave."

Howdy counted his money first. As he counted it, Overby went behind the desk, reached into the open drawer and brought out a .45-caliber Colt semiautomatic, the 1911 model. He removed the clip, pocketed it and worked the slide, ejecting the round in the chamber. He then put the Colt back into the drawer and the ejected round in his pocket.

"Okay," Overby said. "Where're Artie and Durant?"

"The Peninsula," Howdy said, still counting his money.

"Here or Hong Kong?"

"Here. The number's—"

"I know the number," Overby said, picked up the phone, dialed and asked for Mr. Wu. When Artie Wu answered, Overby identified himself and said, "I'm with Boy Howdy, the noted wanker, and we've finished our business so I think I'd better drop by and see you and Quincy." After they agreed on a time, Overby said, "One more thing. I've got a surprise for you." He listened and replied: "It's not a what, Artie, it's a her. Georgia Blue . . . Yeah, you're right. You had better tell Durant."

After Overby hung up he turned to give Howdy a bleak look. "We could still take back the five thousand and have you for nothing, Boy."

Howdy shook his head. "A few years back maybe. But not now. You been away too long, Otherguy. You had yourself an edge once but you went and lost it someplace."

"And you're still fucking hopeless," Overby said as he turned and went to the door. He held it open for Georgia Blue who backed out of the room, her Walther still pointed at Boy Howdy.

When she reached the hall, Howdy said, "I do like my women big, Sweet Georgia Blue."

She didn't reply, nor did Overby as he went through the metal door, closing it behind him. Boy Howdy stood behind his desk for several moments, frowning, then picked up the phone and dialed a number. When it was answered, he said, "It's me and it went about like I said." He listened to a question and then replied, "Nah, he's a lamb. It's Wu and that fucking Durant you gotta keep an eye on."

CHAPTER FOURTEEN

It was past midnight when Artie Wu heard the knock at the door, turned and said, "Let's get it over with."

Georgia Blue rose, her hands unconsciously smoothing and tugging at the gaudy Hawaiian shirt she still wore. Head bowed, she walked slowly across the sitting room of the suite in the Peninsula Hotel. Wu and Otherguy Overby watched her, their curiosity evident. Wu was on the couch; Overby in an easy chair. When she reached the door her bowed head came up and both men seemed to relax.

She let her hand rest lightly on the doorknob. The knock came again, two light taps. She gave her lower lip a quick bite, tightened her grasp on the knob and opened the door. Quincy Durant stood in the corridor. It was difficult to tell whether the sight of her shocked or only surprised him.

His eyes reacted first. They blinked twice, quite rapidly, and then his mouth opened, as if there were something he needed to say. But no words came and his mouth spread itself into a wide pleased grin that she thought made him look about six, possibly seven.

Durant said, "Georgia, by God."

"That's a silly smile, Durant. It makes you look about six. I was hoping for something older—something that maybe needed a cane."

Durant ran a hand through his hair. "Like the gray?"

"Not enough of it."

His smile went away for an instant and then came back, as if taking up permanent residence. "You look almost the same. Except better. I especially like your shirt."

"Otherguy picked it out."

"Otherguy. Well. You're back with him then?"

"I'm his new partner," Georgia Blue said. "I'm also yours and Artie's."

The wide smile slowly went away, an eighth of an inch at a time. "I see."

"No you don't," she said. "But come on in and we'll explain it."

After Durant entered and closed the door, he turned to find Georgia Blue standing only a foot or so away. In her eyes and expression was something he interpreted as either a demand or an invitation, so he tilted up her chin with his left hand and put his right arm around her waist. He kissed her then. It was a chaste kiss of the closed-mouth kind that lasted as long as a kiss ever lasts between distant cousins of the opposite sex. Wu and Overby watched with polite detachment.

When the kiss ended, Georgia Blue said, "The fire's gone out, I see."

Durant's right hand patted the Walther that was still stuck down in her jeans. "Must be your extinguisher," he said.

She reached back and removed the hand. "Years back, Quincy, I had fantasies about you. Real three-in-the-morning S-M stuff that usually ended with my shooting you. But they went away just like cancer sometimes goes away."

Durant studied her briefly. "Whatever you say, Georgia."

Durant turned to find Otherguy Overby up and standing by the club chair. Overby wore his hard merry grin. Durant returned it with a crooked one of his own that was half fond and half wary. "Otherguy," Durant said, a little surprised by the warmth that had crept unbidden into his tone. He crossed the room and held out his hand.

"Quincy," Overby said as they shook hands.

"I hear it's fat."

"You hear right."

"Good," Durant said and turned to the beaming Artie Wu who was still on the couch, hands laced across his belly. "When you called," Durant said, "you kind of forgot to mention Georgia."

Wu shook his great head. "If I'd told you, your heart would've started going pitty-pat and you'd've turned all sweaty and gone looking for roses at one in the morning. This way you open the door and—bang! It's over and done."

"Like a good neat hanging," Durant said.

"Exactly," Wu said and looked at Georgia Blue. "You okay?"

She nodded and sat down on the couch.

"Well, sometimes reunions aren't as bad as we—"

"For Christ sake, Artie, drop it," she said.

Wu smiled agreeably. "Okay. Let's get down to business." He rose from the couch. "I'll pour for whoever's thirsty. After that, Otherguy'll go through it from start to finish without interruption. When he's done, it'll be question time. Any comments or suggestions?"

There weren't any. Georgia Blue asked for a glass of white wine. The three men chose beer. Wu served the drinks, then sat back down on the couch, took out one of his immense cigars and held it up to see whether anyone objected. When no one did, he lit it carefully, blew the smoke up in the air and looked at Overby. "Let's hear it, Otherguy. From the beginning."

"Let me put the price on it first for Quincy," Overby said. He looked at Durant. "It's a five-way even split on five million U.S. There's another loose half million that'll go for expenses and the this-and-that." He paused. "Interested?"

Durant grinned. "Extremely."

Overby told it then, concisely and quickly, leaving out the adjectives and all hyperbole. He pronounced each name carefully and even spelled it. A brief report on the meeting with Boy Howdy was given without rancor, which somehow made it even more damning. When he was done he leaned back in the club chair, picked up his beer, and drank half of it.

There was a brief silence until Durant said, "Our other partner, the one who isn't here?"

"Booth Stallings," Overby said.

"The terrorism expert."

Overby nodded.

"Is he an expert on its cure and prevention, or is he a how-to-do-it man?"

"I read a book he wrote," Overby said. "Well, most of it anyhow. He knows a hell of a lot about it—maybe everything. But . . ." Overby frowned as if his thought had dried up.

"But what?" Durant said.

"Well, when he explains how and why it happens, he stays kind of neutral—you know, like he was above it all."

Artie Wu blew a large fat smoke ring at the ceiling and turned to Georgia Blue. "Tell us about the other one, Georgia. The poet who hired you as shotgun."

"Harry Crites."

Wu acknowledged the name with a wave of his cigar.

"He's a very smooth, well-connected fixer who works Washington out of his Watergate apartment. He has clients in South and Central America, a kind of poste restante office in London, and makes a lot of trips to the Middle East. To Cairo. Nowhere else there. Just Cairo."

"What's his background?" Durant asked.

"Federal," she said. "White House—well, kind of, a long time ago—then DOD and State." She paused. "Varied and murky."

"Langley?" Wu said.

"He says not."

Artie Wu stuck the cigar back in his mouth, locked his hands behind his head and examined the ceiling. He spoke around the cigar.

"Okay. Harry Crites is the tap that turns on the money. It flows through the pipe that's our very own Booth Stallings and lands in the bucket—maybe receptacle would be better—that's Alejandro Espiritu, aging freedom fighter and/or archterrorist."

He took the cigar out of his mouth and looked at Durant. "Except for the fact that he and Stallings were once comrades-in-arms during the war, what else do we know about Espiritu?"

"Fuck all," Durant said.

"Then we'd better get a fix on him. You want to take that on, Otherguy?"

Overby thought about it and finally said yes.

Wu picked up an ashtray and carefully put out his cigar. "Now we get to the real question. Just whose money are we going to lift?"

"Stallings had some thoughts on that," Georgia Blue said. "He thinks it must be dirty money that, once gone, nobody'll send after. I told him Harry Crites'll sure as hell send after it and that he'll probably send me."

Wu raised his right eyebrow. "And what did Mr. Stallings say?"

"He thought it was a pretty notion."

"So do I," Wu said. "Quincy?"

"Very pretty."

"I think it's fucking beautiful," Overby said.

Artie Wu looked at his watch, yawned and stretched. "Somewhere along the way, after the money leaves the tap and before it drops into the Espiritu bucket, we'll have to siphon it off. I can think of several ways we might do that and Otherguy can probably come up with even more."

"At least a dozen," Overby said.

"We'll have to run it on a no-comeback basis," Durant said.

"Absolutely," Wu said.

Durant frowned. "But we can't do that until we know whose money it really is."

Overby squirmed in his chair, asking for the floor. "Want to know my gut hunch?"

Artie Wu leaned forward, elbows on knees, his expression suddenly interested and wide awake. "Very much," he said.

"Okay," Overby said. "We know we're messing with serious money that involves governments or at least multinationals. I mean, nobody's going to spend five million just to bring some old ridgerunner down from the hills unless they stand to get five hundred million back, right?"

"Five hundred million worth of something anyhow."

"Well, I don't much care whose five million it is so long as we can fix up the no-comeback." Overby paused. "But my gut tells me what they want that five million to do." He leaned back in his chair and waited for someone to prompt him, which Durant quickly did.

"Fuck up the Philippines, that's what," Overby said as a look of absolute certitude spread across his face.

There was a lengthy silence while Overby's prediction was digested. Finally, Artie Wu softly said, "Well, I guess it's not going to happen then, is it?"

Dismay and more than a trace of alarm erased Overby's normal confidence. "You mean we don't go for the money?"

"What he means," Durant said, "is that if we make the money disappear, then it can't be used to fuck up the country."

Overby's relief was apparent. "Yeah. Right."

"I can't believe this," Georgia Blue said.

Overby looked at her. "Why the hell not?"

"Because bullshit in the moonlight still stinks. Do-gooders don't steal five million dollars. Thieves do. Grifters like us, Otherguy. If those two want romance, fine. I'll take cash."

"What's so wrong with doing a little good while we're at it?" Overby asked.

Georgia Blue sighed. "Because there's never any money in it."

CHAPTER
FIFTEEN

At 7:15 the following morning Booth Stallings came out of the Manila Hotel coffee shop, where he had been among its first customers, and strolled into the lobby. He dumped the three somewhat strident Manila newspapers that had been his breakfast reading into a wastebasket and turned to watch an ABC television news crew fret over the logistics of loading its equipment into a waiting van.

Stallings wondered what the crew's story might be and what percentage of its viewers would know or care that the Philippines were not, after all, in the Middle East just to the left of Syria. *That's the Philistine Islands you're thinking of, hon.* Maybe ten percent, he decided, but immediately raised that to twenty and then, mostly out of unfounded optimism, increased the percentage to thirty.

Knowing where a country is doesn't make you care what happens to it, Stallings thought, not even if you'd once been enrolled in the ultimate geography lesson of a world war. With a small private grin he recalled what the Marines had said about the Carolines: Who gives a fuck about Truk?

The ABC news team carried out its last big black box and Stallings crossed to the reception desk to see whether he had any messages. The clerk turned, looked and turned back with an envelope. It was a plain white envelope, neither cheap nor expensive.

It was addressed to Stallings in a handwriting that he recognized as Filipino, which he thought to be the prettiest in the world. He also knew his judgment was influenced by the striking similarity of much Filipino penmanship to that of Mary Helen Packer who had sat in front of him in the fourth, fifth and sixth grades, and whose firm but graceful hand had won her a prize every year.

He wondered whether the high quality of Filipino handwriting was a legacy from the Spanish friars or, less likely, from the 540 American schoolteachers who had shipped out to Manila in 1901 aboard the S.S. *Thomas*, a first echelon that had fanned out over the islands, bringing both English and the Palmer method to the provinces. He remembered Espiritu once mentioning that he had been taught by an elderly Thomasite. From Kansas, Stallings seemed to recall.

He crossed to one of the lobby chairs, sat down and examined the envelope. It was handsomely addressed to Mr. Booth Stallings, The Manila Hotel. Down at the lower left-hand corner were the words: By Hand.

Inside was a once folded sheet of good quality white paper. Black ink had been used to write two lines so straight they seemed almost ruled. The lines formed more of a command than an invitation: "Meet me at nine this morning under my name at the American Memorial Cemetery in Makati." The letter was signed Hovey Profette. Stallings used a weak smile to block the chill the dead medic's name was meant to cause.

·　　·　　·

The reception clerk wasn't able to remember exactly who had delivered the letter, although he thought it might have been a small fairly clean boy of no more than nine or ten. Stallings thanked him, turned and walked through the doors of the hotel's front entrance and out into the morning heat.

He put on his prescription sunglasses as the doorman whistled up an air-conditioned taxi. Stallings' eyesight was still close to 20-30 and the sunglasses only served to correct a mild astigmatism that he otherwise ignored.

He knew that benevolent genes had left his sight virtually

intact and permitted him to keep most of his hair and all but
one of his teeth. He also knew it was pure luck that he had
never had an operation, broken a bone, or experienced any real
pain that aspirin wouldn't cure—except the occasional acute
hangovers. For those he relied on Bromo-Seltzer and a beer or
two.

Stallings even regarded his sex life as tolerable, if erratic.
Most of the women he now went to bed with were divorced,
nearly a generation younger than he (in their early forties), and
still puzzled over why their husbands had left them for
someone younger. Stallings always claimed to be as puzzled as
they and the mutual puzzlement provided a never-ending topic
of conversation.

The one thing Stallings occasionally did worry about was his
mind. He feared losing it. He had long recognized that his
mind, if not brilliant, was clever, quick and facile. And if it
had a few quirks and loose boards, it also had a carefully
cultivated streak of objectivity. Should his mind ever really
start to crack, Stallings counted on the objectivity to sort out
the options and go with suicide. He had decided years back
that he would rather be dead than dotty.

* * *

To get to the American Memorial Cemetery the young taxi
driver drove (or detoured, for all Stallings knew) through a
residential section that featured high walls surrounding big
houses that were watched over by tough guards. Stallings
asked what the area was and the driver said it was Forbes Park
and that the rich and the foreign lived there. Stallings caught a
glimpse of the flags of Spain, West Germany and the tricolor of
France. There were also several others, but he sped by too
quickly to identify them.

After Forbes Park came the long U-shaped drive that led up
to the first flight of marble steps at the American Memorial
Cemetery. Beyond the first flight was yet another flight and
beyond that was a five- or six-story tower of marble with a

black door. Above the door were some huge bas-relief figures
that Stallings at first took to be the fallen dead but, on closer
inspection, turned out to be nurturing female nudes.

On the right was a large thick slablike building of white
marble with an American flag on a tall pole. To the left was a
matching building, matching pole and the flag of the Philippines. There were trees behind the memorial buildings and
several acres of nicely kept grass in front. But there were no
cars or visitors. At least none that Stallings could see.

After negotiating the price of a 30-minute wait, Stallings left
the cab and started up the steps. Upon entering the memorial
he found that the names of the dead were listed alphabetically.
Rank was given first, then the name, then the military unit and,
finally, the dead warrior's home state.

Each name was lettered in gold leaf several inches high.
There were, a plaque claimed, 36,279 names. Beyond the twin
memorial buildings was a proper cemetery where the white
crosses and Stars of David grew, row on row, just as they did at
Meuse-Argonne, Château-Thierry and, Stallings presumed,
Shiloh and Little Big Horn, although he had never visited those
last two killing grounds. And he wasn't at all sure whether they
had Stars of David. He resolved to look it up.

The Ps were toward the rear of the breezy, open-sided
memorial building. Stallings walked slowly past the Patter-
sons, the Penningtons, the Phillipses, the Pitts, the Powells
and the Prathers until he came to T/5 Hovey Profette 182
Infantry Arkansas. He stared up at the gold name, third from
the top, and thought what all combat veterans think when
confronted by their own war's dead: Better you than me,
buddy—a first reaction frequently followed by vague and not
easily defined feelings of guilt and pity.

Well, if I'd've shot old Al when I had the chance, Hovey,
said Stallings to himself and the long-dead Profette, maybe all
three of us could've had our names up there in gold leaf. He
was still staring up at Profette's name when the woman's voice

behind him said, "I must apologize for the trick I played on you, Mr. Stallings."

Stallings continued to stare up at the dead medic's name. "No need to apologize," he said and turned to find a young Filipina nun in a modern gray habit. She wore dark glasses and carried a large leather shoulder bag. Stallings noticed she was not very tall and seemed quite fit.

"Al send you?" he said.

"Al?"

"Espiritu."

"Yes, of course. You called him that, didn't you? Al. He wants me to bring you to him."

"When?"

"Now."

"Where is he?"

"Cebu."

"Tell Al I appreciate the offer but I prefer to make my own travel arrangements."

The nun shook her head with regret. "I'm afraid I really must insist."

"No, thanks."

"Oh, dear," she said and reached into the shoulder bag, as if for a handkerchief, fumbled briefly and produced a medium-size semiautomatic pistol. She pointed it at Stallings with what he took to be practiced ease. He also noticed it was at least a .38-caliber and that her hand didn't shake.

"What's that supposed to do?" he asked.

"Make you come with me."

"Guns give people funny notions," he said, trying to make his tone as musing as possible. "If you shoot me, old Al's going to be out a lot of money. Therefore, you won't shoot me. Therefore, I won't come with you." He smiled. "You're not really a nun, are you, Sister?"

Instead of replying, the woman quickly backed up two steps and dropped into a pistol shooter's stance. It was a crouching wide-legged stance that employed a two-handed grip on the semiautomatic. Stallings' first impression was that the stance made her look both silly and faintly erotic, until he realized she actually might shoot and even kill him.

He tried to think of something conciliatory to say, something soothing and full of sweet reason. But before it came to him, a voice snapped out a one-word command: "Don't!"

Stallings was between two walls of gold names. The nun with the pistol had backed two steps into the corridor. The voice came from her right flank and there had been absolute authority in its crackling tone. Stallings recognized the voice. The nun glanced quickly in its direction. What she saw made her flinch and slowly lower the pistol until it pointed at the marble floor.

"Kneel," the same voice ordered.

The nun knelt.

"Put it down."

The nun gently placed the pistol on the floor.

"On your stomach, hands behind your head."

It was an awkward position but the nun managed it with a certain amount of decorum. Georgia Blue appeared in the corridor, the Walther in her right hand. She squatted to pick up the nun's weapon, rose and glanced at Stallings. "How's it feel to be at death's front door?"

"Rotten."

Quincy Durant appeared in the corridor and stood just to the right of Georgia Blue, staring down at the nun. "You can put your hands down," Durant told her.

The nun removed them from her head and placed them palms-down on the floor. Durant knelt and removed her sunglasses. Her head twisted to the right and her shining brown eyes stared up at him.

"You get around," Durant said.

"You know her?" Georgia Blue asked.

"We met on the way down from Baguio where she and four other guys had the kilometer sixteen roadblock concession."

"You're Durant," Stallings said.

The still kneeling Durant looked up at Stallings and nodded. "And you're Booth Stallings."

"Who's she?" Georgia Blue said.

Durant looked back down at the nun who had turned her head away from him. "Let's ask her," Durant said. "You want to give us a name?"

The prone woman said nothing. Durant picked up her large purse and looked through it, itemizing its contents aloud. "Five hundred pesos, an extra clip, a sanitary napkin, some aspirin and no ID."

"She knows Espiritu," Stallings said.

Durant gave him a skeptical look. "Knows him or claims to?"

Stallings took the handwritten letter from his pocket and handed it to Durant. After reading it quickly, Durant passed it up to Georgia Blue who also read it.

"Who's Hovey Profette?" Durant asked as he rose.

Stallings pointed to Profette's gold name. Durant looked at it and then back at Stallings. "He was somehow hooked up with you and Espiritu during the war, right?"

Stallings nodded. "She said she wanted to take me to him. Down in Cebu. When I said no thanks, she pulled the gun."

"Funny," Georgia Blue said to Durant. "I mean it's funny how you and she have already met."

"She also met Artie," Durant said. "Which makes it hilarious." He looked at Stallings. "Otherguy claims you're sole source on this deal."

"So I'm told."

"Then why'd she want to kill you?"

"Let's ask her," Stallings said.

"She won't give us a straight answer," Georgia Blue said.

"Well, what do we do?" Stallings asked, almost beginning to enjoy the improvisation. "Get rid of her?"

There was a silence until Durant said, "If she really is tied to Espiritu, that would send him a message. If she's not . . ." He shrugged.

The woman on the floor turned her head and looked up at Durant. "You won't kill me."

Durant nodded. "I won't but she will." His eyes indicated Georgia Blue.

The woman on the floor sat up quickly. "My name is Carmen Espiritu and I'd like a cigarette, please."

Stallings looked at Durant. "You smoke?"

"I quit."

"Georgia?" Stallings asked.

She shook her head. Stallings squatted beside Carmen Espiritu, his knees up in his armpits, his hands dangling, his rear hanging down between his ankles, an interested look on his face. "Nobody smokes," he said.

The woman said nothing.

"You Al's daughter?"

"Granddaughter."

"Why were you going to shoot me, Carmen?"

"I wasn't."

"Sure looked like it."

"We don't approve of the people you've hired and I was trying to convince you to come to Cebu alone."

"What's wrong with them—the people I hired?"

"Everything," Carmen Espiritu said. "You were observed from the time you met Harry Crites in Washington until you arrived in Manila."

"You mean followed?"

"Observed. Watched."

"By Al's folks?"

"In Los Angeles," she said, "our people talked to that Blondin girl, the drug addict, and paid her to tell us about Overby. That led us to him," she said, looking at Durant, "and also to the big Chinese." Her lip curled slightly. "We already had files on them, but we decided to test their competence." This time she looked at Georgia Blue. "What we saw on the Baguio road was not impressive."

Durant smiled.

"So you really weren't going to shoot me?" Stallings said.

"No," she said. "Of course not."

"Just wanted to scare me into dumping my associates, huh?"

"Associates," she said, looking at Georgia Blue. "A cashiered Secret Service agent." She turned to Durant. "A sociopath adventurer whose Chinese partner suffers from infantile delusions." She turned back to Stallings. "And then, of course, there's Overby, the hooligan. They made my grandfather uneasy. Suspicious. So we were instructed to make you come alone."

Stallings nodded as if it all made perfect sense. He looked up at Durant. "I'll have to send old Al a message, I guess."

"She's already got the message," Georgia Blue said.

Stallings looked dubious. "Maybe. How's your memory, Carmen?"

"Quite adequate."

"I want you to give your granddaddy a personal message from me. You tell Al if he tries to fuck me over again, he'll never see a dime. Got that?"

"If he tries to fuck you over again, he'll never see a dime."

Stallings rose slowly.

"May I leave now?" Carmen Espiritu said.

"Sure," said Stallings.

Durant took a cigarette from his pocket, lit it and handed it down to her. "I lied about not smoking," he said.

"How childish," she said and drew the smoke deep into her lungs.

CHAPTER
SIXTEEN

A s they walked back to his still waiting taxi, Stallings said, "She lied about being Espiritu's granddaughter."

"How d'you know?" Durant asked.

Stallings made no reply until he paid off the young driver and the taxi had driven away. He then turned to examine the four-door Mercedes that was parked just behind where the taxi had been.

"Yours?" he asked.

"The hotel's," Durant said.

"Air-conditioned?"

"Right."

"Let's have some," Stallings said, heading for the car. He climbed into the rear, Durant and Georgia Blue into the front. Durant started the engine and switched on the air-conditioning.

"How old was she, Georgia?" Stallings asked. "Twenty-five? Twenty-six?"

"At least. You could even add on a year or two."

"Old Al's sixty-two now; maybe even sixty-three. And he wasn't married when I knew him. So he and his kids, if he had any, would've had to hump it to produce a twenty-six- or twenty-seven-year-old granddaughter."

Neither Durant nor Georgia Blue disagreed. There was a silence until Stallings cleared his throat and said, "No offense, but I've always been leery of nick-of-time stuff. So how'd you two manage it?"

"Nothing fancy," Durant said. "Artie and I thought the five

of us should meet. So I drove over to the Manila and called Otherguy from the lobby. When he didn't answer, I called Georgia. She and I met in the lobby and she saw you getting into the taxi. We followed in the Mercedes and you know the rest."

Durant watched in the rearview mirror as Stallings smiled coldly. "Checking me out?" Stallings asked.

"That's right."

"Don't blame you."

Durant put the car into gear and drove off. For nearly a minute Stallings stared to his right through the sloppily tinted side window, thinking that it was like looking through a quarter inch of blue Jell-O. "She bothers me," he said, breaking the silence.

"Carmen," Durant said.

"Not her so much as her apparatus, and she and old Al sure as hell have one. Remember the girl she mentioned in L.A.? Blondin?"

"The addict," Georgia Blue said.

"A real space cadet," Stallings said. "I met her at a place Otherguy was house-sitting. In Malibu. Carmen claims her people got to Blondin and then a few days later you guys ran into Carmen herself on the road down from Baguio. I'd sure like to hear about that, Mr. Durant, if you don't mind."

"I don't mind," Durant said. "It had to do with the Cousin."

"Whose cousin?"

"Marcos' third cousin. Ernesto Pineda. Somebody slit his throat and cut off his balls. Carmen and her people take the credit."

"That's an interesting beginning," Stallings said. "How's it turn out?"

Durant told of his and Wu's involvement with Ernesto Pineda, leaving out nothing he thought pertinent. He then spent five minutes answering Stallings' quick, probing questions. After Stallings ran out of questions, they rode in silence for a minute or two until Georgia Blue could no longer suppress the noise that lay somewhere between a giggle and a guffaw.

"My God, Quincy. You and Artie got stiffed."

Durant opened his mouth to reply but changed his mind. Another silence followed. Stallings broke it when he leaned forward from the back seat and said, "Let's suppose, just for the hell of it, that the Cousin's reinsurance deal was legitimate—as legitimate as those things ever are once you factor in the graft. Okay, Georgia?"

She nodded without conviction.

"And let's also suppose, Mr. Durant, that Carmen found out about your deal with the Marcos Cousin just about the time she heard I'd signed Overby on. Now was there anybody else who'd've known that Otherguy was looking for you and Mr. Wu?"

"Here in Manila?"

"Yes."

"Boy Howdy."

"Nice enough fella?"

"The opposite."

"Think he might've talked too much or even sold Carmen what he knew?"

"You could almost count on it."

"Then it's possible," Stallings said slowly, "that Carmen and old Al Espiritu might've preferred the devils they knew."

"That's Artie and me, I take it."

"Sure. She must've known what the Cousin was up to and that you and Mr. Wu were in cahoots with him. Well, why not make sure you two jump at Otherguy's proposition? The best way to do that is to dent your finances. So she and her lads kill the Cousin and you guys are out three hundred thousand and broke—right?"

"Right."

"All cash?"

Durant sighed. "All."

"Which means your money might've provided Carmen with a nice chunk of working capital and also more or less forced you to go to work for me. You know, Mr. Durant, the more I think about it, the more it sounds just like old Al."

"Why'd she stop us on the way down from Baguio?" Durant said. "Just to mindfuck us?"

"Sure. It was typical push-pull intimidation. They love stuff like that."

"You want a second opinion?" Georgia Blue asked.

"Certainly," Stallings said.

"I saw her, Booth. Up close. And she was all set to shoot—not just hijack you down to Cebu. The signs were all there—stance, breathing, everything."

"That your professional Secret Service opinion, Georgia?" Stallings asked.

"It's what they trained and paid me to spot."

"I'm not so sure," he said. "A terrorist's first job is to terrify. Well, she sure scared hell out of me. Another minute and I'd've been on my way down to Cebu alone and I don't much care who knows it. But we also threw a pretty good scare into her. Who terrifies most, controls. Right now I'd call it a draw."

"Carmen's still out front," Durant said. "Ahead on points anyway. About three hundred thousand points."

•   •   •

Otherguy Overby found the man he went looking for in a morning coffee club that was on a side street just off Taft Avenue. It was the third such club Overby had visited and all three seemed to be doing a brisk business of dispensing coffee, rolls, alcohol and sex. The club's customers—off on their morning breaks that might last until one or two in the afternoon—were, for the most part, businessmen, executives, merchants, politicians, lawyers, journalists and a number of well-dressed men who sold things that fell off trucks.

The man Overby went looking for was now in his mid-sixties and had got his start during the Japanese occupation as a young buy-and-sell man in the Manila black market. His name was Abelardo Umali and Overby found him sitting at a table near the crowded bar with two young women and a bottle of something that looked like champagne. Only the two young women drank it; Umali drank coffee.

Overby was dressed in a blue cord jacket, gray pants that looked like flannel but weren't, and a dark blue polo shirt. The only reason he had worn the jacket in the Manila heat was for its inside pocket where the money envelope was. He crossed the room to Umali's table, approaching from the old man's left. When he reached the table, Overby said, "Hello, Abe."

Abelardo Umali turned slowly and looked up. He had a dark brown wrinkled face with a turtle mouth and tiny wet black eyes that looked as if they wept easily. He wore a starched, immaculately ironed white short-sleeved shirt, gray tie and black pants. Overby could not remember him ever wearing anything else. The turtle mouth smiled.

"Otherguy," Umali said. "Somebody claimed you were dead." He frowned, as if trying to remember what he had really heard. "Or maybe it was just that you ought to be. Either way, you've got my condolences. Sit. Join us. Please."

"It's a private matter, Abe," Overby said.

"Private? What kind of secrets have we got?"

"The money I owe you."

The old man's wet eyes widened and the smile returned. "Ah. That money. A real secret." He turned to the young women. "My hearts—could you—would you—please—just for a few minutes?"

The two young women giggled, eyed Overby, giggled again, rose and hurried away. "Sit, Otherguy. Have something cool."

Overby sat down and said he would have a beer. Umali ordered it. When it came, he poured it carefully into a glass and served it to his guest. As Overby took his first swallow, Umali said, "I hear you saw Boy Howdy last night."

Overby nodded.

"I hear it was a warm talk you had. Very warm."

"You ever talk to Boy without raising your voice?"

Umali shrugged. "You paid him good money—or so I hear."

"I paid him to find me Wu and Durant."

Umali's eyebrows went up and down twice in what Overby always thought of as the Cebu salute. The rapid movement of the eyebrows could signal approval, commiseration, agreement, doubt, disappointment or even, Tell me more. "They're at the Peninsula," Umali said. "Have been for a month." He paused. "I would've told you for nothing."

"I want you to tell me something for something, Abe."

"Is there a figure?"

"Two thousand."

"Pesos?"

"Dollars," Overby said. "U.S."

The old man's eyebrows rose and fell again, indicating what Overby interpreted to be interest.

"I hear very little these days," Umali said, obviously lying. "I'm an old man now and I have to pay young women to listen to me. I like to talk to them about the past—about the old days in Cebu. You remember them, Otherguy?"

"They're not so far back," Overby said. "Ten, twelve, fifteen years ago."

"I mean forty, forty-five years ago."

"About the time I was born. Maybe you and I can even talk about that a little."

"For money?"

Overby nodded. Umali's eyebrows went up and down, up and down. Overby took the unsealed Peninsula Hotel envelope from his inside pocket and placed it on the table in front of Umali.

"May I?" he said. Overby again nodded. Umali opened the envelope, peeked inside and sent his eyebrows into motion again. "You can ask," he said. "Maybe I can answer. Maybe not."

"Tell me about Boy Howdy," Overby said. "Tell me why he sort of turned over on his back last night, stuck his paws up in the air, and begged me to scratch his stomach."

Umali looked left, as if in that direction lay orderly thoughts. "You, Durant and Wu, right?"

"Right."

"Interesting," Umali said. "Well, first, you have to understand that Boy's in a state of shock since our leader ran away."

"Boy's afraid Aquino's not going to let the good times roll much longer?"

"It's more complicated than that."

Overby waited. Finally, the old man said, "Boy believes in the second coming."

Overby's hard, merry grin came and went. "Faith is a wonderful thing."

"Boy's willing to back his faith with—what's the saying?—his fortune and his sacred honor, such as it is. His honor, I mean."

"He really wants Marcos back?"

"Many do. But Boy is betting everything he's got on it."

"What're the odds, Abe?"

"For a Marcos return?" He shook his head. "For somebody else?" The eyebrows rose and fell twice.

"Who?"

Again, Umali's eyebrows made a "who knows?" reply.

"Has Boy got a favorite?"

"You'll have to ask him."

"Okay," Overby said. "That was my first question."

"How many more d'you plan to ask?"

"One more."

The eyebrows said one more would be allowed.

"You know Cebu," Overby said. "You were born there."

Umali shrugged.

"Tell me what you know about Alejandro Espiritu."

The old man's thin mouth stretched itself into a wide tight reproachful line. His eyes grew even wetter. He sniffed, either to hold back tears or because he smelled something unpleasant. Then he said, "Go away, Otherguy. Take your money with you."

Overby hitched his chair forward, leaned across the table and tapped the money envelope with his right forefinger. "Two thousand U.S., Abe. Just for a sentence or two."

The old man sighed. "You, Wu and Durant mixed up with Espiritu. Well, you all deserve each other. But I don't want to know about it, Otherguy. For the first time in my life I don't want to be the first to know."

"Espiritu bothers you, huh?"

The eyebrows shot up and down again. "When he was a kid, he only frightened me. Now that he's an old man, he terrifies me. You won't beat him because he's smarter than you, Otherguy. Smarter than Durant. Smarter even than Artie and that's smart-smart. No matter what, you won't win. So I don't care how fat the deal is, drop it. Go run the Mexican General or the Omaha Banker on somebody in Hong Kong or Bangkok. Or even Singapore, for God's sake."

Overby smiled. "He's bad, huh?"

"He's death."

"Pick up your money, Abe."

Umali shook his head.

"I want you to get a message to him."

Apprehension battled with curiosity across the old man's face. Curiosity won. "From you?"

"You can get a message to him without either of us getting mixed up in it. You're good at that, right?"

The old man's hand crept across the table and rested on the money envelope. "What's the message?"

"Out of the five, Overby's it."

The old man stared at him. His turtle mouth went back into a thin line of disapproval. His left eye brimmed over and a single tear ran down his cheek. He didn't bother to wipe it away.

"You're going to stiff Wu and Durant, aren't you?"

Overby made no reply. The old man picked up the money

envelope and tucked it against his stomach beneath his belt buckle.

"I'm talking to a dead man," Umali said. "If Espiritu doesn't fix you, Durant will."

Overby rose. "See to it, Abe."

"I don't like talking to dead people," the old man called, but by then Overby was already walking toward the door.

CHAPTER SEVENTEEN

The first thing Booth Stallings said after Durant introduced him to Artie Wu was, "How'd you get to be the pretender, Mr. Wu?"

"You want a beer or a drink?" Wu said.

"A beer'd be good."

Durant went to the sitting room's refrigerator and took out three beers. He passed the cans around without opening them. Wu popped his open, took a long draught, sighed with pleasure and said, "I'm the illegitimate son of the illegitimate daughter of the last Emperor of China."

"The Boy Emperor?" Stallings said without surprise, popping his own beer can. "Old P'u Yi?"

"The same," Artie Wu said, pleased that Stallings would know, and even more pleased that not much explanation would be necessary.

"Mao threw him in jail for a while, didn't he? And then made him a tourist guide in Peking—or whatever they're calling it now. Died back in the sixties, I think. Sixty-four, sixty-five—around in there."

"Sixty-six," Wu said.

Stallings raised his beer can in a toast of sorts. "Well, here's to Grandpa."

Wu smiled at the toast and said, "You may as well know the rest. My real father was an oversexed Methodist Chinese bishop who either sneaked or snuck into my mother's bedroom. She'd been adopted by a Methodist missionary couple in China who brought her back to San Francisco. She was seventeen when the bishop had his way with her and she died having me. My adoptive grandparents were killed in a car wreck a few years later and I wound up in the John Wesley Memorial Orphanage in San Francisco."

"Where he met me," Durant said.

"And you two've been partners ever since, right?"

Durant nodded.

"Must be a comfort," Stallings said.

Wu's eyebrows moved up into a quizzical look. "Being partners?"

"Knowing where you spring from. Most people don't even know who Grandpa's pa was. I know I don't. A few years back I thought maybe I should, but then I asked myself what the hell difference would it make and got over it. But I can still see how it could be a comfort."

"You have children?" Durant asked.

"Two daughters but no grandchildren."

Wu took out one of his large cigars and went through the ritual of lighting it, talking all the while. "I've always felt that a marketable skill provides far more emotional security than a well-diagrammed family tree. When the rent's due and you're broke, it's not much help to know you're the shirttail relative of some guy who signed the Declaration of Independence, or rode up Cemetery Hill with Pickett, or lent King John a pen."

He looked up and blew one of his fat smoke rings at the ceiling. "On the other hand, when you reach down into your pocket and nothing jingles, and you have to get out and scratch something up, it's nice to know you've got a skill to sell, whether you're a cooper, a parson, a wheelwright, a miller or even a terrorism expert."

Stallings winked at Wu. "I sure like the way you slid into that."

Wu leaned forward, big elbows on broad knees, an interested look on his face. "So how'd you get to be a terrorism expert, Booth?"

Stallings drank some of his beer, thought for a moment and said, "I learned by doing because that's what I did from about the time I turned nineteen until I was almost nineteen and a half."

"Here?" Durant said. "I mean, here in the Philippines?"

"Negros and Cebu. Mostly Cebu." Stallings paused. "You want the rest?"

"Of course," Wu said.

Stallings finished his beer before continuing. "I was a just-commissioned second lieutenant. A replacement. One Hundred and Eighty-second Infantry. The Cebu invasion was set for March twenty-sixth."

"Forty-five?" Durant said.

"Forty-five. There was a pretty fair guerrilla outfit on Cebu that division needed to make contact with. So they decided to send in an eight-man I and R patrol three weeks early—mostly fuckups and new guys like me. Besides me, there were four riflemen, a buck sergeant, a radioman, a T/5 medic and a guerrilla liaison."

"Alejandro Espiritu," Wu said.

"Right. Old Al. Well, they caught us on the beach. Japanese infantry. Four of us never even made it out of the rafts. The sergeant and three riflemen died first. The fourth rifleman bought it the second he made the beach. Then the radioman. That left Al, the medic and me. We ran like hell, lost everything in the surf and finally made it to where we were supposed to hook up with the guerrillas, but they were all dead—all nineteen of 'em. We salvaged an M-1 with no rear sight and about a hundred rounds the Japs'd missed." He paused. "We called them Japs then."

Wu nodded. "I still do when the TV conks out."

"After that," Stallings said, "well, we turned into terrorists, at least Al and I did."

"What about the medic—Profette?" Durant asked. "The guy with his name up in gold letters."

"He went apeshit. Hovey was a Quaker and a C.O. who'd misplaced his faith. We were up on a ridge in the Guadalupes, the three of us, when Hovey spotted two scouts from a Japanese company-strength patrol. They turned out to be Imperial Marines. Big fuckers. Well, Hovey wanted to take out the two scouts with that one rifle we had. The one with no rear sight. Al and I didn't think that was such a hot idea. But then Hovey grabbed the rifle."

There was a silence that threatened to go on and on until Durant broke it with a one-word question. "And?"

"And Al took Hovey out with a bolo."

"Can't say I blame him," Durant said.

Wu nodded slowly several times before he asked the next question. "Then what?"

"Then Al and I hooked up with some other guerrillas, ate fish and rice when we could get it, dog and worse when we couldn't, and turned into pretty fair terrorists."

"When you got back to your own outfit," Wu said, "did they ask about the medic?"

"They asked. I recommended Hovey for a DSC. He got it, too."

"And before you got back . . ." Durant didn't quite make it a question.

The smile that Stallings gave Durant was thin and cold and bleak. His February smile, Durant thought. "Who'd we terrorize is what you want to know, right? Who'd we kill?"

Durant nodded.

"The Japanese were our primary target. We killed a lot of them. Filipino collaborators were our secondary target. We killed a bunch of them, too."

"How'd you know they were collaborators?" Wu said.

"We had a list."

"Whose list?"

"Espiritu's."

"Good list?"

"Good as any." Stallings paused. "Wartime lists, I discovered later, a lot later, often include the names of the enemies of those who draw up the lists. I imagine old Al sprinkled a few of his in."

"You have anything . . . personal against him?" Wu said.

"Espiritu?"

Wu nodded.

"He's a guy I soldiered with a long time ago. That's all. I don't like him or dislike him. But when it comes to trusting him I'm not quite so ambivalent. I don't trust him at all."

"Then neither will we," Artie Wu said. He looked at Durant. "Let's order up some lunch and get Georgia and Otherguy in here. We might as well start."

"I thought we already had," Durant said as he picked up the phone.

•   •   •

Georgia Blue and Overby arrived together shortly before a pair of Peninsula Hotel room waiters wheeled in the lunches Durant had ordered. Durant had asked for three fish and two chicken lunches, which worked out well because Wu, Georgia Blue and Stallings asked for fish. Overby and Durant were content with chicken.

During lunch the talk was desultory. By now, everyone knew about the morning episode at the war memorial. There were several long stretches of silence and occasionally Durant would catch Wu staring off into the distance with a curiously blank expression. It was a look that Durant always thought of as Wu's perfectly rotten plan expression.

After the lunches were eaten—or half eaten—Wu and Durant stacked the dishes, lowered the wheeled table's sides, and rolled the table out into the hall. Stallings watched them work, almost with the efficiency of room waiters, and wondered how many meals they had eaten in how many hotels. Thousands of meals, he guessed. Hundreds of hotels.

Wu went back to his seat on the end of the couch, took out a cigar, and held it up to see whether anyone would object. No one did. Georgia Blue chose the other end of the couch. Stallings returned to his club chair. Otherguy Overby picked out a straight-back chair and sat, feet firmly planted, knees together, arms folded across his chest. Durant leaned against a wall and lit one of his increasingly rare cigarettes.

Booth Stallings noticed how all eyes, including his, were on Artie Wu. Three fat smoke rings headed for the ceiling. Wu watched as they twisted, swirled and finally disintegrated. He then looked at Stallings.

"I've been thinking about our problem," Artie Wu said, "and I may have come up with a solution."

"Let's hear it," Stallings said.

Durant looked at his watch when Wu began to talk. He talked steadily and confidently, as if from a carefully prepared outline. With a change of pitch, he even dropped in the occasional footnote exactly where needed. Stallings leaned forward, listening intently. An admiring smile spread slowly across Overby's face and refused to go away. Georgia Blue gazed at Wu with a look that could have been interpreted as adoration, but which Durant knew to be awe and respect. There was a final summary paragraph and Wu was done. Durant looked at his watch. Wu had spoken without pause or interruption for exactly 26 minutes.

Although he had glanced occasionally at the others, Wu had aimed his sales talk, for that's what it had been, at his primary customer, Booth Stallings. They now waited to hear whether the prospect was buying.

Stallings gave his chin a hard squeeze, his left earlobe a tug and said, "I like it. By God, I do."

Artie Wu beamed and looked at Georgia Blue. She smiled almost helplessly. "Perfect, Artie. As always."

Wu turned to Overby. "Well, Otherguy?"

Overby made an effort to erase his smile, but failed. So, still smiling, he said, "You know what it is, don't you, Artie? It's new. Brand-new. Not just some old-hat change-up. And I haven't heard a new one since the Pommie Bastard, may he rest in peace, came up with the Angel Flight in Saigon and that was what?—eleven years ago when they were all climbing over the Embassy walls. They'll name this one. This one'll go down in the books. They oughta call it the Big Chinaman."

Wu beamed. "I take it you approve, Otherguy."

"I love it."

"Quincy?" Wu said.

Durant shook his head in admiration. "It's really rotten, Artie."

A still beaming Wu turned back to Booth Stallings. "His highest accolade."

Stallings frowned. "I have a question."

"You must have several."

"Everybody has a role to play," Stallings said. "That's normal, I take it?"

"A prerequisite," Durant said. "One turns into an actor. Just as most case officers are top salesmen, all confidence men are actors. You learn your role. You believe in it. You don't stray from it."

"I'm Old Buddy, of course," Stallings said.

Wu nodded.

"You and Durant are the Pair of Knaves."

Again, there was a confirming nod.

"That leaves the Watchman and the Weak Link," Stallings

said, looking first at Georgia Blue and then at Overby. "Which is which?"

"The Weak Link goes to Cebu first," Wu said, "followed a day or so later by the Watchman. I rather like Georgia for the Weak Link."

Durant didn't. "For Christ sake, Artie. People don't like surprises. They like typecasting, which is why there's so much of it. We need to send in a slender reed—not the lady decathlon champion. Look at Otherguy. Go on, look."

Everyone looked at Overby, as if trying to see him for the first time. He glared back. "Okay," Durant continued, "he's a fusspot and neat as two pins. But he lets his beard go for a day or two, sleeps in his suit, wears a little gin on his breath and you've got a perfect Judas."

"That's not exactly how I see myself, Durant," Overby said with that hard curious dignity Stallings had noticed before. "And it's sure as hell not how they remember me in Cebu."

Durant shrugged. "So you've disintegrated."

Artie Wu frowned, looking from Overby to Georgia Blue and back to Overby. "I don't know," he said. "What d'you think, Otherguy?"

"I can do either one, Artie. You know that. If you don't, then fuck it."

Wu shook his head a little, as if still in doubt. "Georgia?" he said.

"I'd do better as the Watchman. I can throw in some exaggerated Secret Service crap for verisimilitude and I also think Otherguy'd be a natural for the Weak Link." She looked at her watch. "I didn't know this was going to run so late. If you'll excuse me, I've got an appointment back at the Manila with a hairdresser."

Wu nodded and Georgia Blue rose and left. After she had gone, Wu looked at the still scowling Overby. "Okay, Otherguy. You fly down tomorrow."

"Not unless you're convinced, Artie."

"I'm more than convinced. So is everyone else—especially Durant."

"You get to play yourself, Otherguy," Durant said. "The role of a lifetime."

The talk went on for another 30 minutes, mostly about the unimportant details that always crop up after the major decisions have been made. Overby was wrangling with Durant over which hotel to use as their headquarters in Cebu when the phone rang. Wu picked it up, said hello, listened and held it out to Durant.

After his own hello, Durant heard Emily Cariaga's voice. Usually calm and even detached, it now crackled with excitement that bordered on panic.

"You have a car, Quincy?" she asked.

"The hotel's."

"Then you can take me to the airport and make sure I get on the plane."

"You're going back to Baguio?"

"Barcelona."

"I see."

"Don't say what's not true. Remember I said I'd ask around to see what I could find out?"

"Yes."

"Well, I asked around and what I found convinced me I'd better go somewhere else for a while."

"But you're going to tell me about it."

"On the way to the airport."

Durant looked at his watch. "I'll be there in thirty minutes."

Emily Cariaga asked him to make it in twenty and hung up.

CHAPTER
EIGHTEEN

Because of impossible traffic, it was not until 36 minutes later at 3:39 P.M. that Durant drove the hotel Mercedes through the open steel gate of the high breeze-block wall that enclosed Emily Cariaga's house in Forbes Park. The house was a little more than two blocks south and east of Epifanio de los Santos Avenue (EDSA) and it bothered Durant that there was no guard on the gate and that a beige Toyota sedan was blocking the narrow asphalt drive.

He parked just behind the Toyota and climbed slowly out of the Mercedes, staring at the house. It was one of the older ones in Forbes Park with wide eaves covering a verandah that wrapped itself around two sides and across the front. The windows were large and deeply recessed into thick stuccoed walls. The solid-looking old place seemed to promise it would be ten or even fifteen degrees cooler inside.

The next thing Durant noticed was the pair of running shoes that poked out—toes up, heels down—from beneath an elegant Traveler's palm. The soles had been worn smooth. The shoes—and the feet inside them—were attached to a pair of jeans-clad legs. The upper legs disappeared into the thick clump of scarlet bougainvillaea that formed a backdrop for the Traveler's palm.

A gravel path led to the running shoes but Durant avoided it, not wanting the gravel's crunch to disturb the man in the bougainvillaea if he were asleep or—less likely—drunk.

Walking on grass, Durant reached the bougainvillaea and parted it, trying without success to avoid the thorns.

The jeans-clad legs belonged to a stocky man in his mid-twenties. He had a wide ugly face, made even uglier by deep smallpox pits. He was obviously dead with an obviously broken neck. But his dark brown eyes remained open and still wore what may have been a look of mild surprise.

The man's name was Placido, Durant remembered. He was one of the two guards who worked for Emily Cariaga. The other guard worked nights and his name was Mario. Durant also recalled that Placido was married and had three children, all boys. He couldn't remember if Mario, the nightwatch, was married.

Durant straightened and turned toward the house. Its front door was ajar, not more than an inch or two. Durant glanced around the carefully tended grounds, looking for something with which to hit or cut or stab. He was hoping for a gardener's machete, even a spade, or at least a rake. He found only a green plastic garden hose with a seven-inch brass nozzle.

Durant unscrewed the nozzle, trotted to the house, went quickly up the steps of the verandah, crossed to the door and kicked it open. The door didn't bang against the wall as it should have. Instead, it hit something soft and yielding that made no noise.

The Filipino giant stepped out from behind the door. In his right hand was a tiny knife. As the knife flashed toward him Durant decided—almost dreamily—that it was actually a big knife, a shakeout with a seven- or eight-inch blade. The giant's huge hand only made it look tiny. Still appraising the knife, Durant spun sideways, arching his body back like a matador anxious to avoid the horn. The knife sliced through his shirt.

Durant drove the brass nozzle into the giant's left eye. The giant grunted and clapped his left hand to the eye. Durant pivoted and slammed the fist with the nozzle into the giant at least six inches below the massive silver belt buckle. The giant said something that sounded like whoof, took one step back and kicked Durant in the chest.

It was a hard kick powered by a telephone-pole leg. If Durant hadn't spun right, bending over, offering only his left thigh, the kick would have caught him in the groin. But it missed the groin and the thigh and struck just below the sternum. Durant discovered he could no longer breathe and that it hurt too much to try. He sank to his knees and then curled up on the cool terrazzo floor.

As he lay on the floor, wondering about suffocation and waiting for the knife blade, Durant felt the giant's hand go through his pockets. He heard the Mercedes key jingle on its ring. He heard the front door slam and wondered whether the kick had broken any ribs and whether the ribs had punctured his lungs. Durant tried for a deep breath but the pain wouldn't permit it. He attempted a single cautious shallow breath. It burned like a poison gas, but some air flowed into his lungs and Durant discovered he wasn't going to suffocate after all.

He heard the Mercedes' engine start. Then a car door slammed. Another engine started, this time the Toyota's, and there was the unique strained sound of a car being driven in reverse. After that, it was quiet.

Durant made himself sit up. He made himself breathe small shallow breaths. The pain in his chest was still excruciating but at least he could pull air into his lungs. He rose slowly, a few inches at a time. He tried to stand up straight, found that he couldn't, and stood—bent over—breathing little sips of air. Finally, he straightened, ignoring the pain, and shuffled into the long living room, moving like a 96-year-old emphysemiac with bad feet.

A tan suitcase and a dark brown carry-on bag were on the floor next to the baby grand piano. The piano's lid was closed. Someone had left a woman's cordovan purse on top of it.

Durant tried to call Emily Cariaga's name, but all that came out was a high-pitched croak. Durant sucked in his first deep breath. It seared his lungs, but again he refused to acknowledge the pain and used the breath to bellow her name. He waited, listening. There was no reply.

He left the living room and walked slowly down the long hall toward her bedroom. The door was closed. Durant reached for the doorknob, hesitated, opened the door and went in.

She lay on her back near the foot of the large spool bed, dressed for traveling in gray slacks and a dark blue blouse. Near her left hand was a heavy dark gray tweed jacket because she always said it turned cold once you reached Hawaii. Her eyes were closed, her mouth open, and she had been stabbed in the chest. Durant knelt beside her and noticed she had been stabbed three times and that there really wasn't very much blood.

He was never quite sure how long he knelt beside Emily Cariaga's body. It could have been one minute, or it could have been ten. But after she at last turned from Emily Cariaga into a corpse, Durant rose, walked around the bed to the telephone and called the police. After that, he called Artie Wu.

•   •   •

The name Hermenegildo Cruz was centered on the engraved business card the Manila detective lieutenant had handed Durant. In the lower left-hand corner was a telephone number. In the lower right, a discreet one-word advertisement in six-point italics: *Homicide*.

Durant guessed Lt. Cruz had had the cards printed at his own expense since it was unlikely the Manila police would have paid for engraving. Durant also found the homicide detective to be almost as novel as his business card—what with the buttery vanilla raw silk suit and the brown and white shoes with their fleur-de-lis toes and almost invisible built-up heels. Then there was the blue chambray cotton shirt with its button-down collar and what Durant suspected to be a Paul Stuart label. Finally, there was the hand-painted tie, featuring a long thin silvery waterfall and tall pines that spoke of either a mischievous regard for camp or extraordinarily bad taste.

Lt. Cruz himself, although not very tall, had one of those long slender faces that perfect bones make almost pretty. Under a small straight inquisitive nose grew a mustache. It wasn't of the American highway-patrol-macho variety, but rather of the suave and immaculate strain much favored by film stars in the thirties and forties. The homicide lieutenant also had a wealth of neatly trimmed thick black hair garnished with a pushed-up wave in front. The wave provided a resting ledge for a pair of expensive aviator sunglasses. Beneath the glasses, the hair, and an unlined forehead were two of the smartest brown eyes Durant had ever seen.

He and Lt. Cruz sat at either end of a couch in the living room near the baby grand piano. Emily Cariaga's purse was still on its closed lid, her suitcase and carry-on bag nearby on the floor. Durant had gone through all three before the police arrived.

There were perhaps a dozen uniformed and plainclothes police in the house. One of them, a middle-aged crusty-looking uniformed sergeant, was on the living room phone, speaking a mixture of English and Tagalog as he notified the victim's relatives of her death. His surprisingly gentle tones were pitched too low for Durant to hear anything that was said.

Lt. Cruz asked Durant the same question for the sixth or seventh time, again phrasing it in a different way. "You're positive you saw nothing or no one out of the ordinary?"

"Two dead persons," Durant said. "That's a little extraordinary for me."

"Setting them aside for the moment."

"Nothing," Durant said and tried for a deep breath, only to cough it out. Lt. Cruz eyed him sympathetically.

"Do you suffer from asthma or bronchitis, Mr. Durant?"

"Asthmatic bronchitis," Durant said, not at all sure there was such an affliction. "Stress sometimes brings it on. I must be allergic to stress." He smiled faintly, hoping the smile would be taken as an apology for his evident lack of sterner stuff.

"Do you smoke?" Cruz asked.

"I'm trying to quit."

Lt. Cruz's manicured right hand grabbed a fistful of air. "You must grasp the nettle."

Durant smiled his weakling's smile again. "And the withdrawal pains?"

"They will pass quickly," Lt. Cruz said in the hectoring tone of a reformed smoker.

"That's good to know," Durant said and coughed two small, almost delicate coughs.

"Were you sleeping with the deceased?" Lt. Cruz asked in the same tone he had used to ask if Durant smoked.

"I beg your pardon," Durant said, letting his inflection measure out just the right amount of resentment.

"Sorry, but I must know the depth of your relationship. Was it casual? Purely social? Intimate? What?"

"We were good friends."

"Lovers."

"We enjoyed each other's company."

"In bed?"

Durant turned his mouth into a thin offended line and let his silence voice more resentment.

Lt. Cruz sighed. "Where did you meet?"

"At the dentist's."

An eyebrow hopped up to signal Lt. Cruz's skepticism.

"We were in the waiting room," Durant explained. "Both of us were scheduled for root canals. We started talking and decided we'd rather have a drink than a root canal and so that's what we did."

"When?"

"About three years ago."

"She was still married when you met her?"

"Yes."

"And her husband died—when was it—six months later?"

"About that."

"You know, of course, how he died?"

"In San Francisco."

"That's where—not how."

"A hit-and-run accident."

"The driver was never caught."

"No."

"The date," Lt. Cruz said, "was August twenty-first, 1983." He paused, as if waiting for Durant to point out the date's historic significance.

Durant decided to oblige him. "They both died the same day, didn't they? Benigno Aquino, gunned down here at the airport, and Patrocinio Cariaga, struck down in San Francisco on Polk Street." Durant shook his head slightly, as if at the wonder of it all. "Emily and I sometimes talked about it and whether it meant anything. We didn't come to any conclusion except coincidence but that's not much of a conclusion."

"You knew him then—Cariaga?"

"Sure. I knew Pat."

"Were you friends?"

"Not exactly."

"Did he know you were sleeping with his wife?"

"He never mentioned it, but then he had no reason to, did he?"

"That's what I'm trying to determine," Cruz said, staring at Durant as if he had finally decided to memorize him. "I believe Pat Cariaga and Ninoy Aquino were political allies, true?"

"Not really."

"They both opposed Marcos."

"But from opposite ends of the political spectrum," Durant said. He gestured with his left hand. "Aquino was sort of over here." He gestured with his right hand. "Pat was sort of over there."

"You talked politics with Cariaga then?"

Durant shook his head. "I listened to his views is all."

"And?"

"I thought they were claptrap."

"Bullshit, you mean?"

"Right."

"Why were they—claptrap?"

"He thought once they got rid of Marcos, the right people would step in and run things the way they should be run." Durant smiled without humor. "Pat always thought he'd make one hell of a foreign secretary."

Before Lt. Cruz could comment, the sergeant with the low comforting voice hung up the phone and left the living room. Lt. Cruz watched him go and then turned back to Durant.

"Did Mrs. Cariaga share her husband's political views?" he asked.

"No," Durant said. "She's one of Mrs. Aquino's strongest supporters." He paused. "Was."

"You sympathized with those views?"

"More or less."

"Then you're a man of the left, Mr. Durant," Cruz said, making it a declaration rather than a question or even an accusation.

"No," Durant said.

"But since you're clearly not of the right, that leaves only the center. Tell me, do you find it comfortable there?"

"There's a guy in Texas called Hightower who claims there's nothing in the middle of the road but yellow stripes and dead armadillos. I tend to agree with him."

"Still, you obviously have more than an academic interest in politics."

"That's because politics affects profits."

"And what kind of business are you in—primarily?"

"Several kinds."

"Insurance?" Lt. Cruz asked. "Reinsurance, to be precise."

Durant nodded, staring at Cruz and longing suddenly for a cigarette. He's even swifter than you thought, Durant realized. "I've considered the reinsurance business."

"You were in business with—or maybe I should say in

league with—the late Ernesto Pineda. I believe you even identified his body. Up in Baguio. True?"

"True."

"Poor Pineda was a distant cousin of our deposed President," Cruz said. "Did you know that?"

"Ernie may have mentioned it in passing."

"Isn't it . . . regrettable, Mr. Durant, that you should be concerned with three horrible murders within the space of a single week? It must affect your asthma most severely."

While framing a reply, Durant again coughed delicately. But before he could say anything, the soft-spoken sergeant returned and whispered something into Lt. Cruz's ear. Cruz replied, "Immediately."

The sergeant left the room. Cruz smiled pleasantly at Durant and said, "We have a visitor."

Both turned to the door as it opened and Artie Wu entered, wearing his white money suit, his Panama hat and his cane. Wu ignored Lt. Cruz, went directly to Durant, and placed a large comforting hand on Durant's shoulder.

"Sorry, Quincy," he said. "I'm just as sorry as I can possibly be."

Durant said nothing.

Wu turned to inspect Lt. Cruz, taking time to admire the vanilla silk suit, the two-tone shoes and the rest of the homicide detective's getup. Artie Wu then nodded, as though in approval, and said, "And you, sir, are . . . ?"

"Lieutenant Cruz," the detective said, smiling and examining Wu's outfit with the frank appreciation of a fellow fop. Still smiling, Cruz rose, extended his hand and said, "Welcome, welcome, Mr. Wu."

CHAPTER NINETEEN

For the next hour, Lt. Cruz peppered Wu and Durant with questions about themselves, about the late Ernesto Pineda (whom even he had begun referring to as "poor Ernie"), and about Emily Cariaga.

"What connection was there between her and poor Ernie?" Cruz wanted to know and seemed dissatisfied when Durant replied none that he knew of. After that, Cruz began asking Wu and Durant about each other.

He inquired of Durant whether Wu was married and if so, what were the given names of Mrs. Wu and the children. Durant rattled them off. He then asked Wu if Durant had ever sought treatment for his asthmatic bronchitis. Wu nodded gravely, replying that Durant had sought out the best specialists in Los Angeles, Denver, Zurich and, in a few weeks, would be consulting a Harley Street specialist who looked promising.

"We have good doctors here, you know," Cruz said, not bothering to mask his jingoist feelings.

"It was my doctor here who recommended the one in London," Durant lied with what Artie Wu noted was his usual artistry.

"We have the best dentists in Asia," Cruz said, apropos of almost nothing.

"In the world, for my money," said Artie Wu.

Cruz seemed to know when he was being gulled so he resumed his questions. "You're obviously a well-educated man, Mr. Wu," he said, his tone clearly anticipating a lying response.

Artie Wu only shrugged. It was Durant who supplied the details. "Princeton. He even made Phi Beta Kappa."

"And you, Mr. Durant. Are you also a Princeton graduate?"

"No. I went but failed to graduate." Durant saw no need to explain how he had sat through all of Artie Wu's classes not as a student, but as the ever-present bodyguard of the pretender to the Chinese Emperor's throne.

Lt. Cruz abandoned all efforts to suspend his disbelief. "What you've been trying to sell me is that two intelligent grown men—well educated, well traveled, a couple of real been-arounds—let themselves get taken by a three-peso buy-and-sell hustler." He gave his head two quick skeptical shakes. "Let's hear it all. Even the dirty parts. You first." He pointed his chin at Artie Wu.

Wu's sigh seemed full of embarrassment. "I'm afraid poor Ernie was, as you say, Lieutenant, nothing but a confidence trickster."

"Really," Cruz said, making sure his sarcasm was heavy enough to be noticed. He then smiled a gleaming smile that had been fashioned in part by one of the best dentists in Asia. "How much did Ernie take you for?"

"Three hundred thousand."

"Pesos?"

Wu shook his great head sadly. "Dollars."

"Mother of God," Cruz whispered. "If you did kill him, they might rule it justifiable homicide."

"But you've already been in touch with the Baguio cops, haven't you?" Durant said.

Cruz hesitated, then nodded.

"So you know we didn't."

"Who do you think did?"

"A guess?" Wu said.

Cruz moved his tailored shoulders in a "why not?" shrug.

"An NPA sparrow team," Wu said.

The answer made Cruz frown. But then the frown went away and he nodded reluctantly. "Makes sense," he said. "A little."

There was a long silence while Lt. Cruz examined Wu, then Durant and then Wu again. "You two," he said softly, "may be the best liars I've come across in years."

Wu smiled. "I take it that means we can go."

"But not far."

"Cebu okay?" Durant asked.

Lt. Cruz bristled. "Cebu! What's in Cebu?"

"Business," Durant said. "We still have to eat."

Lt. Cruz stared at Artie Wu. "Ever been in any of our jails, Mr. Wu?"

"Never."

"They're an absolute scandal."

Wu nodded. "How does one avoid them?"

"One keeps in touch."

"What if one has nothing to report."

"Our jails, although horribly overcrowded, can always hold two more."

"We'll keep in touch," Wu said.

•   •   •

Durant taped his own chest in the Peninsula Hotel Mercedes that Wu had parked across the street from a big Forbes Park house that flew the West German flag. A uniformed Filipino security guard eyed them suspiciously but didn't interfere. Wu cut off strips of surgical tape with a pair of scissors and handed them back, one by one, to Durant who sat in the rear with his shirt off. Wu had bought both scissors and tape at the hotel pharmacy at Durant's request. Durant taped his chest with quick sure movements.

"Cracked?" Wu asked.

"Maybe not."

"Hurts though?"

"Not like it did."

"Okay. Let's hear it."

Durant looked down at his now taped chest, gave it a light thump, grimaced a little, and started putting his shirt back on. "Emily's guard was dead when I got there. The door was open. Just a little. I kicked it all the way open and that Big Stoop who bounces for Boy Howdy came through it with a knife. He missed and I got him in the eye with a brass nozzle—one of those garden hose jobs."

Wu nodded.

"It didn't bother him much and he tried to kick me in the balls and caught my chest instead. Some kick."

"Why didn't he finish you off?"

"Who knows? Maybe nobody told him to."

"Maybe nobody told him to do Emily either," Wu said.

"I thought of that."

"Which is why you didn't tell Cruz about him."

Durant nodded.

"We'd better go talk to Boy," Wu said.

"Let me talk to him."

"What do I do?" Wu asked.

"You hold him."

•   •   •

A $100 bill slipped to the bartender bought Wu and Durant the one-long, two-short buzzer code into Boy Howdy's locked office. Wu rang the code and when the unlocking buzzer sounded he pushed open the metal door and stood there, leaning slightly on his cane and staring at Boy Howdy whose right hand strayed toward the desk drawer that contained the .45 automatic.

"I wouldn't do that, Boy," Wu said. "That fucking Durant might not like it."

"That fucking Durant might rip your face off," Durant said over Wu's shoulder.

Boy Howdy's right hand stopped. "He didn't kill her,"

Howdy said. "She was dead when he got there. The watchman, too."

Artie Wu strolled into the office and looked around. Durant moved to Wu's left, not taking his eyes off Howdy. Wu examined the acrylic-on-velvet painting of the fat carabao and the plump tiger. "Anyone ever mention, Boy, that you have what may well be the worst taste in Asia?"

"He didn't kill her," Howdy said. "She was dead when Ozzie got there."

"Ozzie?" Durant said.

"Osmundo," Howdy explained.

"How is Osmundo?" Durant asked.

"Lost his left eye, didn't he?" Howdy said. "Blinded him, you did."

Wu looked around the room and selected a straight-backed chair, the same chair Otherguy Overby had chosen. He sat down, removed his hat, put it on the floor, and folded his hands over the top of his cane. Durant leaned against a wall on the opposite side of the room, his eyes still fixed on Boy Howdy.

"What was Ozzie doing at Mrs. Cariaga's, Boy?" Durant said.

Howdy made his reply to Wu. "I rent him out, don't I? I mean, if somebody's got a bit of cash they want to see inside the bank safe and sound, they rent Ozzie at five hundred pesos per hour. Nobody in his right mind wants to fuck with a giant. So I get a call this A.M., going on noon. A woman. Says she's Mrs. Cariaga and lives over in Forbes Park. Says she's going to the airport and wants Ozzie to go with her and make sure she gets on the plane. So I ask what time she wants him and she says half past three and I tell her the price and say he'll be there."

"Did you know her husband?" Durant said.

Still looking at Wu, Boy Howdy said, "If his name's Pat Cariaga, then that's right, I've heard of him. Who hasn't? But he's almost three years dead now, isn't he?"

Wu nodded and leaned forward, resting his chin on his

hands that were still folded over the head of his cane. He stared at Boy Howdy with deep interest.

"So Ozzie got there at half past three?" Durant said.

"Right. And there the watchman is in the bushes with his neck broke. So Ozzie goes to the door, finds it open and steps inside. He says hello a couple of times. You know. But nobody says hello back so he looks around. No servants, he says. Not a soul. So he goes to the back of the house and finds her lying there by the bed, stone dead. Well, Ozzie's not all that quick, is he, but he knows when it's time to leave."

Boy Howdy stopped as if waiting for encouragement. When none came, he cleared his throat and continued: "Well, Ozzie hears something then. He hears this car driving in and a bit later somebody running toward the house on the gravel walk and that somebody turns out to be that fucking Durant."

Howdy turned to stare at Durant for the first time. "So Ozzie does what he does and you do what you do and poor old Ozzie ends up blind in one eye." Howdy paused for a moment. "He's thinking maybe you done her and the watchman too. And for all I know, he's right."

"Boy," Artie Wu said.

Howdy looked at him. "What?"

"As I see it, you have three choices. You ever hear of a homicide lieutenant called Cruz?"

"Gildo Cruz? Yeah. Sure. I've heard of him."

"He's one of your choices. You and Ozzie can talk to him. If you don't much like that, then I'll leave you alone with Durant and you can talk to him. He might have a cracked rib or two, but Durant's pretty steamed. Maybe you can handle him; maybe not. I don't think so."

Boy Howdy looked at Durant. "He's not all that much. I've settled worse. A lot worse."

"Leave me your cane, Artie," Durant said. "I may want to slice him up a little."

"As I said," Wu continued, "Durant's a bit steamed. He and Mrs. Cariaga were good friends. Very good friends."

A ribald look began to form in Howdy's eyes. He opened his mouth to say something but snapped it shut when he looked at Durant.

"Your third choice, Boy," Wu said, "is to tell me and Durant what really happened. If it was only business, and Ozzie had nothing to do with Mrs. Cariaga's death, then we can proceed from there." Wu paused. "You have about ten seconds to decide."

"How long've you and Durant known me, Artie?" Boy Howdy said.

Wu lifted his chin from the fingers that were still wrapped over the head of his cane. He leaned back in the straight chair, stuck out his left leg and thoughtfully tapped his shoe with the cane's end. "Years, Boy. Too many, really."

"And we've done our fair share of business together—you, Durant, Otherguy and me. And we've had our giggles, too, we have."

"I can't remember any," Durant said.

Howdy ignored him. "So a piece of business comes my way. That's all. A job of work, it was. A certain party needs a frightener. It seems like the Cariaga lady's been nosing around where she shouldn't've. But the Cariaga lady's quick enough to know she shouldn't've turned up what she turned up and so she's leaving town. Going to Spain, they say. Well, the party that needs the frightener wants to make sure the Cariaga lady don't grass before she gets on the plane. So I rent the party old Ozzie to do nothing—and I swear this—but nervous the Cariaga lady up a bit. And I swear to God it's just like I said it was from the moment he gets there. She's already dead. Her and the watchman both. And that's the sweet Jesus truth."

"Who hired your frightener, Boy?" Artie Wu asked in a soft voice.

"Why don't you ask me to cut me own throat, Artie?"

"Either you cut it or I do," Durant said.

Howdy seemed suddenly bored. He yawned and even stretched. After the stretch his right hand casually drifted down

to the back of his neck. He almost had the knife out of the neck sheath when the huge white blur that was Artie Wu smashed the cane against Howdy's right elbow. He yelled, but by then Durant was around the desk and had the half-drawn knife in his own right hand.

Durant placed the knife point just under the tip of Howdy's chin, forcing his head up. "Tell it," Durant said.

Boy Howdy let a small moan escape from between his almost closed lips. "Give us a rest, Durant," he said.

Durant took the knife point away. Howdy dropped his head, closed his eyes and said, "I'm dead, I am."

Wu sighed. "Get it over with, Boy."

"It was that cunt that rented Ozzie, that's who," Howdy said, his eyes still closed.

Wu and Durant stared at each other, jumping simultaneously to the same conclusion. "The Espiritu woman, you mean?" Durant said. "Carmen Espiritu."

Boy Howdy opened his eyes to glare at Durant. "Quit jacking me around, Durant. I don't know any Carmen whatever the fuck it is."

"Boy," Artie Wu said in a soft and patient voice. "Just give us the name."

"It was that killer bitch of yours that rented herself Ozzie," Howdy said. "Georgia Blue. That's who." Despite his pain he smiled at the accidental rhyme and when he noticed Wu's and Durant's sudden bleak surprised expressions, his smile grew even broader.

CHAPTER
TWENTY

It was 10:33 that night when Georgia Blue arrived by taxi at the Manila Hotel. She slowly entered the vast lobby, sweeping it with practiced eyes as she crossed to the elevators, her right hand down inside the leather bag that hung from her shoulder.

She rode an elevator alone up to the fourth floor. From there she took the stairs to the fifth floor, slipped past the dozing floor porter and hurried down the corridor to suite 542 where she knocked softly. Booth Stallings opened the door a few seconds later.

"I think I'm in a little trouble," she said in a voice not much louder than a whisper.

Stallings poked his head out and looked up and down the corridor. "Come in," he said, opening the door wide enough for her to enter. He then closed the door, shot its dead bolt and fastened the chain. Turning, he found Georgia Blue in the center of the suite's sitting room, her posture awkward, her expression uncertain. Stallings thought she almost looked as if she were missing something, maybe a key part of her body—a foot, or even an arm—until he realized it was her tremendous poise that had vanished. She's lost it somewhere, he decided. Or somebody took it away from her.

"Sit down," he said.

For a moment she seemed not to have understood him. Then she smiled, as if it were the kindest invitation ever offered. The smile vanished as she turned to make her choice of where to sit. It was obviously a difficult choice and possibly the most important of her life. Finally, she decided on a green armchair, which she sank into, keeping her right hand deep in the leather shoulder bag.

"Drink?" Stallings said as he moved to the room refrigerator. She shook her head. Stallings took out a can of beer, carried it back to the couch, sat down, popped open the can and said, "What kind of trouble?"

"I need a place to stay tonight," Georgia Blue said.

"Here, you mean?"

She nodded.

"Wu and Durant are looking for you."

"Oh?"

"Otherguy, too."

"Fuck Otherguy."

Stallings drank some of his beer. "Tell me about it," he said and leaned back, resting the beer can on the left arm of the couch. He draped his own right arm over the couch's back, hoping it was the most nonthreatening posture he could assume. It then occurred to him that a smile might help keep her right hand down inside the shoulder bag. So he smiled.

"Why're they looking for me?" she said.

"They didn't say and I didn't think they much wanted me to ask."

"May I stay here tonight?" she said.

"What about tomorrow?"

"Tomorrow's next year. The future. Tonight's right now and that's all I can handle." She paused and added, almost as an afterthought, "We can do some sex if you'd like."

"Sounds interesting," Stallings said and gave her another smile.

"No it doesn't," she said, bringing her right hand out of the bag. In it was the Walther semiautomatic. "Is this what's bothering you?"

He shrugged. "It's not exactly a turn-on."

She put the pistol back into the shoulder bag and then placed the bag on the floor beside her chair. "Better?"

"Much."

Another silence began to build. Stallings let it. The silence collapsed before reaching 30 seconds when Georgia Blue said, "Shit."

"Go on," Stallings said.

"It happened between the time we got back from the war memorial and had lunch at the Peninsula. That's when he called."

Another silence threatened but Stallings warded it off with: "He being?"

"Harry Crites."

"Ah."

"From Washington."

"I see," Stallings said. "Must've been about midnight yesterday back there, if it was around noon today here. Give or take an hour."

"We didn't talk about the time. Or the weather."

Stallings gave her what he hoped was an encouraging nod. When that failed to produce a response, he said, "What did you talk about?"

"We have a code," she said. "A kind of silly verbal code. He used it to tell me to call a number exactly ten minutes after he hung up. I was to call for instructions."

"Local number?"

"A pay phone. It's always a pay phone."

"Did you call it?"

"I'm supposed to be working for him, right?"

"Right."

"So I called it."

She waited, as if expecting Stallings to prod her along with yet another question. He obliged with, "Who answered?"

"A man."

"Recognize his voice?"

"He had an accent."

"Filipino?"

"I'm not sure. He may have been faking it. Probably not. But I don't know who he was."

"He gave you the instructions though?"

"Yes. He told me to—"

"The guy on the pay phone?"

She nodded. "He told me to call Boy Howdy, identify myself, and say I wanted to rent that giant bouncer of his to throw a fright into somebody called Emily Cariaga. I was to offer Boy Howdy two thousand U.S. Then the pay phone man gave me her address in Forbes Park and told me what he wanted the bouncer to warn her about. Then—" She suddenly stopped talking and for a moment Stallings thought she might have been struck dumb.

"Go on," he said.

"She was flying out late this afternoon. She was going to Spain." Again there was that sudden silence with its air of absolute finality. Stallings felt his irritation growing and decided to vent some of it.

"Goddamnit, Georgia!"

She blinked twice, as if mildly surprised by his tone. "This bouncer," she said. "This monster man who works for Boy Howdy was to warn her she'd better not tell anyone about what she'd learned. No one. Ever. The monster man was to be— extremely firm, the pay phone man said."

"I don't guess he told you what she wasn't supposed to talk about?"

"No."

"So you called Howdy then?"

She nodded. "He wanted his money first. I said he could pick it up at the desk downstairs. I left it there for him. In an envelope. And then I went to the Peninsula and we all had lunch."

"So we did," Stallings said, finished his beer, crushed the

can, rose and headed for the small refrigerator. As he passed Georgia Blue's chair he scooped up her shoulder bag. She turned to look up at him.

"I knew you were going to do that," she said.

Instead of replying, Stallings looked inside the bag.

"I could've stopped you," she said.

Stallings took the Walther out, examined it briefly, and stuck it down into his right hip pocket. He dropped the bag back to the floor. "When'd you find out she'd been killed?" he said.

"Late this afternoon. It was on Radio Veritas, I think. I went downstairs to a pay phone and called the police to make sure it was the same Emily Cariaga."

"Then what'd you do?"

"I went out. I went to the Shoe Mart and Rustan's in Makati near the Peninsula. But I didn't buy anything. Then I went to a couple of bookstores. After that, to the Inter-Continental. They have a cafe there with Jeepneys. I mean with booths that look like Jeepneys. I had a drink. Maybe two. I may have eaten something. I know I'm not hungry."

"And then straight back here?" Stallings said.

She nodded.

"You don't know who she was, do you?"

"No."

"Durant got a phone call after you left this afternoon," Stallings said. "It was from Emily Cariaga. She and Durant were—well, pretty good friends, I guess. It was Durant who found her."

Georgia Blue grew still. Nothing moved. Stallings didn't think she even breathed. There was nothing else for him to say so he waited for her reaction. She finally exhaled the breath she had been holding, drew in another one and used it to say, "I see." There was another long silence until she said, "You'd better call Durant."

"What for?"

"Tell him I'm here."

"What's he going to do tonight that he can't do tomorrow?"

She looked at him with an expression that was both puzzled and confused. And then she asked a question to which she obviously knew the answer although it still seemed to surprise her. "You're . . . you're damned decent, aren't you?"

"Sometimes," Booth Stallings said. "Once in a while."

•   •   •

When Georgia Blue first entered Stallings' suite she had been wearing a brown silk blouse, a tan skirt that looked something like chino but was probably silk gabardine, the brown and white spectators, and the leather shoulder bag containing the Walther PPK. When she entered his bedroom at 1:16 A.M., she was wearing only the brown silk blouse.

Stallings was propped up in bed, reading a book. It was actually a bound set of galleys that a publisher had sent the foundation. While packing for his trip, Stallings had found it on the bedside table in his apartment across from the Washington zoo.

The book was composed of essays by 19 notables of varying rank but identical bent. Each essay set forth the writer's thoughts, often muddled, on terrorism, which none of them could define without waffling. But if they couldn't agree on what terrorism was, they were unanimous about what should be done to its practitioners. Stallings had found the book to be yet another tiresome disquisition of the "Zap the Fuckers" school. In Washington, it had put him to sleep four nights running, so he had packed the galleys instead of the Seconal.

When Georgia Blue came into the bedroom, wearing only the brown silk shirt, Stallings dropped the bound galleys to the floor, locked his hands behind his head, and stared at her. He remembered when—upon seeing her for the first time in the Madison—he had decided she was one of the three most striking women he had ever seen. He now narrowed the field to two and even considered eliminating the remaining contestant who was an Italian actress pushing 50.

"That couch in there too short or are you too tall?" he said, feeling his mouth going into something that he hoped was more smile than leer.

"Both," she said and started unbuttoning the blouse. She undid the buttons methodically, looking down at them as she might have if undressing alone. When all the buttons were undone she removed the blouse, folded it neatly, as though for packing, and placed it carefully on a chair.

She turned back then, neither provocative nor coy, serving up the full course. Stallings devoured it with his eyes, wondering how it would taste on the tongue.

"That does stir the blood," he said.

"Good," Georgia Blue said as she slipped into bed beside him.

Kissing her, Stallings decided, was like kissing your first older woman—the one with all the wicked experience. He then decided not to decide anything else and simply go along with whatever happened, except that what happened was far from simple. Instead, it was intricate, a trifle wild, totally sensual and innovative even to Stallings who thought, until now, that he long ago had crossed his last sexual frontier. At one point he experienced a miser's glow when he realized that this night in this bed in suite 542 of the Manila Hotel would turn into his main account at the Bank of Fantasy—and that he could draw on it without limit for as long as he lived.

•   •   •

It was over in half an hour, give or take five minutes. They lay, staring at the ceiling, her head on his shoulder, Stallings wishing for the first time in years that he still smoked. Chesterfields. Unfiltered. The Destroyers with their "They Satisfy" promise. Or was that Old Gold? He had almost decided to ask Georgia Blue, even if she weren't old enough to remember, when she said, "That fucking Durant."

"Seems like a nice enough fella."

"Not when you think he might kill you."

"Because of the Cariaga woman?"

"He could," she said. "I don't know if he will. But he could."

"He won't kill you," Stallings said. "Not until he gets his money anyhow."

She turned her head to find him still staring at the ceiling. "But what if he never gets his money?" she said. "What if I've blown the whole deal?"

"In that case," Stallings said, still staring at the ceiling, "it won't be just that fucking Durant you have to worry about."

•   •   •

At 8:17 the next morning the venetian blinds went up with a clatter that ended in a small bang. Sunlight streamed in on Stallings and Georgia Blue who lay in the bed, both naked to their waists, which was where the sheet ended. She bolted upright. Stallings opened his eyes to find Otherguy Overby standing at the window, looking out at the bay.

"Nice day," Overby said, not turning. "Except they say it's going to be a little hot later on."

He turned then, looking first at Stallings, then at Georgia Blue who made no effort to pull up the sheet. "Wu and Durant are in there," Overby said, nodding toward the sitting room. "They think we need to talk."

"They order coffee?" Stallings said.

"No, but I did," Overby said, turned and left the room.

CHAPTER
TWENTY-ONE

G eorgia Blue came out of the suite's bedroom, wearing one of those long white terry-cloth robes that the better hotels provide their guests, along with a warning that he who steals it will pay. She came out barefoot, her right hand deep in the robe's pocket where it clutched the Walther PPK that Booth Stallings had returned earlier without comment.

Stallings noticed she had recovered her lost poise. It now seemed almost unshakable as she stopped to look at each of the four men. She nodded at Artie Wu, who sat on the couch in his favorite left-hand corner, a cup of coffee in one hand, a morning cigar in the other. Wu nodded back politely. Georgia Blue's gaze skipped over Overby, seated as usual in a straight-back chair, and lingered only briefly on Stallings, who looked back at her over the rim of his coffee cup. Her gaze came to rest on Durant, who stood by the room service cart with its too many cups and saucers and its twin chrome pots of coffee.

Durant turned to the cart and poured a cup of coffee. "Black, right, Georgia?" he said. "No sugar."

"Please," she said.

Durant turned with cup and saucer, crossed to where she stood in the center of the sitting room, and handed her the coffee. She accepted it with her left hand, keeping her right one wrapped around the Walther in the robe's pocket. She turned then, looking for a place to sit, and again decided on the green armchair with its side table. Placing the cup and saucer on the table first, she sat down, crossing her legs beneath the long robe, keeping her right hand in its pocket.

No one said anything until she picked up the cup with her left hand and sipped the coffee. Then Artie Wu spoke. "Booth told us what you told him last night, Georgia. He made it all very factual, very objective. Anything you'd like to add or clarify?"

"Before I'm sentenced, you mean?"

"I don't think you really meant to say that."

She thought about it, shrugged and looked at Durant who still stood, leaning now against a wall and smoking his first cigarette of the morning. "I didn't know who she was, Quincy," Georgia Blue said. "I didn't know she would be killed. I'm sorry."

Durant stared at her without replying. Finally he said, "Take your hand out of your pocket, Georgia. You're not going to need it."

Georgia Blue's slight sag of relief was almost invisible. She picked up the cup with her left hand, sipped more coffee, put the cup back down and looked at Artie Wu, her right hand still in the robe's pocket.

"Now what, Artie?" she said.

Artie Wu sent one of his fat smoke rings toward the ceiling. "The plan stays the same," he said, "except we speed it up. Emily Cariaga was apparently killed to shut her up. But we don't know what she'd found out or how important it was, and it seems pointless to speculate. We get in and out of this thing fast and hope the Manila cops'll lose all interest in Durant and me."

"I think the Cariaga lady found out who's putting up the five million," said Otherguy Overby to whom speculation was meat and drink.

"Very pat, Otherguy," Durant said.

Overby gave him a cold look. "So I like things neat. But just because I like 'em that way doesn't mean that when nice and neat comes along I've got to toss it out just because I like it so much. That's waste."

"He has a point," Booth Stallings said, turning to Wu. "Can't you guys check it out? See the same people she saw. Find out what they talked about?"

"Quincy and I'll try, of course," Wu said. "But I don't think we'll get anywhere. Emily moved at social heights where the air's thin and the climb up's difficult—if not impossible—for a couple of grifters with no credentials other than their cheerful smiles and witty small talk."

"That's what I thought you two did best," Stallings said. "Separating the undeserving rich from their money. If you can do that, why the hell can't you get them to babble?"

"To part them from their money," Durant said in a too patient tone, "all we have to do is tickle their greed. But we're not going for their money this time. We're going to ask them to confide in us about something that got someone they know killed. And we don't have that kind of leverage."

"But we are going to try, Booth," Artie Wu said.

"You'd better try damned hard," said Stallings.

Wu nodded his agreement and turned to Georgia Blue. "I said we're going to speed things up, Georgia. That means Otherguy flies down to Cebu today on the noon plane and you follow on the three o'clock flight. Booth'll fly down tomorrow, with Quincy and me following the next day, which is—" He looked at the calendar on his watch. "Wednesday, April the first."

"April Fools' Day," said Overby, ever literal.

No one spoke for several seconds. Instead, they watched Artie Wu blow three more smoke rings into the air. As the last one drifted to the ceiling, Wu said, "Let's have some more coffee and then I'm going to deliver a small homily that I trust everybody'll take to heart."

Overby rose, went to the room service table and picked up one of the chrome pots. He moved about the room, filling the cups. Everyone sipped politely at coffee that no one really seemed to want. Booth Stallings kept his eyes on Artie Wu, not quite marveling at the big man's ability to dominate the room—any room, for that matter.

It was partly Wu's great size, Stallings decided, and partly his brilliance that enabled him to lead and command, almost without seeming to. But his real weapon was that effortless easy charm that made virtually everyone like him and, far more useful, seek his approval. Even you aren't immune, Stallings warned himself.

And then there's that fucking Durant, he thought, unconsciously adopting the by now familiar designation. Durant, who's just as smart, or nearly so, and who carefully cultivates that ticking-bomb image, which he damn well might be. The charming, lovable Mr. Wu and his terrible paladin. Some combination.

It occurred then to Booth Stallings—for the first time—that they, the five of them, might really steal the five million after all. The notion was so bizarre that it made him smile and almost caused him to chuckle. But he stifled the chuckle, drained his coffee cup and turned his attention to what Artie Wu had to say.

"With the exception of Booth here," Wu began, "we've all known each other forever, which may be too long. We know each other's strengths, weaknesses, quirks and hang-ups. None of us is perfect, God knows, but each of us is competent. Extremely so. Well, we're going for the lallapalooza—for five million dollars and, as Otherguy says, that's major money. With an even five-way split it should be enough for everybody and I'm convinced we can bring it off. But each of us is human and therefore susceptible to dangling temptation. So if it's ever dangled in front of you, and you've decided you can't resist, just remember this: I'll come after you. And right behind me will come that fucking Durant. One of us will find you. Maybe both of us. And you'll never ever spend the money."

Artie Wu smiled, puffed on his cigar and leaned back in the couch.

Georgia Blue was the first to respond. "Gosh, Artie, that's the most inspirational thing I ever heard." She took her right hand out of the robe's pocket and rose, gathered up the clothing she had left in the sitting room the night before, and disappeared into the bedroom.

After watching her leave, Durant turned to Wu. "I couldn't have said it better," he said. "But I could've made it shorter." He crossed to the door, opened it and looked back at Wu. "I'm going down to the lobby and see if there's anyone around who'll talk to us about Emily."

"I'll be down later," Wu said.

After Durant was gone, Overby rose and looked around the room, nodding a goodbye first to Stallings, then to Artie Wu. "I've got to catch that plane," Overby said.

"See you in Cebu, Otherguy," Wu said.

Overby started for the door, got halfway there and turned back to Wu. "Who was all that shit really aimed at, Artie? Me?"

"You and everybody else, Otherguy."

Overby's answering nod only served to affirm his disbelief. "I bet," he said, turned and left the room.

Booth Stallings rose, went over to the window and looked out at Manila Bay. "You have something on your mind you want to tell me, Artie?"

"I don't think so."

Stallings turned. "No likely suspects, defectors or agents provocateurs?"

"They're all likely," Wu said.

"Me too?"

"You too."

"What about you and Durant?"

"Five million's a lot of money, Booth. Keep an eye on us."

"Everybody watches everybody else, right?"

"It's the only safe way, if we're really going to pull it off."

"Think we are?"

Artie Wu didn't answer for a moment. Then he said, "I think so. I really do."

"So do I," Booth Stallings said. "Well, I'm off."

"Where to?"

"Corregidor," Stallings said. "Thought I'd go see if I can ride out on a hydrofoil and take a look." He patted his pockets to make sure he had his sunglasses, keys and wallet. "Might be the last chance I'll ever have."

Wu smiled. "Not planning to pass this way again?"

"Not if I can help it," Stallings said as he opened the door and left.

. . .

When Georgia Blue came out of the bedroom she wore the same clothes she had worn the night before. The same bag hung over her right shoulder and at the sight of the still waiting Artie Wu her right hand slipped down inside it.

"Sit down, Georgia," Wu said.

She moved to the green armchair and perched on the edge of its seat cushion, her knees together, her hand still down inside the bag and wrapped around the Walther.

"You fucked up, didn't you?" Wu said.

"I didn't know who she was, Artie."

"You could've checked with somebody."

"But I didn't."

"Durant's . . . well, Durant's close to the boiling point." She nodded. "I could tell."

"If he boils over, the deal's dead."

"I know."

"So we can't take any more fuckups—by anyone."

"Especially by me, you mean."

Wu shook his head. "Especially by Otherguy."

Georgia Blue's hand slowly came out of the shoulder bag. It was empty. "Well," she said softly. "What d'you know."

"Down in Cebu Otherguy'll be the Weak Link. You'll be the

Watchman. Your role's going to be for real—and so is his, I'm afraid."

There was a bleak silence until Georgia Blue said, "I've known Otherguy a long time, Artie."

Wu sighed. "So have I."

"You're sure?"

He nodded gravely.

"So . . . 'for a handful of silver he left us,'" she began.

"'Just for a riband to stick in his coat,'" Wu finished.

"Browning, right?"

"'The Lost Leader.'"

"Well, shit."

"Stay on him, Georgia."

She nodded, rising.

"He's smart and he's tricky," Wu said.

"I was once his star pupil, Artie."

"And mine."

"Then I must know all you two know," she said. "And then some."

CHAPTER TWENTY-TWO

 urant noticed the bodyguards first: an almost matched pair of wide thick Filipinos in their late thirties with quick eyes, empty hands and twin lumps on their right hips beneath their sport shirts' squared-off tails.

One of their charges was racing on short fat legs toward the Manila Hotel's newsstand-drugstore. He was followed by a girl of nine who was trying not to hurry so she would appear prim, grown-up and in sharp contrast to her six-year-old brat of a brother, who her parents still swore was not adopted.

Walking between the bodyguards was the mother, a not quite plump pretty woman in her early thirties, who wore a black linen dress with white piping that Durant suspected had come from Neiman-Marcus. He knew that Neiman-Marcus was the only thing the woman had ever liked about Dallas.

Rising from his chair, Durant made a slow oblique approach across the lobby so that the woman and her two bodyguards would see him simultaneously. But the quicker of the bodyguards noticed him first and obviously didn't like what he saw.

The bodyguard snapped something at his partner who shooed the boy and girl into the newsstand-drugstore. The other bodyguard planted himself squarely in front of the woman, his right hand straying back to the concealed lump on his hip. Durant came to a full stop. The woman in the black dress with white piping touched the bodyguard on the arm and said something that made him relax.

The woman who now smiled at Durant from behind and a little to the left of the bodyguard was Restituta Ortiz, mercifully called Tootie by almost everyone. She was married to Cristobal Ortiz who had taken his modest inheritance and invested it at first in banking and shipping, with fair results, and then in politics, which had made him rich.

The dead Emily Cariaga and Tootie Ortiz had grown up together in Manila and later spent a year at Miss Hockaday's in Dallas, hating every minute of it. Back in Manila they were married within a month of each other. When Durant and Emily Cariaga's affair had first begun—and the cuckolded Patrocinio Cariaga was still alive—it was Tootie Ortiz who had served the lovers as go-between, even though she was hopelessly inept at keeping the assignation times and places straight. But she wholeheartedly had approved of the affair because, as Emily Cariaga once said, Tootie likes anything romantic, daring and dirty—as long as it's once-removed.

When Durant reached her, the first thing Tootie Ortiz did was to take his right hand in both of hers and whisper, "It was beautiful, Quincy. It was the most beautiful requiem mass I've ever seen."

"I'd've liked to have been there, Tootie, but—" He shrugged, making the shrug say that the mass was for the dead Emily's family and friends and not for her foreign paramour.

Tootie nodded. "I understand—and so does Emily."

"We need to talk, Tootie."

"About—?"

"Yes."

"Now?"

Durant nodded. She looked at her watch. "Well," she said, her voice full of doubt, "I suppose we could, except—" As was frequently the case, Tootie Ortiz didn't finish her sentence. The almost chronic incompletions were one of her less endearing habits. Durant waited patiently for the question he was sure she would ask.

"Did you really find—?"

"I found her," Durant said.

"Was it—?" The expression on her face was a synonym for terrible.

"It was worse than that, Tootie."

She turned to the bodyguard and said something in a low voice. The bodyguard frowned his disapproval. She snapped at him. The bodyguard gave Durant a glare that was almost a warning, turned and entered the newsstand-drugstore where his partner was reading a comic book to the little boy. The boy's sister was trying to look as if she had no idea who either of them was.

"They'll take the kids to the coffee shop for some, you know—"

"Ice cream," Durant said.

Tootie nodded. "We'll have something nice in the Cowrie Room."

"I don't think it's open yet," Durant said.

Tootie smiled one of her more patronizing smiles. "They'll open it for—"

"Us," Durant supplied.

"Me," she corrected him.

•   •   •

When Tootie Ortiz swept into the empty Cowrie Room, trailed by Durant, the maître d' turned with a frown, saw who it was, erased the frown, slipped into a jacket and ushered them to a corner booth. Tootie Ortiz ordered coffee and caramel pastries for two. Durant didn't want any pastry but made no objection because he knew Tootie would eat his.

But she almost forgot to eat her own when Durant began his heavily varnished account of the discovery of the dead Emily Cariaga. It was almost a duplicate of the report he had given Lt. Cruz, the homicide detective, except he now made it slightly more lurid for Tootie's benefit.

She listened, eyes wide, mouth slightly open. When he had finished, she said, "Dear God, how awful," picked up her fork and attacked the pastry.

Durant waited until she had chewed and swallowed two bites. Then he said, "First poor Ernie Pineda up in Baguio, then Emily."

The fork stopped inches from Tootie's partly open mouth. The mouth closed and she lowered the fork slowly to the plate. "They weren't connected," she said. "They couldn't have been because—" Again, her sentence died prematurely.

"They were in a way, Tootie," Durant said. "Connected."

"How?"

"You know Artie Wu?" he said.

"Of course I know Artie."

"Well, Artie and I were doing some business with poor Ernie and we were the ones who had to identify his body."

She leaned toward him, her pastry for the moment forgotten. "You actually saw—"

Durant nodded.

She looked around and lowered her voice to a whisper. "Did they really—"

"They cut 'em off, Tootie," Durant said.

"But Emily didn't tell me—" She stopped and attacked her pastry again, finishing it in four large bites.

"Didn't tell you what?" Durant said when the last bite was being swallowed.

She reached for his plate, using a small smile to ask him if he really wanted it. He pushed the plate toward her. "Didn't tell you what, Tootie?" Durant said again.

"About you and Ernie."

"You talked to her?"

Tootie, busy chewing, only nodded.

"When?"

She swallowed and said, "When she came back down from Baguio. She called to tell me about Ernie and wanted to know why anyone would, you know, want to do what— Well, I pointed out that Ernie, after all, was *his* third cousin and—"

Again, she arrived at one of her badly timed verbal red lights. Durant pretended not to notice. He took out a cigarette and lit it. After he blew some smoke up and away, he said, "You were saying?"

"Everybody's talking about it."

"Are they?"

"Of course."

"About Emily."

"About poor Ernie."

"Oh. Right. Him." Durant ground out his scarcely smoked cigarette in an ashtray. "Who's everybody, Tootie?"

She moved her shoulders as if to say that everyone knew who everybody was. When Durant still looked skeptical, she said, "Cris," thus proving her point by invoking her husband's name.

"How's old Cris bearing up now that his patron's gone to Hawaii?"

"They still talk."

"Cris calls to cheer him up, I suppose."

"The President calls *him*."

"What do Cris and the old boy talk about?" Durant said. "The dead third cousin?"

"You don't believe me, do you?"

"You haven't said anything yet, Tootie. There's nothing to disbelieve."

"All right," she said, leaning forward again. "I'll tell you exactly what I told Emily."

"Which is what Cris told you, right?"

"Cris knows what's—" She stopped again.

"Going on," Durant finished. "I'm sure he does."

Tootie looked around to make sure there were no eaves-droppers. "He at least knows Ernie was a—"

"A what?" Durant said, surprised at the harshness of his voice.

It also surprised Tootie. "A . . . a communist," she said.

Durant smiled. The smile turned into a broad grin. "Our Ernie?"

She gave Durant an arch look. "*They* thought he was. He was their line into the Palace."

"Ernie was the New People's Army line into Malacañang?"

She nodded.

"What'd Ernie use for bona fides?"

"Money," she said. "He was always getting cut in on those Palace deals. You know that. So he gave half of what he made to the NPA."

"He also gave them information, I bet."

"It wasn't *real* information. It was—"

"Cooked up by the Palace," Durant finished.

She nodded.

"And he fed the Palace whatever he could find out about the NPA."

"Of course."

"What'd they have on him?"

"Who?"

"The NPA. Ernie didn't just wander around until he bumped into some NPA type and said, 'Hi, there. I'd like to be your Palace spy.'"

"They blackmailed him into it," she said. "Pictures of him in bed with—"

"Boys?"

She nodded.

"Ernie didn't give a damn who knew about that."

"But they *thought* he did."

Durant shook his head slowly several times. "The NPA's too smart for that. They took Ernie's money and his cooked-up Palace lies and spoon-fed him their own lies for him to feed the Palace. But when Marcos scampered, poor Ernie's usefulness came to an end and so did he."

"They killed him then, didn't they? The NPA."

"I don't know," Durant said. "Did they?"

"But why would—" Again, Tootie Ortiz didn't finish what she had begun. Except this time it wasn't out of habit, but because of what she saw over Durant's shoulder.

Durant turned. Striding toward the corner booth was Artie Wu, tracked by the two bodyguards. Wu held the six-year-old giggling boy in the crook of his left arm. In Wu's right hand was the hand of the nine-year-old sister who smiled up at him adoringly.

"Tootie," Artie Wu said as he put the boy down and bent over to kiss the mother on her cheek.

"Artie! So good to— Quincy and I were having such a—"

"Nice talk," Artie Wu finished for her.

Tootie looked at her watch. "Oh, my God!" She slipped out of the booth. "I really must be—"

"You're looking great, Tootie," Wu said.

She smiled and turned to Durant. "Quincy, I do hope you won't—"

"Don't worry," Durant said, not at all sure what she was hoping.

Tootie Ortiz smiled nervously, took her children by their

hands, and swept out of the Cowrie Room. One of the bodyguards preceded her. The other one followed, walking backward, his eyes fixed on the booth where Artie Wu was now seated across from Durant.

"Well?" Wu said.

"Guess what poor Ernie is?"

"Is or was?"

"Is."

"No idea."

"He's a real dead double agent."

"Must be a different Ernie," Artie Wu said.

CHAPTER
TWENTY-THREE

At 10:47 that morning Booth Stallings was almost halfway to the island of Corregidor when one of the hydrofoil's two engines failed and the pilot immediately switched off the other one. The Filipino crew, Booth Stallings and nearly three dozen other passengers, including 24 young Japanese naval aviators in immaculate white uniforms, began drifting with the tide in Manila Bay.

One of the aviators and Stallings had been carrying on a kind of conversation, almost shouting to make themselves heard above the engines' scream. The young aviator's English was rudimentary but he seemed determined to make his point, which was that the United States was most fortunate to be led in these times of grave international peril by the greatest President in its history. When Stallings replied that the

President certainly had an unusual grasp of history, the young aviator had nodded his solemn agreement.

They drifted only a few minutes before a twin hydrofoil came alongside and the two Filipino crews held a quick conference. Since the Japanese Navy was a steady repeat customer, it was decided that the aviators would be transferred to the other hydrofoil and ferried on to Corregidor. The remaining dozen or so passengers would remain aboard the disabled craft, which would limp back to port (Do hydrofoils limp? Stallings wondered) where all fares would be cheerfully refunded.

The announcement was met with resignation by all of the seasoned tourists except a gray-haired American who immediately did a rain dance around the bemused Filipino crew, accusing it of incompetence, favoritism and, most of all, ingratitude. The Filipino crew members, ever polite, nodded in agreement and sniggered behind their hands.

When the hydrofoil docked at Manila, the neatly bundled cash refunds were ready. The irate American insisted on counting his twice while Stallings waited in line behind him. Instead of counting his own refund, Stallings simply folded it once and stuck it in a pants pocket.

"Probably clipped you for a hundred pesos," the gray-haired American said.

"Think so?"

"Damnedest thing I ever saw," the American said. "We turn Corregidor into a goddamn shrine and just one hell of a big tourist draw and who do they give priority to? The fucking Japs, that's who—the same fuckers who flattened it during the war."

"Grandsons of the fuckers probably," Stallings said.

"Same thing. Where you headed?"

"Manila Hotel."

"Me too. Wanta share a cab?"

Stallings agreed and they were nearly halfway to the street

before he stopped and turned to examine the American carefully. "What if I'd said no?"

The American gave him a small tight grin. "Then I'd just have to look you up later, Mr. Stallings."

•   •   •

They went to the nearest air-conditioned bar instead of the Manila Hotel. It was a gamey waterfront place called the Shoreleave that featured the usual teenage bar girls and some extremely loud hard rock. When one of the bar girls swayed over to see whether they wanted company, the gray-haired American told her to fuck off and have somebody bring them two bottles of San Miguel but no glasses.

"Might catch AIDS from the glasses," the American explained to Stallings. "All these bimbos like it up the rear, you know. Birth control, Filipino style."

"What's your name today?" Stallings asked.

"Weaver P. Jordan."

Stallings nodded, as though confirming some dark suspicion. "A real spook name."

Jordan smiled his small tight smile and said, "What's a spook?"

The beer came then and Jordan used his palm to wipe off the mouth of his bottle. Stallings didn't. After Jordan drank a third of the beer he put the bottle down and leaned across the table on bare forearms that had too much meat and too little hair.

The hair on his head, by contrast, was long, thick and gleaming gray. Beneath it was the still undefined face of a grumpy baby with wet diapers and a broken rattle. The cheeks were fat and round and the mouth was small, pink and wet. It was a face, Stallings thought, that in a few years would collapse in upon itself like some leftover party balloon.

"I'm with the Embassy," Weaver Jordan said, trying without success to keep his tone confidential and still make himself heard over the hard rock's din.

"Whose embassy?"

"Who the fuck's d'you think?" Jordan snapped, reached into his shirt pocket, palmed something and pushed it across the table. When Jordan's hand lifted, Stallings picked up an ID card encased in laminated plastic. The card claimed Weaver P. Jordan III was an employee of the United States Department of State and should be accorded all the rights and privileges attendant thereto. It also claimed he was 5'10½", weighed 178 lbs., and had been born 43 years ago in Indiana, although the exact place of his birth was left unspecified.

Stallings dealt Jordan back his ID card. It was snatched up and stuck back into the shirt pocket. "What d'you do for the Embassy, Weaver?"

"I'm with the cultural attaché's office."

"I should've guessed," Stallings said.

Jordan drank another third of his beer and then leaned toward Stallings, again trying without success for a confidential tone. "I've got a message for you."

"Who from?"

"Your son-in-law."

"Which one? I have two."

"Secretary Hineline," Jordan said and paused for dramatic effect. "A three-word message."

"Well, I guess three're about all Neal could manage."

"The three words are," Jordan said, "'Cease and desist.'" He leaned back, again wearing the small tight smile that displayed no teeth.

Stallings nodded, as if digesting the message. Then a thought seemed to strike him. "Could I send him a reply through you folks at the Embassy?"

"Yeah. I guess so. Why not?"

"Three words," Stallings said. "Four, if you count my name."

Jordan took a small notebook from his hip pocket and a ballpoint pen from the pocket of his shirt. With notebook open and pen poised, he again nodded at Stallings.

"The message is," Stallings said, speaking at slow dictation speed, "'Get stuffed, Love, Dad.'"

Jordan slowly put his pen down and watched, small pink mouth slightly open, as Booth Stallings rose and headed for the Shoreleave's front exit, pausing only long enough to hand a 100-peso note to the bar girl Weaver P. Jordan had told to fuck off.

•   •   •

At the crowded Philippine Airlines office in the Inter-Continental Hotel, Booth Stallings took a number and found a seat among 41 other prospective passengers. One hour and nine minutes later his number was called. He asked the reservations clerk how soon he could get a seat on a flight to Cebu and was told he could fly out at 4 P.M. Handing the clerk his American Express card and passport, Stallings told her that would do nicely.

Artie Wu received the call from Booth Stallings at 1:39 that afternoon and by 2:14 P.M. he and Quincy Durant were up in Stallings' room at the Manila Hotel, packing the Lew Ritter clothes and surprisingly few personal articles into the old buffalo Gladstone.

The last item was a book that Durant glanced through.

"What's he reading?" Wu asked.

"Auden," Durant said. "Early Auden."

He passed the book to Wu who placed it in the bag and zipped it closed. A knock at the room's door made them look at each other.

"A bad-news knock, if ever I heard one," Wu said.

Durant went to the door and opened it. There were two of them in the corridor, one behind the other, both wearing a "Made in the U.S.A." look. The one nearer the door was in his thirties and rather elegant, which Durant automatically assumed to be some kind of disguise. The number two man, Weaver P. Jordan, afforded no elegance at all.

· The elegant man examined Durant with interest. "I don't believe you're Mr. Stallings, are you?"

"I don't believe I am."

"I'm Jack Cray and he's Weaver Jordan. We're from the Embassy and since Mr. Stallings apparently isn't here, we'd very much like to talk to you, Mr. Durant. And also to Mr. Wu."

"What about?"

Cray erased the polite smile he had been wearing and made himself look serious—even grave. "Prison, I suppose, and how to avoid it."

"Come in," Durant said.

·　·　·

After the introductions were over they all sat down, except Durant, who leaned against a wall. Cray and Jordan took chairs; Wu the couch. "I think I'd like a beer," Wu said with a smile. "Anyone else?"

"Yeah, I'll take a beer," Jordan said, ignoring the chilly look Cray gave him.

Durant served Wu and Jordan beers and then resumed his place at the wall. Jordan popped his can open, drank thirstily and grinned at Durant. "You're the stand-up guy, huh?"

"Piles," Durant said, looked at his watch and then at Jack Cray. "We're a little rushed."

The answering expression on Cray's face seemed indifferent to time. It was a lean face that stretched tanned skin over crags and hollows, planes and ridges. The mouth curved slightly up at one end, down at the other, giving the entire face a look of chronic dubiety. The voice matched the face. It was a baritone, harsh and dark and full of gravel.

"As our beloved Vice-President might put it," the gravelly voice said, "you guys are in deep doo-doo."

"That bad?" Artie Wu said.

Jack Cray ignored Wu and looked at Durant. "You and/or

Mr. Wu did identify or discover the bodies of the late Emily Cariaga and the equally late Ernesto Pineda, right?"

"Right," Durant said.

"And both of you are associated with a Mr. Booth Stallings who arrived in Manila accompanied by a Miss Georgia Blue and a Mr. Maurice Overby, also known as Otherguy Overby?"

Weaver Jordan belched softly and said, "Old Otherguy. And here I thought he was in jail again."

Wu studied Weaver Jordan, nodded as if at some sad conclusion, and turned to Cray. "Was your last sentence an accusation or merely a question?"

"A question."

"Then the answer is no."

"You're not associated with them?"

Wu drank some of his beer and said, "Mr. Durant and I are 'associated,' as you call it. We're partners. We've also known both Miss Blue and Mr. Overby for quite a few years. Mr. Stallings we met only recently."

"Let me put it another way," Cray said. "Are you engaged in any venture with Stallings, Blue and Overby?"

"To put it still another way," Durant said, "that's none of your fucking business."

Cray smiled and shifted his gaze to the ceiling. "I think I'll try delicacy." He brought the gaze down and locked it on Durant. "Two weeks ago, or thereabouts, Booth Stallings was approached to serve as an intermediary to a political figure here in the Philippines. He was smart enough to discuss the proposition with his son-in-law who holds a responsible post at the State Department."

"The car wax king," Durant said.

Cray ignored the description. "Mr. Stallings' son-in-law eventually committed the gist of the proposition to paper and circulated it within the department just at a time when policy toward the Philippines was undergoing an extensive review. The memorandum caused serious discussion at the highest level."

"The shit hit the fan," Weaver Jordan said with a grin.

"His son-in-law wired Mr. Stallings, urging him to abandon his project," Cray went on. "The message was delivered personally to Mr. Stallings today."

"By me," Weaver Jordan said. "Stallings fired back a rocket that said, 'Get stuffed, Love, Dad.'"

"Pithy," Artie Wu said.

"Unfortunately, Mr. Stallings' reply brought our shop all the way into the picture," Cray said.

Wu looked at Durant, apparently puzzled. "Their shop?"

"That big store out in Langley," Durant said.

"Oh."

Cray's sigh was one of nearly exhausted patience. "It was decided at a very high level that Booth Stallings is to be prevented from carrying out his . . . venture." Cray paused to stare coldly first at Durant, then Wu. "Those who aid or abet him, wittingly or unwittingly, will also be . . . discouraged."

Artie Wu turned to Durant. "I'd say old Booth's gone and got himself into a real pickle."

"Dearie me, yes," Durant said as he left his spot by the wall and moved over to where Jack Cray sat. Staring down at Cray, he asked, "What do the Aquino people say about all these crazy Americans running around, trying to interfere with their government?" When Cray made no reply, Durant looked surprised. "Don't tell me you haven't even mentioned it to them?"

Weaver Jordan tossed his now empty beer can into a wastebasket and said, "Why don't we just load these two assholes on the next flight back to L.A.?"

"Yes," Artie Wu said softly. "Why not, Mr. Cray?"

Cray rose. Although he had been sitting for at least 15 minutes there were no wrinkles in his gray suit. He gave Wu and Durant a final inspection.

"Within a week we'll've turned you two inside out." He smiled. "Unless Lieutenant Cruz beats us to it."

When neither Wu nor Durant replied, Cray turned, walked

swiftly to the door and opened it. Weaver Jordan also started for the door, but stopped long enough to give Wu and Durant one of his small tight grins and a wink.

"See you in Cebu, guys," he said and followed Jack Cray out of the room.

CHAPTER
TWENTY-FOUR

With Otherguy Overby buckled into one of its rear portside window seats, the Boeing 707 took only an hour to fly the 365 miles due south from Manila to the long skinny island that centuries before had been called Sugbo, then Zugbu and, finally, Cebu.

Bristling with a spine of green mountains, the island was 300 kilometers long and 40 kilometers across at its widest point. About halfway between its northern and southern tips, facing east into the Bohol Straits, was the port of Cebu City, population 600,000 or thereabouts, and of all the cities in Asia, Otherguy Overby's absolute favorite.

As the Philippine Airlines 707 began its descent to Mactan Airport, Overby thought about why Cebu City still ranked so high in his pantheon of metropolises. For one thing it's old enough, he told himself, and you like real old towns. Cebu City had been founded in 1565—an easy date for Overby to remember because it was exactly 400 years later that he had walked down the gangplank of a Sweet Lines coaster and onto Pier Three with $29 and change in his pocket.

A year after that, he had flown up to Manila and then on to Bangkok with close to $3,000 in a brand-new money belt. And that's why you like Cebu best of all, he decided. Because when you were a kid here you got fat instead of winding up dead broke on the beach.

The Spanish had founded Cebu City 44 years after Chief Lapu-Lapu's spear ended the life of the Portuguese navigator Ferdinand Magellan on Mactan Island, the same island where Overby's plane was landing. They had finally put up a statue to Lapu-Lapu, and named a tasty fish after him, but what the Cebuanos revered far more than the dead chief were the fragments of Magellan's Cross, the first Christian cross ever seen in the Philippines.

The fragments were said to be sealed inside another cross made out of tindalo wood that was on display in a kiosk on upper Magallanes Street. Overby remembered that the shrine, if that's what it was, had drawn pilgrims, beggars and pick-pockets in almost equal numbers. He assumed it still did.

Once inside the airport terminal, Overby ignored the blandishments of a dozen guitar salesmen and found a driver who swore his taxi's air-conditioning still worked. Partly to get back into practice, Overby haggled with the driver over a flat rate to the Magellan Hotel. The bargain struck, they left the airport, drove up and over the Mandaue-Mactan bridge, past the Timex plant, along the south edge of the Club Filipino golf links and into the short drive of the 23-year-old Magellan Hotel that long ago had awarded itself four stars for ambience and five for service.

Twenty-one years had passed since Overby had first checked into the Magellan Hotel. That had been right after he'd run his $29 stake up to $200 in a touch-and-go deal for ten cases of PX Camels, smuggled down from Subic by the second mate on a Panama-registered freighter. As soon as the $200 was safely buttoned into his hip pocket, Overby had checked out of the YMCA and into the Magellan.

The five-story hotel was built in the shape of a Y. It boasted 200 rooms and more bellhops than it really needed. Three of them now saw Overby and his bag out of the taxi and into the hotel. As he entered and glanced around, Overby noticed that the lobby still reeked of maximum tolerance. It was the same atmosphere he'd found the world over in commercial hotels that made a point of not being overly curious about their guests or their guests' friends. He remembered that at one time such hotels could always be found down by the train station. Now they were all out near the airport.

Conservative by instinct, Overby was also pleased to see that almost nothing had changed in the Magellan's lobby. There was still an honest-to-God cigar stand next to the elevators, right where it should be. Across the lobby from the elevators were the reception desk and, next to it, the barred cashier's window. To sit on, there were the same low comfortable chairs and couches, now occupied, he saw, by packaged Japanese tourists in their twenties and thirties who seemed to be wondering where the action was.

At the reception desk, Overby asked about his reservation. The young room clerk sent his eyebrows up and down in the Cebu salute and murmured that the manager would very much like a word with Mr. Overby. The clerk went away and returned with Antonio Imperial.

Overby didn't try to hide his shock. "Jesus, Tony, *you're* the manager?"

Imperial, short wide man with a wide brilliant smile, spread both hands in a gesture that encompassed the entire hotel. "Imperial of the Magellan—at your service," he said and reached across the counter to grab Overby's right hand and pump it vigorously. "How long's it been, Otherguy?" Imperial said, still pumping.

"Eight years," Overby said. "Hell, maybe nine. But back then you were still working the front nights."

"Remember when you checked in here the first time twenty-one years ago and I was the kid who carried your bag up?" Imperial gave his head a "time flies" shake and turned to the hovering young clerk. "Mr. Overby is to have the best of care, Zotico. The very best."

"Yes, sir," the clerk said.

"I've got some other people coming in, Tony," Overby said.

Imperial recited their names from memory. "Blue and Stallings later today; Wu and Durant tomorrow. Correct?"

Overby grinned. "No wonder they made you manager."

"Maybe we could have a drink later, Otherguy—catch up on things."

"I'd like that," Overby said.

When Antonio Imperial, general manager of the Magellan Hotel, turned, banged the bell and barked, "Front!" at the cluster of bellhops, Otherguy Overby felt that perhaps, at long last, he really had come home.

* * *

Seated in front of the window air-conditioning, Overby had just opened his second bottle of beer when the phone rang in his fifth-floor room that offered a view of the golf course. He crossed to the phone and answered with a hello.

The woman's voice said, "Mr. Overby?"

"Yes."

"The same Overby as in, 'Out of the five, Overby's the one'?"

After a moment's hesitation, Overby said, "Could be."

"Then I think we should meet."

"Where?"

"Guadalupe."

"The church?"

"Yes, the church."

"That's way on the other side of town."

"Yes," she said.

Again, Overby hesitated. "All right, when?"

"Four?"

He looked at his watch. "That doesn't give me much time."

"I know."

"Okay," Overby said. "I guess you'll recognize me so I don't have to worry about recognizing you."

"That's right," she said and hung up.

●   ●   ●

When Overby came out of the hotel entrance, the first thing he saw was the large yellow, blue and black sign of the Rotary Club of Metro Cebu that offered a four-question test. "Of the things we think, say or do," the sign read, "four questions should be asked: 1. Is it the TRUTH? 2. Is it FAIR to all concerned? 3. Will it build GOODWILL and BETTER FRIENDSHIPS? 4. Will it be BENEFICIAL to all concerned?"

After reading the sign carefully, Overby answered all four questions with a silent, "You goddamn right," and turned into the adjoining Avis office where he rented himself a gray Toyota sedan.

●   ●   ●

Overby drove west on General Maxilom Avenue, turned right into Rama Avenue and followed it out to the northwest edge of the city. There the Church of Guadalupe occupied an oblong plot of several acres that was encircled by a broken asphalt drive. Built something like a racetrack, the drive ran straight along the stretches, curving into half circles at both ends.

Ever suspicious, Overby drove around the church three times. It was a large structure with a massive gray dome at its center. A concrete cross had been placed atop its gabled south entrance. Below the gable was an elaborate stained-glass window. Two huge doors formed the entrance, which was shielded from rain by an arched concrete canopy. A woman stood beneath the canopy. Overby was too far away to see whether she was young, old or in between, but he could see that she was wearing something blue.

He parked the gray Toyota almost 50 yards away, locked it

and started toward the concrete canopy. The woman turned and watched him approach. As he drew near, he saw that she was young, no more than 25 or 26, and wore a plain pale blue cotton dress that looked cheap. Over her right shoulder hung a tan woven fiber bag. He also noticed that she had large brown eyes and kept her right hand down inside the shoulder bag.

When he was a dozen feet away he stopped and said, "I'm Overby."

"I'm Carmen Espiritu."

"You his daughter, granddaughter, niece—what?"

"His wife."

Overby examined her skeptically. "Been married long?"

"Nearly half a year."

"Well, do we talk here or go somewhere else?"

"First, you tell me in one short sentence why Overby's the one," she said.

Overby smiled slightly. "Twenty-five words or less, right?"

She shrugged.

"Okay, here goes: they're going to cheat him out of the five million, but if he does what I tell him to, he can keep half."

She ran the sentence through her mind, her lips moving slightly. "Twenty-three words."

"I didn't count."

"He gets to keep half, you say. Who keeps the other half?"

"Me."

"Then you're motivated solely by greed."

"What else is there?"

"How're they planning to divide it?" she asked.

"Who?"

"You, Stallings, Wu, Durant—and that woman of theirs, Blue."

"An even split."

"A million each then?"

"Right."

"Aren't you worried about what they'll do when they find you've betrayed them?"

"That's my lookout."

"One last question, Mr. Overby."

He nodded.

"Do you care who ultimately gets the other half of the five million?"

He shook his head slowly. "Not as long as I get my half." He smiled then, that quick hard utterly ruthless smile. "Aren't you afraid of what Mr. Espiritu will do to Mrs. Espiritu when he finds out she double-crossed him?"

"As you say, that's my lookout."

Overby's smile went away. "There'll be risk. A lot of it."

"I'm used to risk."

"So when can I see him and make my pitch?"

"Pitch?"

"Sales talk."

"Yes. Of course. Is tonight satisfactory?"

"Where and when?"

"I'll telephone you," she said. "At the hotel."

"Fine," Overby said, took two steps backward, and looked up at the stained-glass window. "It open?"

"The church?"

He nodded.

"You feel the need to pray?"

"I just like old churches."

"It's open," she said, turned and walked quickly away. After Overby watched her disappear around the far corner of the church, he turned, tugged open one of the massive doors and went inside. Superstitious, if not religious, Overby dropped 50 pesos into the poor box for luck and took a seat in the rear row. There, he folded his arms across his chest and began to figure out his next moves. When he reached the sixth move, he stopped because after the sixth there were too many permutations. But the first move would be to buy the gun, a five-shot revolver, if possible—a belly gun. As he sat on the bench in the old church, arms still folded, Overby wondered

where he should make his purchase and finally decided on Pier
Two. If not Pier Two, then Pier Three. On Pier Three you could
always buy damn near anything although it always cost a little
more.

CHAPTER
TWENTY-FIVE

I t was the Magellan Hotel's general manager, Antonio
Imperial himself, who registered Booth Stallings at 5:41
P.M. on April Fools' Day, 1986. Noting that Stallings was
not burdened with luggage of any kind, Imperial smiled and
said, "Airline lose your bag, Mr. Stallings? They're very good
at that."

"A mix-up in Manila," Stallings said, as he filled out the
registration form. "Some friends are bringing it down."

"Mr. Wu and Mr. Durant?" When he saw Stallings look up
with the beginning of a frown, Imperial hurried on. "Otherguy—I mean, Mr. Overby—checked on all your reservations
and, since Miss Blue's already here, I assumed Wu and Durant
would be bringing your luggage down tomorrow."

The frown was canceled and Stallings smiled slightly.
"Known Otherguy long?"

"More than twenty years."

"He changed much?"

"An interesting question. I'd have to say no, not really.
He's—well, timeless, I suppose." Imperial turned, took
Stallings' room key from its slot, turned back, reached under
the counter, and came up with a small sealed clear plastic bag
that contained a throwaway razor, a toothbrush, miniature

tubes of shaving cream and toothpaste, and a small bottle of shampoo.

"Our compliments," Imperial said, placing the key and the plastic bag on the counter.

"Thanks very much," Stallings said. "What room's Miss Blue in?"

"She's just next door to you, four twenty-six." Imperial snapped his fingers, as if remembering something. He turned again, picked up a small stack of mail, thumbed through it, selected a letter and handed it to Stallings. "This arrived just before you did," he said.

Stallings examined the envelope which was square, white and cheap. His name was printed in ink. Down in the lower left-hand corner, someone had written: "Hold for arrival." Stallings shoved the letter down into a hip pocket, gathered up his room key and plastic bag, and started for the elevator.

"Like a bellman to show you up, Mr. Stallings?" Imperial asked.

Stallings turned back. "No, but you might send up a couple of cold beers."

• • •

It was only after the beer came, and he had drunk half of one bottle, that Booth Stallings took the letter from his hip pocket, held it up to the light, sniffed it, smelled nothing and finally tore it open.

On a single, once-folded sheet of cheap white paper, a precise hand had written:

> Dear Booth,
> Welcome back to Cebu. Someone we both know will
> call on you. Please do exactly as instructed.
>
> > Very truly yours,
> > Al

Still holding the letter, Stallings crossed to the room's window and raised the venetian blind. He reread the letter and then stared out at a red sun setting behind the Guadalupe Mountains, the same mountains in which Stallings and Alejandro Espiritu, the boy terrorists, had done much of their killing. Neither of you, he thought, ever really rid yourself of its fascination. The only difference is that you examined it and poked at it and wrote about it and made a living from it while Al, well, Al just kept on doing it.

Stallings watched what looked like a large Cessna come in for a landing at the old Cebu airport that was now used only by private planes. When his commercial flight from Manila had started its approach to Mactan Airport, Stallings at first thought he had boarded the wrong plane. But Mactan was Cebu's new airport. The one just down the road from the Magellan Hotel was the old one that he and Espiritu, from their vantage point in the mountains, had watched the Japanese military fly in and out of.

Just as the Cessna disappeared behind some trees, there was a knock at the door. Assuming it was either Georgia Blue or Overby, Stallings said, "Come in," and continued to stare out at what was left of the brief tropical sunset. When the door opened and a gruff voice said, "Stallings?"—making it an accusatory question—he turned quickly and found himself staring at a tall old man in his mid-to-late sixties who wore a short-sleeved tan safari jacket with a great many pockets, all of them bulging, and a matching pair of slacks.

The old man had plumb-line posture, silky white hair, a rusted complexion, small blue eyes that needed trifocals and a mouth that obviously liked giving orders. Only the thin-lipped mouth with its pronounced overbite seemed vaguely familiar to Stallings.

"Don't remember me, do you?" the old man said in the gruff baritone that could have belonged to a 30-year-old.

"No," Stallings said. "Should I?"

"Name's Crouch. Vaughn Crouch. Except it was Major Crouch when you knew me."

"Good Lord."

"Finally got to be Colonel Crouch."

"You sent us in."

Crouch nodded. "You and Al Espiritu. I'm the guy."

"What're you—"

Crouch interrupted, as if he didn't have enough patience for fool questions. "I live here."

"In Cebu."

"Here in the goddamn Magellan. Put my thirty in and retired back in seventy-two. Been here ever since. It's cheap and if I need some part fixed, like the prostate, I can fly up to Clark or even back to Schofield in Hawaii and let the quacks there patch me up for free." He raised his head slightly to study Stallings through the bottom lens of the trifocals. "You've changed some. Wouldn't've known you if I'd passed you on the street. You ready?"

"For what?"

"I remember you being kind of quick, Stallings. A little snotty maybe, but quick." Crouch shook his head. "Can't stand dumb. I can put up with goddamn near anything but dumb."

"Espiritu sent you."

"He didn't send me," Crouch said. "He asked. Can't say much for old Al's politics, but he's got a good tactical mind and always did. His fucked-up politics are his business." Crouch paused. "Well, you ready or not?"

"Let's go," Stallings said.

·   ·   ·

The retired Colonel's car was a well-maintained ten-year-old yellow Volkswagen convertible that he drove, top down, with what Stallings quickly decided was far too much dash. The highway up into the mountains started off well enough, but soon disintegrated into broken pavement, patchy gravel, and finally into a twisting red dirt road that was not much more than a trail.

"Why retire here?" Stallings asked. "Why not Fort Sam in San Antonio?"

"With the rest of the old farts?" Crouch said, shaking his head and gearing the VW down for a curve. "I had three wars. Two bad and one good. I sure as shit wouldn't retire to Seoul or Saigon—even if I could—so with the wife dead and both kids either married or divorced, I figured what the hell, you like the Filipinos and always did, so you might as well go live there and see what the fuck happens." He gave his head another shake, this time a satisfied one, and said, "It's sure been interesting."

They drove on without speaking for minutes until Crouch said, "Al lent me that book you wrote."

Stallings' reply was a noncommittal, "Oh."

"I didn't agree with everything you claimed, but you sure got most of it right. So I don't guess I have to tell you that if you're doing a deal with Al, watch him. He's tricky." Crouch glanced at Stallings. "But I expect you must've figured that out by now."

"A long time ago," Stallings said.

They drove on in more silence for what Stallings estimated to be three miles. That made the trip thus far about twelve miles—or not quite halfway across the island. Crouch came to a curve. In the VW's headlights it looked just like any other curve, but he slowed down to fifteen miles per hour, then to ten, and finally stopped.

"End of the line," he said.

"What happens now?"

"You get out, stand around and admire the Southern Cross, if you've a mind to. Somebody'll come fetch you. It won't be long. They're out there somewhere, just waiting to make sure nobody followed us."

"How do I get back?" Stallings said.

"Beats me."

Stallings opened the door, stepped out of the Volkswagen, and looked down at Crouch. "Thanks for the ride."

"Maybe someday you or Al might tell me what the fuck this is all about."

Stallings only nodded.

"And maybe not," Crouch said as he put the car into reverse, backed around and shot off down the rough mountain trail.

Stallings watched until the Volkswagen convertible disappeared around the curve. He decided that once again the grown-ups had sent him out on his own, just as if he had good sense. On the drive up he had remembered more vague details about his elderly chauffeur. In 1945, Crouch had been a 26- or 27-year-old major, a war lover, and somebody who, before the war, had done more than just go to high school. He had either held down a job, or joined the CCC, or bummed around the country, or graduated from Michigan State or Texas A&M. Something anyway.

In 1945 that seven- or eight-year experience gap had seemed unbridgeable to Stallings. In 1986 it still seemed just as wide and just as deep. You'd better grow up fast, sonny, Stallings decided, or you'll slip from acute chronic adolescence into senility with nothing in between. He turned and looked up at the Southern Cross, only to discover—with a trace of surprise—that it, like himself, hadn't changed at all in 41 years.

Stallings wasn't sure how long he stared up at the constellation before he heard them. It was at least five minutes, maybe ten, possibly fifteen. They came down the hill, stumbling and muttering in the dark, indifferent to the noise they made.

Stallings turned to watch their bobbing flashlights approach. He jumped when something hard was jammed into the small of his back by the one who had slipped up silently from behind.

"Please don't move, Mr. Stallings," she said and he recognized the voice of the woman who called herself Carmen Espiritu.

"How've you been, Carmen?"

"Please don't talk either," she said.

The ones who had muttered and stumbled their way down

the hill turned out to be three in number. All were men, none more than 30. While Carmen Espiritu kept the muzzle of her gun in Stallings' back, one of the men searched him with quick, expert hands.

"Nothing," the man said.

She moved around in front of Stallings. With the help of the three flashlights he saw that she wore yet another semiautomatic pistol, a dark T-shirt, jeans and running shoes. The T-shirt advertised a cantina called Hussong's in Baja California.

"How's your health, Mr. Stallings?" she asked.

"Well, I sometimes get a mild touch of sciatica, but it comes and goes."

"I mean can you walk three kilometers into the hills without us carrying you?"

"Sure. Why not?"

"Let's go."

● ● ●

In Booth Stallings' opinion, there was far too much up hill and not nearly enough down dale. But he was pleased by how well he kept up and surprised by how vividly he remembered the way he and Espiritu had once bounded up and down such trails like a couple of goats. Young goats.

They climbed for an hour and 15 minutes before they stopped. One of the men imitated the cry of a bird whose species Stallings didn't even try to identify. After an answering bird cry, they crossed through a cornfield whose rustling stalks provided an effective early-warning alarm system.

Just beyond the cornfield was a large nipa hut of at least three or four rooms. It rested on poles that were the usual five or six feet high. Soft kerosene lamp light came from the hut's open windows and also from those of the three or four smaller nipa huts that made up the compound.

A man who wasn't very tall came through the large hut's

main door and stood, staring down at Stallings as he emerged from the cornfield with Carmen Espiritu at his side.

"How've you been, Booth?" Alejandro Espiritu asked.

"Fine, Al," Stallings said. "And you?"

CHAPTER TWENTY-SIX

After a warm handshake and a somewhat stiff embrace at the top of the bamboo stairs, Stallings followed Carmen and Alejandro Espiritu into the nipa hut, which was really more house than hut.

They came into a combination kitchen-living-and-dining-room. Food was being cooked over a charcoal brazier by a plump handsome woman in her fifties who wore bright red slacks. An old plank table had been set for two with glasses, plates, forks and spoons, but no knives, which many Filipinos seldom use, preferring to cut whatever needs to be cut with the edge of a spoon.

The living room area was furnished with four bentwood chairs and a matching couch. There were no pictures on the wall or rugs on the polished split bamboo floor. But music came from a small battery-powered Sony shortwave set that was softly playing something by the Rolling Stones. The woman in the red slacks left her cooking, went to the radio and turned up its volume slightly, placing her left ear close to the speaker. No one introduced the woman to Stallings.

Espiritu waved his guest to the bentwood couch and chose one of the matching chairs for himself. Carmen Espiritu stood nearby, leaning against a wall, her right hand down inside her woven fiber shoulder bag. It occurred to Stallings that only recently he had seen someone else stand just like that, leaning against a wall, all coiled up and ready to spring. Durant, of course.

"Care for a beer before we eat, Booth?" Espiritu asked.

Stallings said he would and the woman in the red slacks took a bottle of San Miguel from a plastic sack, opened it, crossed the room to Stallings, pausing at the table to pick up one of the two glasses. She handed the bottle and glass to Stallings without a word. He said thank you, but she only nodded and returned to the Sony radio where she glued her left ear back to the speaker.

Stallings carefully poured the warm beer into his glass, indicated the woman with a nod and asked, "Who's she?"

"My little sister," Espiritu said with a smile. "Although not quite as little as she once was."

The plump woman, ear still to the Sony's speaker, gave the right cheek of her buttocks a defiant smack and went on listening to Mick Jagger.

"And her?" Stallings asked, indicating Carmen Espiritu with another nod.

"Who did she say she was?"

"Your granddaughter."

Espiritu giggled and smiled broadly. Stallings noticed that the smaller man's teeth looked absolutely perfect. If he's laid off the sugarcane all these years, Stallings thought, he probably hasn't got a filling in his head.

"Carmen lies as a matter of course," Espiritu said. "She's my bride of six months."

"The present Mrs. Espiritu," Stallings said.

"The only Mrs. Espiritu."

"Well, she certainly keeps busy," Stallings said and drank some of his beer.

Espiritu smiled at his wife. "She's also very ambitious, aren't you, Carmen?"

"I do my part."

Espiritu turned to Stallings. "Who used to say that, 'We Do Our Part'?"

"The Blue Eagle," Stallings said. "Roosevelt's NRA."

"Price fixing was its purpose, wasn't it?" Before Stallings could reply or comment, Espiritu went on. "You're certainly looking well, Booth. Stayed skinny and even grew a little more, didn't you?"

"Half an inch."

"I didn't," Espiritu said with another giggle. "As you must've noticed."

What Stallings had noticed most was the slight tremor in Espiritu's left hand. When the tremor threatened to turn into a shake, Espiritu clutched the left hand with his right. And if the teeth were perfect, or nearly so at 62, Stallings found Espiritu's complexion too sallow and the black eyes too dull.

But the rest of him seems okay, Stallings decided, although it's hard to tell with that white shirt buttoned up to the neck and those sleeves down over his thumbs. He also wondered why Espiritu kept the balled-up handkerchief in his left hand. But when the hand trembled its way up to the left corner of the mouth and mopped away the trace of saliva, Stallings thought he had his answer.

After another swallow of warm beer, Stallings smiled almost gently at Espiritu and asked, "When'd you have it, Al—the stroke?"

"Still very observant, aren't you?"

"When?"

"Months ago."

"I'm sorry."

"No need to be. I'm quite recovered and the prognosis is good." He smiled, dismissing the subject. "Shall we eat?"

Dinner was broiled lapu-lapu, the inevitable rice and a large bowl of fruit. Stallings ate everything set before him; Espiritu only a small portion of rice and a banana. Neither of the women joined the men at table. The plump sister continued to listen to the radio and Carmen Espiritu continued to stand throughout the meal, her right hand down inside the fiber shoulder bag.

"I suppose you were surprised to see old Major Crouch," Espiritu said as he peeled his banana. "Colonel Crouch, actually, retired."

"Very surprised."

"He's grown garrulous, as I suppose we all do. I sometimes think the old tend to talk mostly about the past because there's so much of it. And so little future. My wife finds the past boring, don't you, Carmen?"

"I find it largely irrelevant," she said.

"What was it Santayana said?" Espiritu asked. "'Those who—'"

Carmen Espiritu interrupted the familiar quotation. "Santayana was an ass."

Espiritu smiled at Stallings. "A woman of strong opinions, especially about history. Anything that happened before she was born is irrelevant. As for her politics . . ." He shrugged, still smiling at Stallings. "What do you do for politics these days, Booth?"

"I do without."

"Really? After all those years of studying what you insist on calling terrorism?"

"Terrorism's just a shorthand term."

"Yes, but for what?"

"It's like pornography, Al. Everybody knows it when they see it, but they can't agree on a definition."

"Like to hear mine?"

"Sure."

"Politics by extreme intimidation."

Stallings grunted. "Needs a little work."

"I thought it rather good. Maybe we can discuss it further in the morning."

"In the morning?" Stallings said. "Where?"

"Here, of course. Right after we discuss the five million.

We are going to talk about that, aren't we? Or we could talk about the money now, and my definition over breakfast."

Stallings leaned back in his chair with a bleak smile. "I'm your hostage, huh?" He looked at Carmen Espiritu. "Or hers."

"Yes," Espiritu said. "I believe you are."

Carmen Espiritu came away from the wall, looking at her watch. "That took long enough," she told her husband and turned to Stallings. "I'm leaving now, Mr. Stallings. Our people surround and protect the compound, so please don't go wandering off."

After Stallings nodded, she turned to her husband. "Expect me when you see me."

"As always," he said.

Carmen Espiritu turned and left the room. Twisting around in his chair, Stallings watched her leave through the front entrance. When he turned back he was surprised to find Espiritu's plump sister also gone.

A long silence followed, raising a barrier between the two men. Stallings leaned forward, elbows on the table, and broke the silence, if not the barrier, with a recommendation he made in the form of a question.

"What if we just took off, Al?"

"It's quite simple," Espiritu replied. "You'd be shot."

•   •   •

As far as Otherguy Overby could determine, his rented gray Toyota was parked just where the voice on the phone had told him to park it: 19.3 kilometers from the Magellan Hotel at a curve on the dirt road that led up into the mountains.

Overby also knew he was on time, but he checked his watch anyway. It was two minutes before midnight. The five-shot Smith & Wesson Chief's Special he had bought for US$500 from a buy-and-sell man on Pier Three was tucked beneath his right thigh.

Because all the Toyota windows were open, Overby could

hear them off to his right as they stumbled and cursed their way down the mountain trail. Overby was certain no self-respecting freedom fighters, terrorists, guerrillas or whatever the fuck they were would make that much noise or shine their flashlights around like that.

So he turned his head to the left, just enough for his peripheral vision to become useful. He also removed the five-shot revolver from beneath his thigh and folded his arms across his chest. The pistol, now in his right hand, was pointing at the open left window.

When Carmen Espiritu materialized at the window, Overby wiggled the revolver a little, just to make sure she saw it. "Put both hands on the windowsill, Carmen."

She hesitated, as if calculating long odds, and then put her hands on the sill.

"Call 'em off," Overby said.

She whistled two loud sharp trills. The flashlights went off. Overby switched on the Toyota's headlights, flicking them up to high beam. The headlights illuminated three young men twenty feet away at the edge of the dirt road. Each was armed with what looked like an M-16. Each raised a hand to shield his eyes from the headlights' glare.

"I'm going to slide over into the passenger seat, Carmen," Overby said in a quiet conversational tone, "and you're going to get in behind the wheel. Okay?"

She nodded.

"But before you do," Overby said, "drop that shoulder bag on the back seat. Gently."

Carmen Espiritu took the bag from her shoulder and dropped it through the window onto the back seat. After opening the front door, she slipped behind the Toyota's steering wheel.

"How long will those guys hold still like that?" Overby asked.

"Until I tell them to move," she said. "But if you dim the headlights, they'll sit down."

Overby dimmed the headlights and the three men with the M-16s sat down on the dirt road and lit cigarettes.

"I went looking for Booth tonight at the Magellan and found the old Colonel," Overby said. "Colonel Crouch. Guess what he told me after a couple of drinks?"

"I don't care to guess," she said.

"He told me he'd dropped Booth off about an hour after sunset right here at this very spot where you called and told me to be at midnight. So here I am and here you are and my question, I suppose, is where the hell's old Booth?"

"With my husband."

"Really."

"Yes."

"Let me ask a real dumb question, Carmen. Is your husband alive?"

"That is a stupid question."

"Well, it's just that the only Espiritu anybody's heard from in the flesh is Mrs. Espiritu, and I was just wondering if Mr. Espiritu is alive, dead or maybe in a coma."

"He's quite well."

"Good. And he's planning to hang on to Booth for a while?"

"Yes."

Overby nodded approvingly. "A hostage, huh?"

"Stallings is insurance," she said. "His other use is to convince my husband of the money's . . . legitimacy."

"Jesus, lady. Buy-off money's always a bastard."

"Convince him of the money's existence, not its genealogy. My husband suspects this could be a very elaborate trick to lure him to Hong Kong where there'll be no money and he'll find himself just another penniless exile."

"I like the way his mind works," Overby said. "When was this deal first dangled in front of him?"

"Less than a month ago."

"And he nibbled, but insisted on Stallings as the go-between."

"Yes."

"Who approached him?"

"I won't answer that, Mr. Overby."

Overby grinned. "Don't blame you. If you did, then I'd know what you know."

"How soon do you need to see my husband?" she asked.

"Tomorrow at the latest. And you'll have to get Stallings out of the way for an hour or two so your husband and I can be alone."

She nodded. "Be back here at three tomorrow afternoon and I'll take you to him." She smiled for the first time. "But don't expect me to leave you alone with him, Mr. Overby."

Overby returned her smile. "I didn't think that for a second."

CHAPTER
TWENTY-SEVEN

At 1:43 A.M. Otherguy Overby returned to the Magellan Hotel, parked the gray Toyota and entered the lobby to discover Artie Wu seated on one of the low couches, hands clasped across his belly, eyes fixed on the entrance.

"Artie," Overby said, his eyes darting first to the right where Durant leaned on the counter of the closed cigar stand, and then to the left where Georgia Blue stood in front of the closed cashier's cage, her right hand down inside her shoulder bag. It was then that Overby resolved never again to have anything to do with women who wore shoulder bags.

He also decided to preempt Wu. "I think they've got Booth

Stallings," he said, watching carefully for Wu's reaction, which turned out to be only a polite nod of limited interest.

"They?" said Durant who somehow was now only a foot or so away from Overby. "Who the fuck're they?"

Overby wasn't surprised by Durant's ability to transport himself, as if by magic, but he didn't have to like it. "Christ, you're sneaky," Overby told him and turned back to Wu.

"When'd you guys get here, Artie?" Overby asked. "You weren't due till tomorrow." He remembered the time then and amended his statement. "Or today, I guess it is now."

"Something came up and we chartered a plane," Wu said. "A Cessna, wasn't it?" The question went to Durant.

"A Cessna," Durant agreed.

"We came in at sundown," Wu said, again staring at Overby. "Landed at the old airport up the road. The flight down was quite interesting. We flew at about six thousand and were able to see a lot. The islands all looked very lush, Otherguy, very prosperous." He paused. "Very deceptive."

"Ask him who's got Stallings," Georgia Blue said, crossing from the cashier's cage to stand behind Wu's couch.

"Never hurry Otherguy," Wu said. "He'll tell us after he decides what he wants us to know."

"You want me to tell it down here?" Overby said. "Or up in the room of somebody who's got a bottle because I don't."

"I've got Scotch," Durant said.

Wu rose from the low couch without any help from his hands. "Then let's use your room, Quincy."

·   ·   ·

Durant leaned against the wall as usual. Overby sat in the room's one armchair. Georgia Blue was at the small writing table. Wu sat on the bed, leaning against its headboard. Durant had mixed and served the drinks of Scotch and not very cool tap water after Wu went next door to his room and returned with two more glasses.

After a long swallow of his drink, Artie Wu put it down and

took out a cigar. While inspecting it carefully, possibly for hidden flaws, he said, "So who has Booth Stallings, Otherguy?"

"Mr. and Mrs. Espiritu," Overby said, flicking his eyes from Wu to Durant to Georgia Blue, trying to gauge the effect of his revelation. He was neither surprised nor alarmed when there was none. Overby drank some of his Scotch and water, leaned back in the armchair and waited to see what course Wu would take.

"*Mrs.* Espiritu?" Wu said, raising a mildly perplexed eyebrow.

Overby let himself relax although he didn't let it show. "Carmen Espiritu," he said. "I think everybody's met her at one time or another. Everybody but me."

"She told us she was his granddaughter," Georgia Blue said. "Although Booth didn't believe her."

"From what I hear, she lies a lot," Overby said.

"You hear that where exactly?" Durant asked.

"I'll tell you where," Overby said. "I went looking for Stallings this evening—yesterday evening, I guess—to see if he'd like a drink. I called his room, banged on his door—nothing. Well, the hotel manager's a friend of mine. Tony Imperial. When I first knew Tony twenty years ago he was a bellhop. So I asked him if he'd seen Stallings and he says he saw him with a retired U.S. Army colonel who lives here in the hotel. A guy called Crouch. Vaughn Crouch, like Vaughn Monroe—remember him? And Tony says Crouch and Stallings left in the Colonel's car. An old yellow VW. Okay?"

Wu nodded for Overby to continue. "Well, I hang around and the Colonel comes back alone. So I make a small move on him in the bar, nothing special, and after a couple of drinks he tells me how back in World War II he sent Stallings and Espiritu and six other guys into Cebu on an I and R patrol that only those two came back from. Stallings and Espiritu. So when he retires here in, I think, seventy-two, the Colonel looks up Espiritu and keeps in touch, even after Espiritu goes underground. Well, the Colonel claims it was Espiritu who asked him to drive Stallings up into the hills there. And that's what he did. So I ask him where in the hills did he drop Stallings off and he draws me a map. Well, I got in the car that I rented from Avis next door and drove up to take a look."

"At night?" Wu asked.

"Sure at night. When else was there? You can see things at night, Artie. For all I knew they'd have signs up: This way to the NPA Camp. Except they didn't. So I came back. Oh, yeah. It was the Colonel who told me about Carmen and how much she lies. The Colonel doesn't much like Carmen."

A silence followed Overby's recitation. Wu finally lit his cigar and blew three plump smoke rings at the ceiling. When he spoke, it was more to the rising smoke rings than to Overby.

"That's a very interesting story and I suspect that much of it is even true."

"Thirty percent anyway," Durant said. "Maybe forty."

Overby looked at Durant indifferently. "Just hum me the parts you don't like."

Durant turned to Georgia Blue. "Tell him, Georgia."

She cocked her head to one side, examined Overby with care, gave her head a small shake of wonder and said, "I talked to the Colonel, Otherguy. What you say doesn't quite check out."

"When'd you talk to him?" Overby asked.

"Around midnight."

"Was he sober?"

"Not very."

Overby shrugged. "The guy's on the sauce. He puts away maybe a fifth a day. I can't help it if he can't remember what he said or who he talked to."

"You said you rented a car after you talked to him," Georgia Blue said.

"I said I rented a car."

"*After* you talked to him."

"Not after. That'd be around eight or so. Avis is closed then.

I rented it around three-thirty or four." Overby dug into a pants pocket, came up with the Toyota key and tossed it to Georgia Blue who caught it easily.

She glanced at the key and said, "This doesn't say much."

"The rental agreement's in the glove compartment. The time's on the agreement. The car's a gray Toyota. With the key you can go look." He turned to glare at Durant. "Anything else?"

"You wouldn't still have that map the Colonel drew, would you?" Durant said.

Overby put his drink down and used both hands to pat all his pockets, frowning the while. When one of the pats reached a hip pocket, the frown went away, replaced by a smile. Out of the hip pocket came a folded square of hotel stationery, which he handed to Durant.

Durant unfolded the sheet of stationery, glanced at it, and passed it to Artie Wu who studied it carefully. "It does seem to be a map of some kind and very nicely drawn too. Maybe we owe Otherguy an apology."

"We owe him fuck all," Durant said.

"I apologize for everyone, Otherguy," Wu said. "Especially Quincy."

"Forget it," Overby said.

Wu nodded agreeably. "Now let's go back to what you saw up in the hills tonight. Was there anything at all to indicate that the particular spot you drove to might be used as a rendezvous by the NPA?"

Overby grimaced at the ceiling, as if trying to remember. "I got out and walked around," he said. "There were some cigarette butts. In fact, a lot of them. All in one spot."

"Anything else?"

"Not really."

"Suppose you drove back up there tomorrow and simply waited," Wu said. "What do you think might happen?"

"I think the NPA wouldn't much like it and they'd take me someplace I didn't want to go."

"But that would give you a chance to play Weak Link, wouldn't it?"

Overby shook his head. "They wouldn't buy it, Artie. Not if I just pop up out of nowhere."

"Of course not," Wu said. "But suppose they knew we thieves had fallen out?"

Overby brightened and smiled his hard, merry smile. "Let's hear it."

Wu blew a smoke ring first. "Tomorrow morning downstairs at breakfast, you and Georgia will have a knock-down, drag-out argument. I assume the NPA people will hear it—or about it—and report back to Espiritu. So when you show up in the hills, say tomorrow afternoon, you'll not be altogether unexpected and your credentials, although limited, will have been established."

"I'd be kind of a defector," Overby said.

"A double-crosser," Durant said. "A part you can really lose yourself in."

Overby ignored him and stared coldly at Wu. "I can also get myself shot, Artie."

"This is not exactly a risk-free deal, Otherguy."

"I don't mind shared risk," Overby said. "But up till now it looks like Stallings and me're the only ones sticking our necks out."

"Georgia's goes on the block tomorrow," Wu said. "Mine and Quincy's shortly thereafter."

Overby produced his hardest smile. "Tell me about it."

"Once you've 'gone over,' let's call it, the NPA will naturally wonder if you're a plant. The obvious person for them to question is Georgia. She'll have to bear up under that questioning."

"Okay," Overby said. "That's her. What about him?" Him was obviously Durant.

Wu sighed. "The reason Quincy and I hired the plane and flew down early is because a mismatched pair from Langley came calling. They know what we're up to, more or less, and plan to stop us. We—Quincy and I—can't let that happen."

Durant smiled at Overby. "Want to trade risks, Otherguy?"

Overby shook his head. "I think it's about evened out."

Artie Wu rose from the bed. "Then I think we should all get some sleep unless someone has something else to say."

No one did. Georgia Blue was the first to leave. Then Overby. Wu and Durant waited silently for two minutes. Durant then went to the door, opened it, looked up and down the corridor, closed the door softly and turned back to Wu. "We're slicing it awfully thin," Durant said.

Wu nodded. "And it's going to get even thinner."

•   •   •

Otherguy Overby stood at his room's window 15 minutes later, staring out into the night's nothingness, when he heard the soft knock at his door. He opened it, showing no surprise when Artie Wu entered quickly, closing the door behind him.

"A pep talk, Artie?" Overby said.

"A small warning. It's going to be tricky."

"Too fucking tricky."

"We're going to need luck."

"You never counted on luck before. You don't even believe in it."

Wu moved his lips in what may or may not have been a slight smile. "This time's different, Otherguy. So if you find your luck running out, cut yourself loose."

"Every man for himself, right?"

Wu's answering smile was only slightly larger than his previous one. "Or herself," he said.

CHAPTER
TWENTY-EIGHT

The shouting match ended the next morning at 8:49 in the Magellan Hotel's Zugbu restaurant after Otherguy Overby threw half a cup of lukewarm coffee in Georgia Blue's face and stalked out.

Breakfast was served buffet style in the Zugbu and Overby made sure he had finished his scrambled eggs, rolls and some tasty sausages before he gave Georgia Blue the signal to begin the performance.

It was a vicious although generic kind of domestic scrap with few specifics and much acrimony. Alleged infidelities were recalled. Long-buried grudges were exhumed. Failed joint ventures of a suspect and possibly criminal nature were alluded to, and through it all ran the recurring theme of money and its lack.

The audience, mostly Filipino, Australian and American— plus a contingent of Japanese—found it all fascinating. The Japanese seemed particularly appreciative, despite the absence of subtitles.

After Overby left, Georgia Blue calmly wiped the thrown coffee from her face with a napkin. She lit a cigarette, smoked it for several moments, ground it out and called for the check. She signed it with a hand that trembled only a little, rose and made a slow dignified exit that drew appreciative murmurs from the Japanese.

She used the house phone in the lobby to call Artie Wu.

When he answered, she said, "The son of a bitch threw a cup of coffee in my face."

"Wonderful," Wu said.

"There was a full house."

"Great."

"I'll be at the pool the rest of the morning," she said and hung up.

•　　　•　　　•

Breakfast that morning for Alejandro Espiritu and Booth Stallings consisted of cold rice, more fruit and a can of brisling sardines that Espiritu ate with relish. Stallings passed up the rice and sardines, settling instead for two bananas and three cups of tea.

They had sat up long after midnight, discussing and failing to settle the problems of the world. After six hours of sleep they rose and ate breakfast. When Stallings had finished his third cup of tea he leaned back in his chair and said, "Let's talk about your five million, Al."

"Is there really such a sum?"

"In Hong Kong."

"Marcos once put a price on my head, you know. Two hundred thousand pesos—about ten thousand American dollars. Now that's money you can comprehend—even count. But five million dollars U.S.?" He shook his head.

"What're you going to do with it, Al? Buy guns?"

"Of course."

"If I can figure that out," Stallings said, "so can the money men. Which brings us to the main point. Who the hell are they?"

"You didn't talk to them?"

"Only to a guy who claims to represent them. He says they're a consortium of firms that have a billion or two invested out here and wouldn't mind spending five million to get their money out or even make a few bucks. They think once you're in Hong Kong, your movement will fall apart and Aquino can patch things back together."

"But you didn't believe the lies their emissary told you?"

"No."

"Then why did you come?"

"I was sent for, wasn't I?"

"Yes. You were." Espiritu studied Stallings for ten or fifteen seconds, then frowned and said, "Would you like to know what's really going to happen?"

"Sure. What?"

Espiritu took a deep breath. "First, Aquino hasn't a prayer."

Stallings grunted. "What's two?"

"For four centuries the Philippines have been run by oligarchies of one stripe or another. Mrs. Aquino's a life-long member of the current one and because she's one of them, they'll give her nine months, a year, maybe even longer—until the economy collapses. By then the so-called February revolt will be long forgotten, or remembered only as the great deception. Add disillusionment to total economic collapse and you get general unrest—strikes, riots and the like. Guess who they'll blame?"

"The communists."

"Of course. Harsher military measures will then be proposed and tried, followed by the inevitable military coup. The new junta—or the new exalted maximum leader—will promise to bash the Reds, bring back prosperity and hold free elections in six months, a year, two years—sometime. The elite will breathe its collective sigh of relief. Money to exterminate the terrorists will pour in from Washington and things will return to the status quo ante, which will suit the elite perfectly."

"Historical inevitability, huh?"

"It's inevitable that you and I'll die, Booth. We just don't know when. If we did, we'd spend all we have to postpone it. Well, these money men of yours, whoever they are, don't want to postpone anything. They want to hurry it up."

Stallings' smile was sardonic. "So the sooner you get your guns, the sooner the coup."

"Exactly," Espiritu said and smiled. "They really do need me, Booth."

Stallings nodded thoughtfully. "Five million doesn't sound to me like quite enough."

Espiritu shrugged. "It's seed money. That's all."

"I suppose," Stallings said and looked around the room. "Where's Carmen?"

"She was here earlier, but she left."

"Who the hell is she, Al?"

"My wife."

"Before that?"

"The daughter of an old friend who Marcos had arrested and interrogated years ago. They asked him questions that made him thirsty. So they gave him water to drink—four, five, even six gallons at a time. He died, of course. Carmen was twelve or thirteen then. I arranged for her education and afterward she chose to join us, first in Luzon and later down here."

"So why'd you marry her, Al? It wasn't sex unless you've changed a whole lot."

"Sex always seemed such a—dissipation of time. I married her out of political expediency because I'd just had the stroke and I needed a surrogate. I thought I could trust her. She saved my life, you know." He paused. "I suppose you didn't. She brought a specialist up from Cebu at gunpoint. Blindfolded. I couldn't go to a hospital, of course, and it was a very difficult political time because we had to position ourselves for the snap election."

"You guys sat it out," Stallings said. "You thought Marcos was a shoo-in." He frowned. "Jesus, Al, was that your idea?"

"It doesn't matter now."

"Let's go back to the money then," Stallings said. "When did talk about it first begin?"

Espiritu closed his eyes, as if that helped him to remember. "Around the beginning of March."

"Who approached you? I mean who dropped by one sunny afternoon and said, 'Hey, Al, how'd you like a quick five million?' "

Espiritu smiled again. "You always liked the details."

"My meat and drink."

"Nobody approached me. They went through Carmen."

"She handled the negotiations?"

"Under my guidance."

"They ever meet face-to-face—Carmen and the money men?"

"Of course not. They used a cutout."

"Who was he?"

"Will you write another book, Booth? I liked *Anatomy of Terror* immensely. Did it make any money?"

"Who was the cutout, Al?"

"An Australian. An expatriate Australian."

"What's his name?"

Stallings watched Espiritu's obvious inner debate. When it was over, Espiritu smiled slightly again and said, "A peculiar name. Boy Howdy."

Stallings clamped his teeth together, hoping it would keep his face blank. After a moment he risked a nod and said, "You're right. That is peculiar. Who picked him—Carmen or the money men?"

"They did."

Stallings rose from the table, crossed to the plastic sack, peered inside and removed a warm bottle of San Miguel. He looked back at Espiritu. "Want one?"

After Espiritu shook his head no, Stallings opened the warm beer which foamed up and out of the bottle. He raised it quickly to his lips. Once the foam had subsided, he drank deeply, went back to the table and stared down at the seated Espiritu.

"What're you now, Al—the ventriloquist or the dummy?"

"You're referring to Carmen, of course."

Stallings nodded.

It was seconds before Espiritu spoke again. "I must get to Hong Kong, Booth."

"Boxed in, huh?"

Espiritu nodded. Stallings drank the last of the beer and again stared down at the seated Filipino. "And you really need that five million?"

"Desperately."

"That sister of yours really your sister?"

"Yes."

"And she can come and go?"

Espiritu nodded.

"Could she, say, get down to Cebu and deliver a message this morning to someone at the Magellan?"

"Probably."

Stallings carefully set his empty beer bottle down on the table next to the plate of banana peels. He placed both hands on the table, palms down, and leaned toward Espiritu.

"I'm not in on this deal alone, Al."

Espiritu nodded and said, "Durant, Wu, Overby and Blue, I hear."

Stallings nodded.

"You didn't quite trust me, Booth."

"Couldn't think of much reason why I should."

"What are they—mercenaries?"

"Kind of."

"And you trust them?"

Stallings nodded.

"Then you're as big a fool as ever."

Stallings stopped leaning on the table and straightened slowly, cocking his head a little to the left as if to make sure he heard what came next.

"Say it, Al. Whatever it is."

Espiritu studied Stallings with what seemed to be detached interest. "Very well. At three this afternoon, according to Carmen, one of your trusted colleagues is coming to see me with what I'm told is an interesting counterproposal, the details of which are yet to be revealed."

Stallings was surprised at his sudden rage, which seemed so real and rare and pure that he almost enjoyed it. He leaned across the table toward Espiritu, started to reach for him, thought better of it and again straightened.

"Which one, Al?" he said, making the words grate. "Which one of the fuckers is it?"

Espiritu smiled, still studying Stallings with interest. "You were going to hit me, weren't you?"

"Which one, Al?"

"The one called Overby."

Stallings' anger seeped away, replaced by sadness and disappointment. "Otherguy," he said, more to himself than to Espiritu. "Somehow, I didn't think it would be Otherguy."

CHAPTER
TWENTY-NINE

When the moving mass blocked out the sun at 10:52 A.M., Georgia Blue's eyes snapped open. She was wearing an immodest green bikini and lying on one of the wheeled chaise longues near the Magellan Hotel pool. The shoulder bag was nearby and her hand darted toward it but stopped when the heavy woman in the bright red slacks said, "I'm Minnie Espiritu."

"Minnie?"

"Minerva. And I've got a letter for either Wu or Durant, except they're not in. The desk says you're with them so I guess I can give it to you."

Georgia Blue sat up slowly. "Minerva Espiritu?"

"Alejandro's sister."

"You're from—"

Minnie Espiritu interrupted, as if in a hurry. "From here. Cebu. But I spent a lot of time in California and sure wish I was back there." Wariness spread across her face. "You are Georgia Blue, aren't you?"

"Yes."

Minnie Espiritu dropped a folded copy of *The Manila Bulletin* on the chaise longue near Georgia Blue's feet, fished a pack of cigarettes out of her red pants pocket and lit one, using both hands to shield the match. She blew the smoke out and turned to inspect the pool and the guests. "Inside the paper," she said, still inspecting the pool.

"I'll take it up to my room."

Minnie Espiritu nodded, continuing her inspection. "The Magellan's not bad," she said. "I like nice hotels. If I had my way, I'd check into one and never check out. Well, nice meeting you."

She turned and headed toward the hotel. Georgia Blue yawned, seemed to notice the folded *Manila Bulletin* for the first time, picked it up and carelessly stuck it into her shoulder bag. She then lay back down, her left forearm across her eyes, and waited for five minutes to pass.

•   •   •

In her hotel room, Georgia Blue switched on the air-conditioning, took off her bikini and stood naked in front of the window unit, studying the sealed letter she had found in the folded *Bulletin*.

It was an ordinary white envelope with nothing written on its front. She held it up to the window. After staring at it for a few seconds she picked up a thin silk robe from a chair and put it on as she crossed to her suitcase. From it she removed a packet of plain white envelopes, comparing one of them with the one that came in the folded newspaper.

Satisfied, she used a nail file to slit open the envelope Minnie Espiritu had delivered, slipped the letter from the envelope and took it to the writing desk. It was a two-page letter, folded once.

A rough map had been drawn on the first page. She ignored it and quickly read what was written on the second page. She read it again, this time more slowly. After the second reading she opened the writing desk drawer, selected a sheet of hotel stationery and copied the map with a ballpoint pen.

Finished, she folded the copy she had made of the map and sealed it in a Magellan Hotel envelope. Picking up the telephone, she dialed an outside number. When it was answered, she said, "Room three-nineteen, please."

Room 319 answered on the second ring and Georgia Blue said, "Get a pen and take this down."

She waited until whoever had answered the phone was ready. Then she read into the phone the contents of the letter Minnie Espiritu had delivered. She read at dictation speed, spelling out all abbreviations:

"'Am bringing A. Espiritu out today, starting approx. 4 P.M. from A on map. Meet us with transp. at B on map, 5:30–6:00 P.M. Stallings.'" She paused. "Got that?"

There was a brief reply and a question. The question irritated Georgia Blue. "Where the hell would I Xerox a map? I copied it." Another brief question irritated her even more. "With a goddamn pen, what else?" she said and slammed down the phone.

• • •

At the open-air counter of the Orange Brutus juice stand on the west side of Jones Avenue, Otherguy Overby was lifting a glass of papaya juice to his lips when Carmen Espiritu joined him on the right and something brushed against him on the left.

Overby put his glass down and turned left to inspect a slim man in his mid-twenties who looked uncomfortable in a white shirt, blue tie and dark gray pants. Overby recognized him as one of the three young men from the night before who had squatted on the mountain trail and smoked cigarettes in the glow of the rented Toyota's headlights.

Overby nodded at the man and turned to Carmen Espiritu. "Just him?"

"There're two of them, but you need only talk to this one."

Overby turned to the man again. "Like some juice?"

The man smiled. "Yes, please. Thank you."

Overby signaled the counter woman to serve juice to Carmen Espiritu and the man. After it came and the man took his first sip, Overby said, "Her name's Georgia Blue, B-l-u-e."

"I can spell blue," the man said stiffly.

"She's in room four-two-six."

"Excuse me," the man said. "But what exactly do we ask her?"

"You heard about our big fight this morning?" Overby said.

The man nodded.

"Ask her about that and what caused it and if I need money and how much."

This time the young man looked thoughtful when he nodded. "We are to be very suspicious of you."

"Right."

"What if she refuses to answer?"

Overby shrugged. "Slap her around a little."

A frown expressed the man's disapproval. "That is not . . . nice."

Overby stared at the man for a moment and turned to Carmen Espiritu. "Where'd you find Violet here?"

"He'll do whatever's necessary," she said. "But it's silly. A staged fight followed by a staged interrogation. What good will it do?"

"It'll make Wu and Durant think everything's going just like they've planned it." He smiled. "Even me."

"They're wondering about you, are they?" she said.

"A little."

"You also make me wonder, Mr. Overby."

Overby studied her. "Carmen, would you like me to remind you of something that'll make you feel just one hell of a lot better?"

"What?"

"Your half," Overby said, smiling his hard and utterly ruthless smile, "will be two point five million."

•   •   •

The taxi driver outside the Magellan Hotel knew exactly where the Cebu Plaza Hotel was. But the name of the man to whom he would deliver the sealed envelope that contained the hand-copied map puzzled him. So he asked Georgia Blue to repeat the name slowly.

"Mr. Boy Howdy," she said, pronouncing the name with exaggerated care. "Room three-nineteen. The Cebu Plaza. Mr. Boy . . . Howdy."

The driver nodded dubiously and drove off, silently mouthing Boy Howdy to himself. Georgia Blue went back into the Magellan, stopping at the front desk to ask if either Mr. Wu or Mr. Durant was back. After being told that they weren't she took an elevator up to the fourth floor.

She saw the slim young man in the white shirt, blue tie and dark gray pants as soon as she entered her room. He had plastered himself to the wall next to the door. She automatically feinted a left-handed stab, her right hand darting down inside her shoulder bag for the Walther. When the slim young man ducked to his right as expected, she caught him with a kick to the stomach that doubled him over.

It was then that the huge left arm clamped itself around her neck from behind. The bathroom, she thought. This one was in the bathroom.

A hand that felt like a vise caught her right hand down inside the shoulder bag and immobilized it. She smelled the cloves on his breath although he seemed to be breathing effortlessly. She decided he was immensely strong but not all that good, and that she'd better relax before he snapped her neck out of either incompetence or pique.

She made herself relax and go almost limp. The man in the white shirt straightened slowly, pressing both hands to his stomach. He looked not at her, but at something that seemed to be a few inches above her head and to the right. "Take the bag," the man in the white shirt said.

The enormous left arm stayed clamped around her neck but the other hand released her right wrist and removed the shoulder bag.

"On the bed," said the slim young man who had drunk juice with Otherguy Overby earlier that morning.

The shoulder bag landed on the nearer of the twin beds. The slim young man crossed slowly to the bag, picked it up and dumped out its contents. He examined the Walther, made sure it was loaded, and sat down on the bed, aiming the pistol at Georgia Blue with his right hand, pressing his stomach with the left.

"Let her go," he said.

The arm was removed. Georgia Blue massaged her throat. "May I sit down?" she asked.

The man on the bed nodded. She went to the room's one good chair, turned, sat down and had her first look at the man who had choked her. He wasn't as tall as she had expected— not much more than six feet. But he had immense arms and a massive chest that strained his white short-sleeved shirt. He also had a large head and a curiously placid face with a sweet mouth and dark brown eyes that, for some reason, looked gullible and even trusting.

Georgia Blue turned to the man with the Walther and asked what she thought he expected her to ask. "Who are you and what do you want?"

"Tell us about Overby."

"He's a rotten son of a bitch. Anything else?"

"You're lovers?"

"No. Not now."

"Yet you fought with him at breakfast. Why?"

"Money."

"He wouldn't give you any?"

"Just the opposite."

"He wanted money from you?"

She nodded.

"How much?"

"Fifty thousand U.S. dollars."

"A loan?" asked the sweet-mouthed big man as he moved over to the bed and began poking at the shoulder bag's dumped-out contents with a thick forefinger.

"You don't lend Overby money," Georgia Blue said. "You just kiss it goodbye."

"Why did he want the money?" he asked in a soft and coaxing tone that surprised and bothered Georgia Blue.

"I didn't ask," she said.

"Could you have lent him that much money?" he asked almost idly as he picked up her billfold and started going through its compartments.

"No."

"Then why did he even ask?" the big man said, discarding the billfold and picking up a plain white envelope.

"He thought I could raise it," she said, watching him rip open the envelope.

The big man obviously forgot about Georgia Blue during the seconds it took to read Booth Stallings' letter and examine the crude map. The placidity vanished from his face. The sweet mouth turned sour. A scowl plowed up his forehead. Glaring at Georgia Blue, he handed the map and letter to the slim young man with the gun.

When the slim young man was finished with the map and letter, he looked stricken. "Tricked," he whispered. "We are being tricked."

The big man reached Georgia Blue in two long strides. "Who gave you these—these things?" he demanded, all coaxing gone from his voice.

"It was slipped under the door," she said. "I didn't even open it. I thought it was an advertisement or something."

"Let's kill her," said the slim young man, now using both hands to aim the Walther at Georgia Blue.

"He wants to kill you," the big man said, his tone reasonable. "If you stop lying, he might not."

"I don't know what it is or where it came from," she said, repeating the lies in a monotone the service had trained her to use. "It was slipped under the door. I didn't open it. I don't know what's in it."

The dull flat lies succeeded only in removing the last trace of gullibility from the big man's eyes.

"WHY?" he bellowed, caught up in a sudden rage that threatened to consume him. "Why do you foreign people do these bad things to us?"

Georgia Blue started to ask, "What things?" but there wasn't time because his locked-together hands came smashing down at her like a hammer. She tried to slip the blow but the huge hands slammed into her head, just missing the temple.

There was the imagined taste of something in her mouth, something from her childhood that she couldn't identify. But it lasted only the instant before oblivion came and she could no longer taste anything, not even the copper in her collection of old Indian head pennies.

CHAPTER
THIRTY

S he lay on the floor by the room's one good chair in that discarded rag doll position that only the dead seem able to manage. Artie Wu thought she certainly looked dead. Antonio Imperial, whose passkey had unlocked the door to room 426, was convinced of it. Only Quincy Durant had any doubt as he quickly crossed the room to kneel beside Georgia Blue.

His hands seemed to know exactly where to go and what to do. He felt first for the big artery in her neck. He then peeled back an eyelid. Next he opened her blouse and put his left ear to her chest. Then he sat back on his heels and studied her for a moment before looking up at Imperial.

"She's alive, but you'd better get a doctor."

"Shouldn't she go to hospital?" the hotel manager said.

"That's up to the doctor. But if you don't get her one, she could die on you."

"I'll get one," Imperial said and hurried out.

After the door closed, Durant said, "Let's put her on the bed."

Wu frowned. "Should she be moved?"

"You want to talk to her?"

Wu nodded his reply and helped Durant lift her gently onto the nearer twin bed.

"Get a cold wet washcloth or towel," Durant said.

While Wu was in the bathroom, Durant examined the ugly swelling just above Georgia Blue's left ear. After Wu returned with a wet towel, Durant's practiced hands applied it to the swollen area. Georgia Blue's eyes flickered, opened, closed and opened again. She made a retching noise far down in her throat.

"Get a bucket," Durant snapped.

Georgia Blue threw up into the metal wastebasket Artie Wu held for her. After lying back down and closing her eyes, she asked Durant, "How bad?"

"You'll live, but you'll have one hell of a headache."

"A doctor's on his way, Georgia," Wu said as he came back from the bathroom where he had emptied the wastebasket.

She opened her eyes to look at Wu. "An NPA sparrow team, Artie. One big; one little. The big one was almost as big as you."

"Tell us about it," Wu said. "If you can."

"They wanted to know about me and Otherguy and that stupid fight we put on. And then they wanted to know about the letter from Stallings."

Wu and Durant looked at each other. "What letter?" Durant said.

In sentence fragments and disjointed phrases she told them about Minnie Espiritu delivering the plain white unaddressed envelope. About checking at the desk to see if Wu and Durant were in. About going up to her room and finding the two men, one big, one little. About kicking the little one and being choked by the big one. About the little one finding the Walther and the big one the letter. But she said nothing about opening Stallings' letter and reading it over the phone to Boy Howdy, and nothing about sending a copy of the map to Howdy by taxi.

"Any idea of what was in Booth's letter?" Wu asked.

"He—he read it to me," she lied.

"The big one?" Durant asked.

"Yes. There was the letter and a map. He read me the letter and showed me the map. They wanted to know how I got them."

"What'd you tell them?"

"Lies."

"Can you remember what was in the letter?" Wu said.

She closed her eyes again, as if struggling to recall. "Most of it, I think," she said, opening her eyes.

"Let me get something to write on," Wu said, going to the desk and returning with a magazine and several sheets of hotel stationery. "Okay," he said and clicked his ballpoint pen.

"I . . . I think," Georgia Blue said haltingly, "that it went something like, 'I'm bringing Espiritu out tomorrow from A on map.'" She paused. "And then there was something about when they'd start. Four, I believe."

Wu looked up from his notes. "Four P.M. tomorrow?"

"Yes. Then something like, 'Have transportation at B on map,' except transportation was abbreviated and I'm fairly sure the time for that was between five-thirty and six."

"What about the map?" Durant asked. "Did you get a good look at it?"

"Yes."

Wu leaned forward. "Can you remember where points A and B are?"

"Give me some paper, Artie. Maybe I can draw it."

It took her ten minutes to draw the map on a sheet of hotel stationery. It took that long because she kept hesitating and changing her mind and discarding wadded-up sheets of stationery. Finally satisfied, she handed what she had drawn to Wu. It was another fair copy of the map Booth Stallings had drawn, except that on this second version points A and B were about a kilometer farther west and east, respectively.

Wu studied the map with care. "Nice," he said, passing it to Durant. "You have a good memory."

Durant examined it and looked up. "Some map," he said.

Georgia Blue wearily closed her eyes. "It could be a little off."

"How little?" Durant asked. "Twenty yards? Five hundred meters? A mile or two?"

"You want a money-back guarantee?" she said, opening her eyes to glare at him. "That map and what I told you are all I know. Everything. Except, well, except one dumb question they asked that made no sense."

Wu smiled encouragingly. "And what question was that, Georgia?"

"They asked me, or rather the big one did, what Boy Howdy was doing at the Cebu Plaza. I said I didn't know. So the one time I tell the truth the big bastard hits me." She attempted a smile and nearly made it. "But that's okay, I guess, since the little one wanted to shoot me."

"Why do you think they asked you what Boy's—"

A loud knock at the door kept Wu from completing his question. And before he could get around the twin beds, the door opened and a man in his late thirties strode in, a doctor's bag in his left hand and a worried-looking Antonio Imperial just behind him. The man with the doctor's bag stopped in the middle of the room and glanced around, as if expecting evidence of a riot, revolution or at least a three-day orgy.

He wore an expensive green polo shirt, pale yellow linen slacks and a competent look on a narrow face that featured gentle dark brown eyes and an unforgiving mouth.

"I'm Doctor Bello," he announced to the room at large. "Who the hell are you two?"

"Friends of the patient," Durant said.

"Friends of the patient will kindly wait outside."

•   •   •

Antonio Imperial went away, leaving Wu and Durant waiting in the corridor just outside room 426. He went away somewhat relieved after they both assured him that Georgia Blue had no intention of suing his hotel. When he had gone, Durant unfolded the map and examined it with a sigh. "Some map," he said again. "It's got a rough scale and everything." He handed the map to Wu who folded it back up and tucked it away in his right hip pocket.

"I think," Wu said as he buttoned the pocket, "I think I'd better drop by the Cebu Plaza and have a talk with Boy."

"Want me to go along?"

"I want him talkative, Quincy. Not terrified. And somebody has to stay with Georgia."

"Otherguy can stay with her."

"You're forgetting this is Otherguy's afternoon to defect."

"Mr. Trustworthy."

Wu shrugged. "He's what we've got."

● ● ●

Artie Wu went to his room and telephoned the Cebu Plaza Hotel. He told a room clerk that he had a package for Mr. Howdy and should he send it to room 314 or 514? The room clerk said neither—that the package should be addressed to room 319. Wu said he wished certain people would learn to write legibly and the room clerk said that would indeed be a blessing because Wu was the second person that very day to have the wrong number for Mr. Howdy's room.

Downstairs, Wu took a taxi to the Cebu Plaza, which had been built late in the Marcos reign and was not only much newer than the Magellan but also much taller. As Wu paid off his driver, he noticed the green Subaru four-door sedan that waited with engine running outside the Cebu Plaza's entrance. He noticed it mostly because of the big Filipino who stood by the sedan's open rear door. Artie Wu always noticed men who were nearly as large as he. And this one was especially worth a second glance because of his obvious anxiety. Behind the wheel of the Subaru sat a smaller man wearing a white shirt. Wu couldn't decide whether he was also having an anxiety attack.

Inside the hotel, Wu crossed the lobby to the elevators. Two of them were working and both were on their way down. The first elevator to arrive opened its door with a soft chiming bong and out of it came Carmen Espiritu, wearing an expensive cream silk dress, no brassiere, black pumps, too much makeup

and a black matching leather shoulder bag in which her right
hand was buried.

At the sight of Artie Wu she stopped short and an unfamiliar
left high heel twisted, causing her to stumble. Wu put out a
supportive hand that cupped her left elbow. Carmen Espiritu
quickly recovered, backing away from him, her right hand
bringing up the black leather shoulder bag.

"Don't ever touch me!" she said in a fierce whisper.

Wu smiled. "Buy you a drink, Carmen?"

"You people are such . . . idiots," she said, turned and
hurried away, the wobbling high heels clacking along the
marble floor.

Wu watched her climb into the rear of the green Subaru
sedan. The big Filipino, apparently still stricken with either
panic or anxiety, closed the rear door with a slam and
scrambled into the front seat next to the driver. The Subaru
shot away.

Watching the car drive off, Wu wondered what, if anything,
he should do about it. He decided his only sensible move
would be to go pound on Boy Howdy's door.

He rode the elevator alone up to the third floor, walked down
the corridor until he found 319 and the Do Not Disturb sign
that hung from its doorknob. Wu pounded on the door. When
there was no response, he automatically tried the knob and was
surprised when it turned. He glanced quickly up and down the
corridor, went through the door and closed it behind him,
making sure it locked.

There was the usual short entryway with the bath on the left
and a closet on the right. Beyond the entryway was the room
itself where Wu discovered Boy Howdy sitting in an easy
chair, slumped in it actually, and wearing nothing but the
pillow on his lap.

CHAPTER
THIRTY-ONE

There were two small bullet holes just below Boy Howdy's left nipple. Blood, although not very much, had made some of the reddish gray chest hair even redder. There were also two bullet holes in the thin pillow, which Wu assumed had served as a make-do silencer.

Glancing around the room, he noted the rumpled bed clothing and how Boy Howdy's own clothes formed a kind of trail to the bed. The shirt had been discarded first, then the net undershirt followed by the pants, the Jockey shorts and finally the shoes. Wondering where the socks were, Wu looked back and found a pair of white cotton ones still on the dead man's feet. The socks made him fret a little about his powers of observation.

Wu picked up Boy Howdy's pants and went through the pockets, finding nothing of interest. There was a second thin pillow on the bed, but nothing underneath it. Wu lifted up the mattress and found what he was looking for—Boy Howdy's wallet.

It was a large worn ostrich-skin wallet, very old, very thick, that contained 585 pesos, $800 in American Express traveler's checks, three credit cards, a driver's license, two condoms, some receipts and a sheet of Magellan Hotel stationery, the same sheet on which Georgia Blue had drawn her fair copy of Booth Stallings' map.

Wu put the ostrich-skin wallet back where he'd found it and

carried the map to the writing desk. On the desk were a phone, a bottle of Dewar's Scotch whiskey, a bucket of half-melted ice and two glasses, only one of them used. There was also a nine-sheet stack of Cebu Plaza Hotel stationery. Lying diagonally across the stationery was a hotel ballpoint pen.

Wu switched on the desk lamp, took the map Georgia Blue had drawn for him and Durant from his hip pocket, and compared it with the one he had found in Boy Howdy's wallet. The two maps, obviously drawn by the same hand, were virtually identical, except that points A and B on the map drawn for Wu and Durant had been moved a kilometer west and east, respectively.

Wu smiled and nodded his appreciation of the neat deception. He picked up the Scotch bottle and smelled its contents. It smelled like Scotch whiskey so he had two swallows straight from the bottle. As he used his handkerchief to pat his lips, someone knocked at the door. It wasn't a polite tentative maid's knock, but the hard open-up-in-there kind.

Wu's reply was a loud growl to indicate he was coming as soon as he could get some clothes on. He studied the two maps that lay side by side, put one on top of the other and folded a crease into both just below the Magellan Hotel letterhead. He tore the letterheads off along the crease and stuffed them into his pocket.

Crossing quickly to the bed, Wu took Boy Howdy's wallet from beneath the mattress and put the false map Georgia Blue had drawn for him and Durant into it, returning the wallet to its quaint hiding place. The map he had found in Howdy's wallet went down beneath the elastic top of Wu's left calf-length black sock.

There was more hard knocking at the door. Wu glanced around the room and headed for the door, pausing only to switch off the desk lamp. He opened the door to discover the pair with the "Made in the U.S.A." look. Neither made any attempt to hide his surprise. The older of the pair, Weaver P.

Jordan, recovered first, smiled his tight no-teeth smile and said, "I told you we'd see you in Cebu."

Wu nodded affably. "So you did."

The elegant one, Jack Cray, was wearing a different suit but the same suspicious frown. "Where's Howdy?"

Wu shook his head sadly and replied in an appropriately hushed tone. "Shot dead, it would seem."

Although Wu was already moving back and to one side, Weaver Jordan still said, "Get the fuck out of our way," as he pushed past him into the hotel room followed by Jack Cray.

Jordan slowly circled the dead Boy Howdy three times as Cray stood a few feet away, his eyes not on the corpse but darting around the room, searching—Artie Wu presumed—for the killer. Not finding him he turned to Wu and said, "Who killed him?"

"If you'd asked who wanted him dead, I could give you a long list. Boy had an absolute knack for making life-long enemies."

"You kill him?" Cray said, obviously not expecting much of an answer.

"No."

Weaver Jordan stopped circling the dead Boy Howdy long enough to glower at Wu. "What about Durant?"

"He's sitting up with a sick friend, even as we speak."

"So what're you doing here?" Cray asked in a tone braced for both lies and evasions.

Wu smiled. "Since you have no more official authority than I do, I'll ask the same question."

Jack Cray turned to stare somberly at the naked dead man. When he spoke it was in a voice usually reserved for graveside eulogies. "He was one of ours."

"Boy was one of everybody's," Wu said. "Did he do piece-work? Casual labor? Or did you have him on a retainer?"

When Cray only stared at him bleakly, Wu went on in a half-speculative, half-reminiscent voice. "He was on your books for what—ten years? Fifteen? I'd say fifteen." A thought seemed to strike him. "You did know he was on Tokyo's books, didn't you? And Taipei's, Canberra's, Kuala Lumpur's and, the last I heard, even Bangkok's, although Bangkok doesn't really pay all that much."

"Bangkok," Weaver Jordan said, staring at the dead Howdy with disapproval. "Jesus."

Cray said nothing. Instead, he gave Wu a slow up-and-down inspection, as if curious about what would come next.

"His best customer, of course," Wu continued, "was always the old boy in Malacañang Palace. Howdy was both his supplier and distributor. But you know that, don't you, because you must've bought Palace stuff from Boy so fresh the ink was still wet." Wu turned to examine the dead Howdy, as if for the last time. "I expect Boy really missed the old guy." He paused. "I know he missed the money."

"You jump to nice conclusions," Jack Cray said.

Wu nodded and gave the room itself a final quick glance. "Looks just like a typical honey trap, doesn't it? Boy has something he wants to sell or buy. She walks in. There's some talk. Some business. And then some sex—first on the bed followed by a variation in the chair. And then bang, bang, Boy's dead."

"Through the pillow," Weaver Jordan said. "She was probably kneeling on it—at first anyhow."

Jack Cray looked at Jordan and made a small gesture. "Toss it," he said.

It took only two minutes for Jordan to find the ostrich-skin wallet under the mattress. "Well, lookee here," Jordan said, handing the map to Jack Cray. Wu sidled up behind Cray, as if trying to steal a glimpse over his shoulder. Cray gave him a cold look and walked to the other side of the room where he continued to study the map.

Wu watched Weaver Jordan eye the sheaf of Cebu Plaza Hotel stationery on the writing desk. Jordan first looked at it from above and then squatted so he could look across its surface at eye level. While still squatting and looking, he switched the desk lamp on, off and on again. He produced a pencil and began shading in a portion of the top sheet of stationery.

"I saw a guy do that in a picture once," Wu said.

"We employ all the latest techniques," Jordan said, shading away. "Invisible ink. Poison toothpaste. Real state-of-the-art shit."

He kept on shading the stationery with his pencil for another three or four seconds before he said, "Well, now, by God." He put the pencil down and bent over the sheet. "Listen to this, Jack, will you: 'Am bringing A. Espiritu out—' "

Jack Cray cut him off with a sharp, "Goddamnit, Jordan!" He then turned to Wu and said, "You want to stay around for the cops?"

"Not particularly."

Cray smiled his coldest smile. "Then we'll tell them you weren't here."

"Should it arise."

Cray nodded. "Should it arise."

Artie Wu turned and headed for the door, but turned back. "In that picture I saw," he said to Weaver Jordan. "The guy went to all the trouble of shading the pad with a pencil, but you know what the secret message turned out to be?"

"A fake," Weaver Jordan said.

"I guess we saw the same picture."

"I guess we did," Weaver Jordan said.

CHAPTER
THIRTY-TWO

onvincing Antonio Imperial to hand over Georgia Blue's black attaché case required far less persuasion than either Wu or Durant had anticipated. She had lodged her case with Imperial for safekeeping and they politely looked elsewhere as the hotel manager worked the combination of the large old Mosler safe that dominated his office.

"How is Miss Blue?" he asked, tugging open the safe's door.

"Comfortable," Wu said. "Doctor Bello gave her a sedative."

"She's sleeping then?"

"Dozing," Durant said. "But she needs some of the documents in her case."

"You wouldn't mind signing for it, would you?" Imperial asked as he handed Wu the attaché case.

"Mr. Durant'll be happy to," Artie Wu said.

• • •

Up in Durant's room, Wu watched as Durant used a nail file and a carefully bent paper clip to open the case's two locks. It took five minutes of fiddling and swearing before both locks succumbed. Durant opened the case lid, revealing approximately $200,000 in what Otherguy Overby had called the "this-and-that money." About half was in $100 bills, banded in packets of $5,000, 50 bills to the packet. The rest was in unendorsed American Express traveler's checks.

"How much?" Durant asked.

"Ten thousand for the Colonel?" Wu suggested.

"Better make it fifteen," Durant said, removing three of the packets.

"And maybe twenty-five thousand for the warlord."

Durant frowned. "Think he'll settle for that?"

"Make it thirty thousand then."

Durant removed another six packets.

"And five thousand for incidentals."

Durant nodded, removed one last packet, and closed the attaché case lid.

"Don't lock it yet," Wu said, going to the writing desk where he wrote something on a sheet of hotel stationery and signed his name. He handed the sheet to Durant who read it aloud.

" 'Expense advance in the amount of fifty thousand dollars drawn against miscellaneous gratuities and incidental outlays. A. C. Wu.' "

"Sign your name below mine and date it," Wu said.

"Somehow," Durant said, as he signed his name, "I don't think this'll stand up in court."

•   •   •

After they returned the attaché case to Antonio Imperial and, at his insistence, watched him replace it in the old safe, Wu and Durant rode the elevator to the fourth floor and entered room 426. Georgia Blue lay on the farther twin bed, her eyes closed, her mouth slightly open, a sheet drawn up to her chin.

Artie Wu went over to the bed and said her name softly. When she didn't stir or respond, he whispered to Durant, "How many Percodans did the doctor give her?"

Durant held up two fingers.

"And you?"

Durant held up two fingers of his other hand.

"Let's go," Artie Wu said.

After the door closed, Georgia Blue opened her eyes. She

slowly sat up in bed and managed to swing her feet to the floor. She began to sway slightly and tucked her head down between her knees, keeping it there for at least a minute. After that, she lifted her head, breathed deeply and stood up. She again swayed slightly, but recovered, walked slowly to the writing desk, picked up the phone and dialed the number of the U.S. Consulate in downtown Cebu City.

•   •   •

Durant knocked on the door of room 512 in the Magellan Hotel. Wu stood just to his left. The door was opened a few seconds later by the straight up-and-down old man with the silky white hair and the rust-red complexion. He stared at them, not saying anything, waiting for their pitch.

"Colonel Crouch?" Durant said.

Vaughn Crouch nodded.

"My name's Durant and this is my partner, Mr. Wu. We're associates of Booth Stallings."

"So?"

"We'd like to make you a proposition."

Crouch nodded skeptically. "Am I supposed to buy or sell?"

Durant smiled. "Sell."

Crouch inspected Wu, taking his time, then Durant again. "Okay," he said. "Let's hear it."

The room Wu and Durant entered obviously had been furnished to suit a minimalist's tastes. There were two chairs, a single bed, a pair of lamps, a table that held two bottles—one of gin, the other of Scotch—and four fishing rods that leaned in a corner. It was a room that could be vacated on ten minutes' notice, its valuables either abandoned, drunk or poured down the sink.

"Sit or stand, suit yourself," Crouch said, choosing the bed. Durant leaned against a wall, his arms folded. Wu chose the lone easy chair.

"Drink?" Crouch asked.

"No, thanks," Wu said.

"Well," Crouch said, "which one of you's the spieler?"

Artie Wu smiled and said, "We understand you know Alejandro Espiritu."

"I know a lot of guys."

Wu nodded, as if he had met with confirmation rather than evasion. "Booth Stallings is bringing him down from the hills tomorrow."

Crouch rose, crossed to the gin bottle, poured a measure into a glass, and held up the bottle to Wu and Durant who shook their heads. Crouch tossed the straight gin down, made a face and said, "Al willing to come?"

"That's right," Durant said.

"What the fuck for?"

"For the five million dollars somebody's agreed to pay him if he exiles himself to Hong Kong," Wu said.

Crouch went back to the bed and sat down. "Somebody's yanking your chain, gents," Crouch said. "If Al Espiritu ever got his hands on five million, he'd spend it all on ordnance." He smiled then. "Unless somebody fucked him out of it first."

There was a silence until Durant said, "Would that worry you?"

"Yes and no," Crouch said, after giving the question some thought. "I don't want to see Al hurt or killed or jailed again. But then I don't want to see that bunch of his running things either." He paused. "Maybe a trip to Hong Kong might do him good. He could write his memoirs or something."

"That's why we came to you, Colonel," Wu said. "To keep him from being hurt or killed or jailed."

"I spotted you for a couple of Christians right off," Crouch said with a snort. "Who d'you think wants to stop him most?"

"You tell us," Durant said.

"Well, there's Manila, of course," Crouch said. "Because they're smart enough to know what he'd do with the money once he got his hands on it. Then he's got that bunch of young

Turks who're itching to nudge him out of the way. They wouldn't mind five million either. Washington's probably split right down the middle, not sure which way to crawfish. About the only ones who'd be rooting for Al is the old Marcos crowd because they can't lose. If he's gone, good. If he buys guns, even better because that'd provide an excuse for the coup that's gonna happen sooner or later anyhow." He looked at Wu and then Durant. "That about how you guys figure it?"

Durant nodded. "Except we're not sure about Washington."

"Spooks sticking their oar in?"

"Could be," Wu said.

"So what d'you want me to do?"

"Create a diversion," Wu said.

"You mean stir it up over here while old Al sneaks away over there?"

"Something like that," Durant said.

There was a long pause as Crouch stared at the floor, considering the proposition. A minute went by before he looked up at Artie Wu and said, "How much?"

"What would you say to ten thousand?" Wu asked.

"I'd say fifteen right off the bat."

Durant grinned. "Why fifteen?"

"Because I've got a granddaughter who wants to go to Swarthmore next year and fifteen thousand'll just about cover it. Unless I buy myself a new car. Haven't decided yet." He grinned. "Things don't really change much, do they? Back when I was a kid my old man had to decide whether to send me to Dartmouth or buy himself a new Buick. He sent me to Dartmouth, I flunked out and he regretted his choice till the day he died."

"Okay, Colonel," Artie Wu said. "Fifteen."

"You guys got a plan?"

"A germ of one," Durant said.

"Well, let's hear it and then I'll tell you how to make it work."

•   •   •

The block-long Chinese-owned department store was on Colon Street, the oldest street in Cebu—or in the Philippines, for that matter. Its executive offices were on the fourth floor and it was there that Artie Wu sat on a couch in the reception area, dressed in his white money suit, both hands clasped over the head of his cane, the Panama hat on the arm of the couch. Next to him sat Durant, wearing a light gray suit, shirt, and tie. On Durant's knees was a leather zip-around envelope case large enough to hold a legal brief. Inside it was $30,000 in $100 bills.

The reception area had been done in pale shades of green and yellow. The chairs and the couch looked as if they had been thriftily salvaged from broken suites in the store's furniture department. On the walls were six mass-produced oil paintings, all seascapes, two of them identical or nearly so. From the ceiling came Muzak with something syrupy from *My Fair Lady*. Artie Wu was almost sure it was being played for the third time. At last the green carved door opened and the young Chinese who had introduced himself as Mr. Loh came out. "He'll see you now, gentlemen."

The room they entered was large and filled with fine old stuff from Madrid and Seville, Shanghai and Canton. None of the furniture seemed less than 300 years old and its juxtaposition offered a remarkable study in blends and contrasts.

Behind a desk that Durant guessed to be eighteenth-century Spanish sat a small Chinese who looked only a little younger than his desk. He had miles of wrinkles and not much hair and a pair of gold-rimmed glasses that he wore down on the tip of his nose. Two very black, very young-looking eyes peered over the glasses.

He waved Durant and Wu into chairs. They sat down and heard the green door close behind them. "I am Chang and you obviously are Wu and you, sir, Durant," the Chinese said in a firm high voice that ended in an almost adolescent titter. "Correct me if I'm wrong."

Wu smiled politely; Durant didn't.

Chang tilted his head back so that he could peer down through his glasses at the letter in his left hand. "My dear friend Huang in Manila is well?"

"Mr. Huang is very well," Artie Wu said.

"He writes of you with warm praise."

"He flatters me."

"He asks me to show you every courtesy."

"I would be grateful."

"And urges me to do business with you because it will be profitable."

"A fair profit is only just," Wu said.

Chang put the letter down on his desk, scratched his left ear thoughtfully and said, "Very well. Tell me what you want."

"Mercenaries."

Chang nodded as if he sold them every day on the mezzanine. "Good ones?"

"Mediocre ones."

"Good ones would be expensive."

"And mediocre ones?"

"Less so—depending on how many you want."

"Say, two dozen?"

"And what would you do with these two dozen mediocre mercenaries?"

"They will indirectly help Alejandro Espiritu flee to Hong Kong."

"Flee?"

"Flee."

"And once there, what will become of him?"

"He will enjoy a comfortable retirement and exile."

"And what, please, will the mercenaries be required to do?"

"Surrender."

Chang smiled and tittered again. He had small uneven teeth that seemed to be his own. "How interesting," he said.

"I am pleased you find it so."

"Before we discuss details," Chang said, giving the right ear a scratch this time, "perhaps we should talk of price."

"As you wish."

"Do you have a price in mind?"

Wu shook his head. "Price will be determined by our severely limited resources."

"Are your resources in dollars?"

"They are."

"Then I can offer a ten percent discount."

"Ten percent off how much, may I ask?"

Chang thought about it, his eyes now fixed on Durant. "Two dozen mediocre at fifteen hundred each, less ten percent for cash, would be thirty-two thousand four hundred."

Durant shook his head.

"Say, thirty thousand even?"

Durant nodded.

Chang smiled at Artie Wu. "Your partner drives a hard bargain, Mr. Wu."

Wu looked at Durant with pride. "He does something else equally well," he said, turning back to Chang with a suddenly chill stare. "He makes sure that bargains, once made, are kept."

Chang's wrinkled face went cold and stiff. He's freeze-dried it, Durant thought. Then it slowly thawed and a smile appeared. "I share Mr. Durant's concern," Chang said to Artie Wu.

Wu relaxed. He relaxed even more when Chang bent forward, his eyes glittering, his tone conspiratorial. "Shall we go into the details now?" he asked. "I'm sure I'll find them most tasty."

CHAPTER
THIRTY-THREE

At 3:32 that afternoon, Alejandro Espiritu put down his mug of tea and asked, "What's the most you ever earned in a year from this terrorism diddle of yours?"

"Diddle?" Stallings said with a grin.

"Diddle. A perfectly good word—good enough for Poe, which is where I first ran across it. In one of his short stories."

"You're a treat, Al."

They were again seated at the rough board table in the big nipa hut. Minnie Espiritu had returned a half hour earlier with a sack full of beer for Stallings. She now sat with her ear to the Sony shortwave, listening to a talk program from the BBC.

"Well, how much?" Espiritu asked.

"Fifty-eight thousand in eighty-four."

"What qualifications must you have before setting yourself up as a terrorism expert?"

"Well, you should read a couple of books, maybe even three. Spend at least a week in Beirut and maybe one in either San Salvador or Lima. Then you come back to the States, Washington probably, rent an office, get some cards printed and you're in business."

"You're joking, of course."

"Not much."

"Isn't there some kind of professional organization that sets standards—an American Society of Terrorism and Counter-Insurgency Experts?"

"None that ever asked me to join."

Espiritu drank more tea. "You've talked to many so-called terrorists, according to your book."

Stallings nodded.

"The Polisarios?"

"Nice bunch of people for crazies."

"The Shining Path?"

"They're just crazy."

"Why didn't you ever talk to us, Booth? You gave us just two pages in your book. That's all."

"I only gave the Tupamaros one."

"They're out of business."

"Well, to tell the truth, I figured I already knew all I needed to know about the NPA from that time you and I were in the low-intensity insurgency business."

"The NPA didn't even exist then."

"But you did, Al."

Espiritu started to reply, but before he could the big Filipino who had hammered Georgia Blue unconscious came into the hut followed by his smaller partner. The big man looked at Minnie Espiritu and, with a jerk of his head, ordered her out. She lit a cigarette first, carefully turned off the shortwave set— to conserve batteries, Stallings guessed—and left.

The big Filipino turned to Stallings and said, "Come."

"No, thanks," Stallings said.

"Better go with him, Booth," Espiritu said.

Stallings rose slowly and followed the smaller of the two Filipinos out of the hut. The big man formed a rear guard. When they reached the bamboo stairs, the big man indicated that Stallings should go down them first.

As he started down the thirteen steps, Otherguy Overby started up. Waiting behind Overby on the ground was Carmen Espiritu who looked reasonably cool in her white duck slacks and black T-shirt. Overby, by contrast, appeared hot and tired. His polo shirt and gray slacks were soaked with sweat. He stared up at Stallings silently and backed down the steps.

Stallings went down the bamboo stairs briskly, his two

escorts right behind him. "Hot enough for you, Otherguy?" he said and stopped, as if curious about the answer.

But Overby had retreated into his sealed-off preserve where nothing could touch him. He merely nodded at Stallings, much as he might nod at some not quite despised neighbor, and said, "Almost."

Stallings grinned at Carmen Espiritu. "How you doing, Carmen-honey?"

"You're only going to another house, Mr. Stallings," she said, pointing. "Just over there."

Stallings nodded agreeably and started for it, accompanied by his two mismatched escorts. Suddenly, he spun around and called to Overby who was nearing the top of the bamboo stairs.

"Hey, Otherguy!"

Overby turned, his expression indifferent.

"What d'you want me to tell that fucking Durant?"

"You'll think of something," said Otherguy Overby.

•   •   •

"This is Overby, the one I spoke of," Carmen Espiritu said to her husband who looked up from his mug of tea.

They examined each other, neither trying to hide his curiosity. Overby found just about what he had expected—old dynamite, leaking nitroglycerine. One bump, he thought, and it's big bang time.

"You look hot and tired from your long walk, Mr. Overby," Espiritu said, indicating the chair Booth Stallings had just vacated. "Would you like a beer?"

"Thanks," Overby said, lowering himself into the bentwood chair.

"Carmen would get it for you, but she has to leave," Espiritu said as he rose.

"No!" she said, obviously shocked. "I stay."

Espiritu went to the plastic sack by the Sony shortwave, took out a bottle of beer and brought it back to Overby. "Glass?" Espiritu asked.

Overby shook his head, twisted off the bottle cap, drank thirstily and leaned back in his chair to watch.

"I have the right to stay," Carmen Espiritu said.

"If you stay," her husband said, "there will be no discussion."

Overby smiled at her. "See you, Carmen."

She pointed a trembling finger at him. Anger flushed her face and made her voice vibrate. "This one," she told her husband, "makes his living off old fools like you."

"Could that possibly be true, Mr. Overby?" Espiritu said with obviously feigned shock.

Overby only smiled.

Turning to his wife, Espiritu gave her a final look of dismissal. "Mr. Overby and I have much to discuss, Carmen."

They watched as she turned and strode from the room. When she was gone, Espiritu tilted his head to one side and studied Overby. "Well, now," he said, "where shall we begin?"

"With the five million."

"It really exists—this famous five million?"

"It exists."

"And who's supplying it?"

"You really care?"

Espiritu considered the question. "Not really."

"But you want it?"

"Indeed yes."

"Well, if you keep fucking around with Booth Stallings and them, the odds're about five to one you'll never see a dime. But if you do like I say, you've got a good shot at half. It's up to you. Half or nothing."

"Who gets the other half?" Espiritu said.

"Who d'you think? Me."

Espiritu, still examining Overby with curiosity, smiled and said softly, "You really do deal in greed, don't you?"

"What else is there?" Overby said.

•   •   •

At 4:15 P.M., Georgia Blue drove her rented Honda Accord four kilometers up into the Guadalupe Mountains and the virtually deserted country club whose 18-hole golf course had once been farmed by dozens of farm families. Only one car was in the clubhouse parking lot—a black American Ford sedan with CD license plates.

The clubhouse, which had seemed like such a good idea to the Marcos regime and such a bad idea to the farmers it dispossessed, was built out of beams and glass. The beams were mahogany; the glass was dirty. But it was not so dirty Georgia Blue couldn't see into the clubhouse bar and discover it was empty save for the bartender and two male customers who drank beer at a table. The customers were Weaver P. Jordan and the ever elegant Jack Cray.

Neither man rose when she came in, pulled out a chair and sat down.

Instead of saying hello, Weaver Jordan said, "I didn't tell you about Boy Howdy, did I?"

"You and I haven't talked," she said.

"That's right," he said. "You just left a message. Or was it a summons?"

She ignored Jordan and turned to Jack Cray. "I'd like a vodka on the rocks."

Cray rose, went to the bar and returned with her drink. After she took a deep swallow, Weaver Jordan leaned toward her and said, "Lemme tell you about Boy."

"All right," she said.

"Well, the thing about Boy is—he's dead. Shot. Twice. Up in his room at the Cebu Plaza. Three-nineteen. Buck naked. Except for his socks. He kept his socks on."

"I'm sorry to hear that," Georgia Blue said.

"That he kept them on?"

"Ease up, Weaver," Cray said.

Weaver Jordan ignored him. "Guess who found him up there dead in his room with only his socks on?"

"No idea," she said.

"Artie-fucking-Wu."

"Well," she said. "You talk to Artie?"

"Yeah, we talked to him. One of the world's great cuties, Artie."

Jack Cray drank some of his beer and said, "Why don't we just get to the point, Georgia?"

"The point's the same," Georgia Blue said. "Get Espiritu to Hong Kong, pension him off and make sure he doesn't come back." She looked first at Jordan, then at Cray. "Does that still have everybody's seal of approval? I stress everybody's."

"Yeah, everybody back home's finally on board," Jordan said. "Except for one thing. The five million. Nobody wants Alejandro Espiritu buying Uzis and AK-47s and M-79 grenade launchers with that five million."

"What five million?" Georgia Blue asked.

There was a long silence. Finally, Jordan grinned broadly. Jack Cray only smiled and said, "Then there's no need to mention it again, is there?"

"None," she said. "Can we get on with the rest of it?"

Both men nodded.

"First, Otherguy Overby. I think he's running his own private shitty."

"Sounds like Otherguy," Jordan said.

She nodded her agreement and said, "But we can leave him to Durant."

"Okay," Jordan said. "We leave him to Durant. Who do we leave Durant and Artie to?"

"I want to read you something," she said, reached into her shoulder bag and brought out a sheet of paper. "Listen to this: 'Expense advance in the amount of fifty thousand dollars drawn against miscellaneous gratuities and incidental expenses.' Signed by A. C. Wu and Quincy Durant."

Jack Cray's lips formed a line of disapproval. "Whose fifty was it?"

"I had almost two hundred thousand in operational funds in an attaché case locked in the hotel safe. They conned the manager out of the case, lifted fifty and left me their IOU." She put the receipt back in her purse.

"They're going to fuck everybody over, aren't they?" Jordan said. "You, Otherguy—even Stallings." He smiled. "I like it."

"I thought you might," she said.

"What's the fifty thousand going for?" Cray asked.

"I'm not sure, but I think most of it'll be spent by tomorrow when Booth Stallings brings Espiritu down from the hills."

She leaned back to gauge their surprise. But there was none. Jack Cray reached into his pocket, brought out a much-folded sheet of stationery, unfolded it and flattened it in front of Georgia Blue.

She glanced at the map and up at Cray. "So you already knew about Stallings bringing Espiritu down?"

Cray nodded.

"Artie was up in Boy's room when we got there," Weaver Jordan said. "He could've been there five minutes or fifteen. I toss the room and what do I find? Boy's wallet. So guess what's in it?" He tapped the map in front of Georgia Blue. "This. Now what worries me is how come Artie didn't find it first?"

Georgia Blue studied the map for a moment. "He did," she said and looked at Jack Cray. "Got a pen?"

He handed her a silver ballpoint pen. She used it to alter the rough map. When done, she handed the pen back to Cray and turned the map around so both men could examine it.

"Now your map is just like Artie's."

Weaver Jordan studied it with interest. "So when Espiritu comes down from the hills to point B here," he said, jabbing his finger at a point on the map, "Wu and Durant'll just be in the way, right?"

"Yes," she said.

"And Otherguy?"

"Him too."

Weaver Jordan nodded contentedly. Jack Cray pulled the map over for closer inspection. Still looking at it, he said, "What about Booth Stallings?"

Georgia Blue hesitated. "What d'you think?"

Weaver Jordan smiled his small tight smile. "You're calling it, sugar."

This time her hesitation lasted scarcely a second. "Stallings is a keeper."

CHAPTER
THIRTY-FOUR

The nearly empty warehouse was down on the Cebu docks near Pier Two. Painted on its outside walls in huge letters was the name of the Chinese-owned department store on Colon Street. Inside, Wu and Durant watched as the old man with the silky white hair and the rust-red face inspected his two dozen mercenaries, not much caring for what he saw. The time was 10:17 P.M.

The mercenaries, none of them over 22 or 23, were lined up in two wavering rows of 12 each. Most were armed with M-16s, but a few carried shotguns. Some had regulation canteens and the rest had plastic bottles suspended from their necks by cords. Spare shotgun shells and ammunition clips were jammed into the pockets of pants that were either dark brown or black. All wore very dark green T-shirts, compliments of the old Chinese merchant who had sent somebody out to buy them from a rival store.

Vaughn Crouch made his inspection, looking very much the competent, if somewhat superannuated, mercenary in his short-sleeved bush jacket and dark blue gimme cap. He also wore a webbing belt that supported two canteens and a .45 Colt automatic pistol—or semiautomatic, as he insisted on calling it.

Prior to the inspection Crouch had addressed the mercenaries for five minutes in a mixture of English and Cebuano. When finished he had asked for questions. There had been only one from a very thin man who asked if there would be anything to eat. Crouch replied that there would be plenty.

The inspection over, Crouch told the mercenaries to climb into the two large Toyota vans parked nearby. As they moved to the vans he walked over to Wu and Durant, pausing to pick up a small plastic shopping bag.

Crouch handed the shopping bag to Durant. "Two Smith & Wesson five-shot belly guns," he said. "Also ten extra rounds. If you guys find you need any more'n that, I suggest you take out a white handkerchief and wave it around."

"Sounds sensible," Durant said.

Artie Wu nodded toward the mercenaries. "What d'you think?"

Crouch shrugged. "Average. By the time I get through walking 'em all night, they'll be dog meat." He turned to give the young men a glum look. "I guess I'll let 'em sleep in shifts tomorrow once we get to point B." He turned back to examine Wu carefully, then Durant. "You gents still planning to put in an appearance tomorrow evening?"

"We'll be there," Artie Wu said.

"Yeah, I guess you will at that," Crouch said and turned to go, but again turned back. "What do you think of those Hondas?" he asked Durant.

Durant smiled. "Nice car. But what happened to Swarthmore?"

"If that granddaughter of mine wants to go to college, let her borrow from the government like everybody else."

•　　•　　•

After they returned to the Magellan Hotel, Wu called Otherguy Overby's room from a house phone in the lobby. When there was no answer he and Durant crossed to the reception desk where Wu asked the room clerk if he had seen Overby.

The room clerk's eyebrows shot up and down twice in the Cebu salute, this time signaling surprise mingled with apprehension. "Mr. Overby checked out."

"When?" Durant said.

"An hour ago. He said we should put his bill on Mr. Wu's." The clerk looked up at Wu, expecting the worst. "Have I made a mistake, sir?"

"No, that's fine," Wu said and gave the counter a reassuring slap with his palm. "It's just that we didn't expect him to check out so soon." Forcing an all's well smile, Wu asked, "What about Miss Blue? Has she checked out yet?"

"No, sir. She came in a few minutes ago and went up to her room." The clerk smiled. "She seems to be feeling much better."

"That's splendid," Artie Wu said, started to turn away, but seemed to remember something. "I wonder if I could have Mr. Overby's bill?"

"Yes, sir," the clerk said.

•　　•　　•

Up in Durant's room, the only item of interest on Otherguy Overby's hotel bill was the final charge, which was a long-distance phone call made at 9:14 P.M. to a 202 area code number in the United States. Wu looked at Durant. "Two-oh-two's Washington, right?"

Durant nodded, picked up the phone and placed an international call to (202) 634-5100. While they waited for it to be completed, Durant mixed two drinks of Scotch whiskey and tap water. Artie Wu took a sip of his and asked, "What time is it in Washington?"

Durant looked at his watch. "It's about eleven-thirty here so there it'd be about ten-thirty yesterday morning."

They waited in silence until the telephone rang 15 minutes later and the Manila operator told Durant his call was going through. Durant held the phone away from his ear so Wu could listen to it ring. It rang three times before a man's voice answered with, "Good morning, Secret Service."

"Sorry, I have the wrong number," Durant said and hung up.

Artie Wu went back to his chair with a broad grin. "Otherguy and the Secret Service," he said.

Durant wasn't smiling. "I wonder who that dipshit told them he was?"

"You ever hear him do Overby of Reuters? Very plummy. Or he might've been the Embassy's first secretary calling at the Ambassador's behest. For that he'd've used some Yale gargle." Wu's smile went away and he sighed. "You know who he was calling Washington about, of course."

Durant nodded. "Let's go talk to Georgia."

Wu rose. "See how she's feeling."

•   •   •

It was always Otherguy Overby's theory that if you wanted to lose yourself, you should head for the last place they would ever look. That was why, after checking out of the Magellan Hotel, he had checked into the Cebu YMCA at 61 Jones Avenue. Using his YMCA membership card, Overby had been given a five percent discount off the 40-peso price of his single room with electric fan.

Overby had carefully kept his YMCA membership up to date ever since 1965 when he first had checked into the Christian hostelry on Jones Avenue. From time to time, he had either hidden out or economized in YMCAs from New York to Hong Kong. The one in Kowloon, located just down the street from the Peninsula Hotel, was his particular favorite. It offered the same view as the Peninsula for a tenth of the price. In the early seventies Overby had lived in the Kowloon YMCA for two months while operating out of the Peninsula's splendid next-door lobby. After scoring US$60,000 off a Taipei industrialist, Overby checked out of the YMCA and into a suite at the Peninsula. But first he made sure it offered exactly the same harbor view as did his room at the YMCA.

He sat now in a wooden straight chair in his small one-window room, his shirt off, arms folded across his chest, feet firmly on the floor, a can of cold beer handy. The YMCA's electric fan blew muggy air at him. He was thinking about his phone call to Washington. He had made it because it was a loose end and his finicky nature demanded that loose ends be either tied up or snipped off.

The phone call to the Secret Service had done neither. Instead, it had proved to be a hard tug at a thread that could unravel the entire skein and—if he worked it right—turn into the sweetest no-comeback deal of all time with the chance of retribution so slight as to be almost nonexistent. Except for that fucking Durant. Overby decided he would have to think some more about Durant.

•   •   •

When Wu and Durant came into her room, Georgia Blue waved the $50,000 receipt under Wu's nose. "Just what the hell is this, Artie?" she demanded.

"Precisely what it says. You were asleep. We needed the money. So we helped ourselves and left the marker. If you need a detailed accounting, you can have it when it's over."

"I have a right to know what you blew fifty thousand on—and don't give me any of that 'need to know' crap either."

Artie Wu looked around the room. "I seem to remember a bottle of Scotch somewhere."

"What'd you blow it on, Artie?" she said.

"Where's the bottle?" Durant said.

"In there," she said, pointing to the closet. "Top shelf." She turned back to Wu. "Well?"

"Everything's reached that delicate stage, Georgia, where compartmentalization is best. You don't know what the fifty thousand went for. We don't know what Otherguy's up to. Or you, for that matter. We have to assume that each of us is working along the general outline agreed to in Manila. With individual improvisation and variations, of course."

"Tell her about Otherguy's variation," Durant said as he came back with a bottle of Scotch in one hand and three small glasses in the other. He poured whiskey into the glasses, offering them to Georgia Blue and Artie Wu.

"What about Otherguy?" she asked after a sip of the whiskey.

"He made a phone call and checked out," Wu said. "No forwarding, as the skiptracers put it."

"Who'd he call?"

"A number in Washington." Wu looked at Durant. "You happen to remember it, Quincy?"

Durant looked up at the ceiling and rattled off (202) 634-5100 as if it were printed there.

Wu kept his gaze on Georgia Blue. She was wearing only a thin white silk robe, not quite transparent, but so sheer that Artie Wu almost thought he could see the flush race up her body and pinken her cheeks.

"You fucks," she said. "You called it, didn't you?"

"Recognize the number, Georgia?" Durant asked.

"The Service's number. The Connecticut Avenue office."

"Wonder why Otherguy would call the Secret Service?" Durant said.

"To find out if I'm still working for them. That's how that rat's nest he uses for a mind works."

"And are you, Georgia?" Wu asked softly. "Still working for them?"

"Sure I am, Artie."

Wu smiled. "I didn't think so."

"But you weren't certain, were you?"

Still smiling, Wu shrugged.

"Did you check my calls today?" she asked.

"Just Otherguy's," Wu said.

"If you'd checked mine, you'd've found I called Harry Crites."

"The man with the money," Durant said.

She nodded. "The man with the money. I asked him to transfer it all to Hong Kong. The Hong Kong and Shanghai Bank."

"Which branch?" Wu asked. "That new headquarters they've built on Des Voeux Road?"

"That's the one. I asked Crites to make it a joint account, Artie. Booth Stallings' name and mine. Five million dollars. It'll take both of us to draw it out."

"Then I very much hope that nothing happens to you," Wu said.

"Or to Stallings," she said, turning to Durant. "But you'll make sure of that, won't you, Quincy?"

"Bet on it," Durant said.

• • •

Artie Wu and Georgia Blue were talking about Otherguy Overby again when Durant left them and went to his room. He opened the door, switched on a light and found Carmen Espiritu seated in the chair by the window air-conditioning unit. She wore a light tan dress. Both hands were in her lap. They were also wrapped around a semiautomatic pistol that was aimed at Durant. He thought it looked like a small Browning.

"How're you, Carmen?" Durant said, went to the closet door, opened it, looked inside and moved to the bathroom, which he also inspected. He then crossed to Carmen Espiritu, took the pistol from her, noting that it was a .38-caliber Browning, and shoved it down into his left hip pocket under the squared-off tails of his sports shirt.

"How did you know I wouldn't shoot?" she asked, as if not really interested in an answer.

"Because if you were going to, you'd've done it when I turned to switch on the light. What's on your mind?"

"Overby."

"What about him?" Durant asked as he went to a wall and leaned against it.

"He says you and the woman and Wu are going to cheat my husband out of the money. The five million."

"Overby told you that?"

She nodded.

"What else?"

"He said that if I'd arrange for him to see my husband, he'd present a plan that would let Alejandro keep at least half of the five million."

"And Overby'd get the other half."

"Yes."

"So you set up the meeting and they froze you out."

"I—I don't quite understand what you're—"

Durant interrupted. "Come on, Carmen. You approach Overby—or he approaches you. He warns you that the people he works with are crooks and swears that if you'll work with him, you two'll split the five million. But to make his plan work, he has to talk to the mark—your husband. Alejandro Espiritu. Himself. So you arrange the meeting and they cut you out because you're no longer needed. Overby's going for the whole five million, of course—not just half." Durant paused. "And I'd say so is your husband." He grinned at her. "Some trio."

"Did Overby tell you this?" she said, her voice now cold and angry.

Durant shook his head. "It's just a variation of an old turn called the Omaha Banker."

"A confidence trick?"

"Sure. That's what Overby does. It's his profession."

She stared at the floor. "He's very good, isn't he?"

"Not bad." Durant took a package of cigarettes from his shirt pocket and offered it to Carmen Espiritu. After lighting hers, he said, "Is Booth Stallings all right?"

She blew out the smoke and said, "Yes."

"Why did your husband insist on him?"

"Because he remembers Stallings as a fool."

Mistake number one, Durant thought, smiled slightly and said, "What else?"

Carmen Espiritu looked away. "My husband thought if he insisted on an old American comrade-in-arms as the intermediary, it would demonstrate sincerity. My husband's sincerity."

"And the real reason?"

She looked straight at Durant. "If things went wrong, my husband would have an American hostage."

"That sounds about right," Durant said. "Maybe you can tell me something else. Where's the five million coming from?"

"I have no idea."

Durant made himself look faintly surprised. "Didn't poor old Ernie Pineda tell you up in Baguio before you cut off his balls and slit his throat?"

"You make no sense."

"Sure I do, Carmen. Ernie worked for you—for the NPA anyhow—as well as for the Palace. He knew everything and everybody. So whose five million did Ernie say it was?"

She shook her head, almost as if she pitied Durant. "You don't understand anything, do you?"

"I'm trying. It'd help if you'd tell me what happened between you and Boy Howdy. I mean, what'd Boy do to make you kill him?"

Carmen Espiritu put her cigarette out and rose. "You should ask the Blue woman."

"Think she'd know?"

Carmen Espiritu shrugged. "Are you her lover?"

Durant smiled and shook his head. She slowly walked over

to where he still leaned against the wall. "Just good friends?" she said.

"Not even that."

She put her hands on his shoulders and pressed her body against his. "I haven't taken a lover in months," she said, demonstrating her frustration with small rhythmic thrusts of her pelvis.

Durant kissed her then. He kissed her out of curiosity and because there really wasn't all that much choice. It was a long kiss with much lip nibbling and teeth clicking and a great deal of tongue work. Durant thought she seemed to enjoy it. He knew he did. When it was over, he said, "Let me get the lights."

"I like them on," Carmen Espiritu said in a breathy voice as she gently tugged him toward the nearer of the twin beds.

"Indulge me," Durant said and went to the door. His left hand turned off the lights and the room went dark. His right hand removed the five-shot Smith & Wesson revolver, the one supplied by Vaughn Crouch, from his right hip pocket. With his left hand he opened the door.

Two Filipinos stood there, one large and one small. The large one, who had beaten Georgia Blue unconscious, held a hotel room key in his right hand. His small partner's right hand was darting toward something stuck down beneath his shirttails in the waistband of his pants. Durant slashed the darting hand with the revolver. The small man gasped and raised the hand to his mouth where he kissed and stroked it tenderly.

"She's just leaving," Durant said. "Aren't you, Carmen?"

Durant turned sideways, parallel with the open door, not taking his eyes or his revolver off the two men. Carmen Espiritu stopped in front of him. He didn't look at her when she said, "You still don't understand anything, do you?"

"Such as?" Durant said, still watching the two Filipino men.

"That I win, regardless of what happens."

•   •   •

After Carmen Espiritu and her two chaperones left, Durant closed the door, shot the dead bolt and fastened the chain. He also went to the phone, picked it up and called Artie Wu's room.

When Wu answered, Durant said, "I just heard from Otherguy. Sort of."

"Indirectly, I take it."

"Directly is a path he seldom takes."

"Well, is he still on track or not?" Wu asked.

"Let's put it this way, Artie. Otherguy's either right on track or he's gone completely off the rails."

CHAPTER
THIRTY-FIVE

At dawn, Booth Stallings rose naked from his cot in the smallest room of the large nipa hut and dressed in his freshly laundered and ironed clothes. The night before, Minnie Espiritu—not quite by force—had confiscated his shirt, pants, socks, and shorts.

"They stink," she had said, "so take 'em off and give 'em here."

After Stallings had removed his shirt, pants and socks, she said, "Shorts, too."

When he had hesitated, she grinned. "Old guys don't flick my Bic. They still say that in the States—flick my Bic?"

"I don't think so," Stallings had said, handing her his

shorts. After giving his naked body a frankly curious appraisal, Minnie Espiritu had said, "Not bad. Considering."

•   •   •

Stallings entered the nipa hut's main room to find Alejandro Espiritu seated at the rough board table, drinking a cup of tea. He smiled up at Stallings. "What would you say to a pre-breakfast stroll?"

"What am I supposed to say?"

"'Fine' would do. So would 'Let's go.'"

"Fine," Stallings said. "Let's go."

"You might take this along," Espiritu said, indicating a plastic shopping bag that had been placed on a nearby chair.

"What's in it?"

"Comestibles," Espiritu said with a smile. "And I do believe it's the first time I ever used the word."

Stallings picked up the shopping bag and followed Espiritu out of the hut and down the bamboo stairs. The smaller man wore a blue tails-out shirt, tan cotton pants and a pair of gray Nike running shoes that looked new.

"I like dawn, don't you?" said Espiritu as they strolled across the hard-packed dirt of the compound.

"Not much."

"I like to hold meetings at dawn when everyone else is groggy and I'm wide awake."

"I notice you still like to chatter in the morning."

"Better that you notice the guards," Espiritu said.

"Hard not to."

"They have new orders," Espiritu said. "From Carmen."

"Oh?"

"They've been ordered not to let me leave the compound."

"That's some marriage you've got, Al."

"A marriage of convenience, which is now inconvenient."

They had just walked past the last hut in the compound when Espiritu stopped and turned to face Stallings. "Over my right shoulder. See him?"

"The guard?" Stallings said.

"His name is Orestes. A most conscientious lad who actually stays awake during his shift. He's been on since midnight and he'll be relieved in about ten minutes. Let's go talk to him."

Stallings nodded thoughtfully as he swung the shopping bag back and forth in a small arc. "So we're going now, huh? I mean, really going."

"Yes. We really are."

Orestes, the guard, greeted Espiritu with a cheery good morning. He was a solidly built youth of no more than 19. His equipment consisted of a water bottle and an M-16 rifle. His eyes looked sleepy.

"Long night, Orestes?" Espiritu asked.

The boy grinned and nodded.

"I just noticed that young stand of bamboo—down the path there." Espiritu pointed. Orestes turned to look.

"Think someone could sneak up the path and use it for cover?"

"I don't know."

"Let's take a look."

The three of them went down the path for ten yards, Espiritu in the lead, until they reached the bamboo. It was a small stand and far from mature. Espiritu studied it for a moment and said, "Let's see what it looks like from the other side."

Stallings and Orestes followed him around the bamboo, which now shielded the three of them from the compound. Espiritu backed up a few steps, as if for a better look. Orestes stared up at the bamboo and yawned. He was still yawning when Espiritu landed on his back, clamped a left hand over the still open mouth, and slashed Orestes' throat twice with a right hand that held a kitchen paring knife.

Espiritu rode the guard to the ground, left hand still clamped around the dying boy's mouth. After making sure he was dead, Espiritu wiped the knife blade on the boy's shirt and rose slowly, breathing in short harsh gasps. The hand with the knife, the right one, was rock steady. The left hand trembled. Some drool had formed in the left corner of his mouth and he absently licked it away.

"Jesus Christ, Al," Stallings said as he bent to pick up the guard's fallen M-16.

"What should I have done? Just nicked him a little?"

When Stallings made no answer, Espiritu held out his trembling left hand for the M-16. "I'll take that," he said.

"The fuck you will," Booth Stallings said.

•   •   •

At 6:45 that morning Otherguy Overby sat in his rented gray Toyota, waiting for the owner of the small auto repair garage to show up. The owner arrived at 6:59 A.M. in an aging four-wheel-drive Jeep whose enclosed cab looked homemade.

Overby got out of the Toyota and walked over to the garage owner. They walked around the Jeep together. Overby kicked two tires, nodded, reached into a pocket and handed over a roll of bills. The garage owner counted them rapidly. After he counted them again, more slowly this time, he gave Overby the key to the Jeep. Overby said something to the owner and indicated his parked Toyota sedan. The owner nodded indifferently. Overby climbed into the Jeep, started its engine, backed out of the garage drive and drove off.

By 7:18 A.M., Overby was again standing at the counter of the Orange Brutus fruit juice stand on Jones Avenue, breakfasting on coffee, juice and two freshly baked rolls. He was joined at 7:20 by Carmen Espiritu. She drank a single cup of coffee while Overby finished his second roll. They spoke only a few words. Both wore running shoes and blue jeans. His looked almost new; hers were old and faded. Above his jeans Overby wore a tan loose-fitting short-sleeved bush shirt with six pockets. She wore a dark blue cotton blouse with long sleeves. The blouse was buttoned to her neck.

At 7:30 A.M., Overby looked at his watch and said something to Carmen Espiritu. She reached down to pick up

the woven fiber reticule at her feet. It seemed heavy, but
Overby didn't offer to carry it. They walked to the rented Jeep
and got in. Overby started the engine and drove off in the
direction of the Guadalupe Mountains.

•   •   •

At 8:00 A.M., Artie Wu drove the blue Nissan van he had
just rented from Avis up to the entrance of the Magellan Hotel
where Quincy Durant and Georgia Blue waited. The van was
the panel kind with no side windows.

Georgia Blue climbed into the van and sat next to Artie Wu.
Durant slid back a side panel, lifted a cardboard box the size of
a beer case into the van and climbed in after it, sliding the
panel shut.

The van rolled out of the Magellan Hotel drive and turned
west, heading toward the Guadalupe Mountains.

•   •   •

The retired Colonel lay on his 67-year-old stomach 13 miles
west of Cebu City. He lay on a low ridge dotted with coconut
palms, clumps of bamboo, lush ferns, at least four kinds of
orchids and a dozen fine dipterocarp trees that somehow had
escaped the woodman's ax. Vaughn Crouch lay there, staring
down at the small stream that was spanned by a crudely built
bamboo bridge. The bridge was point B on the rough map
Artie Wu had given him.

The ridge on the other side of the stream was higher than the
one Crouch lay on by at least 15 meters—maybe even 20, he
decided. The opposite ridge also afforded excellent cover, thus
making the bridge and the stream it crossed, in Crouch's
opinion, prime ambush property. He smiled, thinking of Booth
Stallings. Well, Lieutenant, you sure must've learned something about bushwhacking from all those months you and old
Al spent in these hills. Because you sure as shit picked us a
doozy.

The big 23-year-old Filipino mercenary that Crouch had

promoted, almost on sight, to unofficial first sergeant, flopped down beside him, breathing hard from his climb up and down the two ridges.

"Get 'em all in place?" Crouch asked.

The first sergeant nodded, not wanting to waste breath on speech.

"Two hours on, two hours off?"

Again, the mercenary nodded and managed a yes.

"Same thing on this side, understand?"

"Sure."

"How d'you like it?" Crouch asked, giving the bridge and the stream a pleased nod. "Think it'll work?"

"Fuckin' A," the first sergeant said.

Crouch nodded his agreement, sat up and scooted backward until he could lean against the bole of a coconut palm. He pulled the blue gimme cap down low over his eyes, rested his right hand on his holstered .45-caliber semiautomatic, dropped his chin to his chest and told the first sergeant to wake him in two hours.

•　　•　　•

After 129 minutes of hard steady walking it was Booth Stallings who called for a stop. Only minutes after killing the guard, Espiritu abandoned the well-traveled path that led past the young stand of bamboo, and had taken what Stallings thought of as a goat track that headed down and mostly east.

Espiritu stopped and looked back. "You're soft, Booth."

"Not soft. Old."

"It's not far now."

"How far's not far?"

"Another two kilometers. Perhaps three."

Stallings used his already soaked handkerchief to mop sweat from his face. "Okay," he said. "Let's go."

It took them another 23 minutes to reach the stopping place, which was just below a barren rocky ridge. The goat track they had been following suddenly broadened into a steep rutted path that hugged the ridge's side.

"We stop here," Espiritu said.

Stallings looked around, not liking what he saw. "Couldn't you have picked something with shade?"

"I picked something better than shade," said Espiritu with a grin that Stallings thought knocked ten years off his age. "I chose air-conditioning." Espiritu gestured. "Just look around."

Stallings looked around, saw nothing of interest and shook his head.

"You're not only soft, Booth, but you've lost your eye and your memory's in rotten shape. You've been here before, you know."

Stallings looked around again but there was no recollection in his expression. "I give up."

"Crab meat," Espiritu said.

It came back to Stallings then, not in a flood, but in indistinct bits and pieces. It was like trying to remember an indifferent dream. He looked up, scanning the ridge carefully, and saw it—a black, irregularly shaped hole the size of an automobile tire.

"It was bigger then," he said. "Christ, it was ten times as big."

"We filled in the entrance," Espiritu said. "Come on."

The smaller man scrambled up the side of the ridge as if going up a flight of stairs. Stallings followed slowly, wary of the loose shale and rocks. He watched Espiritu duck and disappear into the black hole. Stallings made sure the M-16's safety was off, switched the weapon to automatic fire, and followed Espiritu into the cave.

It was almost as he remembered it, the cave that had been blasted out of solid metamorphic rock by Japanese combat engineers and used to store food. The roof was an irregular dome. The floor slanted up toward the rear. Its dimensions were approximately 15 feet wide by 10 feet high by 35 feet deep. The entrance hole provided perpetual twilight.

As he entered the cave, Stallings saw Espiritu squatting by a large cardboard box. He lifted out two plastic bottles. "Water," Espiritu said, reached back into the box and came up with a revolver. He smiled at Stallings. "Now we both have something to shoot with," he said, sticking the revolver down into the waistband of his pants and covering it with his shirt.

Stallings noticed it was at least 15 degrees cooler in the cave. Handing the shopping bag of food to Espiritu, he said, "You can fix lunch," and sat down, leaning against the cave wall. The M-16 in his lap was pointed in Espiritu's general direction.

From the shopping bag Espiritu took packets of newspaper-wrapped food. Some of them were grease-stained. "How many did we kill in here, Booth?" he asked, unwrapping a mound of cold rice. "Six? Seven?"

"Seven."

"With one grenade. Marvelous." He looked at Stallings. "And then you ate their crab meat." Espiritu chuckled. "There were cases and cases of it, remember? And you ate seven or eight cans."

"Poppy brand," Stallings said.

"What?"

"The cans had an orange poppy on them."

"I was wrong. Your memory's perfect."

"Selective," Stallings said. "I remember the irrelevant best. My seventh-grade junior high school locker number, for instance. Two-twelve. The combination of its lock. Ten right, twenty-five left, ten right."

"Remarkable," Espiritu murmured, unwrapping the last of the packets. He indicated the food with a small gesture.

"So. The perfect lunch. Rice, fish and fruit." He smiled. "Haven't forgotten how to eat with your fingers, have you?"

"No," said Stallings as he leaned forward and took a

handful of cold rice. "After I ate all that crab meat, I got sick. Remember?"

"Indeed."

"Well, I never touched crab again. Never. What I'm saying is that a trick memory like mine can't keep me from making a mistake." He smiled coldly at Espiritu. "But it sure as hell can keep me from making it twice."

*   *   *

Thirty minutes later they heard the low whistle from outside the cave. "They're here," Espiritu said.

"Who?"

Instead of answering, Espiritu imitated the whistle. Stallings could hear feet slipping and sliding on the shale and rocks. He shifted so that he could cover both Espiritu and the cave entrance with the M-16. "Who the fuck's out there, Al?"

"Friends."

The first friend through the cave entrance was Otherguy Overby, hot, sweaty and exasperated. Just behind him came Carmen Espiritu with her woven fiber reticule. She looked cool, fresh and exceedingly stern.

Overby glanced around, taking in the cave. As always, he remarked the obvious. "Christ, it's cool in here."

Booth Stallings aimed the M-16 at Overby and said, "What d'you say, Otherguy?"

"Not a hell of a lot." He nodded at Espiritu. "How're you, Al?"

"Very well, thank you, Mr. Overby," Espiritu said with a wry smile and turned to his wife. "Any difficulty?"

"Not yet."

"You sound as if you're expecting some."

"You have to make the choice."

Espiritu nodded slowly, looking first at Overby, then at Stallings. "Mr. Stallings has an automatic weapon with its safety off that he keeps aimed more or less in my direction. Mr. Overby does not. The choice seems obvious."

Carmen Espiritu's right hand went down into the woven fiber reticule. Espiritu turned away, as if to spare himself some unpleasant sight.

"Sorry," Carmen Espiritu said to Overby.

Otherguy Overby's face turned still and remote as he nodded at some private conclusion and backed up two careful steps.

Booth Stallings kept his gaze on Espiritu. He watched him turn away and then spin back, aiming the revolver he had taken from the cardboard box at his young wife.

Stallings opened his mouth to yell, but Carmen Espiritu had already seen the pistol. If rage hadn't driven her to curse her husband, she might have had time enough to tug her own weapon from the reticule. But it snagged on something and Alejandro Espiritu shot her twice—first in the chest and again, lower down, in the midsection. The two rounds drove her back against the cave wall, which provided enough support to keep her standing for a moment or two, looking far more surprised than hurt. She then pitched forward onto her face.

Carmen Espiritu twitched two or three times after she fell and then lay still. Overby was pressing both hands against his ears as if they hurt. Espiritu had clapped his left hand to his left ear, but his right hand still held the revolver. Because Booth Stallings had opened his mouth to yell just as Espiritu fired, his ears didn't bother him. Both his M-16 and his eyes were still trained on Espiritu.

Seconds passed before anyone spoke or took their hands down from their ears. The first to speak was Espiritu whose voice sounded even more Kansas and toneless than usual, as if he couldn't quite hear what he was saying.

He used the flat voice to deliver a kind of eulogy about his dead wife. "Carmen had many fine qualities and one glaring fault," he said. "She thought everyone was a damned fool. Except her."

Another silence followed. Overby cleared his throat, but said nothing and kept his expression cold, remote and wary.

When Booth Stallings spoke, it was in a tone he might have used if speaking to the slightly deaf. "I'll take that now, Al."

Alejandro Espiritu looked down at the revolver in his right hand, as though faintly surprised it was still there. He smiled and pointed it at Booth Stallings. "No, Booth," he said, as if addressing a child. "I don't think so."

There was another silence as Stallings and Espiritu stared at each other. Without looking at Otherguy Overby, Espiritu gave him instructions. "Take his rifle, please, Mr. Overby."

Overby, his face a study in neutrality, shook his head. "It's not my play."

"Well," Espiritu said. "We seem to have a—what do they call it—a Spanish standoff."

"Mexican," said Overby.

"Yes, Mexican," Espiritu said and stuck his revolver back into the waistband of his pants. He looked up quickly at Stallings. "Tell me, Booth. Am I the mistake you don't intend to repeat?"

"You're it, Al," Booth Stallings said.

CHAPTER THIRTY-SIX

They came out of the cave, Overby first, Espiritu second and then Booth Stallings who kept his M-16 pointed at the Filipino. They left the dead Carmen Espiritu where she lay, next to the empty cardboard box.

After walking nearly a kilometer along a steep rutted track that was not quite a road, they reached Overby's rented Jeep. "You could've driven closer, Mr. Overby," Espiritu said.

"If I had, I couldn't've turned around," Overby said as he slipped behind the wheel and watched curiously to see how Booth Stallings would climb into the Jeep's small rear seat without exposing his back to Espiritu.

Stallings managed by backing through the Jeep's flimsy homemade door and into the rear seat. Espiritu, half-smiling, climbed into the seat next to Overby.

The rutted track was still so narrow it took Overby four back-and-fill tries before he got the Jeep turned around. He drove down the track slowly, never more than 15 miles per hour, hugging the right side of the ridge. To the left was a sheer drop of at least 300 feet.

Stallings leaned forward and asked, "So why'd you kill her, Al?"

"To keep myself alive," he said, turning to look at Stallings. "It was all her idea—having someone pay me five million to go into exile. Carmen's scheme was that I'd go to Hong Kong, grab the five million, use it to buy arms and then slip back into the country."

"Sounds okay," Overby said.

"She'd go to Hong Kong with me, naturally."

Overby grunted. "Bad idea."

Espiritu smiled his agreement. "I suspected that if she did, I'd suddenly be leaving behind a very rich widow. But I told her to go ahead and make the initial contact."

"Who with?" Stallings asked.

"Ernesto Pineda. He was a devious sort from up in Baguio who sometimes worked for us—and sometimes for his third cousin who'd be putting up the money."

"This third cousin with all the millions," Overby said. "You happen to remember his name?"

"Ferdinand Marcos—who else," Stallings answered, deciding that the world was far more deceptive and dangerous than he had ever supposed. It was Wu and Durant's kind of world. And Otherguy's, of course.

Espiritu, still turned around in the front seat, looked at

Stallings with something like approval. "So you didn't really believe that nonsense about it being an American business consortium?"

Stallings only shrugged.

Espiritu nodded sympathetically. "Americans always seem to be swinging from utter naïveté to raging paranoia and back again. But how could anybody believe a group of hardheaded American businessmen would spend one peso, let alone five million dollars, to get rid of me? I'm their blessed communist menace, Booth, that doesn't cost them a cent. I'm what's going to justify the coup that'll dump Aquino and get things back to normal where deals can be cut and profits made."

"If I was them, I'd pay you to stay on," Overby said.

"Precisely."

"And Marcos?" Stallings asked.

"As usual, he's being more subtle. Maybe too subtle. He's only agreed to pay me to go into exile. But he thinks he knows what I'll really do once I get my hands on the money. He thinks I'll buy weapons, sneak back here and raise hell. That, I suppose, is our unspoken agreement. The rest is foolishness."

"And Marcos will wind up financing the NPA."

"He prefers to think he's financing a quick coup."

"What would you really do, Al—with the money?"

Espiritu smiled. "I'm still not quite sure."

Hungry for details, Overby asked, "So it was Carmen who worked out the deal with the cousin, what's his name, Pineda?"

"Yes," Espiritu said.

"Then what?"

"After the five million was transferred to Luxembourg—I think it was Luxembourg—Marcos could no longer control it. So Carmen quite sensibly executed the cousin who, after all, was our only real link with Marcos. She had a good mind, did Carmen."

"The guy in Washington, Harry Crites," Stallings said.

"The one who recruited me. Does he know whose money it really is?"

"No."

"Then who—" Stallings said, but was interrupted by Overby who had a question of his own. "Now which way?"

Espiritu turned around to look. They had reached a fork in the track. "To the right," Espiritu said, "and I'd like to make a comfort stop, if you don't mind."

"Up around that bend okay?"

"Perfect," Espiritu said.

When the Jeep was around the bend, Overby pulled it over to the edge of the track that had almost widened into a road. Espiritu got out and walked over to a thick wall of tropical foliage where he stood with his back to the Jeep. Stallings climbed out, slung his M-16 over his right shoulder, and joined him. Overby, now out of the Jeep, leaned against its front right fender and waited.

As they stood urinating, Espiritu said, "Remember my definition of terrorism, Booth?"

"Sure. Politics by extreme intimidation."

"You said it needed work."

"Still does."

Espiritu zipped up his fly. "What about: 'Politics without moral compunction'?"

Stallings thought about it as he zipped up his own fly. He shook his head and said, "That doesn't quite cut it either."

"I really don't have any, you know," Espiritu said. "Any moral compunction."

Stallings turned to find Espiritu aiming the revolver at him.

"Well, shit, Al," Stallings said.

"This will simplify things."

Stallings looked at Otherguy Overby who still leaned against the Jeep's right front fender. "Guess you'd like things simple too, Otherguy."

Overby's only reply was his remote, sealed-off look.

"You want to turn around, Booth?" Espiritu asked.

Stallings thought about it and was surprised by his decision. "Yes, by God. I think I do."

Stallings turned slowly, discovering that of all places, Cebu was absolutely the last place he'd have chosen to die. He was almost completely turned around when he heard the two shots. They were fired so closely together they sounded like one. He tensed, waiting for the pain, even as his mind told him there would be none—not if he'd heard the shots. Finally, he turned to find Alejandro Espiritu sprawled facedown in the dirt, part of the right side of his head gone. The second round had made a hole dead center in the back of his blue shirt.

Otherguy Overby, the pistol he had paid $500 for on Pier Three dangling from his right hand, stared down at the dead Espiritu from less than six feet away.

He looked up at Stallings. "I don't guess I've got a whole lot of moral compunction either," Overby said.

"You've got enough," Stallings said.

They heard the unmistakable sound of a Jeepney's diesel engine long before it chugged around the bend in the road and came to a stop. Five armed men scrambled out. Stallings recognized them as five of the young guards who had been posted around the perimeter of the Espiritu compound.

Minnie Espiritu was the last one out of the Jeepney. She climbed down slowly from the rear, wearing her bright red slacks and a black cotton sweater. In her right hand was a machine pistol—an Ingram, Stallings saw, wondering where she had got it. She nodded at Stallings, gave Overby a sour look and walked over to where her brother lay dead.

She stared down at him for several moments before looking up at Stallings and Overby. "Which one of you killed him?"

When neither answered, she said, "Whoever it was saved me the trouble." She looked back down at Espiritu. "We found Carmen in that silly cave of his. He kill her?"

"Yes," said Stallings.

"He would." She sighed heavily. "That Orestes kid, too?"

"Him, too."

She shook her head, as if in disbelief. "The kid was my son. Picture that? Alejandro killing his own nephew?" She turned to look at both men again. "Yeah, I think you can picture that."

She sighed again, even more heavily than before, and said, "He went bad by stages, you know. Not all of a sudden." She looked at Overby. "Think he might've had a tumor on the brain or something?"

"I couldn't say," Overby replied.

Minnie Espiritu indicated the M-16 that was still slung over Stallings' right shoulder. "That Orestes' piece?"

He nodded.

"I'll take it unless you wanta come help out with the revolution."

"No, thanks," Stallings said, unslinging the rifle and handing it to her. She gave it to one of the young guards and said something in Cebuano. The five young guards turned and headed toward the Jeepney.

Minnie Espiritu gave her dead brother a long look, turned to nod goodbye at Overby and Stallings, and started after the young guards. She turned back at Stallings' question. "What do you want to do with Al, Minnie?"

She gave her brother one quick final glance. "The wild pigs'll eat him by noon," she said, turned and slowly walked to the Jeepney. After she climbed into its rear, the Jeepney bumped off down the rough road.

Otherguy Overby, ever literal, said, "There aren't any wild pigs up here."

"So?"

"So is that what they say when they don't want to say, 'Who gives a fuck?' "

"How would I know?" Booth Stallings said.

CHAPTER
THIRTY-SEVEN

It was 10:29 that morning and already sweltering hot when Artie Wu ran out of road. He had driven the rented Avis van as close as possible to point B on Booth Stallings' map, but the point still remained some four kilometers away. The mountain road Wu had followed out of Cebu City had disintegrated into a rutted trail two kilometers back. He stopped the van when the trail suddenly narrowed into a trace just wide enough for two small goats or one fairly large human.

He turned to Georgia Blue who sat beside him, studying the crude map. "This it?" Wu asked.

She nodded. "This is it."

Without turning his head, Wu spoke to Durant who sat on the floor in the van's seatless rear. "What d'you think, Quincy?"

"I think we should eat."

"I think you're right," Wu said.

•　　•　　•

After they finished the box lunches provided by the Magellan Hotel, Artie Wu reached into the cardboard carton Durant had loaded into the van that morning and removed a three-inch stack of Filipino 50-peso notes that was bound with a rubber band. He also took out a 35mm Minolta camera.

"Here," Wu said, handing the camera to Georgia Blue who gave it a brief inspection before placing it in her shoulder bag.

Wu divided the stack of 50-peso notes into guessed-at halves, giving one half to Durant who folded the currency and stuck it down into a hip pocket where it created a noticeable bulge. Wu slipped his own unfolded half into his right pants pocket.

"Okay," Artie Wu said, "we'll take it slow and easy and try not to hurt anybody."

"These guys are pros, Artie," Georgia Blue said.

"Then we'll try not to kill anybody." He looked at Durant. "You going to flank from right or left?"

"From the right, I think," Durant said, moved ten feet off the trace and began inspecting what seemed to be an impenetrable barrier of green and black tropical rain forest. Georgia Blue used two seconds to give the contents of her shoulder bag a final check. When she looked up, Durant had disappeared.

"Still the show-off, I see," she said to Artie Wu.

Wu smiled. "Why hide hidden talent?" He nodded at the trace that led into the rain forest. "Point or drag?"

"You giving me a choice?"

Wu nodded.

"Then I'll take drag."

Wu took out and inspected the five-shot revolver provided by Vaughn Crouch, shoved it back down into his right hip pocket, hitched his pants up over his big belly and strolled off down the trace, as if beginning his regular morning constitutional.

Georgia Blue slipped her right hand down into her shoulder bag and waited until Wu was 20 feet away. She followed after him then, walking with an athletic stride so smooth and effortless that her heels seemed to make almost no contact with the ground.

•   •   •

They walked like that for 21 minutes, Artie Wu in the lead, Georgia Blue 20 feet or so behind him, both moving at an unhurried but steady 105 paces a minute, both listening in vain for Durant on their right flank, but hearing only the fuck-you geckos and the scolding of angry birds.

Wu was wondering for the third or fourth time how such deep cool-looking shade could produce such insufferable heat when he heard the man's voice shout the order.

"Freeze, Wu!"

Wu stopped but didn't freeze. Instead, he raised his hands and turned slowly around. Ten feet away Weaver P. Jordan was in what Artie Wu always thought of as the TV Crouch: wide stance, knees bent, both hands holding the weapon—in this case a revolver with a three- or four-inch barrel.

"Morning," Wu said just as Georgia Blue slipped out of the tropical rain forest and struck Jordan from the rear with a left-handed chopping blow that immobilized his left arm. Despite the pain, Jordan tried to swing his right arm around and bring the revolver into play. It seemed to be exactly what Georgia Blue expected. She grabbed his right wrist and brought it down and then up behind him, giving it a twist that dislocated the elbow. Jordan went to his knees, dropping the revolver. Georgia Blue kicked it away and then stamped on his left hand which he was using for support. Jordan collapsed, howling.

Just as the howl died away, Wu heard something metallic off to his right that sounded like the slide being pulled back on some kind of automatic weapon. With his hands still raised, Wu turned left just in time to see Durant use a stick to knock a machine pistol out of the hands of a man who wore what appeared to be designer jungle fatigues. The man wearing the camouflage fatigues was the elegant Jack Cray.

Although disarmed, Jack Cray was undismayed. He dropped into a slight crouch, both hands extended and weaving around in some kind of martial arts stance that apparently puzzled Durant who dropped his stick and backed up. With an odd wordless cry, Jack Cray leaped at Durant, trying for a knuckled jab to the throat. Durant slipped it easily and gave Cray a hard open-palm slap to the right ear.

"Fuckhead," Cray said, abandoning his martial arts stance to put a soothing palm to the boxed ear.

"I'll look after Mr. Cray, Quincy," Artie Wu said with a solicitous smile. "You go tend to Mr. Jordan."

"What's wrong with him?" Durant asked.

"Georgia dislocated his elbow," Wu said. "At least, I hope that's all she did."

•   •   •

Weaver P. Jordan looked up at Durant and said, "Will it hurt?"

"For a second."

"Then fix it."

With Wu, Georgia Blue and Cray looking on, Durant placed both hands on Jordan's right arm—one on the bicep, the other on the forearm. "Look away, if you want to," he told Jordan.

Jordan looked away just as Durant pulled so quickly his audience wasn't even sure it heard the soft pop as the elbow was snapped back into place. Jordan howled again.

When he was through howling he glared at Jack Cray and said, "Trust her, you said. She's practically one of us, you said."

"I was obviously wrong," Cray said and turned to Wu. "So where does all this leave us?"

"At a point of mutual distrust," Wu said with a beaming smile.

Weaver Jordan got to his feet, glaring now at Georgia Blue. "You worked us pretty slick, Georgia."

"Assholes are always easy," she said.

"Everything is not lost, gentlemen," Wu said, turning to Durant. "Wouldn't you agree, Quincy?"

"Plenty of glory to go around."

Jack Cray raised an elegant eyebrow. "What form does this glory take?"

"Human form," Durant said. "Alejandro Espiritu."

The raised eyebrow dropped back into place as Cray

narrowed his eyes, giving his face an almost crafty look. The expression made Durant reflect that the only thing worse than being half-dumb was being half-smart.

"You want to sell us Espiritu?" Cray said.

Artie Wu looked almost hurt. "Sell him? Good Lord, no. He's a gift—from all of us to all of you."

"A gift?" Jordan said. "For free, you mean?"

"If it's not for free, Weaver," said Durant, "it's not a gift."

Jordan worried over Durant's clarification as if it were a particularly abstruse concept. "I guess I don't hang out enough with swifties like you."

"Just why," Jack Cray asked, "are you giving us Espiritu if, in fact, you are?"

"Bullshit aside?" Wu said.

Cray nodded.

"Because we'd like to spend our money without the Federales peering over our shoulders."

Jack Cray nodded approvingly. "At last, a half-sensible answer."

Which is all, Durant thought, a half-smart question deserves.

CHAPTER THIRTY-EIGHT

Thirty-one minutes later the five of them reached the crude bamboo bridge that spanned the stream that flowed between the two steep ridges. It was point B on Booth Stallings' rough map and Jack Cray, looking around, didn't at all like what he saw.

"Who picked this place?" Cray asked.

"Why?" Durant said.

"It's a perfect trap."

Durant looked up and around, nodding in what seemed to be surprised agreement. "I believe it is."

"So who picked it?"

"Espiritu, probably."

Jack Cray raked one ridge with his eyes, turned and did the same to the other one. "There're bandits up on those ridges, aren't there?"

"Why do you say that?" Artie Wu asked.

"Because you can feel the fuckers, that's why," Weaver P. Jordan said. "Because when some guy's got a bead on you, you damn well sense it."

Jack Cray moved as close to Artie Wu as he could without touching him. "Who's up there, damn it?"

Wu sighed. "Mercenaries."

"Mercenaries! Whose mercenaries?"

"They could be ours. Possibly Espiritu's. Maybe even yours. It all depends."

The shock appeared first in Cray's eyes, popping them wide, and then flowed down to his mouth, giving him a dim, slack-jawed look. When he asked his question, it was in a low monotone that shock had robbed of all expression, even the normal rising inflection. "That was just a shuck about giving us Espiritu, wasn't it?"

Wu gave the far ridge his own long look before replying. "There's a small problem with that," he admitted. "You see, to keep the mercenaries away from Espiritu and their hands off whatever price is now on his head, we had to promise them a couple of profitable hostages."

Weaver Jordan turned apoplectic red. His voice was a shout. "Us? You promised them me and him?"

"You were handy," Georgia Blue said.

Durant studied the glassy-eyed Cray and the crimson-faced

Jordan. "How much would Langley pop for you two?" he asked. "A rough guess."

Cray answered as if by rote. "Not a dime. The agency will not negotiate with terrorists."

"No one need ever know," Wu said.

"You'd know," said Weaver Jordan.

Artie Wu nodded sadly. "Yes, I suppose we would, wouldn't we?" There was a silence and then Wu smiled, as if suddenly struck by an idea so wise and wonderful that it bordered on pure inspiration. "You could, of course—" Wu broke off. "Well, never mind."

"We could what?" Cray asked.

"You could make your own deal with them." Wu turned to Durant. "What d'you think, Quincy?"

Durant appeared to give it some thought. "Sure. Why not?"

"Georgia?" Wu asked.

"It'd be better than your playing hostage up in the hills for a year or six months," she said to Cray and Jordan. "Unless you're both crazy about fishheads and rice."

Resignation spread across Cray's face, erasing the last vestige of shock. Cynicism, in the form of a slight smile, moved in to replace resignation. "Isn't this where I ask: I don't suppose they take American Express?"

Wu's frown was one of deep concern. "Money does present a problem."

"But not an insurmountable one, right?" Cray said.

Wu looked a question at Durant who nodded his answer. "Yes, well, I suppose Quincy and I could lend you the money and you could give us an IOU or something."

"A promissory note would be best," Durant said.

"You fucks," said Weaver Jordan.

Jack Cray again looked first at one ridge, then the other, turned to Wu and said, "Write it out."

Wu smiled at Georgia Blue. "Georgia."

She reached into her shoulder bag and removed an envelope.

From the envelope she took a thrice-folded sheet of bond paper, which she unfolded and handed to Jack Cray.

He looked at it. "Neatly typed, I see."

"What's it say?" Weaver Jordan asked.

"It's headed 'Promissory Note' and then it says, 'For value received we promise to pay to Arthur Case Wu and Quincy Durant on demand the sum of forty-eight thousand Filipino pesos or twenty-four hundred U.S. dollars with simple interest accruing at the rate of six percent per annum.' And then there're places to fill in the date and sign our names."

"Who's got a pen?" Weaver Jordan asked. "I'll sign the fucker."

Georgia Blue silently handed him a ballpoint pen. Using Durant's back as a desk, Jordan signed his name with a flourish and handed the promissory note to Cray who glared at Wu. "We're signing under duress, of course."

Wu smiled politely. "We'll let the lawyers argue about that, should it ever come up."

Cray signed, handed the note to Wu and said, "Okay. Let's get it over with."

Durant turned toward the far ridge, took a white handkerchief from his pocket and waved it back and forth above his head.

"What the fuck're you doing?" Weaver Jordan said.

"Surrendering, what else?" Durant said.

•   •   •

Up on the far ridge, Vaughn Crouch grinned down at the handkerchief-waving Durant, turned to his temporary first sergeant and said, "Well, son, you know what to do."

"Right," the first sergeant said.

•   •   •

Barking out his orders, the first sergeant had lined up his 23 armed mercenaries in two neat rows near the bamboo bridge. Twelve men stood at near attention in the front row; 11 in the rear. Weaver Jordan and Jack Cray were the paymasters. Carrying the thick stack of Filipino 50-peso notes, Cray counted out 2,000 pesos at a time. He handed each payment to Jordan who in turn handed it with his undamaged right arm to the next mercenary in line. The first sergeant approved each payment with a grunt and a nod.

When Cray and Jordan were halfway down the front row, Georgia Blue took the 35mm Minolta from her shoulder bag and began snapping pictures of the payments. Jack Cray stopped, turned and started to say something, but changed his mind when the first sergeant clapped a large but gentle hand on his shoulder. Georgia Blue captured Cray with his mouth open and the first sergeant's hand on his shoulder.

After the last mercenary was paid, Cray and Jordan walked over to Wu and Durant, accompanied by the first sergeant.

"Now what?" Cray said.

"Well, we come now to the glory part," Wu said. "You and Mr. Jordan will escort these brave ex–NPA freedom fighters back to Cebu City where they'll meekly surrender to the proper authorities. Just how the CIA talked them down out of the hills we'll leave to your imagination. But whatever you guys dream up, they'll swear to. Right, Sergeant?"

"Absolutely," the first sergeant said.

There was a silence that went on and on until Jordan looked at Jack Cray and said, "You know. It just might work."

After a moment, Cray nodded and looked at Durant. "What else?"

"One last item," Durant said. "If ever asked, you know nothing about anyone called Wu, Stallings, Overby, Blue or Durant. Nothing pertinent anyhow."

Cray turned the threat over in his mind. "If we know nothing about you," he said slowly, "then you can't know anything about us, can you? And you'd have no use for that promissory note or the photos."

"What a good boy," said the beaming look that Artie Wu

gave Jack Cray. Aloud, he said, "And thus we all arrive safely at the perfect stalemate."

"Otherwise known as mutual blackmail," Durant said.

"I like détente better," Weaver Jordan said.

Wu beamed again. "Then we'll call it détente."

•   •   •

They came out of the tropical rain forest at 3:31 P.M., both limping a little, Otherguy Overby in the lead, Booth Stallings a dozen or so feet behind. They saw the bamboo bridge first and then, a little to the right of it, seated in the shade of some flourishing nipa palms, Wu, Durant and Georgia Blue.

Durant was up first and trotted toward Overby who stopped and waited for him. "Where the hell is he?" Durant demanded.

"Right behind me the last I looked," Overby said and turned to find Booth Stallings moving slowly toward him. "Yeah. There he is."

Durant waited patiently until Stallings joined them. "I mean Espiritu."

"Oh," Overby said. "Him. Well, he couldn't make it."

"Espiritu's dead," said Stallings.

"What happened?"

Neither Overby nor Stallings apparently wanted to speak first. Finally, Stallings said, "We'd like to sit down in some shade, have a drink of water and maybe a sip of whiskey, if anybody's got any, and then I'll tell you what happened. And if Otherguy doesn't like my version, he can tell his."

•   •   •

They sat in a row in the shade of the flourishing nipa palms, three big wide-eyed kids named Wu, Durant and Blue, listening transfixed to the tale told at storytime in the jungle kindergarten. At least, that's how Otherguy Overby would later remember it.

Stallings, the tale teller, began with the death of Alejandro

Espiritu's nephew, Orestes; continued with the death of Carmen Espiritu in the cave; reached his climax with the death of Espiritu himself ("Otherguy shot him twice in the back before old Al shot me. Afterward, Otherguy felt a little bad about it but I sure as hell didn't"); and ended with the arrival of Minnie Espiritu and her five young guards.

When Stallings was done with his story, he asked, "Anybody think to bring a bottle?"

Georgia Blue reached into her apparently bottomless shoulder bag and produced a half-liter of Black and White Scotch, which she handed to Stallings. He twisted off the cap, had a long swallow and passed it to Overby who drank and offered it to Artie Wu who shook his head. So did Durant. Overby gave the bottle back to Georgia Blue and then crept into his private sealed-off place to wait and see who would get blamed for what.

Wu looked at Overby and nodded sympathetically. "Is that about what happened, Otherguy?"

"That's it."

"So what d'you think went wrong?"

"Overall?"

Wu nodded.

Overby thought before answering. "You came up with a real smart plan, Artie. One of your best. Maybe a little tricky here and there, and maybe a little too egg-crated, but what the hell, there was a big score involved and none of us, except you and Durant, have worked together for a while. So that was okay. And everybody was given a job to do and, as far as I can tell, everybody did their job—except one person."

"Who?" Durant asked.

Although sweat still flowed down over Overby's face, the smile he gave Durant was one of chilly disapproval. "Espiritu. You guys sort of forgot to give him the whole script. Especially the last act. If you had, well, maybe, things would've turned out better."

"Maybe," Artie Wu said. "Maybe not." He leaned toward

Overby, his expression frankly curious. "What if you hadn't shot him, Otherguy?"

Overby sighed. "Well, Booth here'd be dead and I—well, I probably could've been five million bucks richer." He paused. "Two and a half million anyway."

Durant glared at him. "You were going solo, weren't you?"

Overby returned the glare. "Was I?"

Artie Wu smiled. "Let's assume the thought crossed your mind—fleetingly, of course."

Overby only shrugged.

Booth Stallings looked at Overby with a wry fond smile. "That was a hell of a choice you made, Otherguy."

Overby nodded. "Well, I made it," he said. "And now I'll just have to live with it."

CHAPTER
THIRTY-NINE

When Booth Stallings came down to breakfast at 6:30 the next morning after three and a half hours' sleep, the only other customer in the Magellan Hotel's Zugbu restaurant was the retired Colonel, Vaughn Crouch. Stallings helped himself to rice, fruit and scrambled eggs from the breakfast buffet and sat down at Crouch's table.

"What time'd you get back?" Crouch asked, spearing the last piece of ham on his plate.

"A little before three this morning."

"I got back yesterday afternoon—around four-thirty."

"You didn't have to walk as far."

"The rest of your bunch sleeping in?"

Stallings nodded and tried some of the eggs, which tasted like eggs had tasted when he was a child.

"Then I guess they haven't seen this yet," Crouch said, handing Stallings a Cebu City morning newspaper. "My kids made the front page," he announced proudly. "Had themselves a hell of a time."

Booth Stallings read the headline first, which claimed in 48-point Bodoni bold italics across three columns: 'SURRENDER' REPORT DISPUTED. He then read the story, or at least its first three paragraphs:

> CEBU CITY—Yesterday's surrender of 24 rebels in Catmon Town, north of this city, was immediately branded as an "elaborate psy-war operation run by the CIA and the army's Regional Unified Command to demoralize revolutionary forces."
>
> The statement challenging the alleged surrender was issued by the Cebu Provincial Operational Command of the New People's Army (POC-NPA) and signed by "Commander Min," the nom de guerre (war name) of Miss Minerva Espiritu, sister of NPA legend, Alejandro Espiritu.
>
> The 24 alleged rebels who "defected" yesterday were accompanied by two men eyewitnesses described as "European males." Catmon Town police refused to identify the two European males and later denied their existence.

Stallings gave up on the story, handed the paper to Crouch and went back to his breakfast. After another forkful of eggs, he said, "Where were you?"

The retired Colonel grinned. "Once I shadowed the kids and those two Langley shitbirds down from the hills, I kind of disappeared." He indicated the newspaper. "Sure you don't want to finish the story?" he said. "It gets better."

"Who cares?" Stallings said and pushed his breakfast plate away.

Crouch slipped on his trifocals to give Stallings a closer inspection. "Something happened, didn't it—up in the hills?"

Stallings nodded. "Al got himself killed. I guess you could call that something—something you'd better not tell anyone."

"By God. Old Al," Crouch said, leaned back in his chair, took off his glasses and stared off into blurred nothingness for almost a minute. "Well, I think he was just about due, don't you?"

"I don't think Al thought so," Booth Stallings said.

•   •   •

At a few minutes after nine that morning, Otherguy Overby came out of the entrance to the Magellan Hotel, heading for the air-conditioned hotel van that would take him, Wu, Durant, Stallings and Georgia Blue to the Cebu airport and the eleven o'clock flight to Manila.

Something blue, yellow and black caught his eye. It was the Rotary Club of Metro Cebu's four-question billboard whose fourth question still wondered: "Will it be BENEFICIAL to all concerned?"

"All but one," Overby replied, surprised that he had spoken aloud and even more surprised to find Artie Wu standing just behind him. Wu looked where Overby had been looking, read the Rotary Club billboard and smiled.

"In Manila, Otherguy," Wu said, "we'll talk about it."

"What?" Overby said.

"The correct answer to question four."

•   •   •

Booth Stallings was assigned a window seat on the port side of the Philippine Airlines plane. Next to him sat Quincy Durant. Across the aisle were Georgia Blue and Artie Wu. Otherguy Overby sat by himself in an aisle seat two rows forward.

After the plane gained altitude, Stallings stared down at the long green skinny tropical island of Cebu until he could no longer see it. As he leaned back in his seat, Durant lowered his newspaper and said, "Did you find it?"

"What?"

"Whatever you were looking for."

"I was looking for a nineteen-year-old second john who went in on an I and R patrol armed with a carbine, six grenades and the collected poems of Rupert Brooke."

"And?"

"I found him."

"How was he?"

Stallings turned to look at Durant. "Older. That's all. Just older."

"And wiser?"

"Not so you'd notice."

•   •   •

At 12:06 P.M. that day, Quincy Durant walked into the Manila International Airport's main entrance concourse. Ahead of him were Artie Wu and Otherguy Overby. Just behind him were Booth Stallings and Georgia Blue. At 12:07 P.M., he was arrested by the Manila homicide detective who had two of the smartest brown eyes Durant had ever seen.

As another detective snapped the handcuffs on, Durant said, "May I ask why?"

"No," said Lt. Hermenegildo Cruz.

"May I call a lawyer?"

"No."

"What about my rights, such as they are?"

Lt. Cruz smiled, as if enjoying the exchange. "What rights?"

Artie Wu had now turned back and was striding toward Durant when a third detective stepped in front of him, blocking the way. Wu stopped and glared down at the five-foot-seven detective with such menace that a fourth detective hurried over to form a two-man barrier.

Lt. Cruz led Durant over to where Wu stood, still blocked by the two detectives. "You wanted to say something?" Lt. Cruz asked.

With as much bombast as he could manage, Wu said, "You can't do that—he's an American citizen."

"Dear God, I had no idea," Lt. Cruz said as he led Durant away.

      •   •   •

Two of the plainclothes detectives put the still handcuffed Durant into the front seat of a black Nissan Maxima and waited until Lt. Cruz slipped behind the wheel. The detectives then melted away into a small crowd of airport gawkers who had gathered to see whether something awful would happen to Durant.

Lt. Cruz backed the Maxima out of a parking space whose stenciled sign claimed it was reserved for the assistant airport manager. Neither man spoke until they were well past the airport and turning into EDSA.

It was then that Lt. Cruz said, "I think I'll charge you with the murder of your lady friend, Emily Cariaga."

"I notice this isn't the way to police headquarters," Durant said.

"I could build a very tight case against you—opportunity, motive, all that."

"A crime of passion, right?"

"What else?"

"You can take the cuffs off now."

"Later," Cruz said and drove on in silence except for the sound of his horn, which he honked every four seconds regardless of need. "I know who killed her," Lt. Cruz said after four blocks of verbal silence.

"So do I."

Lt. Cruz flicked a glance at Durant and then looked back at

the traffic, which he decided could use another toot from his horn. "How long've you known?"

"Days."

"And you didn't come forward."

"I was busy."

"Down in Cebu."

"Yes."

"A pleasure trip, wasn't it?"

"Strictly business."

There was another silence, four blocks long this time, until Lt. Cruz said, "I know who killed her but I can't prove it."

"I probably can," Durant said, "but it'll have to be done my way."

"That would pose some rather delicate problems."

"Not as delicate as the one you've already got."

"I'll think about it," Lt. Cruz said.

"You've got until eight tomorrow morning."

"What happens then?"

"I fly to Hong Kong."

Lt. Cruz said nothing. Instead, he turned off EDSA and onto Ayala Avenue, which led into the heart of Manila's financial district. It was down Ayala Avenue that Mrs. Aquino's white-collar and middle-class supporters had liked to parade.

Lt. Cruz drove past the Ritz Tower on the right and the Rustan's department store on the left. After he drove past Fonda Street and the Rizal Theatre and crossed Makati Avenue, Durant said, "My hotel's back there, the Peninsula."

"I know," Lt. Cruz said but didn't slow the car until he reached the Associated Bank Building and pulled over to a stop. A man of about 30, wearing a Hawaiian shirt, silently opened Cruz's door. The shirt covered but didn't conceal the gun lump on the man's right hip. After Lt. Cruz climbed out of the car the man slipped behind the wheel.

Durant was now on the sidewalk and staring up at the building when Lt. Cruz joined him. "A bank," Durant said.

"A bank," Lt. Cruz agreed and used a nod to indicate they

should go inside where they rode an elevator to the fifth floor, walked down a long corridor, went through a door with no name on it and into a receptionist's office that contained no receptionist. Lt. Cruz crossed the small room to a dark slab door and knocked. A voice behind the door said, "Enter."

"That means you," Lt. Cruz said.

"I'm still flying to Hong Kong at eight tomorrow."

"I'll talk to you long before then," Lt. Cruz said and removed the cuffs from Durant's wrists.

Durant nodded at the slab door. "Does what you do depend on who's in there?"

After a moment, Lt. Cruz answered with a slight nod.

Durant turned, opened the door and entered a large office whose furniture consisted of two gray metal chairs. One of them had arms; the other didn't. In the one without arms sat a woman in her middle thirties who wore a dark blue dress that looked like silk.

Before Durant could say anything the woman said, "We met once at Emily's."

"I remember."

She indicated the chair with arms. "Please."

Durant sat down, deciding she was easy to remember because of her eyes and mouth. The eyes were far too large and much too sad. Her mouth was too full, too wide and too melancholy. Emily Cariaga had claimed that men made fools of themselves just to see if they could make that wide mouth smile.

Durant also remembered that before being richly wed, the seated woman had been expensively educated in Switzerland and Dublin. She also had two children, played the piano well, wrote moody quatrains and spent just one hell of a lot of money on clothes. And now, he thought, she's going to tell you who she really is and why you're meeting in a room with two chairs and no witnesses.

"First, let me apologize for what must've been the rudeness

at the airport," she said in her low contralto whose slight Filipino accent was flavored with a hint of Gaelic.

Durant nodded but said nothing.

"We've been receiving reports from Cebu about your dealings with Alejandro Espiritu."

"We?"

"The government."

"The Aquino government?"

Her large eyes grew even larger. "You don't think that—"

"I don't think anything."

"The government is anxious to . . . to neutralize Alejandro Espiritu. It's our understanding that he's been offered twenty million U.S. dollars to exile himself to Singapore."

She paused as if waiting for Durant's confirmation or denial. When he offered neither, she said, "You're making this very difficult, Mr. Durant."

"I'm listening."

"The government would have no objection if Espiritu were to exile himself to wherever he chooses, providing, of course, that he is not supplied with funds to purchase arms."

"Like Aguinaldo was."

She almost smiled. "Yes, like Aguinaldo."

"What you seem to be looking for is another crooked British consul like the one who cheated Aguinaldo out of his money."

"You know your Filipino history, Mr. Durant."

"Not really."

"He need not be British," she said. "He could also keep the twenty million dollars."

"What if I say no thanks."

"Oh dear. I do hope you're not refusing."

"I'm exploring the alternatives."

"If you refuse, we'll simply have to charge you with poor Emily's death."

"I don't think so."

"I didn't say convict you. I said charge you. It could be terribly . . . well, inconvenient."

Durant smiled sympathetically. "You're not very good at this yet, are you?"

She looked away. "Not really."

"It takes practice."

She looked back at him coldly. "As does everything worthwhile."

"Well, to begin with, it's not twenty million, it's five million, and the exile's to Hong Kong, not Singapore."

A hard slap couldn't have surprised her more. "Five million?"

Durant nodded, thinking that if her next question was what he thought it would be, she might have a future in her new career.

"Whose money is it?" she said.

The right question, Durant thought. "What do your intelligence people say?"

"That it's being supplied by a consortium of American and Japanese corporations."

Durant sighed. "You'd better find yourself some new assets. It's Marcos money."

"Oh dear," she whispered.

"And it's all to be spent on weaponry."

She nodded. "Of course."

"Which could build up the red menace and speed up the coup. What's the government's timetable on the coup?"

She bit down on her full lower lip, as if trying to decide whether to lie. "Within a year," she said. "Perhaps nine months. They'll make an attempt anyhow."

Durant rose. "Okay, I can guarantee that Espiritu will never get his hands on the five million."

"Guarantee?"

He nodded. "Guarantee. But you'll have to give me Lieutenant Cruz."

"Give him?"

"Assign him to me."

"For how long?"

"A couple of days—beginning now."

She made her decision quickly. "All right. What else?"

"How do you want Espiritu? Dead or alive?"

It was another hard blow, but she absorbed it more easily this time, although Durant thought he could see tears welling up in her enormous eyes. "I can't—rather, I won't tell you to—"

"You do need practice," he said. "It's a theoretical question. Would you prefer Espiritu bribed, disgraced and hiding in exile, or dead of natural causes down in Cebu?"

She took a full minute to decide, staring down at the rugless floor as if the answer might lie there. When she looked up, Durant thought her eyes had gone from sad and teary to cold and implacable.

"Dead," she said in a low firm voice.

"Okay," Durant said.

CHAPTER
FORTY

After Otherguy Overby knocked on the door of Artie Wu's fifth-floor suite in the Manila Peninsula Hotel, he was told to come in. He entered to find Durant up and leaning against a wall. Wu was seated on a couch, looking freshly barbered and wearing his white silk money suit. Overby would have preferred to find them feet up, shoes off and drinking beer.

"Sit down, Otherguy," Wu said. "Like a beer?"

Overby shook his head as he sat down in a straight chair, folding his arms protectively across his chest and planting his feet firmly on the carpet.

"Everything set?" Durant asked.

Overby looked at him. "I called the old Colonel down in Cebu and he got word to Minnie. She's agreed to meet us in Hong Kong but she wants proof it's all on the up-and-up. Otherwise, no deal. Okay?"

Wu said it was fine and Overby continued. "Welcome-Welcome got the telex confirmation on our rooms at the Hong Kong Peninsula and it'll send a couple of cars to meet us at the airport." He paused and looked again at Durant. "What about that homicide cop, Lieutenant Cruz?"

"Manila contacted Hong Kong through a back channel and got him wired into the CID there," Durant said. "He's to get full cooperation."

"No trouble with the airline, I trust?" Wu said to Overby.

"None."

Wu gave Overby a long look of what seemed to be genuine liking. "I was just trying to tell Quincy about that Rotary Club billboard in Cebu, Otherguy. How'd it go? 'Will it benefit all concerned?'"

"'Be beneficial to all concerned,'" Overby said.

Wu nodded, as if grateful for the correction. "And it really looks as if it might be beneficial, doesn't it?" he said. "Except to one of us." He stared at Overby. "Or possibly two of us."

"Get to the point, Artie," Overby said. "You can shine me on some other time."

Wu sighed. "I think I will have a beer, Quincy."

"Me, too," Overby said.

Durant went to the room's mini-refrigerator, took out three cans of San Miguel and passed them around. Wu opened his, took several swallows and said, "Who were you, Otherguy, when you called the Secret Service from Cebu?"

"Reuters," Overby said and drank some of his beer.

"Inquiring about?"

"October, last year."

"Any special date?" Durant said.

Overby shrugged. "October eighteenth, around in there."

Wu and Durant looked at each other. Durant shook his head. The date meant nothing.

"October eighteenth where?" Wu said.

"New York."

"It's like pulling teeth," Durant said.

"Otherguy tells things his own way," Wu said. "Where in New York, Otherguy?"

"The United Nations."

"Ah!" Wu said.

"What the fuck does 'Ah!' mean?" Durant said.

Wu ignored him and smiled again at Overby. "You're doing fine, Otherguy. What happened last year on October eighteenth at the U.N.?"

"An acting foreign minister made a speech. At a commemorative session of the fortieth anniversary."

Durant smiled mockingly at Wu and said, "Ah, so!"

Wu ignored him and gently asked Overby, "Whose acting foreign minister, Otherguy?"

Overby had another drink of beer and said, "The acting foreign minister of the Philippines."

Durant got there first and said, "Jesus."

Artie Wu, scarcely a beat behind, nodded at Overby and said, "Imelda Marcos, right?"

Overby shrugged again and drank more beer.

"What was in her speech, Otherguy?" Wu said.

"How the hell should I know? We live in terrible times. We should all pull together. Stamp out injustice. What they always say at the U.N."

"It wasn't the speech, Artie," Durant said.

"No. Of course not," Wu said, staring at Overby. "It was Georgia, wasn't it?"

Overby looked first at Durant, then at Wu. It was an amused, speculative look. "Good thing you guys don't play this game for money."

Artie Wu smiled, as if in complete agreement. "The Secret

Service had assigned Georgia to watch Imelda Marcos' back, right?"

"That's it."

"How'd you pry it out of them?" Durant asked.

"I told them Georgia was applying for a job out here with Reuters and I was checking her references and work history. And is it true, I ask, that Miss Blue was once assigned to Mrs. Marcos who's listed as a reference? And they say yes and give the dates and places. So then I ask if Georgia had quit the Service or been fired or what, and they say she quit. Resigned. Although she tells everybody else, Booth anyway, that she got canned."

"You got all this over the phone?" Durant asked with unconcealed skepticism.

"From their personnel section, which is what it's there for. Credit checks. References. And if I've got to say it myself, Quincy, I'm the best fucking phone man who ever lived."

"You are indeed, Otherguy," Wu said. "But tell me. What exactly made you pick up the phone?"

"Artie, nobody—and I mean nobody—sends out five million dirty unless they've got a trace on it. A trace they can trust. Well, I eliminated me first, of course, then Booth and you two last. That left Georgia. Then I remembered Booth saying Georgia'd told him that Treasury assigned her mostly to the wives of visiting big shots. So I play the hunch, pick up the phone, ask a couple of questions and bingo."

"Nice," Artie Wu said. "Very nice. Almost brilliant."

"And that's when you almost went solo, right?" Durant said.

Overby looked up with his unassailable, nothing-can-touch-me stare. "Like I said, Quincy, it crossed my mind." He smiled his hard merry smile. "Just like it would've crossed yours."

Wu rose, walked over to the seated Overby and put a friendly, almost comforting hand on his left shoulder. Overby looked down at the hand suspiciously.

"It was thoughtful of you to confide in us, Otherguy," Wu said.

Overby rose and turned to Durant who was still leaning against the wall. "Now that Espiritu's dead, you guys know what she'll try to do, don't you?"

"We know," Durant said.

Overby nodded. "Yeah. I thought you might."

After he had gone, Wu turned to face the suite's open bedroom door. He raised his voice slightly and said, "You can come out now, Lieutenant."

Lt. Cruz walked into the suite's sitting room. "You get all that?" Durant asked.

The homicide detective nodded. "Fascinating. He has a very good mind, doesn't he?"

"Too good sometimes," Durant said.

Lt. Cruz smiled, obviously pleased. "Yes, well, I'll see you in Hong Kong then."

•   •   •

The Hong Kong Peninsula Hotel had dispatched two Rolls-Royce sedans to the airport. One of the two uniformed chauffeurs carried a neatly lettered sign that sought "Mr. Wu and Party." Artie Wu served as tour director, assigning Durant, Overby and Booth Stallings to the lead Rolls. He and Georgia Blue settled into the rear one. As the two-car procession rolled toward Kowloon, Wu pushed the button that raised the glass partition.

"Been to Hong Kong before, Georgia?"

"Twice," she said. "I drew the Secretary of State's wife the first time; the Vice-President's the second."

Wu smiled. "Fun trip?"

"Nothing but girlish giggles."

"I can imagine." There was a block-long silence until Wu asked, "What about Harry Crites back in Washington? Think he'll kick up a fuss?"

"When Espiritu's death is announced?"

Wu nodded.

"What can Harry say? Espiritu flew to Hong Kong, picked up his five million, changed his mind, flew back home and died of a second stroke. The NPA won't deny he's dead. They'll deny the five million and all, but I don't think Harry is going to sue."

"Then we're virtually home free, wouldn't you say?"

She considered the question. "I think so. It certainly beats trying to throw a switch on a live Espiritu." She grinned at Wu. "You really were serious about running the pigeon drop on him, weren't you?"

Wu smiled almost wistfully, as if at some lost chance. "An elegant variation thereof. It would've been beautiful." He sighed. "And no comeback. None at all."

"There won't be any this way either," she said.

"Let's hope not," said Artie Wu.

•   •   •

Booth Stallings decided that royalty wouldn't have received a much warmer reception than the one the Hong Kong Peninsula gave Wu, Durant and Otherguy Overby. The hotel obviously cherished its trio of free-spending guests and even made a small fuss over Georgia Blue. By virtue of his membership in Mr. Wu's party, Stallings himself was treated with the deference usually reserved for visiting ministers of sport and culture and fading rock stars.

After Stallings was shown to his room, he took a shower, had a nap, read, ordered a room service dinner and waited for the phone to ring. It rang at 8 P.M. After he said hello, he heard Durant say, "Let's take a walk."

"What for?"

"Because I want to," Durant said.

•   •   •

They walked a block up Salisbury Road to the Kowloon YMCA, once the residence of Otherguy Overby.

"Let's have a cup of tea," Durant said.

"Tea?"

"Tea."

"Well, I guess we are in China, sort of."

The YMCA restaurant offered Formica tables, plastic chairs that wobbled and the smell of cheap food cooked in vast quantities. Durant examined the almost empty room before selecting a table that was occupied by a Filipino in a well-cut suit of tan linen whose jacket sleeves had cuffs that really buttoned. The Filipino nodded coolly at Durant as he sat down. Stallings chose a chair across from the Filipino.

Durant made the introductions casually. "Lieutenant Cruz, Booth Stallings."

Stallings stared at Cruz and said, "At the Manila airport, right?"

Lt. Cruz nodded.

"You were a lieutenant of what when you picked up Durant?"

"Homicide. I still am."

Durant asked Cruz, "You talk to the Hong Kong cops?"

"I called them from Manila and then saw them after I got here. They gave me this." He picked up a leather attaché case from the floor, opened it on his lap, removed an envelope and handed it to Durant. The empty letter-size envelope bore the name of the Hong Kong and Shanghai Bank. Durant carefully put it away in his inside jacket pocket.

Lt. Cruz used his chin to point at Stallings. "Does he know?"

"Not yet."

"Know what?" Stallings said.

They ignored the question as Lt. Cruz raised an eyebrow at Durant who shrugged. The detective leaned toward Stallings and spoke in a low rapid voice.

"Listen carefully. The Hong Kong police will arrest Miss Blue when she comes out of the bank tomorrow."

"For what?"

"The murder of Mrs. Emily Cariaga—who was a friend of his." Lt. Cruz indicated Durant with a nod.

"So far, it sucks," Stallings said.

"We have evidence," Lt. Cruz said, "that Miss Blue, directly or indirectly, is in the pay of Ferdinand Marcos or his wife, Imelda. Possibly both."

Stallings chuckled. It sounded to Durant like glass being ground up. "Their hired gun, huh?" Stallings said.

"I'm saying only that the late Mrs. Cariaga, apparently through her extensive social or political connections, learned that Miss Blue was in the Marcoses' pay. The information frightened her. So much so that she decided to leave the country."

"Who says she was frightened?" Stallings asked.

"I do," Durant said. "She called and told me she was and asked me to drive her to the airport."

"She tell you about Georgia and the Marcoses?"

"No."

"Why not?"

"Because when I got to her house she was dead."

"So you think somebody tipped Georgia off that the Cariaga woman knew all about her and the Marcoses, and that's why Georgia killed her?"

Lt. Cruz nodded.

"Sounds weak to me," Stallings said. "Who tipped Georgia off—one of the Marcoses?"

"Possibly."

"Since when does 'possibly' hack it in a murder case?"

"It doesn't," Lt. Cruz said. "But an eyewitness does."

"And you just happen to have one, huh?"

Lt. Cruz sighed in exasperation. "Miss Blue hired herself a frightener who worked for a very undesirable alien called Boy Howdy."

"A friend of yours, wasn't he?" Stallings said to Durant.

"Not quite," Durant said.

"She hired this frightener," Lt. Cruz went on doggedly,

"ostensibly to throw a scare into Mrs. Cariaga. But actually to blame him for the murder. She and Howdy may have conspired in this. The poor brute is very, very large and very, very dumb."

"So Georgia and Howdy set him up?" Stallings said.

Lt. Cruz nodded. "As I said, the man is none too bright. He got the time mixed up and arrived at Mrs. Cariaga's early, only to find her day guard dead from a broken neck—which, I understand, Georgia Blue is quite capable of doing."

"Is she?" Stallings said.

Lt. Cruz ignored the question. But Durant said, "Yes. She is."

"After finding the body," Cruz continued, "the dummy hid in the shrubbery, not sure what to do next. He saw Georgia Blue come out of Emily Cariaga's house. After she drove away, he went in the house and found Mrs. Cariaga dead. Stabbed. He panicked and tried to leave, only to bump into Durant here. They fought. Durant lost, or so he says. When sufficiently recovered he quite sensibly called the police."

"And told you about the dummy," Stallings said.

Lt. Cruz gave Durant a disapproving look. "Not right away, unfortunately."

Stallings smiled slightly at Durant. "Held out on the cops, did you?"

"For a while."

Stallings turned back to Lt. Cruz and asked, "Do you find him and his partner kind of devious?"

"Extremely so."

Stallings nodded thoughtfully. "But you've talked to the dummy—the so-called eyewitness?"

"At length," Lt. Cruz said. "He freely admits what I've told you."

"So who shot Boy Howdy down in Cebu?" Stallings asked in a quick hard voice, as if trying to rattle Lt. Cruz.

"Carmen Espiritu, of course," Lt. Cruz said. "Probably because Howdy worked for whoever paid him—for the

Espiritus, for Georgia Blue, even for the Palace. Apparently, Georgia Blue paid better than anyone else and his loyalty, such as it was, went to her. We can only presume the Espiritus found out about his duplicity and killed him. We'd like to question Carmen Espiritu, but I hear she's dead. I do hear correctly, don't I, Mr. Stallings?"

Booth Stallings sat at the Formica table on the wobbly plastic chair, thinking not about Lt. Cruz's question, but about the night he had gone to bed with Georgia Blue. He probed, rather gently, for feelings of revulsion or moral outrage, but found none. He did turn up a lot of regret and a measure of sadness. But what you regret, he decided, is that you won't be jumping into bed with her again. And what you're sad about is that these guys are going to ask you to do something to her, something high-minded, like bringing her to justice, and you're going to say yes, although what you really want to do is run off to New Caledonia with her.

He looked at Lt. Cruz and said, "You asked if Carmen's dead?"

Lt. Cruz nodded.

"Yeah. She's dead."

Lt. Cruz made no comment, as if waiting for Stallings to continue. Instead, Stallings asked a question. "Why don't you and the Hong Kong cops go arrest Georgia right now?"

"Because," Lt. Cruz said, "you and she haven't come out of the bank yet."

"You want to bust her with the money on her, right?"

"I pray to God she won't have it on her."

"I think I missed a beat there."

Lt. Cruz looked away. "For reasons of national security we prefer not to arrest her until she comes out of the bank."

Stallings nodded glumly, as if at the familiar punch line of some bad old joke. "In my dictionary, national security's a synonym for politics."

"You have an excellent dictionary, Mr. Stallings," Lt. Cruz

said and rose. "Good evening, gentlemen." He turned and walked out of the YMCA restaurant.

Durant and Stallings sat in silence until Durant said, "It's not the principle of the thing, Booth. It's the money."

All Stallings said was, "We never did get that tea."

Durant rose. "Somebody else'll buy you a cup."

Stallings also rose to follow Durant out of the YMCA and into the night. Durant's eyes roamed over the sidewalk and the street, poking into the darker corners. Otherguy Overby seemed to materialize out of the shadows.

"He's all yours," Durant said.

Overby nodded toward the corner. "Let's go, Booth."

Both men turned, but Overby turned back when Durant called to him. "Otherguy."

"What?"

"Buy him a cup of tea, will you?"

·   ·   ·

Their walk took them six blocks north of the Peninsula Hotel and two blocks east. The streets narrowed and the tourists thinned out as the shops grew junkier. When they came to a small restaurant with a Chinese sign, Overby said, "Take a good look because you'll be coming back here tomorrow."

"I'll never find it again," Stallings said.

Overby handed him a slip of paper with the name and address of the restaurant written in both English and Chinese. "Give it to any taxi driver."

They went in. A young Chinese woman seemed to know Overby because she smiled at him and asked him a question in Chinese. After Overby replied in English she led them toward the rear of the nearly deserted restaurant. They went along a row of booths whose seat backs rose to the ceiling, transforming the booths into small semiprivate cubicles.

The young woman asked Overby another question in Chinese. He again replied in English. "Tea for three, please."

After the woman left, Overby waved Stallings into the far

seat of the last booth. As he slipped into it, Stallings saw the woman diagonally across the table, almost huddled into the corner next to the wall.

She smiled at him wanly. "So how's it go, Booth?" Minerva Espiritu said.

"It goes, Minnie," Booth Stallings said.

Otherguy Overby sat down next to Minnie Espiritu. "Any problems?" he asked her.

"Not yet."

After looking around for eavesdroppers, Overby leaned toward Stallings and spoke in the low soft tones of the born conniver. "Okay, Booth. Now here's what's really going to happen."

CHAPTER
FORTY-ONE

The next morning, shortly before ten o'clock, two of them went to Hong Kong Island by ferry and three went by car. The two who took the Star Ferry were Georgia Blue and Booth Stallings. She wore a serious dark gray dress and a black leather shoulder bag. Stallings wore the tan suit Otherguy Overby had picked out at Lew Ritter's in Los Angeles. He also carried a slim brown leather attaché case that looked new.

Georgia Blue noticed the case and said, "Window dressing?"

Stallings shrugged. "I don't want to walk in, ask for five million dollars and then have no place to stick it, except my hip pocket."

"It won't be in cash, Booth."

He grinned. "Still."

They took seats forward in the first-class section of the ferry during the crossing from Kowloon. The only time they spoke was when Georgia Blue asked, "What'll you do with your share, Booth?"

"Endow myself," he said.

• • •

The car the other three rode in was a rented Jaguar sedan. Artie Wu drove, of course, and much too fast as always. Durant, seated next to him, kept closing his eyes at the near misses and close catastrophes. Otherguy Overby sat silent and relaxed in the rear, looking out the window.

Wu turned to look at Overby. "Do you think—"

"For Christ's sake, Artie," Durant snapped.

Wu turned back just in time to avoid a bus and then finished his question. "—Booth can handle it?"

"I kept him up till two this morning practicing," Overby said.

"How was he?" Durant asked.

"I don't think he's got his heart in it."

"That's not what I asked."

"He did okay."

"Why don't you think his heart's in it, Otherguy?" Wu said, keeping his eyes on the road.

"I think he'd rather fuck Georgia again instead."

"Instead of going for a million?" Wu asked, sounding more interested than surprised.

"At sixty, that could be a tough call, right, Quincy?"

Durant smiled slightly. "With her, it's a tough call at thirty."

• • •

Booth Stallings, who doted on anachronisms, grinned at the 88-year-old double-deck streetcar that dinged and clanked its way down Des Voeux Road past the silver and gray Hong

Kong and Shanghai Banking Corporation's startling new 60-story headquarters.

He and Georgia Blue had walked the two or three blocks from the Star Ferry terminal to Des Voeux Road and were now waiting for a green light. Staring up at the towering bank building, which seemed to be mostly glass and exposed girders, Stallings said, "You can't tell if it's supposed to cash a check or launch a space probe, but I sure like that two-story Toonerville Trolley going by in front."

"Where's Toonerville?" Georgia Blue asked.

Instead of answering, Stallings said, "Light's green." They crossed the street and rode an escalator up to an entrance that led into an atrium 17 stories high. A bank guard directed them to the desk of Mr. Henry Pow, an assistant cashier.

Pow's desk was in an open space just off the main banking hall. The bank apparently liked to do its business in full view of its customers. Confidentiality was assured by spacing its officers' desks ten feet apart. Pow, a Chinese in his late thirties, wore a genial look and a dark blue suit. He glanced up at Stallings and Georgia Blue with what seemed to be genuine pleasure.

"Miss Blue and Mr. Stallings—am I correct?" he said as he rose.

Stallings replied that he was and Pow waved them to chairs beside his desk. Stallings made sure he got the chair closer to Pow and sat down, his new attaché case on his lap.

"We've been expecting you," Pow said with another bright smile that displayed a gold crown far back on the left.

"Any problems, Mr. Pow?" Georgia Blue asked.

"No problems, none at all," he said and chuckled. "Unless you forgot to bring along identification."

"Passports do?" Stallings asked.

"Perfectly."

Georgia Blue handed hers over first. Pow inspected it with care and made a few notes. Stallings opened his attaché case, took out his passport and gave it to Pow who examined it even more closely than he had Georgia Blue's, glancing from the passport photo to Stallings and back to the photo at least three times.

With yet another smile and another small chuckle, Pow said, "You are what you are."

"Like Popeye," Stallings said.

"Yes. Quite. Now if you'll just sign these release forms where the red check marks are. All three copies, please."

He handed the forms and a ballpoint pen to Stallings who signed and passed pen and forms to Georgia Blue. After signing, she handed them back to Pow, along with the pen. He compared the signatures with those in the passports.

Satisfied, Pow handed the passports back, unlocked his center desk drawer and took out five buff checks. He examined each one deliberately before passing them to Georgia Blue. As he looked at them, one by one, Pow said, "You'll notice they are certified checks for one million U.S. each and are made out to cash as requested."

Georgia Blue nodded and handed the checks to Stallings for inspection. He looked at each one and then at Pow. "Got an envelope?"

"Of course," Pow said as Stallings handed him the five checks. The envelope Pow removed from his desk drawer was a white number ten that bore the bank's logo. It was also an exact duplicate of the one Lt. Cruz had given Quincy Durant the night before in the YMCA restaurant.

Stallings watched, almost mesmerized, as Pow slowly counted the checks again, slipped them into the envelope, ran his tongue across the mucilage on its flap, sealed it carefully and, with only a moment's indecision, handed it to Stallings. The expert on terrorism raised the lid of the attaché case, as Otherguy Overby had instructed him, just enough to slip the hand with the envelope inside. It was then that Stallings went into the rest of his act. Frown first, he thought. So he frowned, as if struck by a sudden thought, and looked at Georgia Blue.

"Maybe it'd be better if you carried them," he said.

"If you like," she said, her relief nearly invisible. He
brought his hand out of the attaché case. In it was a sealed
white number ten envelope that bore the bank's logo. He
handed it to her and watched as she tucked it down into her
black leather bag.

"Thank you very much, Mr. Pow," she said, rising and
offering the assistant cashier her hand. Pow also rose, his smile
at the ready as he shook hands with her and Stallings. "Thank
you for your custom," he said. "And whenever you have other
banking needs, please keep us in mind."

"We'll do that," Booth Stallings said.

•   •   •

Stallings stepped onto the down escalator first, Georgia Blue
only two steps up and behind him, her right hand now deep
inside her shoulder bag, her eyes back into their Secret Service
mode and darting from face to face, classifying each one at a
glance.

She didn't spot them until she and Stallings were across De
Voeux Road and walking through the park that was bounded by
the Prince's Building on the left and the courthouse on the
right. She was walking one step back of Stallings and to his
right. He couldn't see them but he knew she had when her left
hand took his right arm just above the elbow, as if she needed
some slight support. Iron fingers dug into the elbow nerve
then. The pain was immediate and awful. Stallings sucked in
his breath, making a hissing noise.

"See them?" she demanded.

"Who?"

"Two at eleven o'clock and three at one."

Stallings looked. He saw two Chinese men in their thirties
wearing casual clothes and bent slightly forward, right hand
back on their right hips. To the right at one o'clock he located
three more men, two Chinese and one European. The Chinese
were young, not yet 30, but the European was at least 45. He
wore a gray suit. He also had a red face and well-chilled blue

eyes that drilled into Georgia Blue. Stallings thought he might as well have had cop tattooed across his forehead.

"See them?" she demanded again.

"Sure."

"Notice my bag right against your gut?"

"Hard not to."

"Just keep walking, Booth, and shake your head no at the guy with the red face."

Her fingers again dug into the elbow nerve and again Stallings sucked air at the pain. The red-faced European was staring now at him instead of Georgia Blue. As they drew near, Stallings shook his head no. After what Stallings knew was a week or ten days, the red-faced man jerked his chin down in an abrupt and angry nod.

Once past him, Stallings said, "What the fuck're you doing, Georgia?"

"Catching a boat," she said as she steered him into the crowd that was heading for the Star Ferry.

It was at that exact moment that Booth Stallings, whose life study had been terrorism, came to a profound and utter understanding of his chosen topic. He even settled on a definition, which, although not particularly original, was immensely satisfying. Terrorism, he decided, was that which terrifies. The headline for his soon-to-be-printed obituary seemed to write itself: Terror Expert Slain By Ex–Secret Service Terrorist.

Normally, the labored irony would have made him chuckle or at least smile. But he did neither because of the new wave of fear and terror that rolled over him as he realized with absolute certainty that he would never make it back to Kowloon. Not alive anyhow, he decided. And dead doesn't much count.

•   •   •

Artie Wu and Otherguy Overby stood on tiptoe on the green iron bench in the park between the Prince's Building and the

courthouse and watched Stallings and Georgia Blue lose
themselves in the crowd heading for the ferry.

"Well," Wu said, almost approvingly, "she made it."

"Told you she would."

"We listened to you, Otherguy—Quincy and I."

"The Hong Kong cops wouldn't."

"They're only trying to avoid a massacre," said Wu as he
stepped down from the park bench, frowning and puzzled.
Overby also stepped down. "But why the ferry?" Wu asked.
"She must know it's a floating death trap."

"Well, that's his problem now, isn't it?" Otherguy Overby
said. "That fucking Durant's."

•   •   •

As the Star Ferry pulled out, Georgia Blue and Booth
Stallings stood outside the enclosed first-class section, their
backs to the rail. Georgia Blue was on Stallings' left, her hand
down in her shoulder bag, the bag still pressed against his side.

"Artie set me up?" she asked, her eyes jumping from
passenger to passenger.

"Durant."

She didn't seem surprised as she glanced quickly at her
watch. "This is what you do, Booth. You count to sixty, very
slowly and just loud enough to let me hear you. When you
reach sixty you hand me that nice new attaché case."

She glanced at him briefly and resumed her vigil, smiling at
the surprise that had splashed across his face. "That was about
the worst switch I ever saw," she said.

"I thought I was pretty good."

"You're an amateur," she said, turning the noun into an
epithet. "Now start counting."

When Stallings' low soft count reached 16, a man's voice
shouted, "Look out, Georgia!"

Stallings felt himself being grabbed, pushed and then pulled
back against something hard which he knew was Georgia

Blue's gun. Now out of her bag, the gun was jammed into the small of his back.

He found Durant then, no more than 15 feet away, the five-shot revolver that had been furnished by the retired Colonel held in an unwavering two-handed grip and aimed right at Stallings' chest. The ferry passengers had also seen it and were yelling, screaming and scrambling away.

"Let go the case, Booth," Durant said.

"If you do, you're dead," Georgia Blue promised Stallings in a quiet tone. He believed her promise.

"I'll blow right through him, Georgia," Durant said.

Stallings also believed Durant. He dropped the attaché case to the deck and kicked it toward him. Durant didn't glance down. Stallings drew in a deep breath and turned slowly to face Georgia Blue. Her pistol was aimed at his belt. Her dollar-green eyes, steady and unblinking, were aimed at Durant over Stallings' shoulder.

"Back again at death's front door, right, Georgia?" Stallings said.

"Could be, Booth," she said, not taking her eyes off Durant.

"Better make your jump."

"You blocking for me?"

Stallings nodded.

She backed quickly to the rail. In one smooth flowing motion she was over it, holding on with her left hand, her right hand still aiming the Walther at Stallings. Her feet were braced on the edge of the deck. She bent her knees slightly and then used them to propel herself back and away from the ferry.

In four strides, Durant was at the rail. Stallings joined him. Below they could see Georgia Blue treading water. An open speedboat was bearing down on her. She waved at it. The hard-faced Chinese at its helm reduced speed.

It was then that Quincy Durant raised the revolver, aimed carefully and fired five shots at the speedboat. He hit only water, but the speedboat swerved away and sped off, leaving

Georgia Blue in its wake. Stallings and Durant watched her, bobbing up and down in the water.

"How do we stop this thing?" Stallings asked.

"The ferry?"

"Christ, yes, the ferry."

"We don't," Durant said.

It was then that the ferry changed course slightly. A few seconds later they could see only dirty water and nothing at all of Georgia Blue.

CHAPTER
FORTY-TWO

At 1:45 that afternoon Artie Wu entered his suite, accompanied by Otherguy Overby, to find Durant leaning against the wall and Booth Stallings pacing up and down the sitting room, a glass of what looked like straight Scotch whiskey in his right hand, the attaché case in his left.

Wu turned to Durant and said, "What's wrong with him?"

"He thinks we should've stopped the ferry."

"To rescue Georgia?"

Durant nodded.

"You didn't tell him?"

"How could I?" Durant said.

"Of course. You didn't know for certain."

"Sit the fuck down, Booth, will you?" Otherguy Overby said. "The cops fished her out."

Stallings stopped pacing and turned quickly to face Overby. " She didn't drown?"

Overby grunted. "Do fish drown?"

"Where is she?" Stallings said.

"In jail," Overby said. "Where the hell'd you think she'd be?"

Artie Wu went over to Stallings and put a comforting hand on his shoulder. "Sit down, Booth. Please."

Stallings sat down in an easy chair, the attaché case on his lap, the dark drink still in his right hand. He looked up at Wu who was staring down at him with an extremely gentle expression. "Let's have a beer, Otherguy," Wu said.

"Sure," said Overby and went to the room refrigerator.

"All of us, Booth, are very fond of Georgia," Wu said. "Some of us, at one time or other, have been even more than fond of her. Therefore, we wouldn't do anything to her that she didn't deserve."

"Unless we had to," Overby said, handing beers to Wu and Durant.

"It was Otherguy who thought she'd make it past the cops," Wu said and took a swallow of his beer. "I didn't. It was Quincy who suspected she'd use the ferry and make the jump. Again, I didn't think so. But when you two headed for the ferry, I went to the Hong Kong police—the red-faced man, did you notice him?"

Stallings nodded.

"And suggested that he send a police launch after the ferry. Which he did. The reason we're so late is that Otherguy and I had to find Georgia a lawyer. A solicitor, actually."

"The first thing he wanted to talk about was money," Overby said.

"What about extradition to Manila?" Stallings said.

"He'll try to delay it."

"What about bail?" Stallings said.

"I don't think so," Wu said.

Overby grinned. "If she got bail, it'd be goodbye, Georgia."

Durant left the wall and went over to Stallings. "It's over, Booth. All over."

Stallings nodded.

"Except for one thing," Durant said. "Are you sure you gave her the right envelope?"

Stallings thought about it. "Christ, I don't know. I was getting nervous in the bank. But I think so. I sure as hell hope so."

Overby looked at Wu. "Did she still have her shoulder bag when they pulled her out of the drink, Artie?"

Wu slowly shook his head no.

"Jesus," Overby whispered.

Durant cleared his throat. "May we take a look, Booth?"

"You do it," Stallings said and handed the attaché case to Durant.

Durant went to the couch, sat down and put the attaché case on the coffee table. He stared at it as Overby and Wu gathered round.

Durant looked up at them, shrugged, undid the brass snaps and raised the lid. A Bank of Hong Kong and Shanghai envelope was all the case contained, except for Stallings' passport. Durant tossed it to him.

Again, Durant stared at the envelope, then snatched it up and ripped it open. Inside were five buff-colored checks.

"I think I'm going to cry," said Otherguy Overby.

• • •

At 4:15 that afternoon, Booth Stallings stepped out of a taxi and again entered the small Chinese restaurant that was two blocks east and six blocks north of the Hong Kong Peninsula Hotel.

The same young Chinese woman smiled at him in recognition and led him back to the same last booth. Sitting there, gazing into a glass of beer, was Minnie Espiritu.

She looked up as Stallings slid into the booth. "I didn't think you'd show," she said.

"I wasn't sure you would," Stallings said.

"Beer?" she asked.

"Tea."

"One tea," Minnie Espiritu said to the young Chinese woman who turned and left.

"Well?" Minnie Espiritu said.

"You want the ground rules again?"

"Just the catch."

"No catch. I give you one million bucks that you can spend any way you want."

"Providing?" she said.

"Providing you give Al his funeral. The biggest one Cebu's ever seen."

Minnie Espiritu leaned back in the booth and examined Stallings coldly. "They don't know Alejandro's dead, do they? Manila, I mean."

"No," Stallings said. "They don't."

"But they think you guys are going to kill him."

"That's right."

"For the five million. That way they're not out anything."

"Right again."

"I could blow both you and Manila out of the water, couldn't I?"

"It'd be a one-day story, Minnie. Maybe two. And you'd be out a million bucks."

Seconds went by before she nodded. "Let's see it."

Stallings reached into an inside breast pocket, brought out a buff-colored check and handed it to her just as the Chinese woman returned with his tea. Minnie Espiritu clapped the check against her breasts until the Chinese woman left. She then stared at the check, her lips moving silently as she carefully counted its six zeroes.

"Made out to cash and certified, I see," she said and silently counted the zeroes for the second time.

"No way to stop payment on it either," Stallings said and sipped his tea.

"One . . . million . . . dollars."

"One million," he agreed.

"I could run it through our Panama account," she said more to herself than to him as he took another sip of tea. When he looked up he saw two tears rolling down her cheeks.

"I spent five years in the States begging for money," she said, "and in all that time I didn't even raise one third of this." She smiled a winner's smile. "Okay, Booth, he'll get his rotten funeral."

Stallings raised his cup of tea to her. "Have a nice revolt, Minnie."

•　　　•　　　•

When he returned to the Peninsula Hotel at 5:21, Stallings called Artie Wu's room. When there was no answer, he asked hotel information for the room numbers of Durant and Overby. A few moments later, the operator said, "I'm sorry, but Mr. Durant and Mr. Overby have checked out."

"What about Mr. Wu—Mr. Arthur Wu?"

It took her another five seconds to check. "I'm sorry, but he too has departed."

Booth Stallings thanked her, hung up the house phone, and wandered over to a table in the lobby where he ordered a Scotch and water. As he waited for it, he took out the other buff check and, like Minnie Espiritu, counted the six zeroes silently, wondering how he would spend the money.

CHAPTER
FORTY-THREE

At 12:45 P.M. on the sixteenth of May, 1986, a Friday, Booth Stallings sat on his favorite bench in Dupont Circle, his face turned up to the spring sun, waiting for his luncheon guest and remembering, for no very good reason, that on this date in seventeen-sixty-something, Boswell had first met Dr. Johnson.

Two minutes later, Harry Crites sat down next to him on the bench, cracked a smile and said, "What's for lunch?"

"Drugstore chili dogs," Stallings said, offering a white greasy paper sack.

"I like chili dogs," Crites said, took one, unwrapped it and, leaning forward to avoid the drip, bit into it.

Stallings slowly unwrapped his own chili dog. "Sorry about your employee, Harry. But there was nothing I could do."

Crites nodded, chewed and smiled slightly, remembering not to show any teeth. "Georgia, you mean?" he said after he swallowed.

"Georgia," Stallings said, curious about what kind of self-absolution Crites would offer.

Harry Crites finished his chili dog in two enormous bites, chewed some more, swallowed, wiped his mouth and hands carefully with a paper napkin, rose and stared down at Stallings.

"I didn't hire her, Booth," he said. "She hired me."

Stallings stared back at him, unblinking, determined not to let his face betray anything—not surprise or disappointment or sadness. Especially not sadness. "She hired you to get me fired and recruited," he said, not making it a question.

"You were sole source, remember?" Crites said. "All it took was half a dozen phone calls, a dinner at the Madison and a trip to L.A." He smiled the smile of a superior mind. "I imagine you'd like to know how much I cost her."

Stallings only nodded, despising himself for the curiosity he was unable to stifle.

"Fifty thousand plus expenses." Crites produced his superior smile again. "But hell, Booth, it all worked out okay. I saw on TV a few weeks back that big funeral they gave Espiritu in Cebu. So in a way you must've brought him down from the hills after all." He shook his head in what seemed to be a mixture of regret and admiration. "That Georgia," he said. "She's something, isn't she?" When Stallings made no reply, he added, "You heard what happened, didn't you?"

Stallings, still seated, stared up at him and, after a moment, shook his head.

"She cut herself a deal. Traded everything she knew about how Marcos sluices his money around for reduced charges. Christ, she ought to be out in a year or two. Maybe even sooner." He paused just long enough to give Stallings a cruel smile. "Think you can wait, Booth?"

"Why not?" Stallings said, adding, "Who told you about the deal she cut, Harry?"

Harry Crites seemed almost on the point of answering, but shrugged instead, turned and walked away. Stallings watched him go. He then leaned back against the bench, closed his eyes and lifted his face up to the sun, wondering what Georgia Blue was doing and thinking at that very moment. When this proved both pointless and adolescent, he wondered whether Harry Crites might have been lying.

It was then that it came to him—struck him actually—with startling clarity. And he realized what it was that he missed, needed and even wanted to do and be now that he was all grown up. Or nearly so.

Stallings picked up the empty white paper bag, crumpled it, rose quickly, hurried to the trash basket and tossed it in. After crossing the street to the bank of pay phones near the Peoples Drugstore, he dropped in a quarter, the only coin he bothered to carry, and tapped out the office number of his son-in-law, the criminal lawyer.

As it rang, Stallings was convinced that his son-in-law would have a new phone number where Otherguy Overby could be reached. And he was equally certain that by now Otherguy would have something going. Something Stallings could buy into. Something interesting and different out on the Rim perhaps—or, for that matter, almost anywhere.

MORE MYSTERIOUS PLEASURES

HAROLD ADAMS
The Carl Wilcox mystery series

MURDER	#501	$3.95
PAINT THE TOWN RED	#601	$3.95
THE MISSING MOON	#602	$3.95
THE NAKED LIAR	#420	$3.95
THE FOURTH WIDOW	#502	$3.50
THE BARBED WIRE NOOSE	#603	$3.95

TED ALLBEURY

THE SEEDS OF TREASON	#604	$3.95

ERIC AMBLER

HERE LIES: AN AUTOBIOGRAPHY	#701	$8.95

ROBERT BARNARD

A TALENT TO DECEIVE: AN APPRECIATION OF AGATHA CHRISTIE	#702	$8.95

EARL DERR BIGGERS
The Charlie Chan mystery series

THE HOUSE WITHOUT A KEY	#421	$3.95
THE CHINESE PARROT	#503	$3.95
BEHIND THAT CURTAIN	#504	$3.95
THE BLACK CAMEL	#505	$3.95
CHARLIE CHAN CARRIES ON	#506	$3.95
KEEPER OF THE KEYS	#605	$3.95

JAMES M. CAIN

THE ENCHANTED ISLE	#415	$3.95
CLOUD NINE	#507	$3.95

ROBERT CAMPBELL

IN LA-LA LAND WE TRUST	#508	$3.95

ANNE FINE
THE KILLJOY   #613 $3.95

DICK FRANCIS
THE SPORT OF QUEENS   #410 $3.95

JOHN GARDNER
THE GARDEN OF WEAPONS   #103 $4.50

BRIAN GARFIELD
DEATH WISH   #301 $3.95
DEATH SENTENCE   #302 $3.95
TRIPWIRE   #303 $3.95
FEAR IN A HANDFUL OF DUST   #304 $3.95

THOMAS GODFREY, ED.
MURDER FOR CHRISTMAS   #614 $3.95
MURDER FOR CHRISTMAS II   #615 $3.95

JOE GORES
COME MORNING   #518 $3.95

JOSEPH HANSEN
The Dave Brandstetter mystery series
EARLY GRAVES   #643 $3.95

NAT HENTOFF
THE MAN FROM INTERNAL AFFAIRS   #409 $3.95

PATRICIA HIGHSMITH
THE ANIMAL-LOVER'S BOOK
  OF BEASTLY MURDER   #706 $8.95
LITTLE TALES OF MISOGYNY   #707 $8.95
SLOWLY, SLOWLY IN THE WIND   #708 $8.95

DOUG HORNIG
WATERMAN   #616 $3.95
The Loren Swift mystery series
THE DARK SIDE   #519 $3.95

JANE HORNING
THE MYSTERY LOVERS' BOOK
  OF QUOTATIONS   #709 $9.95

P.D. JAMES/T.A. CRITCHLEY
THE MAUL AND THE PEAR TREE   #520 $3.95

STUART M. KAMINSKY
The Toby Peters mystery series
HE DONE HER WRONG   #105 $3.95
HIGH MIDNIGHT   #106 $3.95
NEVER CROSS A VAMPIRE   #107 $3.95
BULLET FOR A STAR   #308 $3.95
THE FALA FACTOR   #309 $3.95

JOSEPH KOENIG
FLOATER   #521 $3.50

ELMORE LEONARD
THE HUNTED   #401 $3.95
MR. MAJESTYK   #402 $3.95
THE BIG BOUNCE   #403 $3.95

ELSA LEWIN
I, ANNA   #522 $3.50

PETER LOVESEY
ROUGH CIDER   #617 $3.95
BUTCHERS AND OTHER STORIES OF CRIME   #710 $9.95

ARTHUR LYONS
The Jacob Asch mystery series
FAST FADE   #618 $3.95

ED McBAIN
ANOTHER PART OF THE CITY   #524 $3.95
The Matthew Hope mystery series
SNOW WHITE AND ROSE RED   #414 $3.95
CINDERELLA   #525 $3.95
PUSS IN BOOTS   #629 $3.95

VINCENT McCONNOR
LIMBO   #630 $3.95

GREGORY MCDONALD, ED.
LAST LAUGHS: THE 1986 MYSTERY
  WRITERS OF AMERICA ANTHOLOGY   #711 $8.95

CHARLOTTE MacLEOD
The Professor Peter Shandy mystery series
THE CORPSE IN OOZAK'S POND   #627 $3.95

REX STOUT
UNDER THE ANDES   #419 $3.50

JULIAN SYMONS
CONAN DOYLE: PORTRAIT OF AN ARTIST   #721 $9.95

ROSS THOMAS
CAST A YELLOW SHADOW   #535 $3.95
THE SINGAPORE WINK   #536 $3.95
THE FOOLS IN TOWN ARE
  ON OUR SIDE   #537 $3.95
CHINAMAN'S CHANCE   #638 $4.50
THE EIGHTH DWARF   #639 $4.50
OUT ON THE RIM   #640 $4.95

JIM THOMPSON
THE KILL-OFF   #538 $3.95
THE NOTHING MAN   #641 $3.95
BAD BOY   #642 $3.95

COLIN WATSON
SNOBBERY WITH VIOLENCE: CRIME
  STORIES AND THEIR AUDIENCES   #722 $8.95

DONALD E. WESTLAKE
THE BUSY BODY   #541 $3.95
THE SPY IN THE OINTMENT   #542 $3.95
GOD SAVE THE MARK   #543 $3.95
The Dortmunder caper series
THE HOT ROCK   #539 $3.95
BANK SHOT   #540 $3.95

TERI WHITE
TIGHTROPE   #544 $3.95
MAX TRUEBLOOD AND
  THE JERSEY DESPERADO   #644 $3.95

COLIN WILCOX
The Lt. Frank Hastings mystery series
VICTIMS   #413 $3.95
NIGHT GAMES   #545 $3.95

DAVID WILLIAMS
The Mark Treasure mystery series
UNHOLY WRIT   #112 $3.95
TREASURE BY DEGREES   #113 $3.95

CHRIS WILTZ
The Neal Rafferty mystery series
A DIAMOND BEFORE YOU DIE   #645 $3.95

CORNELL WOOLRICH/LAWRENCE BLOCK
INTO THE NIGHT   #646 $3.95

■■■■■■■■■■■■■■■■■■■■■■■■■■■■■

AVAILABLE AT YOUR BOOKSTORE OR DIRECT FROM THE PUBLISHER

Mysterious Press Mail Order
129 West 56th Street
New York, NY 10019

Please send me the MYSTERIOUS PRESS titles I have circled below:

103 105 106 107 112 113 209 210 211 212 213 214 301 302
303 304 308 309 315 316 401 402 403 404 405 406 407 408
409 410 411 412 413 414 415 416 417 418 419 420 421 501
502 503 504 505 506 507 508 509 510 511 512 513 514 515
516 517 518 519 520 521 522 523 524 525 526 527 528 529
530 531 532 533 534 535 536 537 538 539 540 541 542 543
544 545 601 602 603 604 605 606 607 608 609 610 611 612
613 614 615 616 617 618 619 620 621 622 623 624 625 626
627 628 629 630 631 632 633 634 635 636 637 638 639 640
641 642 643 644 645 646 701 702 703 704 705 706 707 708
709 710 711 712 713 714 715 716 717 718 719 720 721 722

I am enclosing $_____ (please add $3.00 postage and handling
for the first book, and 25¢ for each additional book). Send check or
money order only—no cash or C.O.D.'s please. Allow at least 4 weeks
for delivery.

NAME _____

ADDRESS _____

CITY _____ STATE _____ ZIP CODE _____
New York State residents please add appropriate sales tax.